MW00790434

STACY M. JONES

The Founders

First edition

ISBN: 978-0-578-85694-0

This book was professionally typeset on Reedsy.
Find out more at reedsy.com

For Carmen - hope you enjoy your character

Acknowledgement

Years of working as an investigator with a forensic psychology background have given me unparalleled access to some of the top law enforcement agencies in the United States from local and state police to the FBI. I'm grateful to detectives, special agents, and forensics teams I've had the pleasure of working with through the years and the knowledge and expertise you have shared with me.

Special thanks to 17 Studio Book Design for bringing my stories to life with amazing covers. Thank you to Dj Hendrickson for your insightful editing and Liza Wood for proofreading and revisions.

Thank you to my readers who enjoy these stories and were excited about a new series as much as I was writing it.

CHAPTER 1

Two loud raps, deliberate and insistent, reverberated off the door. "Kate Walsh," a deep male voice called out. "We need to speak to you immediately." Three more loud raps, knuckles meeting wood, pounded the message home.

Kate blinked an eye open and then the other. The incessant knocking continued. She roused herself from her bed on the second floor of her parents' brownstone in Boston's Back Bay, one of the city's wealthiest neighborhoods. She padded barefoot through the hallway, past her parents' closed bedroom door, and down the front staircase, adjusting her cotton shorts and wiping the sleep from her eyes as she went. She tried unsuccessfully to tame the mane of dark hair that framed her heart-shaped face.

She yanked open the front door, not even stopping to see who was out there first. All Kate wanted was for the knocking to stop. She'd had a late night studying for her last two final exams at Harvard. Graduation was in two weeks. Kate would finish her undergrad studies in linguistics and psychology early, just four days shy of her twentieth birthday on May fifteenth. Then it was on to grad school.

Pulling open the heavy front door, Kate stopped short when she came face to face with two men. They flashed their credentials and stuffed them back in their pockets before she even had a chance to register which three-lettered agency they were from. They shoved past her, stepping into the foyer. She pointed to the living room without saying a word.

They moved into the room but didn't sit. One of the men, the taller of the two, peered down at Kate, his intense blue eyes on her. He didn't waste any time. There were no niceties, no build-up, just the plain cold truth.

"There's been an explosion at the U.S. Embassy in Kenya. We are sorry to inform you that Ambassador Joseph Walsh and his wife have been killed."

Kate stumbled back at the mention of her parents. Dead? They couldn't be dead. They were on their way to Boston for her graduation. She reached a hand out behind her for support, a wall or piece of furniture, but found none, just empty space. She stared at the two men. The first man was still moving his mouth, but she couldn't make out what he was saying. His words were clouded by the piercing static in her ears. A thousand thoughts flew through her head, but she couldn't grab ahold of any.

The man stepped toward her and placed his hands on her upper arms. She watched his mouth, dotted by a line of crooked front teeth. "Do you have anyone to call for support?"

Kate shook her head. "I'm an only child of only children." That wasn't technically true. Her mother had a sister she hadn't spoken to since their twenties, and her father had two brothers who had been killed in Vietnam. It was true enough though. She didn't have anyone.

"How did this happen?" Kate stammered out. She jockeyed from one foot to the other, hoping to steady herself, but her legs shook.

The two men looked at each other then back at her. "Terrorism. The CIA had been watching a cell but couldn't stop them in time."

Kate's heart all but stopped beating. A wave of nausea took hold, and she dropped to her knees sucking in sharp breaths. The room spun.

CHAPTER 2

18 Years Later

Kate jerked awake. She sat upright in bed with the sheets twisted around her left leg. She looked around the room, working to adjust her eyes. The dream, a nightmare really, had happened again. It played out exactly as it always did. She relived the worst moment of her life over and over again. It had been more than eighteen years, and it never stopped.

Kate untwisted her leg from the sheet, threw back the covers, and planted her feet on the cold hardwoods of her parents' brownstone. Well, her brownstone as it had been since their deaths. No matter where work had taken her, from the farthest corners of the globe to the bustling streets of New York City, her little slice on Marlborough Street in Boston had always been home. The brownstone was all she had.

There had been time in her life for nothing else. Until now. No children and no husband. Kate searched the far recesses of her mind to see if she could even remember the last date she had been on. There had been that one guy in Marrakesh, but spiced mint tea in her hotel room and frantic groping of two people who had been in the field too long could hardly be called a date.

Clothes were hastily shed in a heap on the floor. Bodies slick with sweat and desperation. Her head slammed into the wall with every thrust. It ended as quickly as it had started. No, she definitely couldn't call that a date. Kate could barely remember his name. John or Jim or something as commonly American. He had been CIA or NSA. She couldn't remember which agency paid him a living. It didn't matter now. It didn't even matter then.

On that particular mission, Kate had been summoned to Morocco to profile a bombing suspect and interrogate three men from a suspected terror cell. That was her bread and butter. Old school FBI-style profiling and interrogation. Not the tortuous kind that had played out in black sites after 9/11, but back to old tried and true techniques. It had been her specialty. A mix of instinct, forensic linguistics, and psychology her only weapons. The FBI held her leash, but she had been a pawn of many government agencies. In truth, Kate had allowed herself to be farmed out as a mental gun for hire.

They all came recruiting after grad school. The daughter of a murdered U.S. Ambassador intent on revenge, armed with fluency in multiple languages, a knack for profiling, and an ability to secure confessions from even the most hardened criminals. She had done an internship with the FBI, and her field supervisor had been floored at her technique and skill. It was something she didn't even think twice about. Interrogation was as innate for her as breathing. A mental chess game she rarely lost.

She traveled the globe, saw far more than she ever should have in her thirty-eight years, and stockpiled money away. Not that she needed it. The brownstone, one of the few fully-intact that hadn't been carved into apartments and condos, was already paid off. The last time a real estate agent came calling, they had slipped her a piece of paper with twenty-five million written on it. She'd never sell. Her parents had left her a fortune, more money than she could ever spend. It's what afforded her this luxury of a break now. A life reset so to speak.

The FBI had balked at her taking an extended leave, but she

threatened to quit. With millions in the bank, she didn't need the government pension. Kate was pretty sure if she went private, they'd all come calling, paying hand over fist in consultant fees. She had the power and the Bureau knew it.

Kate padded down to the first floor and walked the length of the brownstone to the back kitchen. Her stomach rumbled. She needed her staple of oatmeal and coffee. Kate flipped the switch of the coffeemaker without even giving it a second look and pulled a bowl from the cabinet. She busied herself making her breakfast. She'd had the kitchen remodeled in late 2016, even though she was rarely home. Kate knew she'd quit soon enough and wanted more modern living. She'd been happy with the choice. The gray shaker cabinets offset by the mosaic-tiled backsplash felt warm and inviting. It was a nice contrast to the cold hardwood floors.

With breakfast ready, Kate sat on one side of the large island instead of at the table in the nook where she had eaten nearly every meal as a child. The first spoonful of oatmeal had barely reached her stomach when clanging at the back of the house drew her attention. She raised her eyebrows and glanced to the backdoor. Behind the brownstone sat a postage stamp of a yard, a small space for parking, and a public alley that ran the length of her street. No one came to the house that way – except one person.

Kate got up and unlocked the deadbolt. She slid back into her chair at the island and lazily spooned oatmeal into her mouth.

A few seconds later, without even so much as a knock, a man with thick, wavy dark hair that he had a tendency of never combing, threw open the back door. He stood at nearly six-two and fit. His seafoam green eyes still held a glimmer of mischief. He threw his muscled arms open wide. "Katie, you're back among the living."

"Declan James. Still keeping tabs on me, I see." Kate hitched her head toward the counter. "There's coffee. You should have some. It might lessen the smell of the cheap booze you've bathed in."

Declan frowned. "Now is that any way to speak to your oldest, and dare I say, only friend." He laughed the good-hearted belly laugh that tugged on Kate's heartstrings, what was left of them anyway. Declan made his way to the coffeemaker and poured himself a cup, only a half because he filled the rest of the mug with milk and generous amounts of sugar.

Instead of sitting next to Kate at the island, Declan took a seat at the table in the kitchen's nook. The half-circle space had windows that ran floor-to-ceiling. He stretched out and made himself at home. Kate turned back to her food but could feel his eyes on her.

Declan took a noisy sip, smacking his lips dramatically. "This is good. I missed the way you make coffee. You missed me, too, just admit it."

"Missed isn't the word I'd use." Kate smiled into her oatmeal. Even if she had missed him, she wasn't going to let on. He was right though about one thing. Declan was her oldest and probably only true friend in the world. They had met at the FBI academy when they were both wide-eyed and eager to take on the world.

Hailing from South Boston, Declan had been too roguish at the time for her. He was the youngest in a big Irish Catholic family, and his father was a long-time Boston cop. His handsome good looks and charm intimidated her as much as his hot temper and off-the-cuff approach terrified her.

Declan had asked her out several times in those early days, but she watched him make his way through a sea of women in Virginia bars far too often to let herself go down that path. They had enough in common with their Boston Irish Catholic roots that they had bonded well enough. She had offered friendship, and he had taken it. It was a good thing, too, because Declan was the one constant and stable force in her life. Her romantic relationships had been anything but constant and stable.

Declan had been her partner for a long time at the FBI. For the last few months, since a case they had together in Paris, Kate had been sent from one terrorism case to the next while Declan made the FBI Boston field office his home.

"Come on, Katie. Come sit here. I haven't seen you in months," Declan pleaded.

Declan was the only one who called her Katie. She hated it, but she had long since stopped reminding him. Kate grudgingly picked up her coffee and bowl and made her way to the nook. She pulled up a chair across from him. "How's Lauren?"

Declan looked down at the table and toyed with his mug. "She kicked me out a month ago."

"You knew that was coming. You had enough time to straighten up. She wanted kids and isn't getting any younger."

Declan raised his head to meet her eyes. His signature devastating smile streaked across his face. "Lauren and I drifted apart."

"Is that what you're calling it?" Kate chuckled. "I thought it was the booze and the hooker she found you with?"

Declan slapped the table. "The hooker was part of a case. She was an informant for the Irish mob. You know that."

"I told you eight years ago the night before you married her that she wouldn't understand our work. Frankly, I told you that six months into dating her. I think at the time you suggested I was jealous." Kate took another satisfying bite of oatmeal.

Declan reached across the table for her hand. He stroked her palm with his thumb. "See, Katie, that's why we're friends. You get it. Lauren didn't get it. She didn't even get our friendship. Actually, when Lauren kicked me out, she told me I could go back to you."

Kate ignored that. Lauren had always been jealous of their partnership, but Kate never remained stateside long enough to care.

"I don't want to talk about my failed marriage." He got up and poured himself more coffee and sat down again. "Where were you last, Egypt?"

Kate nodded. "It started in Egypt and ended in San Francisco."

"How'd it go?"

"It's done. The perp is going away for life. The young girls who were trafficked are seeking counseling and shelter. It's going to take the FBI and local cops time to figure out where all the girls came from and get them back home, if home is even an option. Some of the girls had been gone so long who knows what will happen."

"How'd the FBI field office out there treat you? Did you get the confession?"

"The field office was fine. Good group of guys working the case. A couple of them weren't happy I led the interrogation, but I secured a solid confession in under two hours so they were happy on the backend getting to wrap up the case and being able to go home early. I heard he's pleading guilty so it will save me a trip back out there to testify."

Declan sat up straight and leaned forward on the table. He eyed her. "What are you doing now? Just quitting on us? Giving up your security clearances?"

"I'm not quitting. I'm keeping my creds until I decide what I'm doing. I'm taking a break. Waking up one day in the states and the next day farmed out to a CIA black site in Poland. Day in and day out, I'm faced with the scum of the earth. It wears on you..."

Kate stopped talking as Declan pulled his phone from his pocket and checked the screen. He held it up. "Office. Got to take it."

Declan listened to the caller, then his eyes snapped up to Kate. "Yeah, she's here. Got back yesterday." He listened some more. "She's on leave."

Kate shook her head. She didn't care who was on the other end of that phone. She wasn't leaving Boston.

Declan ignored her. "We'll be right there. Secure the scene until I get there." He disconnected from the call and put the phone on the table.

"I just told you—"

Declan stood. "Get dressed. You have ten minutes. We need to be at the scene."

Kate sat back in her chair and folded her arms. "I'm not going anywhere."

Declan slammed his fist on the table, his voice filled with impatience. "You're going even if I have to throw you over my shoulder and carry you there. Now go get dressed. I'll brief you on the walk over."

Kate stared at him, debating if he was serious. Declan took a step toward her. He had a few inches on her and outweighed her by at least sixty pounds of muscle. If he wanted to carry her to the scene, he would do it easily. She softened slightly. "Is it really that important?"

"Kate, the killer left you a note along with a victim sliced ear to ear at Granary Burying Ground. You don't have an option on this one." Declan checked his watch. "We're wasting time."

Without saying a word, Kate dropped her dishes in the sink and made her way to the front stairs. Declan followed right behind.

On the third step, she turned to him. "I'm going to get dressed. What do you think you're doing? You're not coming with me."

Declan ran a hand down his stubbled face. He looked up at the winding staircase. "Listen, Katie, don't be mad. When Lauren kicked me out, I had nowhere to go. I've been living on your third floor ever since. I left yesterday when I knew you were coming back. I figured I'd give you a night all to yourself."

"You moved into my house without telling me!" Kate shouted.

Declan shrugged calmly. "I didn't have an option. We don't have time to get into this now." He nudged her up the stairs. "There will be plenty of time to yell at me later."

CHAPTER 3

Granary Burying Ground sat on the northeastern end of Boston Common on Tremont Street. Kate and Declan walked from her house and cut through the Boston Public Garden. Kate had loved playing there as a child. She had her first kiss as a teen near the pond that took up much of the middle of the garden. In college, when her parents were home, she'd sit with her father on a park bench while he read her the classics. Henry James had been his favorite. Kate shoved the memories down like choking on water. She coughed and sucked back the emotion.

Declan reached for her hand and laced his fingers through hers. "You okay?"

Kate pulled her hand back and shoved it in the pocket of her heavy, long cardigan sweater. She didn't need his sympathy. They walked side by side in silence. When they reached the edge of Charles Street, they waited for a light and the flow of traffic to stop. Kate steadied herself with each step, trying to get her mind back on work. "Tell me what you know about the case."

"A male victim. We haven't found a wallet yet, but he looks to be in his early forties. From what I'm told, he has been propped up against Paul Revere's grave and sliced from ear to ear. His head is nearly off. There's a note attached to his shirt that's addressed to you. They've not read it yet."

"He's around the age Paul Revere was on his midnight ride in 1775 to alert that the British were coming," Kate said absently.

"That's the first thing that comes to mind when I tell you a man is nearly decapitated. Why do you know that?"

Katie's mouth set in a firm line slightly upturned at the corner. "As you know, my father was an American history professor at Harvard obsessed with the Revolutionary War. It was a constant source of discussion in my house growing up."

At the far northeast end of Boston Common, Kate and Declan stepped onto the sidewalk and continued north for less than a block passing Park Street Church. Immediately the wrought iron gates of the cemetery came into view as did the throngs of people standing in groups murmuring about what had happened. Kate shut out the chatter.

They continued walking until they reached the stone archway. Boston police blocked steps up into the cemetery. Declan flashed his creds and they moved out of the way. It's amazing what an FBI badge will do for access.

Kate tried to recall where Paul Revere's gravesite sat in the cemetery. It had been a long time since she'd set foot on the hallowed ground. Her memory strain wasn't needed. The swarm of cops at the end of the central walkway told her exactly where they needed to go.

Paul Revere's grave was a straight shot back from the main entrance, slightly off to the right in the farthest back section. It was a simple stone for a man who had proven such a central figure in the country's history. The stone itself was blocked from her, but as two local Boston cops stepped to the side, the victim came into view.

Until today, Kate had thought she'd seen it all. She'd been to every kind of crime scene imaginable. Some bothered her more than others. The sight before her would stay with her for a long time.

The victim slumped against the gravestone with his head down and hands folded in his lap as if he were praying. It might have been the case, but his blood-soaked shirt told another story. Kate walked toward the grave with Declan at her side. "There are too many people out here, trampling over the crime scene."

"I was just thinking the same thing. Let me see if I can get the local guys out of here." Declan moved in front of Kate and headed directly for a group of cops milling around. He pulled a trio of them to the side and began to gesture with his hands. Working with locals wasn't always the easiest for the FBI. Jurisdictional issues created as much of a problem as egos. In a sensational case like this, everyone wants a piece of the action.

Kate pulled her sweater around her tighter and brushed a strand of hair out of her eyes. She was glad she at least had the good sense to throw a scarf around her neck. Late October wasn't supposed to be this cold.

"FBI Special Agent Kate Walsh?" a man standing next to the body asked. He stood about Kate's height, athletic build, dark eyes and skin tone. His black hair was cropped close to his head. He had a Boston Police Department windbreaker on, and the crease down the front of his pants had been starched into place. Kate assumed he might have been military at some point. He had blue gloves on his hands, the kind cops wore at a crime scene. Otherwise, Kate was sure he would have shaken her hand.

"I'm Harris Briggs, Boston Police Detective, homicide unit."

"What do we have, Det. Briggs?"

He went over the details that Declan had just told her on the walk to the cemetery. From Kate's angle, she couldn't see the man's neck wound, only the blood. As Det. Briggs spoke, he handed her a pair of gloves, which she snapped on her hands. She crouched low enough to see the wound. It was a clean slice nearly decapitating him. She looked to the left and right and then tilted her head toward Det. Briggs. "Is there blood someplace else in the cemetery?"

"Why do you ask that?"

"With a slice across his neck like that, the blood would have sprayed farther away. There would be a mess at his feet and in front of him. Besides, to make the cut, the perp would have to have been standing behind him, and that's not possible with the gravestone. He wasn't killed right here. The perp probably did it close by and moved his body here."

Det. Briggs said solemnly, "It's back here behind the stone."

Kate stood and moved to the back of the stone. Thankfully, the cops had sectioned off the area so it wasn't trampled. From the blood spatter, it looked like the altercation with the perp and victim had started behind the stone. As Kate assessed the area something struck her as odd. The blood spatter didn't leave the spray-like pattern she expected.

"I don't think the neck wound is the first injury," Kate said, turning to Det. Briggs. "I think the victim was killed another way, and when he was dying, the perp caused the neck injury."

"Why do you say that?" Det. Briggs asked, his confusion evident.

Kate didn't respond. Instead, she waved Declan over. He had an eagle eye with crime scene investigation. He could pick out something strange from a mile away. It was a skill Kate wished she had and part of what made them such good partners. She pointed to the ground. "Take a look at the crime scene and tell me what you see."

Declan stepped back from the body. "Well, right off, it's obvious the perp wanted to horrify whoever found the body." He moved around the gravestone and scoped out the area. When he got to the back of the stone, Declan pulled up short. "Does the victim have another injury?"

"Lack of blood spatter, right?" Kate asked. When Declan confirmed, she moved around and crouched low again in front of the victim. She let her eyes roam over his body. She didn't want to touch him and potentially destroy the scene. She'd let her eyes do the work first. But she didn't see anything unusual.

"Let me look," Declan said, crouching low next to her. Kate got up and moved out of the way. She watched as Declan inched his gloved finger toward the fabric of the shirt, assessing an area right near the man's heart. He stood quickly. "There's a slice through the fabric. I need a crime scene tech."

A crime scene tech walked toward them at once. The young woman looked at both Kate and Declan. "What do you see?"

"There's a weird rip in his shirt near his heart." Declan pointed to the area on the victim's shirt. "Right here, look at this."

The crime scene tech carefully unbuttoned the man's shirt and pulled the fabric back to reveal what looked to Kate like a stab wound. The area around it had already bruised.

"Is that a pattern bruise?" Kate asked, squinting down at the man's bloodied skin.

"Looks like from the handle of the knife," the tech said, snapping photos of the area. "I don't see much evidence to collect, but the medical examiner will know more."

Det. Briggs cleared his throat. "We have this under control, Agent Walsh. We called the FBI in because the killer left you a note."

His comment was akin to a mother slapping a child's hand away while baking. Det. Briggs didn't want the FBI taking over the scene. Kate offered him a sympathetic smile. She didn't want to get involved any more than he wanted her to, but it came as second nature to her. She stepped toward Det. Briggs. "Agent James mentioned the note. Do you have it?"

Det. Briggs stepped away and walked over to where the other cops stood. The cop handed him a clear plastic evidence bag and Det. Briggs walked back over to Kate and Declan, giving it to her. "It's addressed to you. A crime scene tech opened it a moment ago. We didn't know when you'd get here. We waited as long as we could."

"Understood." Kate squinted down at the evidence bag. It was more than a simple note written or typed on paper. She had never seen handwriting so precise and perfect, on parchment paper no less. It was almost like the author had lined the parchment with a ruler and wrote with what appeared to be a fountain pen. Kate brought the note closer to her face. There were only a few lines.

Special Agent Walsh, we find ourselves on opposite sides of this battle once again. You are the only worthy adversary. This time, we shall not lose. You will not repeat the sins of your forefathers. Your patriots were pathetic excuses for men. General Thomas Gage

Kate blinked a few times at the note, unsure of its meaning. She handed it to Declan. He read the note aloud, and when he was done, he held it up. "What's this supposed to mean? Do you know General Thomas Gage?"

Kate stood for several moments running through names of people she'd met, adversaries she'd gone up against, criminals she'd put away, and nothing clicked. She was about to tell Declan she hadn't heard of him but one of her father's history lessons popped into her head.

"It can't be," Kate said quietly to herself. "No, that's ridiculous."

"What is?" Declan pressed.

"General Thomas Gage was commander-in-chief of British forces in North America and governor of Massachusetts Bay during the years leading up to the American Revolution. For many in Britain at the time, it was Gage who failed to squelch the uprising. Obviously, he's been deceased for more than two centuries."

CHAPTER 4

"What are you saying exactly?" Det. Briggs asked, looking at Kate skeptically and taking the note back from Declan.

"I don't know what I'm saying," Kate responded, meaning it. She had no idea what they were looking at or why the note would have been directed to her personally. "We need to have this analyzed not only for a handwriting sample but for the type of parchment and the pen used to write it."

Declan pointed. "You think that's real parchment from 1775 and a fountain pen?"

"They used a quill and ink then," Kate corrected. "I'm not saying anything of the sort. I don't know what we are looking at here that's why I'm saying we need to have it analyzed. Look at this scene and where we are. Paul Revere's grave. Granary Burying Ground. Boston. Read the words he chose to use – patriots, forefathers. He's sending us a message. I'm just not sure what that message is yet."

"You don't know why he addressed this note to you?" Det. Briggs asked.

"I have no idea. I don't think this is a run of the mill homicide. I can tell you that much. Have you identified the victim yet?"

"No," Det. Briggs said, frustration on his face evident. "We haven't moved his body so his wallet could be in his back pocket, but we don't have any information otherwise."

"Where did you find the note?"

"It was lying on the ground next to the victim. We called the FBI office right away looking for you." Det. Briggs locked eyes with her. "I had hoped you'd be more helpful in identifying the killer."

Kate gestured with her palms up in a shrug. "I can't tell you what I don't know."

Declan looked down at the victim. "When is the medical examiner getting here?"

"Dr. Oliver Graham should be here with his team any minute now. I can call you when I know more."

"I think we should stick around and talk to him ourselves." When Det. Briggs exhaled loudly and shook his head, Declan reassured, "I'm not trying to take over your crime scene. When a killer leaves a note for an FBI agent, we need to fully assess what's happening."

Kate waved Declan off to the side. "Take care of what you have to, Detective. We don't want to be in your way. I'll spend some time thinking about who could have written that note."

Det. Briggs stalked off to talk to a crime scene investigator while Kate and Declan walked to the far side of the cemetery out of earshot of other police.

When they were alone, Declan asked, "What do you think we're dealing with here? Do you have some ideas about who wrote the note?"

"Not a clue. I said that to buy us some time." Kate glanced back toward the body. "That's not his first kill. I can tell you that much. I think we're looking at a serial killer, but you and I both know the locals aren't going to call it that. What instruction did Spade give you when he called?"

"Spade didn't give any instructions other than to figure out why a killer is leaving you a note. You know how he is – cryptic, bossy, and lacking in details."

Martin Spade was their FBI handler and supervisor. He made the determination what cases Kate and Declan got involved with. They rarely saw the man and only referred to him as Spade. He was an enigma at the FBI and had run the unit Kate and Declan were assigned to for nearly all thirty years of his career. If Spade wanted them on a case, they'd be on the case, even if Kate had threatened to resign if she didn't get some time off. She hated being bullied, but she hated a killer connecting her to a horrific crime even more.

"We wait then and see what the medical examiner has to say." Kate looked out toward the front of the cemetery the way they had come in. "We won't have to wait long. He's here," she said spotting the medical examiner van pulling up to the sidewalk.

Declan and Kate stood off to the side while the medical examiner and his team spoke to Det. Briggs and then to some of the crime scene investigators. The medical examiner did a cursory overview of the scene and the body and then made quick work of getting the body in the body bag and on the stretcher for transport back to the office for an autopsy.

Before they left, Kate and Declan walked over and introduced themselves. Kate made sure to stress the FBI had limited involvement but would still like to be read in on the autopsy results when he was done.

Dr. Graham pursed his lips. "Anything the FBI wants, the FBI gets." With that, he walked off with his team back toward his waiting van.

"I've been thinking," Det. Briggs said evenly with a slight hesitation in his voice, "I think it would be a good idea for the FBI to stay involved."

Declan waited to see if he'd say anything else. When Det. Briggs didn't elaborate, Declan asked, "Why is that?"

Det. Briggs pointed to a group of Boston police standing in a circle on the other side of Paul Revere's grave. "When I was over there talking, one of the beat cops mentioned a shooting a couple of weeks back. I'd like you to take a look at it. It might be connected."

That piqued Kate's interest. "Why would you think so? This was a stabbing and that one a shooting. What's the connection?"

Det. Briggs toed the dirt in front of him. He looked uncertain about what he was about to say.

Declan encouraged him. "Tell us even if it's just a theory. I don't care if it comes across as the craziest thing you've ever thought, we've all been there before. Just tell us."

Det. Briggs swallowed and cleared his throat. "We were called to a scene late in the evening of a man who had been shot in front of the Old State House. The victim was a black man in his late forties. He was shot once in the chest. I didn't think much of it at the time. Not that shootings happen often in Boston in that area of the city, but it's not completely out of the question. Dr. Graham and I have been wracking our brains about the case since it happened. He pulled round lead bullets out of the victim – two of them. They aren't bullets you'd find today. I couldn't even get a ballistics match on the weapon."

"You're thinking it's homemade?" That's what it sounded like to Kate anyway. She was far from a weapons expert though.

"Not exactly. We think the victim was shot with an antique gun, but we have no leads. No suspects at this time. We believe it was a random attack. There is nothing in the man's background to suggest otherwise. He worked for a financial firm. His wife said he had gone to meet friends for dinner. She had been on the phone with him and he said he was going to catch a cab and be home soon. He was shot shortly after that. He had his wallet, so there was no robbery. No motive we can discern."

"I still don't understand how you think it could be connected," Declan said, shifting his weight from one foot to the other. Kate wasn't sure if he was antsy or cold. The wind had started to whip up around them.

"I'm getting to that," Det. Briggs started. "One of the cops over there just told me that a few days after that shooting, his brother-in-law, a reporter from the *Boston Globe*, received a letter with similar parchment paper to what we saw tonight with a note that read: *Crispus started the Revolution. Victory will be ours this time.* No one connected that random note to the shooting though. Why would they? The reporter joked about it in the newsroom and told his brother-in-law. I don't even know if he still has the note."

Declan shifted his eyes over to Kate, waiting for an explanation. He didn't know American history the way she did.

Kate explained, "Crispus Attucks is widely reported to be the first person killed during the Boston Massacre, which happened right outside of the Old State House. Scholars believe that was the turning point in bringing the Colonists together in supporting independence from England. It was a pivotal moment in American history."

Kate stopped speaking and turned around looking across the graveyard. "Crispus Attucks and the other four Boston Massacre victims are buried here. They were interred in a mass grave, and there is a stone that lists their names." Kate didn't wait, she stalked off from Declan and Det. Briggs in search.

She couldn't quite remember where the stone was in the cemetery, but it didn't take her long. She went up and down a few rows and then found the simple stone marker. It was wider and larger than the stone for Paul Revere and had a good deal of writing down the front. It mentioned the names of all five of the Boston Massacre victims with the date. It was also the burial place for Christopher Snider, a twelve-year-old boy who was killed in his home by loyalist Ebenezer Richardson when a mob had formed outside of the house of a loyalist informer.

Kate scanned down the gravestone in the front and the back. For some reason, she thought the killer might have left them a message, but she didn't see anything. Declan and Det. Briggs caught up to her. "I think you're right, Det. Briggs. This could all be connected."

"What should we do first?" Det. Briggs asked, looking down at the stone.

Kate pulled her sweater around her tighter. "We need to be read in on the shooting. I'd need everything you have to date including the autopsy report, crime scene photos, and interview notes. We also need to interview the *Boston Globe* reporter and hope he still has the first letter. Let us know if you can get ahold of that if he still has it." Kate glanced up at Declan. "You want to go back to the house and strategize?"

"I think we should." Declan turned to Det. Briggs. "I appreciate you calling us on this. The FBI has authorized us to focus on this case, so we are at your disposal for whatever you need." Declan paused for a moment like he wanted to say something else. He bit at his lip and said cautiously, "I don't want to cause any alarm or speak for Kate, but I don't think it would be a bad idea to quietly pull together a task force to address these cases. These two murders won't be the last."

Det. Briggs raised his eyebrows. "You think this is a serial killer?"

"I don't know yet," Declan said, "but it has all the hallmarks of that. Better to be ready."

Det. Briggs thanked them, and Kate and Declan made their way across the row of gravestones to the center walkway and out of the cemetery past the throngs of news media and onlookers.

CHAPTER 5

"That was brave," Kate commented when they were past the crowds. "Local cops don't usually react too well to hearing they might have a serial killer."

Declan turned his head to look at her. "I thought we better prepare ourselves. Do you think I should have held back?"

"I'm not saying that. I don't know what we are working with yet. I might have waited until we explored the shooting case first. I think the shooting and the note to the newspaper are connected, but we can't be sure right now. I would have been more cautious."

Declan laughed. "That was the appropriate response. Now, tell me what you really think."

"I think someone isn't done fighting the Revolutionary War. Someone is mighty aggravated the Patriots won." They kept walking the few blocks to her house. Kate pulled out her key and unlocked her front door. "I've heard comments of people still acting like they are fighting the Civil War, but who is still angry over the Revolutionary War? It's bizarre to me."

Declan held the door for Kate as they walked into the house. "What we need to figure out, Katie, is why a serial killer is targeting you with his notes."

"That's exactly what we are going to do after I shower and change." Kate started up the stairs, but stopped midway and turned to look back down at Declan. "We are also going to discuss you living on my third floor."

"I'll start some coffee, honey, so you have something warm to drink while you yell at me." Declan walked out of sight before Kate could yell at him.

Kate opened the door to her bedroom, realized she hadn't made her bed, which is something she did every morning without fail. Declan had been back in her presence for less than a few hours and already her routine changed. She made her bed quickly, peeled off her clothes, dropped them in the hamper, and stepped into the shower. She had the length of the shower to decide what she was going to do with Declan.

The third floor of the brownstone hadn't been used in years. Kate's father's study took up the entire back half of the house. She sometimes used it as an office. There was a bedroom and bathroom along with a library in the front of the house. The library still held her parents' collection of books. Kate had added books she had read through the years and used the space as a reading room ever since. She hadn't had much of an occasion to be up there in the last few years given the constant travel her job required.

Kate finished her shower, having decided about Declan. She dried her hair in soft waves and threw on just a touch of makeup. Kate slid worn comfortable jeans over her narrow hips and pulled an old Harvard sweatshirt over her head. She couldn't imagine she'd be going anywhere else today, so she might as well be comfortable.

Kate found Declan sitting in the living room in a brown leather chair that had been her father's favorite. He had started a fire in the fireplace and had a cup of coffee for each of them on the coffee table.

"I can have my things packed in an hour and be gone," Declan said as soon as Kate hit the last step of the stairs.

Kate walked to the coffee table and picked up a cup of coffee.

She took a sip and savored the taste. He had complimented her on the coffee she made earlier, but she could have easily returned the sentiment. He knew just how she liked it.

Kate sat down on the couch and pulled her legs up under her. "That won't be necessary—"

"You're going to let me stay?" Declan asked, interrupting her.

She held up her hand. "There are a few house rules. If you can abide by them, you can stay." She took another sip, watching him over the rim of the cup.

"I'll do my homework, pick up my clothes, and be in bed by ten," Declan promised with a wink.

"Not what I had in mind." Kate relaxed back into the couch. "It might be nice having some company here for a change. That said, you know I'm a neat freak and I like my alone time. If you disturb my peace, I'm kicking you to the curb. No women here either. If you feel the need to hook up, go to her house."

Declan held his hands up in surrender. "There will be no hooking up. I'm going to get on the straight and narrow. I take no pleasure in messing up my marriage, but it's for the best. There were more issues between Lauren and me than just my drinking."

Kate had no desire to wade through the remnants of Declan's failed marriage. She thought of something else. She peered over at him with a mischievous grin on her face. "You have to cook a few nights a week. I hate cooking and you're so good at it. I could use some homecooked meals."

"You can't cook anything decent anyway. What do you want for rent?"

"Nothing." Declan started to argue, but Kate wouldn't hear of it. "You are in debt anyway or will be once Lauren gets you in court. Cook for me, stay out of my way, and the place is yours. If you want to take one of the bedrooms with the ensuite bathroom on the second floor, feel free. The front right corner room is nice. It has a sitting room and a desk."

Declan took a sip of his coffee. "How long are you letting me stay?"

"As long as you want. This house is too big for me. Rents in the city are insane. I think we can manage to share the house until you want to move out."

"That's a generous offer," Declan said, peering over at her. "You sure?"

Kate nodded. "Now that we have that settled, let's talk about the case."

Declan got up and grabbed Kate's cup. He went off into the kitchen while Kate grabbed the throw blanket and wrapped it around herself. She thanked him for refilling her coffee. Declan sat back in the chair.

"Tell me why you think this killer is targeting you." Declan took a sip and then set down his cup.

"Maybe he's read articles in the news about me profiling serial killers. There was that one case in Nevada I received a good deal of press coverage on. I think it also mentioned that I'm from Boston." Kate had been thinking about this since leaving the cemetery, but she didn't believe it was as simple as she just said. By the look on Declan's face, he didn't either.

"My father was fairly well known in some academic circles for his lectures on the Revolutionary War. His family goes back to the 1600s in New England. His ancestors left England and came to America. They were Patriots during the war. My mother is descended from Robert Treat Paine, who was one of the signers of the Declaration of Independence. He was a lawyer and a representative of Massachusetts. He also served as the state's first attorney general and as an associate justice of the Massachusetts Supreme Judicial Court. My family on both sides is fairly steeped in American history." Kate took a breath. "If this killer, who I assume is a man, is so keyed up about England losing the war, then maybe he went in search of descendants of Patriots."

Declan nodded. "When he realized you were an FBI agent, he probably felt like he struck gold."

"If that's even his motive." Kate had no idea what they were dealing with yet. She had dealt with many serial killer cases in her career, but none that had a particular tie to anything historical or political. She'd dealt with acts of domestic and international terrorism that certainly had political, religious, and even historical ties, but not a serial killer. This was new for her.

Declan snapped Kate back to the present. "You said yourself both notes showed a connection to the Revolutionary War, and the body was propped up against Paul Revere's grave. Det. Briggs said the guy was shot with antique bullets. Then there is the parchment paper and fountain pen. What more evidence do you need?"

"I concede this is probably exactly what it looks like. You know me, I don't like making judgments early about a case."

Declan sat forward in his chair. "Between you and me, can you profile him yet?"

"Declan, I'm not psychic. It's not how it works."

"Kate, I know you. The wheels are already turning. I can see his personality shining through in the crime scene in the cemetery today, so I know you can as well."

Kate stayed quiet. Even if it was just with Declan, she didn't want to get ahead of herself. Profiling was as much a science as it was an art. A blend of many factors. She didn't have enough information to say anything definitively. Before Declan could press her further, the knocker on the front door slammed against the wood three times.

Wide-eyed, Declan looked at Kate. "Expecting company?"

"Do I ever have company beside you?" Kate got up to go check the door, but Declan called her back.

"Let me go," he said standing. "It's Sunday, there are no deliveries and a serial killer just left you a note on a dead body." Declan grabbed his gun, which he had left on a side table in the living room when they had come home earlier. He moved quickly into the hall. Kate thought he was being a bit paranoid.

Declan opened the front door, which creaked on its old hinges. "Are you sure you don't have a boyfriend?"

Kate walked the rest of the way to the door and expected to see someone standing there. Instead, on the stoop sat a beautifully gift-wrapped package. The gold wrapping paper with glitter foil was topped with a sheer lace ribbon tied in a perfect bow. The sender had left a small card tucked into the bow.

Neither one of them touched the gift. Kate had no idea who sent it. She wasn't expecting any presents. Her birthday was in May. There was nothing she celebrated in October.

"I have no idea who that could be from," she said.

Declan bounded down the front steps and looked in both directions. For a Sunday, there wasn't much foot traffic on the streets, and Declan didn't see anyone.

As Declan came back up the steps, he inched opened the folded card and read it aloud to Kate. "I never leave my adversary unarmed. Enjoy this piece of history and use it well. Your life will depend on it." He glanced up. "Same cursive in fountain pen. It's not ticking, so it's probably not a bomb."

CHAPTER 6

"Probably not a bomb isn't good enough for me," Kate said, her brow furrowed as she looked over the package. "Can you get a crime scene unit from the Boston FBI field office here?"

"On it." Declan moved past Kate into the house. Within seconds he made a call and said he needed a unit to Kate's house. When he ended the call, he stood by Kate in the doorway. "They should be here soon. Do you want to leave it out there until they arrive?"

"I don't want to touch it at all." Kate turned to Declan. "He knows where I live."

Declan reached his arm across Kate's shoulder and pulled her into his side. "I'm not going anywhere."

Kate relaxed into him. "He is probably in his fifties. College-educated and might even have advanced degrees. He is intelligent and well planned. These aren't frenzied crimes. There's no sexual component. I have no idea of motive."

"I knew you were already working up a profile." Declan bent down to take a closer look at the gift. "Do you want me to call Det. Briggs and get the locals involved?"

"Not right now. I want to know what's in the box first. I want the FBI techs to have the first crack at this. We have better resources than the local cops. This won't win me any favors with Det. Briggs, but I don't care. Not when we are dealing with a killer who knows my home address."

They waited together on Kate's front stoop until the crime scene techs arrived. It was two guys Declan knew well. He explained about the murder in the cemetery and the potential connection to Kate. It was a brief overview, only enough for them to get started in assessing the gift.

The tech with dark hair looked up at Kate. "Do you want us to open this here or take it back to the lab and open it?"

"Will you lose evidence if you open it here?"

"We shouldn't. The lab is just more sterile and secure."

"I understand," Kate said evenly, and she did. She didn't want to wait until later to learn what the killer sent her. She wanted to know now. "Just open it here. I need to know what he sent. We are going to have to call Det. Briggs with the Boston Police Department when you're done. I want to make sure FBI forensics are on this first."

The crime scene techs went to work. When they were ready, one untied the bow and carefully unwrapped the package, preserving even the tape that was used to keep the wrapping paper closed. A simple brown box sat under the wrapping. One tech carefully lifted the lid and exposed an antique dagger. Kate guessed the silver blade to be about eight to nine inches long. The handle had an ornate scrolled design and where the two pieces met was a silver plate that jutted out with two round balls on each side, one facing the handle and the other curved up toward the blade.

Declan cleared his throat. "How old do you think that is?"

Kate wasn't sure. The blade itself wasn't new. It had been worn and wasn't as shiny as it had probably been when it was crafted. It was well-preserved but definitely an antique.

"We can analyze that at the lab," one of the techs said.

Declan went to get his phone and when he returned, he took several photos of the dagger. Kate asked the tech to lift it out of the box since they were wearing gloves and she wasn't. "Do you see anything engraved on it? Any writing or any markings?"

The tech examined the dagger carefully. On the end of the handle, there was an engraving, but Kate had a hard time seeing what it was. The techs couldn't discern it either, but it looked to one of them as a part of a family crest.

"We can get this back to the lab and analyze more." The techs slipped the dagger into an evidence bag. They did the same with the gift wrapping and the box. They left promising to call when they knew more.

As soon as they were gone, Kate and Declan stepped back into the house. The looming thought that someone was watching them plagued Kate. "Do you think the guy was watching us out there?"

"I thought the same thing," Declan said and went into the living room and picked up their coffee cups and carried them to the kitchen. He poured himself some more coffee and offered more to Kate, but she declined.

He stood leaning against the kitchen counter watching her as she sat at the island. Kate felt small, childlike under his intense gaze. "Why are you looking at me like that?"

"The killer just left you a gift on your front stoop. You need to start using the security system you have but never use," he scolded. Declan walked over to the back door and fiddled with the bolt lock. "We need to beef up security around here. How accessible is your address online?"

Kate had been wondering the same thing. She wasn't on social media, but even so, everything was accessible if you knew enough these days. "I'm sure it's out there if you look hard enough. This was my grandparents' brownstone. My father grew up here in this house and moved back in after his parents passed away. Who didn't know Harvard Professor Joe Walsh? My mother, Madeline, went to all the society functions in Boston. People knew them. They knew me growing up and eventually that I joined the FBI. Locally, it's no secret and easy to find out."

Kate thought for several moments. "I think this killer is local to Boston and probably has been for a long time."

"Do you want me to check with my parents to see if we can stay at their house?"

Kate loved Declan's parents. They had been there for her as much as her own would have been over the years, so if a killer was after her, the last thing she wanted was to bring a killer to their front door. Kate explained as much. "You'll be here. I think between the two of us, we'll be fine."

Declan raised an eyebrow. "Do you want me to call my brothers for added protection?" Declan was the youngest of a family of five boys who grew up in South Boston, blocks from Carson Beach. His parents still had the same home Declan grew up in. They went to Catholic schools in the neighborhood and were regulars at their local parish.

The oldest son became a criminal defense attorney in New York City. The second oldest a doctor here in Boston. The next two ran with street gangs in their youth and were "mobbed up" as Declan put it. His biggest fear was having a mob case and finding his brothers were the targets of the investigation. But they'd protect Declan to their deaths. The family was loyal to the end.

Thinking about Declan's loud Irish-Catholic family made her smile. "I think we can leave your brothers out of this. It's probably the last thing we need. Do your parents know about you and Lauren?"

Declan shrugged. "I didn't tell them, but I'm sure she did. You know how my parents feel about divorce. I'm surprised my mother hasn't called to yell at me yet."

Kate reached up and brushed strands of hair that had fallen over her face. "Text those photos to Det. Briggs if you can. We need to set up a call with Spade and let him know what's going on."

Kate got up from the center island and went upstairs to the third-floor office. Years ago, after she first joined the FBI, she had installed a secure phone line since she rarely made it to the small office that she kept in the Boston FBI field office. She and Declan used that line to call into headquarters when they were in Boston.

She pulled the desk chair out, lifted the phone off the receiver, clicked speakerphone, and dialed the familiar number. Spade answered on the first ring like the man had been sitting there waiting for their call. He probably had. Declan and Kate often joked that he probably had their houses and phones bugged.

"Looks like you're not going to get that vacation, Walsh." Spade blew out a breath. "You can tell me you're quitting all you want. I need you on this case. Boston needs you on this case."

Spade didn't have to give Kate the hard sell. She was already invested. "That's fine, Spade. I've already made my peace with it."

"Read me in on the case. What do we know so far?"

Kate and Declan took turns explaining everything that had transpired over the day. Declan motioned with his hand for Kate to explain the dagger. She said seriously, "I don't know who this person is or why I've been targeted. It's a strange case, Spade, because this seems like it would be politically motivated, but it's not the typical domestic terrorism."

"Criminals adapt all the time and we must, too," Spade said, leaving no room for debate. Not that Kate had anything else to add. She had grown accustomed to his responses. In her early years, she would have debated him, but it was a waste of effort.

"Declan already sent the information about the dagger to Det. Harris Briggs, the homicide lead with the Boston Police Department. We had our forensic team go over it first though."

"Good. Give me an update when you review the details of the shooting. We need to dig into the victims' backgrounds as well. It's important to know if this is random victim selection or if he's targeting them."

Neither Kate nor Declan disagreed with that. Kate said, "They are both local Boston cases. How much access do you think the local cops are going to give us?"

"It shouldn't be an issue," Spade reassured. "Let me know if you have trouble because I want you both leading up the investigation."

Declan balked. "We can't just take over their case, Spade."

"You can and you will." The click resounded, and Kate and Declan shared a look. If Spade said they were taking over the case, they were taking it over. He had probably already called the police chief or governor if he had to. Spade's influence went far and wide.

CHAPTER 7

The next morning Kate and Declan sat at a large conference table in the homicide unit of the Boston Police Department. Dressed professionally, badges around their necks and guns on their hips, they were all business.

Det. Harris Briggs entered the room looking like he'd been read the riot act by someone, probably his boss. He had an evidence box in his hands that he set down on the table and shoved toward them. "I was informed you're taking over these cases, and I need to give you whatever you want." He turned to walk out of the room, but Declan called him back.

"Det. Briggs, that's not accurate," Declan said his voice constrained. Det. Briggs turned around and folded his arms across his chest. He was at least willing to listen to what Declan had to say. "We spoke to our boss, Martin Spade, yesterday. He wants us in charge of this case, which we don't have much say in. However, we can't work on this case without you. I meant what I said yesterday that we need a full team – a task force. I wasn't saying that to appease you. We need your expertise on this case."

Det. Briggs shifted his eyes toward Kate. "I looked you up last night. You have an excellent record. Do you want the same?"

Kate nodded. "Without question. We are here this morning to go over the evidence with you. Our FBI boss can pull all the strings he wants, but we know how it works in the field. I looked you up too, Det. Briggs. You have the highest closure rate of any detective in Boston and have for years. There's no way we can work this case without you."

Declan and Kate hadn't gone over what they'd say to Det. Briggs before the meeting, but they had anticipated there would be much to smooth over. No local police department liked it when the FBI swooped in and took over their case. There was typically a good deal of politics going on behind the scenes the detectives weren't involved in and couldn't stand. Declan and Kate meant what they said. Det. Briggs would be an integral part of the team.

Kate knew he'd have to swallow a bit of his pride to join them. She was glad when he did just that. Det. Briggs pulled the box back and opened it for them. "This is all from the shooting. The victim Jordan Williams was forty-seven, and from what we can tell, in the wrong place at the wrong time."

Kate wasn't sure that was right. "You said earlier nothing in the man's history has given any clues to a suspect, correct?"

"Correct. We think this was random." Det. Briggs pulled another file out and slid it over to Kate. "The autopsy indicates two gunshots – one to his gut and the fatal one to his chest. He bled out right there on the street. A few bystanders rushed to his aid after the shooting, but no one can identify the shooter or even where the shots came from."

Declan clicked his tongue. "Antique bullets indicate antique gun most likely. That tells me the victim wasn't shot by a sniper on a roof. For that kind of accuracy, the killer probably wasn't more than three hundred or so feet away, possibly closer."

Det. Briggs agreed. "That's what we thought. There is an alleyway and a few spots the killer could have shot from and stayed out of view of bystanders."

Kate flipped through the autopsy report. Nothing stood out. The victim had a low blood alcohol level indicating he might have had a drink or two with dinner, which is what he had told his wife he was doing that night. He wasn't intoxicated and no drugs in his system. There was no indication of a robbery or mugging.

Kate glanced up at Det. Briggs. "Why do you think this was random?"

"There's no other explanation we could come up with. We've talked to fifty people who knew him from his colleagues to his friends and family. I can't come up with a single shred of evidence he knew his killer."

"Right," Kate said cautiously. It wasn't what she was getting at. Det. Briggs maintained eye contact with her waiting for her to explain. "At first look, I think you were on the right track, but now with the note referencing Crispus Attucks, we might need to revisit. I think he was probably targeted that night."

"How so?" Det. Briggs asked with hesitation tinging his voice.

"Crispus Attucks was of African and Native American descent and by all accounts was a freed black man in Boston. Some believe he escaped slavery. My history on his background isn't exact, but suffice it to say, he was a free black man," Kate explained. "Your victim was black. I believe he was targeted that night. Now, I can't say if the killer stalked him for a while before he killed him or if the killer laid in wait until he had the right victim selection, but I believe Jordan Williams was chosen for a reason. If I were to guess, I'd say it was more than the victim just happened to fit the right race."

Det. Briggs pinched the bridge of his nose. "Are you saying this is a hate crime?"

"Not at all. I'm saying the killer chose a victim representative of a historical figure, no more no less." Kate waited until she was sure Det. Briggs understood. "I want us to dig more into Jordan Williams's ancestral background. The killer is targeting me for a reason. He might be targeting others for the same."

Det. Briggs sat down at the table. "You know why the killer is targeting you?"

Kate explained her family background, including her father's doctorate in American history and her mother's lineage back to a signer of the Declaration of Independence. "It occurred to me this morning, if the killer spent this much time targeting me, he might be doing the same with the other victims. Does the journalist still have the note?"

"Charlie Crain still has the note. I told him we'd be expecting him around ten." Det. Briggs looked at his watch. "He should be here in about thirty minutes."

Declan tapped Kate's arm. "Are you thinking we should interview the wife of Jordan Williams?"

"That's exactly what I'm thinking. I want more background on him now that we are looking at the case from this angle." Kate continued flipping through the case file. Det. Briggs and his team had done a thorough investigation. They took the same course in the investigation she would have given the information they had available at the time. Nothing was missed. Now they had a potential lead, they could go a different direction.

As Kate scanned another document summarizing items picked up at the crime scene, she said, "This is great work, Det. Briggs. How long have you been in homicide?"

"Nearly fifteen years." His phone rang before he could explain more. Det. Briggs looked at the screen and excused himself from the room.

Declan sat back. "At least we smoothed that over. You think this killer is going to the trouble to hunt down people like you who have a tie to the American Revolution?"

"I don't know, but it's worth exploring." Kate shifted in her seat to look at Declan. "It occurred to me last night the kind of legwork the killer would have to put in to get ancestral information about me. It's not as simple as reading my father's bio. Someone would have to dig."

They went back to reading over the case file on Jordan Williams until Det. Briggs arrived back with a man who was an inch or two shorter than Declan. He had bright blue eyes and sandy brown hair. He was dressed in a light jacket, polo shirt, and pressed khakis and had what looked like the note in a Ziplock freezer bag.

Det. Briggs made introductions. "Charlie is the senior crime reporter with the *Boston Globe*."

Charlie smiled awkwardly and sat down across from Kate and Declan. "This has my fingerprints all over it. I feel a bit stupid now. I thought this was a stupid prank. We get all kinds of crazy letters to the newsroom. At first, I thought it was one of my friends giving me a hard time about my obsession with American history. I told my brother-in-law, who is a cop, about it, too. He laughed it off. I had no reason to believe it was serious."

Kate felt bad for him. He wouldn't have any reason to believe the note was as serious as it turned out to be. Kate picked up the bag and examined the contents. It had the same look as the parchment paper found yesterday and the same scrolling style of cursive. She'd put money on it being from the same writer. "We appreciate you bringing this in. When was it sent to you?"

"I don't remember the exact date but about two weeks ago. I'm fairly certain it was a Thursday or Friday. I saw some buddies that weekend and I gave them a hard time about sending it to me. No one took credit."

Declan hitched his jaw toward the note. "Did any of your friends, family or colleagues touch it?"

"No, believe it or not, I put it in the bag right away. My desk is a mess, and I didn't want to spill anything on it. I thought it was a stupid prank but someone had done some work to make it look legit.

I wanted to keep it."

"Happy coincidence," Declan agreed. "Do you have any idea who the sender might be? Anything about the envelope that might give a clue as to who sent it?"

Charlie ran a hand over the top of his head and winced. "I threw out the envelope. There was nothing special about that. Standard letter-size white envelope. It was addressed to me but typed and had basic postage. The postmark was Boston, the same zip code as the newsroom."

It was a shame they had lost the envelope, but it happens. Kate set the bag with the note down on the table. "Charlie, did you cover the shooting of Jordan Williams? The man who was found in front of the Old State House."

"I did," Charlie said, confusion on his face. "I was out there that night. I was the first reporter on the scene. I got a statement from Det. Briggs. I've written two articles about the shooting, but there haven't been any breaks in the case."

"Until now," Kate said, carefully watching his reaction.

CHAPTER 8

Charlie narrowed his eyes. "You think the letter that was sent to me has something to do with the shooting?"

"Not just the shooting," Det. Briggs said, glancing at Kate, in what she assumed was a request for permission to give details. She nodded and Det. Briggs went on. "We believe that the letter was the first communication with the killer. Yesterday, the man found murdered in Granary Burying Ground also had a note near him in similar parchment, ink, and writing. The FBI is involved because the cases are connected. We are concerned there will be more."

Charlie blew out a breath and sat back. He looked at both Kate and Declan and then up at Det. Briggs. "I don't understand. Are you saying there is a serial killer in Boston?"

Kate held up her hand. "This is an off the record conversation. Under no circumstance should you run a story informing the public of that. We've not made any determination yet other than we suspect the shooting and the case yesterday are connected. We are in the middle of trying to piece together what all this means."

Charlie started to argue, but Det. Briggs rested a hand on the man's shoulder. "I promise you that we'll give you the exclusive once we know more. We don't want to alarm the public until we know what we are working with here."

Charlie pointed to the note on the table. "Can I write about this letter in connection to the shooting?"

"Not yet," Kate said. "There are a few witnesses we need to interview. Give us a day or two and then you can run it. We'll give you a quote. Everything else needs to be off the record for right now."

Charlie didn't look too happy with that, but he said he understood. "What more do you want to know about the note I received?"

"I think the most obvious – do you know who sent it?" Declan asked, picking up the evidence bag and examining it.

Charlie shook his head. "No, absolutely not. As I said, I thought it was a prank. I asked my friends and family but everyone denied it."

Kate believed him. There was no reason for him to lie, and his open body language indicated his honesty. She thought about something he had said earlier. "Charlie, you mentioned that you have a love for American history. Is that something well-known about you?"

"It is," Charlie said, offering a smile. "I have a master's in journalism from Columbia, but I've taken several graduate courses in American history over the years. I attend guest lectures at Harvard when the school opens them up to the public. I have shelves of biographies and history books at home, too."

Kate had thought as much. Normally, she wouldn't share this, but Kate believed Charlie was targeted by the killer as well. She didn't want to say that to him and freak him out though. Instead, Kate explained, "We believe this killer has a love of American history as well. His views might be a bit warped, but we suspect he is targeting people for a reason. Beyond your love of history, do you have any ancestry going back to the Revolutionary War?"

Charlie's face grew red and his eyes opened wide. "I do," he said hesitantly. "Benjamin Franklin was a distant cousin of mine. Years ago, my mother used a genealogist and traced our family line back. We were both shocked to find Benjamin Franklin in our family tree."

"Who would have known that?" Det. Briggs asked, taking a seat next to Charlie.

Charlie expelled a breath and rubbed at his chin. He was quiet for a moment and then finally he shrugged. "Probably everyone that knows me." He laughed. "I'm a journalist and so was he. I was psyched when I found it out. I told everyone." His face grew even redder from embarrassment.

Any other time Kate would have enjoyed his childlike excitement for his connection to a historical figure. Right now, it was another clue.

"I was targeted with the second letter," Kate explained. "I also have family connections going back to the founding of America. My father, Professor Joseph Walsh—"

Charlie slapped his hand down on the table startling everyone. His eyes grew wide with excitement. "Your father was Professor Walsh from Harvard?"

"Yes," Kate said hesitantly. "He taught there before your time, I'm sure."

Gesturing with his hand, Charlie said, "I never had the pleasure of meeting him, but a professor at Harvard, whose classes I've sat in, mentions your father all the time."

"Who is that?"

"Professor Anthony Holt. He said he was a pre-doctorate fellow and your father was his advisor." Charlie grew quiet. When he spoke again, his voice was filled with sincerity. "I'm sorry that happened to your parents. I can't even imagine losing them like that."

Det. Briggs glanced at Kate and then at Declan. He had no idea about Kate's parents. She had no desire to explain.

"Thank you," Kate said simply. "What does Professor Holt teach?"

"Exactly what you need. He is a history professor with a focus on the American Revolution, the years leading up to it, key turning points, and the founding of America. He's the most well-studied and well-versed professor I've ever met. His lectures are incredibly nuanced."

"You think we need to talk to an academic?" Declan asked Kate, giving her a look that told her he disagreed.

"I'd like to just to get some insight," Kate explained, ignoring Declan's look. He didn't like to pull too many people into an investigation unless it was necessary. Declan was incredibly intelligent, but he didn't put too much stock into the opinions of academics in murder investigations. There were times when Kate agreed. This wasn't one of those times.

"I can set up a meeting if you'd like," Charlie offered.

"Please do and give him my direct cellphone number if it's easier." Kate reached into her bag and pulled out her business card. "If you have any other communication from the killer or anything suspicious at all, let us know immediately. We will be in touch about when you can run with a story."

Charlie took the card and toyed with it in his hand. "Do you think I'm safe? If you think this killer is targeting people, should I be concerned about my safety? He knows where I work and possibly about my background."

"I think there is reason to assess your current safety," Declan said evenly. His tone was serious but not trying to instill fear. "We don't know what we are dealing with exactly so if I were you, I'd beef up security at home, vary routes to work, put the newspaper on notice, and be aware of your surroundings." Declan glanced over at Det. Briggs. "I don't want to speak for the Boston police, but if you're that concerned, they might be able to offer you a patrol car outside of your house or at least some extra watches in your neighborhood."

Det. Briggs agreed that was possible, but Charlie waved them off, letting them know he'd take precautions. He'd been writing the crime beat for a long time and had gone up against the mob and other nefarious characters.

"Thanks for coming in, Charlie," Det. Briggs said as the two men stood and shook hands. Declan reached across the table and shook his hand too before Det. Briggs escorted him out.

Declan picked up the note in the evidence bag. "Let me call the forensic team and have them come over and pick it up for analysis."

Before Declan could place a call though, Det. Briggs entered the conference room walking in step with Dr. Graham. Kate perked up. "Are you done with the autopsy?" she asked as he dropped a file folder on the table and sat down.

Dr. Graham nodded. "As soon as you mentioned the involvement of the FBI yesterday and that this case could be connected to another, I thought I'd better do this one myself. I've put my team on other pending autopsies."

"We appreciate that." Kate gestured to the file and Dr. Graham gave her permission to read it.

"What do you know about yesterday's case?" Dr. Graham asked.

"Nothing, not even the victim's name," Declan said. "We were focused on the prior case this morning. Any information you can share would be a good start."

Dr. Graham began, "Nathan Hammond was forty years old. He died from a puncture wound to the heart. Someone yesterday told me you had questioned the amount of blood from the neck wound."

Kate explained she had. "I'm not an expert, but I've been to enough crime scenes to know the blood spatter didn't add up."

Dr. Graham continued. "You were correct about that. The neck wound occurred after the chest wound. The victim was close to death." He motioned for Kate to hand him back the autopsy report, which sat opened but unread in front of her. She slid it across the table, and Dr. Graham glanced down. He read and then went on. "Hammond also had bruising around the chest wound, which I believe is indicative of the knife that was used. I believe the perp slammed it into his chest with such force it left bruising."

"Any defense wounds?" Declan asked.

"Not many. I'm waiting for the toxicology report to be back, but based on stomach contents, Hammond was drinking a considerable amount before death so I'd say he was inebriated, possibly to the point of passing out." Dr. Graham went on to explain more details in the autopsy, none of which were particularly relevant to the crime.

When he was done, Det. Briggs asked, "What was the time of death?"

"It was around two in the morning."

Kate reached for the autopsy report and scanned the pages as Det. Briggs and Dr. Graham continued their discussion. As she read, Kate tried to figure out some chronological order for the crime. The victim could have been coming home from a bar at that hour. Bars close at two in the morning with last call typically around one-thirty.

She caught just a few words Dr. Graham said and snapped back to attention. "Did you say you think the knife used was an antique?"

Dr. Graham refocused his attention back on Kate. "Det. Briggs sent me a photo of the dagger that was sent to you. I believe the victim was killed with a similar dagger." He paused and considered. "Similar might not be going far enough. He might have been killed with that very weapon or its twin. Even the bruising on the victim's chest matches the design of that dagger."

Kate's breath caught in her throat. It was one thing to be sent a bizarre gift from a killer. It was another to be sent the actual murder weapon.

CHAPTER 9

Soon after leaving the Boston Police Department building, Kate and Declan were on their way back to the FBI field office to talk to their forensics team. They had walked back to Kate's house and Declan drove them. The FBI field office was in Chelsea across the Mystic River from Boston. Kate needed to know if there was recent blood evidence on the dagger, and she didn't want to wait a minute longer.

"What if there is blood?" Declan asked as he navigated the city streets. "How does that make what he sent you any better or worse? The killer is still targeting you either way."

Kate didn't know how it made it worse, so she couldn't explain her reasoning to Declan in any sort of rational way. She remained silent. It galled her to be irrational. It was the trait she liked least about herself. He glanced at her across the front seat in such a way that told her he knew she wasn't being rational. Thankfully, he didn't press further.

"After we talk to the forensics team, I'd like to go talk to the widow of Jordan Williams." Kate opened the file folder on her lap that she had taken from Det. Briggs. "It says her name is Simone and they live in the North End."

Kate flipped through the file and read Simone's statement. She was an emergency room doctor at Massachusetts General and Jordan had been a financial analyst at a big firm in downtown Boston.

They drove in silence the rest of the way. It had been months since Kate had been to the FBI Boston field office. Declan parked and grabbed the evidence bag with the killer's note before exiting the car. Kate got out and followed him into the eight-floor glass and metal building. There was nothing attractive in its design. It looked like every other nondescript government building, but it was newer than many. The FBI Boston Division employed close to six-hundred agents and professional staff and provided supervision of ten resident agencies across Massachusetts, Rhode Island, New Hampshire, and Maine.

Declan might be stationed there, but no one in the FBI Boston Division had oversight of his work. He still belonged to the same unit as Kate. He had been farmed out to help other agents while Kate was working cases overseas and had grown familiar with a few local agents and the forensics staff. The Boston forensics unit was one of the best in the country and had been integral during the investigation to catch the Boston Marathon bombers in 2013. Kate trusted them like no other.

They took the elevator up to the forensic lab. As the door opened, there stood a short, fit, dark-haired woman who appeared to have been waiting for them. She must have been a new hire because Kate had never met her.

"I'm Sharon Esposito, the new supervisor in charge of the forensic unit," she said smiling and offering her hand to Kate. "Nice to meet you. I would have been to your house yesterday, but I was off. I sent my best crime scene techs though."

Turning to Declan, she added, "Good to see you, Agent James. Now that your work wife is back does that mean we'll be seeing less of you in the office?"

"Work wife?" Kate asked, snickering.

Sharon rolled her eyes and playfully punched Declan in the gut. "He talks about you nonstop, Agent Walsh. I couldn't tell if he had a crush on you or if you were his idol."

Declan blushed but laughed. "Sharon, you're telling all my secrets. Before you embarrass me any further, what have you got for us on that dagger?"

"Come this way," she said and took off like a shot toward the lab. The woman may have been five-foot-nothing, but she was fast. She rounded corners in the hallway like the building was seconds from exploding and this was her only way out. She glanced back at them. "Keep up or you'll lose me in this maze."

"Sharon runs marathons," Declan whispered to Kate.

"I can believe that." Kate followed Sharon into her office. The woman hopped up on a stool in front of a wide workspace with microscopes, a mess of file folders, and other equipment.

"That note found in the cemetery was something else." Sharon whistled loudly. "Someone went to a lot of trouble to make that look old, but it's not. The parchment paper can be found in any store. You could go to Walgreens right now and find the paper. The ink isn't from your run of the mill pen though."

Sharon motioned for Kate to have a look through the microscope she had set up. The parchment paper was under the glass with a portion of the writing magnified. "Right there, you can see the heavy sharp strokes, breaks in the writing, and ink splotches."

Kate focused her attention on the things Sharon mentioned, and she was right. This wasn't written with a regular pen. Kate had been right the day before when she suspected it had been written with a quill and ink. Kate moved out of the way for Declan to take a look.

"You think that's from a quill and ink?" Kate asked.

"That's exactly what I think it is." Sharon leaned back on the stool. "Now, I can't be certain how old it is. Calligraphers still use quill and ink so for all I know it's another fake like the parchment paper, but he went a long way to make someone believe it's old. You have a killer into theatrics."

Kate swallowed and she almost didn't want to ask, but she had to. "What about the knife?"

"That is the real deal. I called an expert on antique daggers about an hour before you arrived. I sent him photos. He'd have to examine it more, but he believes it's from right around the Revolutionary War." Sharon picked up a business card from the table. "He said he might be able to help narrow down ownership. He said a dagger in that good a condition is rare. All we have to do is say the word, and he'll put some feelers out to see if it can be identified."

Declan stepped back from looking at the parchment and looked over at Kate. He must have seen the worry line crease across her forehead because he asked Sharon, "Were there any traces of blood on the knife?"

"No, none that I found. It's void of fingerprints, too. Someone wiped it down thoroughly over the years." Sharon hitched her jaw toward the bag in Declan's hand. "What do you have there?"

Declan held up the bag. "It's another letter from the killer. We think it's the first letter or at least the one before the killing at the cemetery."

Sharon got off the stool and walked down to the end of the table. She pulled a fresh pair of gloves from the box and snapped them on. "I'll take a look while you're here." Sharon took the bag from Declan and carefully slid out the piece of parchment. "He's not writing much on these. Short little statements, but it certainly packs a punch."

Sharon shooed Declan out of the way so she could access her microscope. Kate and Declan stood back while she went to work. A few minutes later, Sharon confirmed, "Looks like it's the same paper and ink. I'm not a handwriting expert but that looks about the same as well." Sharon took the parchment and slipped it into an official FBI evidence bag and labeled the outside accordingly.

When she was done, she handed it to Declan. "Boston police will want to have a look I'm sure. It was like pulling teeth to get a look at that other letter. I heard a rumor you're heading up this investigation now."

"That's what they tell us," Declan said, rocking on his feet.

"How'd that happen?" Sharon asked curiously.

"The same we get involved in anything," Kate said.

"Martin Spade," the three of them said in unison.

Sharon laughed. "That man needs to retire. Any idea how old he is?"

Declan shook his head, laughing. "Probably older than the dagger." He reached out a hand and patted Sharon on the back. "We appreciate the quick information. I'll let you know if we need anything else."

"Nice meeting you," Kate said.

Sharon raised her eyes to Kate. "I heard rumors you were quitting."

"It was more like an extended break so I could sort out a plan, but that's not going to happen now."

"Hopefully, you'll stick around. The FBI needs more female agents. I heard you're top-notch."

"Thanks," Kate said, feeling slightly embarrassed. She had earned a reputation in the FBI, but it wasn't always easy to live up to.

Kate and Declan left the lab and made their way back down to the first floor. Declan saw a few agents along the way and introduced Kate to those she didn't know. When they walked out the front door, Kate shielded her eyes from the sun. "You like working at this office, don't you?"

Declan shrugged, but the grin on his face gave him away. "I like the camaraderie that being a part of a normal field office gives me, but I miss working with you. I think here I'm getting the best of both worlds. It might be different if I had to report to a supervisor like everyone else. Spade has let me do my own thing while you were gone."

"We all know how you hate authority." Kate got in the car and they left to see Simone Williams. While Declan drove, she placed a call to make sure the woman was home and not at work. Simone answered quickly and let Kate know it was her day off and she'd be happy to speak with them.

"You going to tell her a serial killer killed her husband?" Declan asked when Kate ended the call.

Kate bit her lip thinking about just that. She had no idea what she planned to tell Simone, but she only had about ten minutes to make a decision.

CHAPTER 10

Parking on the street in the North End, Boston's "Little Italy", proved impossible so Declan headed right for a parking garage. The small streets, the majority still cobblestone, packed rows of homes filled with apartments and restaurants into the oldest neighborhood in the city. Visitors flocked to the area for the history, architecture, and food.

Kate's stomach growled just thinking about the food. The streets were lined with authentic Italian eateries. She couldn't even pick a favorite they were all so good. They walked the few short blocks to Prince Street and found the house where Simone lived in a second-floor apartment. The brick building had three floors and a small foyer at the bottom. They climbed the stairs and Declan knocked on the door.

A moment later they were greeted by a tall, thin, black woman who had an easy smile and warmth and calmness about her Kate assumed made her an asset in emergency medicine. Simone welcomed Kate and Declan into the apartment.

"If you're comfortable, we can sit in the living room, but if you'd rather the dining room, I can clear some space on the table." Simone reached up and touched her forehead. "I've been overwhelmed going through all the paperwork since Jordan's death."

"I'm so sorry for your loss," Kate said as she looked at a photo of the couple on the end table. They were an attractive pair and clearly in love with each other. "The living room is fine, and we won't take up too much of your time."

Simone sat on the edge of an ottoman. "Take all the time you need if it means you can find who killed my husband. None of it makes any sense to me. I know Det. Briggs hasn't been able to narrow in on a suspect." Simone took a breath and held back her emotion.

Declan started. "I know it's difficult, but if you could recount the evening your husband was killed that would be a helpful place to start."

Simone nodded and looked to the ceiling. When she focused back on Declan and Kate, her voice was filled with emotion. "It was like any other night. I worked a later shift than usual at the hospital and wasn't home until around seven in the evening. Jordan met with some clients for dinner and then stopped by a bar to have a drink with a friend he hadn't seen in a while. I called him and he was on his way home. He never made it." Simone choked back a sob. "Sometime later that night, I couldn't even tell you the time, there was a cop at my door explaining my husband was dead. They had his identification from his wallet, but I insisted on going to the morgue to see him."

Kate understood, and it took an effort to hold back from commenting. If it were her husband, she'd have done the same. "Were you questioned by police right away?"

"Of course," Simone said. "I think they always look at the spouse. They asked if we had money issues, inheritance, cheating. They ran the whole gamut. There's nothing. My husband worked in finance. He was squeaky clean." Simone let out a short ironic laugh. "I'm an emergency room doctor. We are probably boring by most people's standard of living. We have no kids, little debt, and no drama in our lives. We go to work, pay our taxes, are good community members, and travel occasionally when we can get our schedules to match up.

We had a great life together. Our marriage was a happy one. The only complaint we ever had was not enough time together. We are about as low risk for crime as you get."

"Have there been any threats made against your husband?" Declan asked.

"None," Simone replied, expelling a frustrated breath. "No family issues, no issues with friends, and none with colleagues I'm aware of. He would get the occasional unhappy client from time to time, but that's common in his field. There was nothing that would have raised the alarm for murder." Simone looked between Kate and Declan. "Det. Briggs thought maybe Jordan was just at the wrong place at the wrong time, but that didn't make any sense to me. A robbery I could understand. But his watch and wedding band weren't taken. He had his wallet in his back pocket full of cash and credit cards. I can't see how it would be a robbery."

Declan asked a few more questions, trying to rule out every possible motive for the murder. While he exhausted himself of questions, Kate crossed her legs and looked around the living room. There was no hint the couple was into anything historical, but they did have a bookshelf filled with paperbacks. She looked back to Simone. "Do either you or your husband have an interest in American history?"

"Not particularly. We were more math and science kind of people, but as you can see, I do enjoy reading occasionally. All fiction though."

"What about your backgrounds? Do either of you have ties to Boston and the American Revolution in your family trees?"

Simone cocked her head to the side. "Not that I know. Neither one of us has explored our ancestry much if that's what you're getting at. I don't recall that Jordan had an interest in his. He knew his parents back to his great-grandparents on both sides. I did as well. I never saw a need to go back further. It wasn't even something we talked about."

"What about your connections to Boston?" Kate asked.

"We aren't from Boston. Jordan was from Miami and I'm from Chicago. I did my residency at Mass General. That's what brought us here going on close to twenty years ago. I got a job at the hospital after my residency and we've been here ever since."

Declan clasped his hands together. "You have friends and good ties to the community?"

"Very good friends. We don't get to see our families much, but we've created an entire community of friends that are as close as family now."

"No issues with any of them?"

Simone's eyes grew wide. "None of them could have killed Jordan. Every one of them has been here since it happened, helping me get through this. I think Det. Briggs checked everyone's alibis, too. He was thorough on nearly everything." Looking at Kate suspiciously, she asked, "Is there a reason you're asking me about our ancestry and ties to Boston? It seems like a strange question for a murder investigation."

Knowing the information about the letter and the entire case would be made public eventually, the last thing Kate wanted was to lie to Simone. She explained the note from the killer that went to the *Boston Globe* and the murder at the cemetery as gently as possible. Simone's face registered shock, then disgust, and then anger.

She sat back shaking her head like she couldn't believe it. "I lost my husband because some freak is on a killing spree because England lost the Revolutionary War? Isn't there a statute of limitations on asinine grudges?"

Declan offered her a sad smile and shifted in his seat. "I understand your reaction. I've had the same, but I've come to learn, especially working with Agent Walsh who has a specialty in analyzing the motive and behavior of these types of killers, that it's impossible to make rational sense out of the irrational."

"When you say these types of killers are you talking about a serial killer? Do you expect there will be more murders?"

Kate gave the only answer she could. "We don't know, but the FBI and the Boston Police Department are expecting it. That's why it's so critical we find any connection your husband might have had to this killer or reason your husband might have been targeted."

"I have no idea," Simone said sadly, getting up from the ottoman and walking out of the room. "I'll be right back," she called over her shoulder as she left. A few moments later, she returned and handed Declan a black eight-by-eleven soft-cover book. "It's Jordan's day planner. He wrote everything down in there. Det. Briggs looked through it and gave it back to me. Maybe you'll find something in there. Jordan was meticulous with his schedule. Every client appointment, meeting with work, outing with a friend, doctor's appointment, and even our date nights, he wrote down. He had so much going on it was the only way he kept track."

Declan held the planner in his hands. "Why didn't he use his phone?"

Simone smiled. "He didn't trust it. Jordan never embraced technology. He kept things old school. We still have a record player. If there is any clue that he knew the killer, it's in there. I was surprised Det. Briggs didn't keep it longer, but he gave it back a few days after I retrieved it from Jordan's office after his death."

Kate asked a few more questions but didn't learn anything useful. She and Declan would have to take the time to go through the planner. She, too, was surprised that Det. Briggs hadn't spent more time, but maybe it was where he had garnered the names for the fifty interviews he had conducted. Kate and Declan thanked Simone for her time and headed back to the front door.

Kate reached her hand out to the woman. "I promise you I'm going to do everything I can to bring this killer to justice."

Simone nodded. "Just catch the psycho, please. I don't want to see any other family have to go through this. I want justice for Jordan. He wasn't just my husband. He was an incredible man who still would have done great things in this world."

Kate followed Declan down the stairs. At the bottom of the stairs, she turned back to see Simone watching them out. Kate gave a half-hearted smile and then hit the street. She opened her mouth to suggest lunch before they headed back, but sirens wailed in the background, growing louder by the second. Then both Kate's and Declan's phones rang.

They scrambled to answer and stepped apart so they could each hear their caller. After listening intently Kate turned back to Declan and they shared the same terrified look as they received the information.

Declan cursed as he hung up the phone. "That was Det. Briggs. The caretaker just found a body at the Old North Church."

Kate had received the same message. Charlie had called her. "The *Boston Globe* received another note. It came in this morning's mail and Charlie received it at his desk when he got back to the office from meeting with us. He left a message for Det. Briggs. About a half-hour later, he received a call from someone claiming to be the killer letting him know where to find the body. I guess the killer didn't want him to disregard the letter like he did with the first one. He called Det. Briggs right away."

"Det. Briggs told me that much. He said he called units immediately to get to Old North Church. He said a crime scene unit and Dr. Graham and his team are already on their way, too." Declan looked in the direction of the Old North Church a few blocks away. "Let's head there now."

CHAPTER 11

Declan and Kate took off toward the Old North Church, located a few blocks north on Salem Street. It had been years since Kate had visited the church. As they made their way there, she tried to recall the last time she'd been inside. It had to have been a high school history trip. She couldn't pinpoint a more recent time. There wasn't much reason to visit.

They slowed their pace as they rounded the corner. Cops had already secured the road to not allow cars or foot traffic near the church. Kate and Declan flashed their badges to the beat cop standing guard and he waved them through.

Declan pointed to a sign near the front door. "The church has been closed for a few days for cleaning and repairs. I wonder how the killer got in."

The door to the church was propped open and Declan and Kate walked through. The Georgian architecture featured stained glass windows and white pews. The church had been a sharp contrast to the simplicity of other churches at the time.

Det. Briggs stood in the middle aisle talking to a crime scene tech. He stepped away from him when he spotted Declan and Kate. "Glad you two could make it so quickly. I haven't even made it up to the bell tower yet."

"That's where the body was found?" Declan asked, looking in the direction of the tower stairs.

Det. Briggs explained, "The caretaker came in this morning and did some work. They have a small crew making some repairs to the church. He hadn't had a reason to go up to the bell tower, but then he remembered he needed a hammer he left up there yesterday. When he got up there, he found the victim's body in the middle of the floor." Det. Briggs swallowed hard and tried to stay composed. "The victim's hand that had been severed is sitting on the window ledge."

Even Declan knew this history. He rubbed his hand across his jaw. "The same window ledge that the lanterns were hung to let Paul Revere know the British were coming by sea?"

"That very one." Det. Briggs motioned for them to follow. As they got farther into the church, they stopped when a cop handed each of them gloves and foot coverings. When they were prepared, they followed Det. Briggs.

Kate didn't have much to say. She strained to remember the history. She'd have to double-check, but she thought it was Robert Newman and John Pulling who left the lanterns for Paul Revere to see.

Declan went first up the steps and Kate followed behind. The boards creaked with each step they took. Kate held onto the hand railing on each side as she ascended the stairs. The small space could only accommodate one person at a time. There was no way the killer had carried the man's body to the top. That much she knew for sure.

As they reached the top landing, they passed two cops standing guard and entered the bell tower. The brick walls showed their age but that was part of the charm. Dirt and dust littered the floor and ropes and pulleys hung from the ceiling. A few benches used for school tours and such lined the walls. The oval window where the lanterns had been placed that fateful night now held a severed hand. It sat with the fingers facing them like some twisted Halloween decoration. The skin on the fingers had shriveled and already turned a putrid gray.

Kate turned away and focused her eyes on the body on the floor. Blood pooled under the man and stained his shirt. He lay there prone on the ground legs in front of him and arms at his sides as if maybe he was sleeping off a bender from the night before.

Declan bent down and looked over the man, careful not to touch him. Kate had to resist the urge to remove his shirt and see if the chest wound looked like the one on the victim yesterday. If the murder weapon had been sent to her, it meant the killer would use something else. If the wounds were the same, it assured Kate she wasn't sent the murder weapon.

A scuffle behind them drew their attention. A man had raced up the stairs and was trying to push his way past the two cops standing guard. "I need to make sure that's not my brother!" the man yelled. "Let me through."

Declan stood and walked to the stairs. He waved off the cops and asked the man a few questions, confirming he was the foreman of the local construction crew that had been hired to handle some of the repairs.

His voice laden with emotion, he explained, "My brother has been missing since late last night. His wife called me this morning and said he hadn't made it home after work. I left before he did last night and got a call from the caretaker that there was a body found up here."

Declan turned back to Det. Briggs and Kate. "Any identification found?"

"We haven't even looked for it," Det. Briggs said. "We were waiting for the crime scene unit to arrive first."

The man tried to shove Declan out of the way to get into the room. Kate saw Declan take a step back and then wrap his arms around the man and shove him out of sight. Kate hoped Declan would take him back down the stairs.

To Det. Briggs, Kate advised, "Let's check the body for a wallet at least. I don't want this guy in here messing up the scene. If it is his brother, we can at least interview him downstairs while we wait for the forensics team."

Det. Briggs bent down and reached into the front pocket of the man's jeans and found nothing. Kate helped roll the man to his side while Det. Briggs searched his back pockets. He came away with a wallet and opened it. "Massachusetts driver's license and union card. He's in construction. There's a good chance the man is his brother."

"Name?" Kate asked, wincing. She hated having to give a death notice.

"Pete Amato. Forty and lives not far from here in the North End."

Before Kate left the room, she took a cursory glance around the small space. As she turned to the left she saw the toolbelt and tools strewn on the floor. Had the victim been working and attacked? That certainly would make more sense than the killer luring him to the bell tower. Kate pointed to the toolbelt before she went downstairs to make sure Det. Briggs saw it.

Once back downstairs, Kate found Declan sitting in a pew up near the front of the church talking to the man, who he introduced as Christopher Amato. Kate introduced herself and asked cautiously, "Is your brother Pete Amato?"

The man dropped his head and sobbed. Declan reached his arm out and put it around the man, patting his back as he sat forward in the pew. The man sobbed for several minutes. This was sometimes the hardest part of their job, sitting with people in extreme emotional pain and not having anything to make it better at that moment.

"Christopher," Kate said gently, "I'm very sorry for your loss. There are victim services we can connect your family to. We can go with you when you tell his wife if you'd like."

Christopher sat up and wiped his eyes with the backs of his hands. He focused up at Kate. "I can handle that. I didn't mean to lose it like that. My brother and I are very close." He took a breath and let it out slowly. "I don't understand. What happened to Pete? I left him here working at ten last night. We've been working here for nearly a month. Had to close down the church for a few days for some bigger repairs, but we were nearly finished with the job. Pete was fixing some loose bricks up there in the bell tower. We were hoping to finish the job today."

"Did you lock the door after you left?" Declan asked.

Christopher shook his head. "We only had one key. Pete needed it to leave. I yelled from downstairs that I was leaving. I told him to come down and lock the door behind me, but he said he would be done in thirty minutes and didn't see a reason to. It's a safe area, you know? Who is going to hurt him in a church?"

"That makes sense. We just wanted an idea of what the killer did to get in the building, but it sounds like he could have walked in off the street."

"Yeah, but when I left, I didn't see anybody out there." Christopher sat back as if thinking. "There were maybe a handful of people leaving restaurants, but that was it. They were mostly couples. I didn't see anyone that might raise suspicion."

Kate took a seat in the pew in front of them, propping up her knee on the seat so she could turn around and speak to Christopher at eye level. "Who else knew Pete was here?"

"A couple of the guys on the crew who were working here, but they had all gone home around eight. Pete's wife Jenn knew, but she was with my wife last night. The caretaker here knew we were working at night. He's the one that gave us the key. I'm sure people walking by saw the lights on and us moving equipment in and out of here over the last few days. I was the only one who knew Pete was alone here late last night."

Kate would have staked her life on the fact that it was the same killer they were after, but she had to be sure. An image of the hand on the window ledge came to mind. She looked at Christopher. "Was Pete involved in any criminal activity?"

"Not that I know of, and I think I'd know."

"What about mob connections?" Kate caught Declan's eye and she knew he thought the same thing. The hand might be an indication that Pete was stealing from the mob. They'd seen it before.

"Absolutely not," Christopher assured. "I know Italian last name, living here in the North End and working construction we must have some kind of mafia connections, right?" He paused and looked at them both. Neither Kate nor Declan responded because he wasn't wrong. Christopher shook his head. "Not my family, I swear. My mother would have killed us herself. Is there a reason you're asking this? Do you think it was like a mob hit or something?"

"There are questions given—" Kate started to speak, but Christopher cut her off.

"If it was a mob hit, they got the wrong guy. Pete didn't drink, he didn't gamble and he wasn't involved in anything illegal. He's been married to the same woman since his senior year of college."

"I understand," Kate said and then paused, waiting to see if he'd continue. When Christopher remained silent, she asked, "Where were you last night and this morning until you arrived here?"

Christopher cursed at Kate and sat forward in the pew, his anger brimming over. Declan reached a hand out. "Settle down. It's a routine question. The faster we can rule you out, the faster you'll get information."

Christopher turned to Declan, and for a minute Kate thought he might take a swing at him, but at that moment, Dr. Graham arrived with his team. As they rolled the stretcher with the empty body bag on top, Christopher lost it again. Deep wracking sobs consumed his body.

CHAPTER 12

Declan guided Christopher out of the church while Kate went to brief Dr. Graham and his team. She filled them in about what she knew before they made their way up to the bell tower. She was glad she wasn't going to be the one to try to navigate those narrow stairs with a stretcher, but Kate assumed they had probably encountered worse conditions. When she was done, Kate made her way out to the street to talk.

As she stepped out of the church, she expected to see Declan but he was nowhere in sight. Turning to one of the cops, she asked, "Did you see where the other FBI agent went?"

The cop pointed down the street. "He was with a guy. They said something about going to a house down the street."

Kate stepped around several officers and headed in the direction the cop pointed. She didn't see Declan anywhere. She stepped to the side to let other people pass on the sidewalk and pulled her phone from her pocket. Thankfully, Declan had texted her an address. She pulled it up on GPS and realized that they were just a block away. Kate walked to the house and knocked on the front door of the modest brick home.

A moment later, Declan appeared behind the door. "I hoped you'd check your phone. Christopher said we could speak to his wife. Pete's wife is here as well. I did the death notification and would like to give the family a moment before we head back in."

Kate waved him outside. "What do you think?"

"Christopher's wife Tara corroborates his story. He got home a few minutes after ten. He told Tara and Jenn, who were both at the house, that Pete was going to finish up and then he'd be home. Christopher took a shower and then relaxed in front of the television. Pete and Jenn live on the second floor. Jenn said she went home to bed. Christopher had no idea his brother was missing until Jenn told him a little while ago."

Kate turned in the direction of the church. She could see it from where she stood. "Didn't Jenn notice her husband didn't come home last night?"

"I guess not. Jenn said that sometimes if Pete came home late, he'd sleep in the spare room so he wouldn't wake her up. She got up this morning and saw that the bed hadn't been made and assumed he went out for a run. He does that sometimes. She tried to text him and when he didn't come home or get back to her, she called Christopher."

"That doesn't make any sense to me. Who slept in the bed?"

Declan stepped down to the sidewalk. "I asked her that. Jenn admitted that maybe she hadn't gone in the room for a few days so maybe he had left the bed unmade from the last time."

Kate still didn't understand. Her house was three times the size of this one and while there were rooms she rarely went into, she'd know whether a bed was made or not. "I think we're going to have to pin down a better alibi than that."

"Agreed, but I figured since they liked me, you could be the bad cop." Declan smiled a sneaky grin and bounded back into the house.

Kate sighed and followed Declan into the first floor and through a comfortable-looking, if not small, living room, and found the family sitting at the dining room table. Declan introduced Kate.

"Jenn, do you think there's someplace you and I could speak

privately?" Kate asked, hoping she didn't have to address the issue in front of Pete's family.

"Sure, let's head up to my place." Jenn stood from the table, shared a look with her sister-in-law and took Kate the backway through the kitchen and up a flight of stairs to her flat. They entered through a backdoor into a kitchen with the same layout as the one below.

As they passed from one room to the next Kate noticed the small bar set up in the dining room with bottles of expensive gin and vodka. There were also several empty beer bottles stashed in the bin next to the bar. Kate had initially thought Jenn's puffy face had been from crying too much, but it might be bloat from alcohol. She tucked that information away for later.

"I'm sorry we have to be meeting like this," Kate said as Jenn pointed to a straight-back, maroon-colored chair for her to take a seat. Jenn sat across from her in the chair's twin.

"I don't understand what happened." Jenn wrung her hands in her lap and didn't look at Kate.

"I'm not sure either. Crime scene techs are assessing the scene. It's going to take us some time to know for sure, but you can be of help right now."

Jenn nodded. "I'll try."

Kate crossed her legs at her ankles and sat back. "Was it common for Pete to work late?"

"All the time. Pete worked a lot of overtime and took construction jobs here and there. He didn't just work with his brother." Jenn paused and then added, "Pete didn't usually work past ten-thirty though so I should have known when he didn't come home."

"Is there a reason you didn't know?" Kate asked gently, trying not to sound like she blamed the woman.

"I was passed out asleep. This morning, I thought he had already left for a run. Pete liked to exercise first thing."

"Agent James said that sometimes Pete slept in the spare bedroom, but you hadn't been in there for a few days."

Jenn finally looked at Kate. "What do you want to hear? That I'm an alcoholic and occasionally pass out drunk and me and Pete were having problems because of that?"

Kate shook her head and offered a sympathetic smile. "Jenn, I'm not here to judge you. I'm working to find out what happened to your husband. Part of that is to understand where you were and what you know about Pete's schedule and movements."

"Pete and I fought before he left for work last night. Christopher was probably too nice to tell you that." Jenn wiped a tear from her eyes. "We fought and had been fighting for the last few nights. That's why Pete has been sleeping in the spare room. I haven't been sober much this week, so I can't tell you when that bed was made or not. Pete sometimes made it and sometimes didn't."

"Fair enough," Kate said, believing her. She didn't think going down this line of questioning any longer would serve any purpose. "Do you know of anyone who might have wanted to hurt Pete?"

"No, Pete was everybody's friend. He's always been like that. That isn't just something to say either. There wasn't anyone Pete wouldn't help if they needed it."

Kate glanced around the living room. It was much like the one downstairs. "Did you or Pete like American history?"

"What do you mean?"

"You live right here in the center of where the American Revolution took place. Did you or Pete ever study history or go to lectures or have a general interest in the subject?"

"Not me, but Pete watched the History Channel a lot, but not anything more than that."

Kate asked more questions about Pete's interests, other guys in the construction crew, and people he knew. She also asked about their ancestry to see if there were any ties back to the founding of America. Jenn didn't know nor did she seem like she cared.

Before she wrapped the interview, Kate asked if Jenn or Pete knew the two other victims. Jenn didn't recognize the names and didn't think they were people her husband knew.

As Kate got up to leave, Jenn stopped her. "Why did you ask me about American history and our ancestry?" she asked with an edge of concern in her voice.

Kate explained briefly that she believed Pete's murder might be connected to others in the city. "We don't know for sure exactly what we're dealing with, but we have reason to believe there is a historical tie for this killer." There was something about Jenn's expression that told Kate the woman might know more than she was saying. Kate nudged her. "Is there something you might know about that?"

"I don't know anything about the murders, but talk to Christopher. Pete told me there was a guy who came into the Old North Church a couple of times while they were there and talked about the American Revolution and said that the British should have won that war. He went on and on about how the British were the true founders of America. Pete laughed that the guy seemed a bit off." Jenn smiled as if reliving a memory.

She turned her head to Kate. "That was Pete. Even when he didn't like someone, he didn't talk bad about them. He called him a funny duck. He'd come home and laugh and say, 'That funny duck was in again tonight telling us his version of history.'"

It was the first inkling of a clue Kate felt like they might have. "Pete sounds like he was a wonderful guy. Do you know anything about this guy? A name? What he looks like? Where he works? Anything?"

"No, nothing like that. Pete would just laugh when the guy came in. He distracted Pete from doing his work. Pete said he was a nice guy and didn't think he meant any harm, but he was annoying at times."

"You said Christopher might know more about this guy."

"Yeah, Christopher would know. He'd met him a few times."

Kate narrowed her eyes. "This man bothered them that much?"

"I'm not sure how many times, to be honest with you," Jenn said. "Pete mentioned him three or four times to me. There might have been times he showed up that Pete didn't mention that's why I think Christopher would know more."

"Understood." Kate thanked Jenn for the information. Jenn rubbed her temples and told Kate she was going to stay upstairs unless they needed her. Kate assured her they'd call if needed and headed back downstairs alone.

CHAPTER 13

Declan was in the same place Kate had left him, sitting at the dining room table talking to Christopher and Tara. They all glanced up when Kate entered the room.

"Jenn said she's going to stay upstairs until she's needed."

Christopher and Tara shared a look of concern. Tara pushed her chair back from the table and stood. "I'll go check on her."

When Tara was out of earshot, Kate sat and said, "It must be a lot to have to take care of your sister-in-law."

Christopher nodded. "She's been an alcoholic for years. We all partied pretty hard in our twenties, but we stopped. Jenn continued, and it was manageable for a few years, but lately, it's gotten worse. This is going to send her right over the edge."

Declan reached for his wallet and pulled out a business card. He slid it over to Christopher. "There's support out there if you need help. The FBI victim service office can send a counselor out and help you connect to local services."

Christopher picked up the card and glanced at it. He put it in his pocket. "Was Jenn able to tell you what you needed to know?"

"She was very helpful. She mentioned that there was a man who came by the Old North Church a few times and talked about history."

"Yeah, there was a guy." Christopher sat back and tapped at his head with his index finger and then he snapped his fingers. "Mark Boyle was his name. I'd say he's in his early fifties. Quirky guy. He stopped in the Old North Church sometimes during the first week we were working on the job."

"What did he talk to you about?"

"He didn't talk to me, specifically. He tried to talk to some of the other guys, but they brushed him off. Mark shouldn't have been in there while we were working and we told him that a few times. The guy just wouldn't take a hint. Pete talked to him, but Pete would have talked to anyone."

Christopher snapped his head up to look at Kate. "You don't think that's who did this, do you?"

"I can't say for sure, but he's someone I want to speak with. Can you tell me more about him? Jenn said he talked to Pete about history. Was that something your brother was interested in?"

Christopher laughed. "No. Pete didn't care at all, but he wasn't going to be mean or ignore the guy. Pete was like that. Mark rambled on about history. He said some weird things."

"What things?" Declan asked.

"I don't know..." Christopher started and then paused to think. "He said that the British did it wrong. They should have attacked that night by land and not sea. He said that some British general was railroaded and that the history books made him look like a fool. He told all of us a few times that we wouldn't be where we were if it wasn't for the British. That they were the ones who made Boston what it was. After all, most of the so-called founders of America were from England."

Declan asked, "Was this man British?"

"No, he was from here. Pretty thick Boston accent like yours. The guy was weird, but I would never say dangerous. He looked like a nerdy guy."

"Did Pete ever argue with him?" Kate asked, leaning forward to rest her arms on the table.

"Pete wasn't like that. He humored him. Mark would get going about something, and Pete would tell him what he was saying was interesting or a unique perspective. Pete didn't argue with anyone even when he thought what they were saying was absolute crap."

"Anything else you can remember about him? Where he lived? What he did for work?"

"I don't know. Pete might have known, but I didn't pay too much attention to the guy." Christopher shrugged. "He might have lived close because once he had his dog. I got the feeling going past the Old North Church was a nightly ritual for him, but I can't say that I've seen him in the neighborhood otherwise."

Declan glanced over at Kate, but she didn't say anything. He asked, "Anything else you can think of?"

Christopher drummed his fingers on the table and thought for a moment. "You know, Pete told me once that Mark said something about a group that he was in. They called themselves The Founders or something like that. That might be it because I remember a night Mark said he was off to TF, and I asked Pete what that meant."

It wasn't a group Kate had heard of and by the expression on Declan's face, he hadn't either. "Any idea the purpose of the group?" she asked, wanting to reach for her phone and look it up.

"I assume by the name and the other things he said that maybe it was a bunch of other people like him who think we should still be loyal to England."

Declan and Kate asked a few more questions about the group, none of which Christopher could answer. There was nothing else Kate needed to know at the moment. She certainly appreciated the family's time and she said as much to Christopher.

As he walked them to the front door, he said, "Anything you need to help find who killed my brother, I'm there. Day or night call me or show up here. I'm not going to rest until we get justice for Pete."

Kate believed him. When they were on the street and a few houses away, she asked Declan if he had learned anything important while she was interviewing Jenn.

"Jenn and Pete were in some serious debt. In addition to Jenn's drinking problem, she had a gambling addiction. She'd take off with friends to the casino and lose big. Pete was working so much to pay off her debts. It got so bad, Christopher said, that Pete had to cut off all access to the credit cards and bank account so Jenn wouldn't blow all their money."

Kate couldn't imagine. She had never gambled a day in her life and she had no interest in doing so. Co-addictions like that would have taken its toll on Pete. It surprised Kate that he was still so nice and giving of his time with an annoyance like Mark Boyle. "They are going to have a lot to deal with now."

"Yeah, but Christopher said his parents are there for them. One of the benefits of a big family." As soon as the words were out of his mouth, Declan regretted it and walked it back. "Kate, I'm sorry, I know—"

Kate cut him off. "What are you sorry for? I'm glad they have a big family to help out. I can still be happy for people even if I don't have it in my life."

Declan reached his arm out and went to put it around Kate's shoulder, but she brushed him off.

"Why are you the only person that treats me like I'm about to break at any second?"

He winked at her. "I'm the only one who knows you, Katie."

Kate looked at him and then looked back toward the church. "Let's go catch a killer."

Declan laughed. "I've never met a woman who avoids emotion as much as you do. But I'll let it slide for now. What's the plan?"

"I think we need to loop Det. Briggs in and see what else he might have found."

Kate and Declan walked quickly back to the church. Kate took out her phone and looked up The Founders but didn't find anything. The cops waved them into the church again. While Declan made his way over to talk to Det. Briggs, Kate slid into a pew and plugged a couple of different search terms into the search engine.

After several tries, she came back with a message board that referenced The Founders. The group, it seemed, was made up of academics and others who would have been deemed Loyalists back at the time of the Revolutionary War. It was speculated that those in the group came from families who had lost great economic wealth when the Colonies cut ties with England. They still believed that America would be better off today under British rule.

Kate kept reading comments and then clicked several links until she ended up on another site that listed an email address to contact for membership. Kate took a screenshot so she wouldn't lose it later and scrolled down to more comments. A few commenters noted that members were often frustrated with the American political system and thought that the country was headed down the wrong path. The only way to save America from itself was to go back under British rule.

Kate had no idea that people like this existed. She had worked more domestic terrorism cases than she cared to remember, but serial killing wasn't their typical method of causing destruction. They usually went for a mass casualty sort of event. It was why she was both drawn to this group and equally ready to dismiss them from being suspects. It might just be that one member took it too far. Either way, it needed to be explored.

She shoved her phone back in her pocket and walked over to meet Det. Briggs. Declan stopped talking when he saw her. He turned and said, "Det. Briggs asked me something interesting I hadn't given any thought to. Given the group we were just talking about it might be of interest."

Det. Briggs had a tone of uncertainty, but he pushed forward. "I asked Agent James if he had any idea why the killer didn't cut off both hands. If he's replicating things that happened, wouldn't he have put both hands in the window like the two lanterns that night?"

Impressed with the detective's insightful observation, Kate said honestly, "I hadn't considered it, but as Agent James just said it might give some credence to information we received about a potential suspect." Kate paused and held her hand up. "That's probably going a bit too far. I wouldn't call him a suspect just yet, but rather a person of interest." Kate explained to Det. Briggs about Mark Boyle's visits to the Old North Church and his conversations with Pete.

Det. Briggs glanced back to the stairs and then at Kate and Declan. "I don't think there is any more we can do here. Dr. Graham and his team have already removed the body. A forensic scientist named Sharon Esposito from your team is upstairs now working on the scene. Let's head back to my office to discuss a plan of action. Charlie said he was going to bring the other letter by when we were done."

CHAPTER 14

The day had worn on at an exhausting pace for Kate. They made it into the Boston Police Department office just as the gray sky opened up and torrents of rain fell to the ground, making instant puddles on the sidewalk. Charlie sat waiting in the conference room for them. The worried expression on his face instantly jacked up Kate's nerves and made her wonder if something more had happened.

"Is everything okay?" Kate asked as she and Declan took a seat across from him. Det. Briggs pulled out the chair next to Charlie and sat down.

"Of course not. There is a deranged killer out there sending me letters. If this is right, he has killed three people. We have to alert the public." Charlie slid the bagged letter to Kate.

She picked it up and assessed the letter. It was written by the same hand with what looked like similar ink and on the same paper as before. This time the killer addressed Charlie specifically.

Charlie Crain,

The great-nephew of the infamous Benjamin Franklin. None a greater traitor than he. You will atone for your uncle's sins. The pen is mightier than the sword, but my sword is mighty and swift. I'd rather not have to use it on you. To avoid such a punishing fate, you will print my letters and inform the public that I am on the hunt and will right the wrongs of the past. If you think this is in jest, I've left the police another reminder of how serious I am in the bell tower of the Old North Church. The British should have come by land and cut off that wretched rabble-rouser on that fateful night. If only I had been there then, it might have all turned out differently. People will pay for that now.

A Devoted Determined Loyalist

The killer's words reinforced Kate's original theory that the killer was intelligent and college-educated. He had a strong, if incorrect interpretation of history and was driven to right what he felt were wrongs. He had done significant research and had planned carefully. They were the hardest killers to catch. It was only when their egotism got the better of them that they started to take too many risks and slip up. She handed the letter to Declan for him to read.

"Was there a body in the Old North Church?" Charlie asked, sitting back with his face twisted in fear.

"There was," Kate said matter-of-factly. She explained about the construction happening in the church and the man's body found in the bell tower. Kate hesitated to tell Charlie about Pete's severed hand, but the family knew, so it might become common knowledge at some point. They might as well get in front of the story now, so she gave him that final detail about the murder.

Charlie's face registered shock and then more fear. "I'm a news guy who has worked the crime beat for most of my career. Nothing shakes me. I've gone up against mob bosses, but this scares me to death. This killer is deranged and on the loose in the city. He's killed three. We have to go public with this."

"No, no," Det. Briggs said. "We can't go public and terrify the city. How is that going to help anything?"

Declan shared a look with Kate, and she knew he was thinking the same. They didn't have a choice but to go public. It would be irresponsible at this point not to. Declan bent his head to read the letter, but she knew he did it to avoid being the one to deliver the news to Det. Briggs.

As Charlie started to argue the merits of going public, Kate politely interrupted. "Det. Briggs, I completely understand we don't want to cause panic, but at this point, we know what we are dealing with. We have to go public, not only to warn the community but to ask for their help. Someone might know this killer. I think we can schedule a press conference tomorrow after we attempt to speak to our person of interest."

Charlie slapped his hand down on the table. "You have a suspect."

Declan raised his head. "No, we have a person of interest and that's not being published. We don't know anything about this guy other than he stopped occasionally and spoke to the victim at the Old North Church. From what the victim's brother said, the man might have some information that can help the case. We have to be cautious not to tip him off or accuse him of anything."

Kate agreed with Declan and was proud of his cautious approach for once. "Charlie, we will give you the exclusive as we promised and you can run it online tomorrow after we give you the go-ahead. We can't release enough right now for you to make the morning print edition, but we are fine with you running it before the press conference. Fair enough?"

Charlie nodded once. "Will you give me an interview today so I can work on the article overnight to have it ready before the press conference?"

Before Kate responded, she looked to Det. Briggs who still hadn't said anything about the FBI wanting to hold a press conference. She needed him on board. "Are you okay with this, Det. Briggs?"

He scowled. "Do I have a choice?"

Declan passed the letter across the table to Det. Briggs. "Read that. It sounds like he's just getting started. I agree with Agent Walsh that we have to warn the public. Speculation about these murders is going to spread across the city, the state, and probably across the country. Do you know how many tourists have probably already heard about the man murdered in Granary Burying Ground? Information is going to be out there whether we like it or not. We must get in front of the story and look like a united front in the hunt for this killer."

Det. Briggs sat back, read the letter, and seemed to consider what Declan had to say. After a moment, he relented. "Do you want me to get our public information officer involved or will the FBI handle it?"

"I think we can handle it right here," Declan said, glancing at Kate. "We need to control the information as best we can. The fewer people we loop in, the better. If you need to because that's your protocol let us know."

"We can handle it here," Det. Briggs said.

"Good," Declan said. "Can I use one of your workstations to search for this guy we want to interview? I need an address and see if he has any priors. I figured I could do that while you and Agent Walsh give Charlie an interview for the paper."

"Sure, I can set you up." Det. Briggs headed with Declan out of the room and into the hall.

Kate wanted to take a moment anyway to check in with Charlie. "Listen," she said softly, "I want to see how you're doing. This killer has targeted me with a note and delivered an antique knife to my home. That isn't for the public to know, but I understand you might be freaked out by all of this."

A hint of relief washed over Charlie's face. "I'm not glad this is happening to you, too, but it's nice to know I'm not alone. I know you said you have an ancestral tie to the American Revolution, but do you think that's all it is?"

"I don't know right now, but I want to make sure that you're okay."

"I'm fine. As I said the other day, normally, I'm on the outside looking in on criminal cases. This one has been brought right to me, so it adds a new dimension to my involvement."

"I get it," Kate said honestly. "It's the same for me. You mentioned a professor the other day that maybe I should speak with. Professor Anthony Holt was his name. Could you set that up for me? I think I'd like to ask him a few questions just for context."

Charlie nodded. "I can give him a call later today. What time works best for you?"

"I can make any time he's available work for us."

As they were finalizing a potential meeting with Professor Holt, Det. Briggs walked back into the room. "Agent James is all set. Let's get down to the interview. I have a few other things to take care of before the end of the day."

Kate and Det. Briggs sat with Charlie for the next hour providing him the details that could be made public about the three murders, details about each victim, and specific details that were important to include and those they didn't want made public right now. While Kate didn't want the information about the knife left at her home included in the story, she didn't mind if Charlie detailed the note that was left for her near the victim's body. It was an important part of the larger story about these cases. Det. Briggs had some insightful information and quotes for Charlie to use as well. All in all, it would make for a compelling story.

When they were done, Det. Briggs added, "If we need the help, I can have our public information officer set up the press conference here tomorrow afternoon. She has all the relevant media contacts at her fingertips."

Kate sat back in her seat, feeling for the first time that they had a solid plan for moving forward. "That sounds perfect."

Charlie gathered up his things to go, promising Kate he'd be in touch as soon as he was able to reach Professor Holt. When Charlie left, Det. Briggs looked at her for an explanation.

"Charlie mentioned he knew an American history professor at Harvard. I figured since this case seems to have a historical motive it might not be a bad idea to connect with an academic, especially if this lead about The Founders pans out."

Det. Briggs seemed to understand. "Are you going to want me to sit in on that meeting with you?" he asked hesitantly.

"Sure, if you'd like to."

Det. Briggs finally cracked a smile. "I don't, so enjoy that meeting alone. Have I ever mentioned how much I hate history? I barely squeaked by in school. I was focused on other things."

"Well, then you certainly won't be a target of our killer." Kate returned the smile. "I won't make you come to a boring academic meeting. I'd make Agent James go with me, but he'd be as bored as you. I doubt much will come of it. I just want to talk a few things out."

As the conversation lulled, Declan shoved open the conference room door. "I got Mark Boyle's address right here. He has a prior arrest for an assault but looks like it was dropped in court. That was a few years ago. Not much in the way of details in the system." Declan slapped Det. Briggs on the back. "You want to go with us in the morning?"

"If you need me, I'll be there, but I think the FBI showing up at his door might be enough. We don't want to spook him too badly," Det. Briggs reasoned.

Kate agreed, but he had already declined to go with her to meet Professor Holt. She didn't want Det. Briggs to feel too pushed out of the investigation. "We'll be back here when we are done to brief you on anything we find. We appreciate your willingness to work with us."

"It's good to share the workload. I have a few leads I want to run down on the Nathan Hammond murder. I'll share those when we meet."

CHAPTER 15

"That was too long of a day," Kate said as she walked with Declan. They got in his car, which had been parked in the Boston Police Department visitor's lot. As they were headed back to her house, Kate asked Declan if he wanted to stop for dinner on the way. "I don't have much in the house to cook for dinner and we skipped lunch."

He smirked. "Do you ever have anything to cook?"

Declan knew her too well. Her culinary skills weren't even close to her interrogation skills. Kate might even venture to say she was a terrible cook. "Let's go back home and ditch the car, change, and we can go someplace close."

It sounded like a good plan. She leaned her head back and took a few deep breaths. "This is the worst vacation ever." She laughed. "I was really stupid enough to believe the Bureau was going to give me time off."

"You'll get it eventually." Declan changed lanes too fast and had to slam on his brakes. Kate jerked forward but stopped against the seatbelt. "I hate driving on city streets."

"You think Spade is killing people to keep me working?" Kate asked, only half-kidding.

Declan laughed. "I wouldn't put it past him."

Martin Spade was an enigma. Neither she nor Declan knew him

well even though they had worked for him for years. He was well-respected by the FBI and had been Special Forces in Vietnam but other than that, no one knew much about his background or family life. Many joked Spade was more cut out for the CIA than the FBI, but he had made the Bureau his home and never left.

Even with heavy traffic, they made it back to Kate's house faster than they thought. They went inside, changed, and were back out on the sidewalk within twenty minutes. They only made it half-way down the block when a young man with dark hair and glasses approached.

"You Declan James?" the kid asked.

"Who wants to know?" Declan said, reaching his hand instinctively to the gun on his hip.

The kid thrust a thick envelope at Declan. "You've been served."

Declan groaned but took the envelope from the kid who was just doing his job. He turned to Kate. "I'll give you two guesses what's in here."

Kate reached her hand out and put it on his arm. "You said Lauren wanted a divorce. You had to know she was going to file sooner or later."

"I thought it would be later."

"Are you still up for dinner? I can go pick something up and bring it back?"

Declan looked down the road and back to the house. "Would you mind? I want to see what this says. I'd be terrible company now anyway."

"I'll be back. Go inside and get settled." Kate felt for Declan, but this was of his own making. He shouldn't have married Lauren and he hadn't been the best husband. In their line of work, it was hard to keep a marriage going.

Kate went down a few blocks to her favorite upscale restaurant. She sat at the bar and ordered a beer while she waited. Kate garnered the amorous glances of more than a couple of men dressed in business attire. She could have flirted if she wanted but that wasn't where her mind was tonight.

Kate kept a watchful eye around the bar area and into the restaurant to see if anyone looked like they might be a deranged serial killer with a hard-on for the British. She chuckled for being so silly. A serial killer wasn't going to stand out like that, but the killer knew where she lived. He had walked the same streets as her and probably ate at the same restaurants. Kate was so lost in thought she didn't hear the server announcing that her food was ready and pushing the bag to her across the bar.

"Sorry," Kate mumbled, grabbing the heavy white bag and leaving cash with a generous tip on the bar.

Kate made it out of the restaurant and back to the house quickly. She found Declan nursing a glass of whiskey and sulking in the living room. "I got you salad, steak, and a baked potato. I figured that might cheer you up."

Declan made his way into the kitchen to fix his plate. "Lauren put in the divorce papers that I was having an affair. I was undercover!"

"Does it matter what she puts in the divorce papers? Divorce is divorce."

"I know," Declan grumbled. "I don't like the idea of putting something in a legal document that isn't true. Will you talk to her for me?"

"Absolutely not, Declan." Kate turned on him with her hands on her hips. "I'm surprised Lauren didn't write in there that we are having an affair. She hates me. Besides, this isn't high school. I'm not going to make things all better with your wife. Just suck it up and do what you have to do." Kate finished making her plate and headed for the living room just as a crack of thunder ripped overhead.

"She's always been jealous of our relationship," Declan said, following right behind Kate. "We should give her something to be jealous of."

"Not if your life depended on it." Kate sat on the floor and rested her plate on the coffee table. She clicked on the television for some noise, hoping nothing about the case broke into the local news.

Declan pouted dramatically and took a seat on the couch. "I'm sure if I were the last man on Earth, you'd change your mind."

Kate laughed. "Maybe not even then."

The thunder clapped loudly overhead and the rain pelted the windows with such force it sounded like tiny pebbles being thrown against it. The lamp on the table flickered.

"I hope we don't lose power," Declan said through a bite of food.

They both dug into their food, listening to a sitcom on the television neither of them had ever seen before. Declan wasn't much of a television watcher other than sports, and Kate wasn't in one place enough to enjoy anything.

As they were nearly finished with their meal, Kate looked up at him. "Tell me what you found out about Mark Boyle during your search."

Declan took his last bite of steak and wiped his mouth. "Not much to tell. He's fifty-six and lives alone from what I can see. He graduated from Boston College with a degree in business and finance. He works for a local accounting firm. He does okay for himself from what I can see. If he hadn't told Pete Amato about The Founders, we wouldn't have known. There is nothing in his file or from what I can see from the outside that he even has an interest in history."

That didn't dissuade Kate. "Everything fits the profile so far. I would assume most accountants are planners and meticulous about what they do. They'd have to be to do their job effectively." Kate took a sip of her drink and leaned back, stretching her legs for the first time. The pull in her calf muscles told her she needed to get back to at least doing some yoga regularly. "You said there was a prior for assault.

What was that about?"

Declan leaned back and rested his hands across his full belly. "There was a dispute with a neighbor five years ago and they got into an altercation. It seems like the neighbor's wife called the cops, and when they came, both were arrested for assault. I think from what I can see the judge dropped it to a fine for disturbing the peace. I wouldn't say it constituted a real assault. Seems like a situation between neighbors that just got out of hand."

"Possibly," Kate said, weighing what it meant. "I mean, you don't see me throwing punches with Mary next door."

Declan laughed so loud he snorted. "I would hope not. Mary is ninety if she's a day. She kept asking about you while you were gone. You should check in with her."

Mary had been Kate's neighbor all of her life. When her parents passed, Mary became downright motherly toward Kate. "I'd be checking in sooner if I got my time off."

"You can rest when you're as old as Mary." Declan stood and grabbed Kate's plate and headed for the kitchen. Kate leaned back and stretched some more. With all her travel, her body had stiffened up over the years. Cramped plane rides, countless hours interrogating subjects, and research to create psychological profiles. She had frequented hotel gyms to keep up on exercise when she could, but in most places she had been, Kate hadn't the freedom to exercise like she needed and wanted. Her naturally thin frame might not show that she was getting out of shape, but she felt it.

Declan came back into the living room and sat down. "What's the plan for tomorrow?"

Kate sat back and crossed her legs under her. "I've been thinking about that. I'm not sure you should come with me. I've been thinking we might need to infiltrate The Founders, and if we are both seen tomorrow, it means neither one of us can go undercover."

"You think I could go undercover with The Founders? Kate, are you crazy? I'm as Irish as you get in Boston. South Boston. Southern Ireland. I can pull off undercover for the IRA, but there is no way I can pull off convincing anyone the British should still be in charge. I'd have ancestors rolling over in their graves."

Kate sighed. "You are so dramatic. You're great undercover and all we have. I want to keep this as close to the vest as possible."

"Katie," Declan said seriously. "Think about it. If this killer knows where you live, he's seen me, too. It's a no go."

Kate cursed. She hadn't thought of that. "We are going to have to figure out something then because this guy is going to keep on killing until we stop him. I'm most worried that he doesn't even have a cooling-off period like most serial killers. He killed at the cemetery and the next day at the church. Well technically, it might have been Sunday morning and late Sunday night. We still don't know Pete's time of death. The killer might very well have his eyes on the next target as we are sitting here."

Declan stood from the couch and offered Kate his hand to help pull her off the floor. She took it. "We'll stop him. Have we ever failed?"

"Paris."

Declan groaned. "I'm never living that down, am I?"

"Not as long as I'm alive."

CHAPTER 16

The next morning at seven, Kate, Declan, and Det. Briggs stood on the front stoop of Mark Boyle's home in the North End of Boston. At the last minute, they decided if they were confronting a killer, it would be better to have Det. Briggs with them.

The simple two-story brick house fit in with the rest of the neighborhood. Kate wondered which neighbor he had the altercation with. The streets were mostly quiet, but soon there'd be a rush of people heading off to work and school. They had gotten there early enough to catch Mark before he left for work.

Declan reached out and rapped his knuckles against the door three times and then stood back and waited. None of them were expecting an altercation, but they were all armed and ready if that's how it went. The seconds ticked by and Kate worried he might have left already, but soon she heard footsteps coming toward the door and a man calling out that he'd be right with them.

A short man with dark hair answered the door. His ruddy cheeks and slightly winded breath gave away how hurried he was. "I'm sorry, I didn't hear you. I was getting ready for work." He shoved the bottom of his shirt into his pants, which were unbuttoned. "Can I help you?"

Det. Briggs and Declan held up their badges at the same time, but Declan was louder. "Agent James and Agent Walsh with the FBI. This is Det. Briggs with the Boston Police. We need to speak with you."

Kate watched the man's face for any sign of recognition that he knew her or was surprised that she'd be standing on his porch, but there was none. Mark stammered out a few words Kate didn't understand, but he opened the door wide and stepped out of the way for them to enter his home. "Have a seat in the living room or the dining room table if you'd rather."

"Is there anyone else in the home?" Declan asked.

"What?" Mark asked and Declan repeated. "No, just my small dog who is upstairs. She's harmless though." They opted for the dining room. Mark quickly picked up stacks of magazines and papers that littered one side of the table. As he carried the stack to a sideboard that held a stack of dishes and decorative items, Kate noticed the image on the magazine on top of the pile.

"Is that an antique gun?" Kate asked, pointing to it.

Mark set the stack of magazines down and lifted the top to show her. "It's a magazine for old war antiques – guns, knives, war medals, uniforms, and such."

Declan sat down at the table. "Is that something you're into, Mark?"

Mark dropped the magazine down on the pile and sat at the table. "I'm interested in all sorts of antiques. The sideboard there is from 1839, for instance. It's a hobby of mine."

Declan started to speak, but Mark cut him off. "I'm sorry, Agent James, but can I ask what this visit is about? It's not everyday law enforcement shows up at my home." Mark wrung his hands, showing off his nervousness. "I assume this might be about one of my clients, but I can assure you, if they are doing something illegal, I don't know about it. We pride ourselves on not handling those kinds of clients."

Det. Briggs waved his hand dismissively. "Not why we are here. Where were you Sunday night into the morning?"

"Here at home," Mark said. "I didn't have anything going on this past weekend. During the week, I usually get out of work around six, back home to take the dog out, and I spend most evenings here. I take my dog for a walk late, usually around nine or ten, and back home again for the night."

That was good and exactly what Kate had wanted. The goal that morning was to lock Mark into his alibi before telling him why they were there. It rarely worked as most insisted on knowing why the cops were speaking to them. His forthrightness didn't knock him off the suspect list because no one could confirm his alibi if he was here alone.

"How about early Sunday morning before dawn?" Det. Briggs pressed again.

"Here, alone." Mark rubbed his head. "I don't mind answering your questions, but I'd like to know what this is about. You're suggesting I might have done something wrong. I can assure you I didn't."

Declan drew Mark's attention to him. "Do you know Pete Amato?"

Mark sat back and seemed to think about it. "I don't think so."

"What about any of the construction workers down at the Old North Church? Have you ever spoken to them?"

Mark nodded. "On a few occasions." Mark paused and then amended his earlier answer. "Now that I think about it, one of the guys that I've spoken to most often might be Pete. I don't know his last name. Is this what you're here for? You want me to stop talking to them? I know the church is closed, but I was only curious about what they were doing. Pete seems like an affable guy. We got into a conversation and I stopped in from time to time."

Declan shook his head. "No, that's not why we are here. The FBI doesn't get involved in things so trivial."

"The Boston Police Department either," echoed Det. Briggs.

Kate had been quiet until then, but they had decided she'd be the one to tell Mark that Pete had been murdered. "Mark, did you speak to Pete on Sunday night?"

"I haven't spoken to Pete since early last week. Sunday night I walked a different direction and didn't go by the church." Mark glanced at all three of them and breathed heavily. "I've been accommodating here, more than most people would. Please, tell me what this is about or I'm going to have to ask you to leave."

Mark had a backbone. Kate had started to wonder about the man. She leveled a look at him. "Pete Amato was murdered at the church late Sunday night into Monday morning. We are still waiting for the time of death to be confirmed."

Mark stammered. "You think I had something to do with that?"

Declan downplayed it for now. "We aren't accusing anyone. Our goal right now is to find who killed Pete. We spoke to his brother and his wife and some of the other construction workers. We are speaking to everyone who had contact with Pete. You were in the Old North Church when you weren't supposed to be and sought Pete out. It was natural we speak to you."

Kate added, "Mark, there's a chance you might have more information than you realize. You could help us catch Pete's killer." Mark relaxed his shoulders, and Kate knew what she said had eased off some of the tension. "Did you ever see anyone suspicious around the church late in the evening?"

"No," Mark said his eyes roaming over them seeming unsure where to land. "I only saw construction workers in the church and people I usually see in the neighborhood on the street. I wouldn't have any idea who'd want to harm Pete. What happened to him?"

"He was stabbed," Det. Briggs said forcefully, "with an antique knife."

Mark opened his eyes a little wider and glanced in the direction of the stack of magazines. He let out a small gasp. "I'm sure having those magazines makes me even more of a suspect."

"It doesn't look good," Declan said, leaning back in the chair and appraising the man. "Do you have weapons in the house?"

Mark nodded once. "Upstairs in the spare bedroom." He stood from the table. "I might as well just show you. I'm sure you could get a search warrant anyway."

Declan raised his head to meet Mark's eyes. "You're going to voluntarily give us permission to search your house?"

Mark stood with his arms wide open. "I have nothing to hide. I swear to you I didn't kill Pete. I liked the guy. I was going to visit him tonight."

"You didn't hear about the murder before now?"

Mark shook his head. "I don't talk to many of my neighbors. I haven't seen anything on the news. I worked late yesterday, and by the time I got home, I was exhausted."

Declan and Det. Briggs stood to follow Mark out of the room to see the weapons. Kate asked if he would mind if she stayed downstairs and had a look around. Mark waved her off and told her to look wherever she wanted to so that's what Kate did.

She first flipped through the stack of magazines and then pulled out drawers on the sideboard. She didn't find anything but silverware and other dining items. She went into the kitchen and pulled open cabinet doors and slid out drawers. There was nothing beyond the usual kitchen items. Kate even opened the fridge and freezer. She pulled out some frozen meat and vegetables, but there was nothing.

She had learned to look in the freezer from a case years ago. A mob boss had built a false back in the freezer and stuffed stacks of cash there. But there was nothing of interest in Mark's. A door led off the kitchen to a small spare room in the back of the house that looked like Mark's home office. Kate stepped into the room and ran her hand on the wall next to the door until she found a light switch. She flipped it up and an overhead light illuminated the room.

A laptop sat on a neatly arranged desk. Kate walked over and hit the mousepad with her index finger, but the computer was off. She made a mental note of the make and model in case later they needed forensics on it. She bent down and pulled open the desk drawers and rifled through the papers, pens, and paperclips. She pulled out a stack of letters, but it was mostly bills.

Kate sighed. Not that she expected to walk in and find a trove of evidence, but Mark's place was clean. Before she left the room, she pulled open a closet door and pulled the string that clicked on the light, which wasn't even encased in a light fixture. The naked bulb's brightness made Kate blink several times until her eyes adjusted to the light. Four winter coats hung neatly in the closet. More magazines were stacked on the top shelf. Two pairs of boots were on the floor and next to it sat a blue plastic bin. Kate crouched down and unclasped both sides to take off the top. She couldn't believe her eyes.

A stack of parchment paper like the killer had used sat in a neat stack encased in plastic. To the side of that were an antique inkwell and a feathered quill pen. Kate stood and stepped back. She pulled out her cellphone from her pants pocket and snapped a few pictures. She scrolled through her phone until she landed on the FBI field office main number and called, navigating through one receptionist after another until she had Sharon on the line.

"What's up, Agent Walsh?" Sharon said. "Busy morning. Just got off the line with Agent James."

"Oh," Kate said surprised. "He's upstairs in a house we are searching. I found something and wanted a forensic team here as soon as possible."

"We are getting ready to leave right now. See you in a few."

Kate ended the call and made a quick dash out of the room and headed for the stairs to the second floor.

CHAPTER 17

Kate met Declan on the stairs as he rushed toward her. "Sharon said you called her," she said, stopping him.

Declan pointed up to the second floor. "We found antique knives upstairs and need to have them tested for blood residue. He could have cleaned them off. Det. Briggs said better to call the FBI lab than Boston. He said we'd probably get the results sooner." Declan caught his breath. "Did you say you called Sharon, too?"

"I found an inkwell, quill pen, and parchment similar to what the killer used." Kate glanced behind Declan but didn't see Mark or Det. Briggs.

Declan asked, "Do you think we have enough to make an arrest?"

"No, not yet. Sharon said the paper is available at any store. Many people have antique weapons. We only have a circumstantial connection to one victim. Where is he?"

"We are keeping him up there in his bedroom. He's quite distraught. What do you want to do about a search warrant? I think we should at least try to get one."

Kate had thought the same. Even if Mark had agreed to a search it was better to get a search warrant in case he backed out later and claimed he had never given permission. "Can you take care of the warrant? I'd like to sit down and talk to him some more."

Declan moved past Kate down the stairs. "I'll call Sharon and stall her. I'll call you as soon as I have a signed search warrant in hand." Declan ran down the rest of the stairs and out the front door, closing it behind him.

Kate made her way to the second floor and down a narrow hall with three bedrooms off it. She found Mark and Det. Briggs in the last bedroom on the right. It was the largest of the three and had an ensuite master bath. Mark sat in a chair near the window holding his head in his hands, either looking at the floor or with his eyes closed. From where Kate stood, she couldn't be sure.

Kate motioned for Det. Briggs to join her in the hallway. He came right out to her and Kate whispered close to his ear. "I found parchment paper downstairs. Agent James went to get a search warrant to cover us."

Det. Briggs nodded. "I said as much to him when he left. I don't trust that Mark will decide later he didn't authorize a search."

"Has he asked for a lawyer?"

"Not yet, but he asked if I thought he should call one. I told him it was up to him. So far, he hasn't. I haven't Mirandized him yet. I don't think we have enough for an arrest."

"Let me see if I can talk to him while we wait for Agent James to come back."

"I have to make a call to my office. He has no weapon on him and he's fully cooperated. I'd take him downstairs though. I'll be outside the front door if you're comfortable with that."

Kate patted the gun on her hip. "I'll be fine."

"Mark," Kate said softly, walking back into the bedroom. "Would you like to come back downstairs with me? We can talk in the dining room. There are a few questions I have for you."

Mark raised his head but shifted his eyes away from Kate. "I'm okay with that."

Kate wasn't going to walk in front of him down a flight of stairs or turn her back on him at all, so she stepped out of the way and let him pass. He did so hesitantly, but Kate wasn't going to budge regardless. If they had to stand in the hallway all day that's what they'd do. Mark glanced behind at her, and Kate offered a stiff smile.

Once at the table, Mark said, "I need to call my office and tell them I won't be in." He reached into his pocket and pulled out his cellphone. The act made Kate sit up a little straighter until she was sure it was a phone. He placed the call, spoke to someone quickly, and then rested the phone on the table when he was done. Mark glanced over at Kate. "We can talk now. I rarely miss work, and they would have been looking for me."

"Understood." Kate wasn't sure where she wanted to start, and since she hadn't seen the knife, she would start with something easy. "Did you read about the murder in the Granary Burying Ground that happened on Sunday?"

"I saw it briefly on the news. The reporter said something about the dead guy being propped up against Paul Revere's grave. Was that true?"

"It was," Kate said. "It was a horrific scene. Do you see any similarities between that murder and what happened to Pete?"

Mark didn't say anything for a moment, but then he shrugged. "I'm not sure what you mean. I don't know how either of them was killed or much about the murders at all."

"What about where they were found?"

"Tourist spots in Boston, I guess."

"Also, significant historical spots in the founding of America."

"You're right," Mark said, "but I don't get it. What does that have to do with me and why you're here?"

Kate tapped her finger on the table. "Other information has come to light that leads us to believe you're involved or you know who is involved."

Mark shook his head. “That can’t be true. I had nothing to do with this.”

“What can you tell us about The Founders?” Kate watched the man’s face as it went from shock to recognition to fear.

“You don’t think The Founders had something to do with this, do you?” he asked incredulously.

“We don’t know, but we believe whoever killed Pete had a political motivation. From what I know about The Founders, they are Loyalists to England still, nearly two-hundred and fifty years later.”

“Is that what you think The Founders is about?” Mark asked.

“I don’t know, that’s why I’m asking you. I’ve heard you’re a member.”

“I am a member, but that’s not all we are about.”

Kate caught how Mark said that. It was significant. “You said that’s not all The Founders is about. So, you are focused on wanting to be loyal to England? What else does the club do?”

Mark smirked. “We aren’t a club. We are an academic society focused on dissecting and discussing the founding of America and where it all went wrong. Some of those in the society do believe we should have remained loyal to England and are still quite hung up on the loss. Others, like myself, simply enjoy the historical and political conversation.”

“Who makes up your membership?” Kate asked, noting that Mark was holding something back in his explanation. She’d get to that later.

“We have people from every walk of life, but the majority are academics, scholars, and American history enthusiasts.”

“Do you have any professors among your ranks?”

“Yes, of course,” Mark said without naming names or elaborating. “I still don’t understand what this has to do with The Founders or how you think I could have killed Pete.”

Kate still wasn’t prepared to answer that question, so she didn’t. “If you claim that you're innocent, do you have any extremists in your society? Maybe someone still fighting the war or threatening war again – to make people pay for the Patriots winning."

Mark shifted his look toward the kitchen. Kate wasn't sure why, but she wondered if he knew she had found his parchment and quill. After a moment, Mark looked straight ahead. "There are extremists in every group, aren't there?"

"I'm not talking about every group," Kate cautioned. "I'm talking about The Founders and if there is anyone there you think capable of these murders."

Mark's head snapped in her direction. "Murders? Now you think two of them are tied to me."

He was paying attention. Kate offered a smug grin. "It's three murders."

Mark's breath caught in his throat and he vehemently shook his head. "That can't be. I would never. No one I know would ever."

"Well, we have three dead men, and we believe each case is connected. That means a killer is lurking around Boston with an agenda."

"What agenda?" Mark screeched.

"You tell me."

Mark dropped his head into his hands. "I swear to you I don't know what you're talking about. I've let you search my home, which now has only gotten me in more trouble, and I don't even know why. I'd tell you what you want to know, but none of this makes any sense to me."

Kate had pushed him far enough, and she knew pushing more wasn't going to yield what she wanted right now. "Mark, the killer has written two letters to the *Boston Globe* and left one for me at the cemetery murder. The letters indicate his anger over the outcome of the Revolutionary War and his desire to settle the score. The writer of those letters believes that America should be back under British rule." Kate waited for Mark to say something, but he didn't. "That sounds a lot like The Founders."

Mark didn't argue her point. He only had one question in response to hearing all of that. He finally lifted his head and locked eyes with Kate. "How does any of this connect to me?"

"The murder weapons are antiques and the letters are written on the same parchment paper you have in the closet in your back room."

"I was holding that for a friend!" Mark yelled.

Det. Briggs must have heard him yell because two seconds later he came crashing through the front door. "Everything okay in here?"

Kate appreciated how quickly Det. Briggs had raced into the house to make sure she was okay. She explained the conversation she and Mark were having and that his excuse for the parchment was that a friend had asked him to hold it.

Det. Briggs let out a chuckle. "I said the same thing when my mother found pot in my bedroom when I was sixteen." Looking over at Mark, he added, "I think you can come up with something better than that."

"I'm telling the truth."

"We'll see about that," Det. Briggs said. "Agent James called me while I was outside. We have the warrant and your forensics team will be here soon. Mark, I think it's time you come down to the police station with me."

"I'll come with you," Kate said. Mark knew more than he was saying, and while he still wasn't asking for a lawyer, she wasn't going to let up on him.

CHAPTER 18

Late that afternoon, just before four, Kate sat in Det. Briggs office at the Boston Police Department and lamented the fact that as soon as they had arrived at the station, Mark Boyle lawyered up. "I thought we had him," she said for the fifth time.

"He's an accountant who knows how the game is played. What did you expect?" Det. Briggs said leaning back in his chair. They were waiting for Declan who had called about thirty minutes ago to say that he and Sharon were headed to meet with them about what they found at Mark's house. Mark had been let go as soon as his attorney arrived. He was given specific directions not to return home until the FBI forensics team was done. His attorney assured Kate and Det. Briggs that he wouldn't.

"Mark didn't seem all that savvy to me, and I usually know when someone is faking it." Kate checked her phone again to see if Declan had called. He hadn't, but he had texted to say they had arrived. "Agent James and Sharon are here." Det. Briggs stood and walked with Kate to the conference room.

They had pushed back the press conference until five so they had an hour to strategize. Charlie Crain had broken the story earlier online so other news stations were chomping at the bit for information. They still needed to decide what they were going to release to the public.

Kate found Declan leaning against the table smiling and laughing with Sharon. "Do you have good news for us?"

"Agent Walsh," Sharon said as a greeting. "I'd like to tell you we have good news, but we don't. I tested some of those weapons right in that weaselly little man's home and nothing. Either he wiped them clean or he's not your guy. We bagged all the knives for evidence, and of course, I'll run more tests back at the lab, but it's not looking good."

Declan pushed himself off from the edge of the table. "We don't have anything on him right now. Not connected to those weapons anyway. Most were in a display case. Nothing else in the home. There wasn't anything else found. A ballistics expert took the two guns back to the lab, but he texted me right as we walked in here and said neither had been fired in a long time."

Kate sighed. "What about from the three crime scenes? Do we have any fingerprints or DNA to match?"

"Not a drop so far," Sharon said as she propped her hands on her hips. "As you know, the FBI lab didn't test anything from the first crime scene with the shooting victim, but the last two, nothing so far. There is still a mountain of evidence to go through, but right now it's looking like this killer didn't leave a trace. I don't like this guy. He's too clean, too much of a neat freak."

Kate understood that statement. Not that anyone liked a killer, but when there wasn't a drop of evidence behind, it didn't give them much to go on. "Keep digging, there might be something still left to uncover."

Sharon smacked her lips and grinned. "Oh, I'm going to keep digging, you can be sure of that. I'm not letting some creep keep killing people in my city that's for sure."

Kate turned to Det. Briggs. "Can your forensics team share the evidence from the shooting victim with the FBI forensics team? Can't hurt to have two sets of eyes on it."

"Absolutely," Det. Briggs said already reaching for his phone to place the call.

While he did that, Kate turned back to Sharon. "What about the paper and quill?"

"Unfortunately, the parchment paper can be bought at any store. They have it all over the place. The quill looked unused and there wasn't ink in that inkwell. It looked newly bought if you ask me. We bagged it for safekeeping until we can rule this guy in or out. Looks alone, I'd tell you I think he's good for it, but not a drop of evidence so far."

That's why Sharon did her job and Kate and Declan did theirs. Perps can't be arrested on looks alone, or at least, that's not how the FBI operated. Kate reached up and rubbed her forehead. She told Declan that he had lawyered up. "We don't have much of anything right now. Certainly, not a late-breaking bombshell for the news."

Kate slumped down in a seat at the conference table. Declan and Sharon sat as well. "What do you want to do?" Declan asked her.

"We have to prepare a statement for the press. We are going to have to let them know there have been three murders and mention the letters. Charlie already posted as much online. Now, we have to go out and let them know the FBI and Boston Police are working together. People will be in a panic. I'm sure the mayor is going to go ballistic. Tourists are flocking into the city for the fall, but the public has a right to know there's a deranged serial killer bent on carrying out a political agenda from more than two hundred years ago."

Sharon squinted. "What's so great about the British? I mean if we wanted to get things straightened out, send in my Italian momma. She'd have things in order right quick."

Kate laughed. "I have no idea why this killer is focused on this agenda."

"You think he's got a dog in the fight?" Sharon asked with her dark, perfectly-arched eyebrows raised.

"What do you mean?" Declan asked.

"Think about it," Sharon said, looking at Declan like he was a child being scolded. "Agent Walsh was targeted and she has a connection to a signer of the Declaration. Declan, you told me Charlie Crain is distantly related to Benjamin Franklin. What if this killer is related to someone on the British side from back then? Maybe it's not political but revenge. Righting the wrongs of the past."

No one said a word. Kate had heard crazier ideas before, but the more she mulled over what Sharon said, the more it made a certain kind of sense.

"Have I stunned you all into silence with my spectacular observation skills?" Sharon laughed but continued talking before anyone could say anything. "You have to think if this guy, and I'm assuming it's a guy, can track Agent Walsh's history that far back, he's probably gotten on one of those ancestry websites and traced his family line. Maybe he stumbled on something that set him off. That's how these serial killers work, right? They are budding little killers in their youth and then there is a trigger when they are older."

Sharon wasn't wrong. Of course, not every serial killer takes the same path. There were some commonalities – bedwetting, fire starting, and animal abuse when they are young. Sharon was right though when she said there is typically a trigger when they are older. A humiliation, a buildup of abuse from childhood that manifests itself in acting out, or even sex and violence linked in their minds that are no longer fulfilled in fantasy life alone. There was always something.

Kate raised her head to look at Sharon in respect. "I'm supposed to be the profiler and I've been down too far in the weeds with this one in the last two days. I think you're onto something. I don't know much about this ancestry stuff though. It was never something I was too interested in. My parents told me my history, and I've never felt a real desire to explore further. Where do we even start?"

Det. Briggs offered, "I can pull some research help in to start looking at some ancestry websites and digging into the family trees of prominent people from that time."

"It's like looking for a needle in a haystack," Declan lamented. He was right, but they had nothing to go on.

Kate said as much. "Let's also check with Mark Boyle, if his lawyer will let us ask, and see if he ever did his family tree. We have enough information that we can start building a family tree on him regardless and see what we find in his background."

Declan leaned back in the chair and kicked his long legs out in front of him. "We also need a way into The Founders. There is a ripe suspect pool right there."

"True," Kate said, thinking. "If we can rule Mark Boyle out as a suspect, do you think there is any chance he'd be willing to wear a wire when he goes to The Founders' meetings?"

Declan laughed. "I doubt it. Plus, we have no idea if he knows the killer. He might not be the one committing the crime, but there's no telling what goes on in that society. It might be a case of conspiracy to commit murder rather than him doing it himself."

"Do we have anything we can charge him with and dangle cooperation over his head for getting off the hook?" Det. Briggs asked.

That was usually how it worked, but it didn't sound like they had Mark on anything, yet anyway. "Let's focus on getting the information ourselves," Kate said, backtracking on her original idea.

"There's that professor that Charlie Crain wants you to meet. Maybe he knows something about The Founders," Declan reminded her.

"That's a good idea." Turning to Det. Briggs, she asked, "Do you have some paper and a pen? I'd like to sit here and sketch out a statement for the press conference. You said your public information person was also going to issue a press release. Do you have that on hand?"

Det. Briggs said he'd track down the statement and bring Kate what she needed. Sharon decided to leave, saying she'd be better off heading back to the FBI lab. Declan offered to walk her out. It was just as well. Kate needed a few minutes to collect her thoughts before making the statement.

Kate closed her eyes and mentally prepared her statement before she wrote it out. Normally, she'd have an FBI spokesperson handle this for her because she was behind the scenes. It's how it went down in most cases, but she and Declan were on their own right now.

Det. Briggs came in and dropped the press release on the table and the other items Kate wanted. She thanked him and he said he'd be in his office until it was time. Kate checked her watch. They had twenty minutes before they'd need to be downstairs. Kate read over the press release, which was void of any serious details other than the FBI and Boston Police Department were working together and would issue updates on the cases periodically. It was the standard press release for this kind of case – giving enough without giving away the farm.

Kate finished writing a succinct statement, and before she knew it, Declan was back asking if she was ready to go. "Ready as I'm going to get," she said as she gathered up the pages and headed out with him.

CHAPTER 19

Kate gripped the edges of the wood podium with her hands and tried not to look at her statement so she could project a sense of confidence and calm to the media standing before her with video cameras aimed and microphones out. Declan stood on one side of her and Det. Briggs on the other. Behind them were a few Boston Police Department officials, who Kate hadn't met and didn't think she'd ever see again.

Kate introduced herself, Declan, and Det. Briggs. She began, her voice strong and steady, "The FBI and Boston Police Department are working together on a joint task force to address three murders that have occurred in the city in the last few weeks. We have reason to believe these cases are connected." Kate continued with the statement, providing a smattering of evidence including mention of the antique weapons, letters to the media, and one addressed to her. She finished the statement with what she knew the media would focus on the most – the letters, but purposefully left out how the killer signed them.

"Through the letters that were sent from the killer and where the bodies were left – the Old State House, Granary Burying Ground, and the Old North Church – we are confident in saying this killer is out to make a statement about their feelings on the outcome of the Revolutionary War." Kate looked right into the cameras. "I know that might seem ridiculous to some, but that's what we are dealing with. It would not surprise us if this were less politically motivated and more an indication this killer is out for revenge."

What felt like a million flashbulbs went off in Kate's face all at once. Reporters' questions came fast, and Kate stepped back from the onslaught. She asked the crowd of reporters to be quiet so she could hear them and then tried her best, with the information she could disclose, to answer every question. Most questions she had to dodge and weave like a prizefighter. After a few minutes, Kate stepped out of the way and gave the mic over to Det. Briggs.

It was clear how much more comfortable and practiced he was giving press conferences than Kate. He commanded their attention and answered directly and honestly. He was even so affable that when he couldn't give a reporter the details they wanted, they still ate it up. Kate watched in amazement. Det. Briggs was an absolute rock star in front of the media. Even Declan glanced down at Kate with a wide grin, a sure sign he was impressed, too. Det. Briggs closed the press conference moments later, promising to provide more information as soon as it became available.

As the media started to make their way back to their news vans, Kate came up and rested her hand on Det. Briggs back. "That was incredible. From now on, it would be great for you to take the lead on all press conferences if you're willing. Agent James and I will be here as added support and to answer questions they might have of the FBI."

Det. Briggs gave a sheepish grin. "I know it probably sounds strange, but I don't mind speaking to the media. I ended up a detective, but, for a long time, I toyed with being a sports broadcaster."

"You could have done that easily," Declan said. "You still can if you want to retire."

The Boston officials who stood in the background congratulated Det. Briggs and Kate on a job well done and then headed back into the police station. As Kate, Declan, and Det. Briggs stood there talking a news anchor from a local news station approached.

The man introduced himself as Walter Kelly from News 10, the NBC affiliate in Boston. "Det. Briggs, I have some information that might prove to be useful, but I'd prefer to speak with you somewhere more private."

"Certainly," Det. Briggs said, hitching his head toward Kate and Declan to head inside. The four of them made their way into the building. They rode the elevator in near silence. It was only once they were seated around the conference room table that Walter Kelly started talking about anything serious.

"Let me start by saying I'm no longer a member of this society," Walter started, and Kate had a feeling where this was headed. "I had belonged to The Founders, a local society for those focused on exploring history and its intersection to the current political and social climate in the United States."

"We've been made aware of this society," Kate said but didn't elaborate. "We'd love to understand your perspective on it and why you left. Also, why you think it might be relevant to this case."

Walter sat back in his seat. "I had been a society member for probably ten years when I quit. This society was founded back in the early 1900s, and throughout its history, had a board of five people that directed the discussion. There were elections to decide who held these positions and term limits so there was a rotation of members into those positions. That is until a man took over the role of president on the board, garnered a group of people in support of him, and the board shut down all elections. It wasn't even done by vote, but all approved by the board and that's how it went. He essentially hijacked the society and no one seemed to know how to stop him. This man wanted to stay in power, push his agenda, and the purpose of the society started to take a turn."

Walter glanced at each of them as he spoke. "When I initially joined the group, it was focused on discussing the role of historical figures and how their personalities and experiences shaped America. For instance, how did George Washington's background and role during the American Revolution shape the political and social climate of today? How did FDR's polio shape his perspective on World War II?" Walter smiled. "We had some heady spirited debates. It was fascinating conversation, and I hate that I'm no longer part of it. But it changed."

"You said that," Declan mentioned. "Tell us more about how it changed."

"Most of the society members were men. We'd occasionally have a woman join and that was fine. It was by no means meant to be a boy's club. When I first joined, we wanted a diverse range of opinions and had pretty much open admission into the group. There were no large fees either that would have excluded people who could not afford it."

"Did that change too?" Kate asked, not meaning to interrupt, but she thought it was important for looking at potential suspects.

"It did, very much so," Walter said frowning. "During my last year there, the board decided to add yearly membership fees that were quite high. The last I paid was close to five thousand dollars. The discussion also started to change. Where once we also discussed important female historical figures, those discussions were shut down. Women in the group were often interrupted when speaking. It became more male-dominated. They stopped accepting applications from women altogether at one point. The society also started getting cliquey, and over months the few black men who had been involved started to feel downright uncomfortable coming to the meetings. With the heavy fees, it also made anyone of a lower socio-economic status drop their membership as well. The whole group started to become monolithic. That's when it took a strange turn."

Det. Briggs stopped him from going on. "You stayed when all of these changes were being made?" Walter's face fell, but Det. Briggs was quick to clarify. "I'm not judging you. I'm simply trying to understand if it was something you saw firsthand or only what you heard about from other members."

"Understood," Walter said. "Yes, I stayed during this time and saw it firsthand. You have to understand though these weren't abrupt changes and they weren't overt. It wasn't like they said let's change these fees so only wealthy people join. It wasn't like they said let's start keeping women out and limiting the diversity of our members. It was in the way they shaped conversation and how they treated people that the intent was obvious. No one ever came right out and said it. In fact, when called on it by members, the board denied it and said others were just trying to create an issue where there wasn't any. For those of us who had been long-time members, the change and reasoning for it were obvious."

"What made you decide to finally leave The Founders?" Kate asked, finding the entire conversation captivating. She had seen other groups take the same path. Some ended up labeled cults.

"I was planning to leave anyway. A few of my friends in the society had decided it wasn't enjoyable anymore. What's the point of debate if there are no diverse opinions and voices at the table? It stops becoming a learning exercise and becomes something else." Walter sat back and took a breath. He let it out slowly. "I left when the discussions started taking a strange turn. The board stopped allowing any discussion about any historical figures other than those connected to the American Revolution and the founding of the United States. That's it. Forget the rest of history and all that came after. The discussion also started being incredibly pro-England. As you can imagine, for those of us who grew up in Boston and were incredibly proud of our American roots, this was a slap in the face and also strange."

Kate folded her hands on the table. "You said the other changes were slow and somewhat covert. How about that change? Did the conversation start slowly moving to be more about the American Revolution?"

Walter shook his head and scowled. "No, that was quite abrupt. We met every Thursday evening and sometimes on Sunday afternoons. One Thursday evening, the board came in and said there'd be no more discussion about historical figures outside of specific years, and that was it. A few board members started to express Loyalist views. We lost two-thirds of the membership at that time. I stayed on solely to see what was going to happen. It's the news guy in me. I wanted the story. Within a few weeks, the board members started recruiting others with Loyalist views, and within a month or two you had only wealthy, educated men sitting around talking about how we should have remained loyal to England. It was disturbing."

"I don't remember ever seeing a story on The Founders. Did you run one when you left for good?" Det. Briggs asked.

"No, and Agent Walsh and Agent James might know more. There had been rumblings from a few members who were discussing overthrowing the government and bombing historical sites around Boston. I made a call to the local FBI office and they came out to speak with me. The agent I spoke with asked me not to run a story, so I didn't. I left The Founders and never looked back."

This was news to Kate. By the look on Declan's face, he hadn't heard anything either. "Do you know the agent who took your statement?"

"No, I'm sorry, I don't. This was going back probably five years ago. I don't recall his name, but nothing ever happened in Boston so I figured they took care of the problem. I stopped thinking too much about them until now. I figured I should tell you. This sounds like the kind of thing this group would do."

Kate sat stone-faced trying not to give too much away. "Do you know other members of the society who are still active?"

"A few but mostly those on the board."

"Do you know Mark Boyle?"

Walter raised his eyebrows. "Do you think he's killing these people?"

"Do you think he's capable of it?"

"I don't know. Mark is a follower and easily swayed. He might be out to prove himself. I wouldn't rule him out."

Det. Briggs leaned forward on the table. "You've yet to mention the name of the president who took over and never left power."

Walter grimaced and leaned into the table "That wasn't intentional. He's someone I abhor so I try not to give him more power than he deserves. Parker Gage, a distant relative of General Thomas Gage."

CHAPTER 20

Later that night, Kate and Declan sat in the living room as they had the evening before – eating dinner and discussing the case. They had spent another hour with Walter Kelly gathering more information about Mark Boyle and Parker Gage. He knew quite a bit about both men. They thanked Walter for coming forward and had assured him they'd be in touch if they needed more.

Tomorrow Declan planned to run down some leads that Walter had provided and hunt down any potential witnesses around the Old North Church. The Boston cops had done a good job of canvassing neighbors and taking statements, but Declan wanted to speak to them himself.

Without anything else to do for the day, Kate and Declan had left the police station and picked up dinner on the way home. With dinner finished, Declan sat reclined on the couch nursing a beer and getting a history lesson from Kate about General Thomas Gage's role in the American Revolution.

Kate sat curled up in an oversized plush chair reading from one of her father's history books she had pulled off a shelf in the upstairs office. This was twice now Thomas Gage had been mentioned – as the killer's signature on the letters and his distant relative who had overthrown The Founders, taking them essentially from a democratically run organization to a monarchy. Parker Gage would have made his ancestor proud.

Kate kept her eyes focused on the lines of text in front of her, but explained to Declan its contents rather than reading word for word. "There's history lore that Thomas Gage's wife, Margaret Kemble Gage, may have been a spy for the Patriots. It's speculated that she told Dr. Joseph Warren on April 18, 1775, that her husband's troops planned to arrest Paul Revere and John Hancock at Lexington and then raid the armories at Concord."

"Ratted out by your wife. I know the feeling." Declan took a swig of his beer. "Why would a British woman want the Colonies to win?"

Kate ignored Declan's pity party and explained, "Margaret was from a prominent family in New Jersey, which is where she had met Gage. They had moved to and from England as his military orders required him. They had ten children, too."

"Do you think the killer will go after a woman given Margaret's possible treachery?"

"I don't know," Kate said, but she had wondered it as well. So far, only men had been victims, but historically several prominent women of the time had been spies and had helped the Patriots' cause. "I think Sharon might be right about her theory of revenge. At first, I couldn't quite pin down why it all felt off to me. The killer's letters come across like they have a political agenda, but we know that isn't generally a serial killer's mindset. It's more personal to them. Revenge checks that box."

"Either way, he's scum." Declan took another swig of his beer. "Anything else the history book says we need to know? I should have paid more attention in high school history instead of flirting with all the girls."

Kate rolled her eyes and focused her attention back on the text. "Not too much. Most historians feel Gage went back to England disgraced for his failures in America. He did continue to serve in the military there though. He was officially recalled in June 1775 to England by Lord George Germain, the secretary of state for the American Colonies at the time." Kate read a few more lines and closed the book. "I think that's it for now. I need to get ready for that meeting tomorrow with Professor Holt."

"Do you think you're going to get much from that?" Declan asked, eyeing her skeptically. He wasn't always thrilled with Kate's reliance on academics instead of good old fashion fieldwork.

"I think it can't hurt to have a conversation with him." Kate stood, set the book down on the chair, and picked up the plates on the coffee table. She left Declan sitting there.

The grouchy look on his face told her he was itching for a fight that had nothing to do with her. Kate wasn't going to give it to him. She loaded the dishes in the dishwasher and closed the door. She fiddled with the knobs to get the right wash setting, shut off the kitchen lights, double-checked the back lock, and headed upstairs. Kate said goodnight to Declan as she made her way past the living room, but he merely grunted a response in return. Once in her room, Kate quickly got ready for bed and then read for an hour before finally turning off the lights.

The next morning, Kate took her time getting ready. She didn't have to be over to the Harvard campus until ten that morning. She had heard Declan's shower turn on around seven, but she didn't get out of bed until eight, which was late for her. Kate knew exactly why she was dragging her feet that morning, but the last thing she wanted to do was to confront the feelings. She hadn't been back to Harvard's history department, where her father had worked, since his death. She had hoped Professor Holt would have been willing to meet with her off-campus, but Charlie had texted her that his schedule was tight and in between classes was the best he could do.

Kate finished getting ready and made her way downstairs, realizing then that Declan had already left without saying goodbye or even leaving her a note. She made breakfast and found her keys. She hated driving and even more so in the city, but Harvard was too far to walk.

Kate made it to the campus in record time and found her way among the eager throngs of students to Harvard Yard and Robinson Hall where the history department was located. She stood outside the brick rectangular building and looked up. The building had undergone a renovation to upgrade the facilities, including adding an elevator and modernizing offices and classrooms.

A pang of missing her father washed over Kate the way she knew it would. She pushed it aside and glanced at her phone for Professor Holt's office number and then entered the building. Her shoes squeaked over the polished floor, which when she thought about it, she had never seen unpolished. Kate smiled when she spotted the two lions that sat on either side of the few steps up into the main interior of the building. Students were sitting in the main lobby. Kate smiled as she walked past them. Years ago, she had studied there.

Kate found her way to Professor Holt's office and knocked on the door. He called her in. Kate turned the handle and nudged open the door not quite sure who she expected to see, but she was surprised by his appearance. Professor Holt was a tall man with a lean swimmer's body of sinewy muscle and an affable smile that matched the warmth of his eyes. He had a full head of dark hair and a closely trimmed beard and didn't look older than fifty.

"I'm Agent Kate Walsh. Charlie Crain set up a meeting for us today," she said as a way of introduction.

Professor Holt stood and reached out his hand. "I'm Anthony or just Holt, whichever you prefer. I spent a few years in the Army after high school before going to college and got used to being called by my last name."

Kate smiled. "It's the same with the FBI. You can call me Kate if you'd like."

He waved her over to sit down at a chair in front of his desk. "I remember you as a young woman," Professor Holt said. "Your father had pictures of you all over his office. I'm sorry for your loss. Joseph Walsh was a mentor to me and a dear friend."

"Thank you. I spent a good deal of time in my father's office when I was young before he became an ambassador."

Professor Holt sat back and rubbed at his jawline. "Charlie said you had some questions about history and how it might intersect with one of your cases. I assume it's the one you spoke about on the news last night."

"It is," Kate said, sitting. "I'm not even sure what to ask, but Charlie thought it might be helpful for us to speak. I assume he told you that there was a letter from the killer at a crime scene addressed to me and that he's also received a letter."

Professor Holt nodded. "He mentioned it and why. Do you think the killer spent the time tracing your family's ancestry or do you think it was just an accident you were targeted?"

"We were targeted. I do not doubt that." Kate didn't want to spend precious time going back and forth, so she gave an overview of what she knew to date, sharing more details than they had given the news. "I came here because I want to understand the mentality of someone who could be obsessed with history in this way."

Professor Holt sat back and appraised her. "Do you think this is political?"

"At first, I did, but domestic terrorism doesn't usually take this form. It's been suggested that it might be revenge."

"Revenge?" he asked, confusion in his voice. "Revenge for what?"

"The United States winning the war and possibly beating or humiliating someone's ancestor in the process."

Professor Holt's eyes grew wide and he tapped the pads of his index fingers together. "That would be a long grudge to hold. Wouldn't it make more sense if the killer was your classic serial killer and this was a signature for his crimes?"

Kate shook her head. Professor Holt had watched too many television shows about serial killers. "A signature doesn't work like that. A signature is normally something that is part of the killer's internal fantasy that shows in their rituals and behaviors, which over time shows up as a pattern."

"Right," Professor Holt said, "I get that. But what if he's fantasizing that he is a historical British figure. Couldn't all of this just be a part of his persona?"

"Possibly, but then I'd say the killer would be pretty deep into psychosis and it would show itself more in a disorganized murder. These killings are researched, planned, and executed with such precision that he's leaving nearly no forensics behind. I don't think someone that deep in psychosis could pull that off."

"Fair enough. You're certainly the expert on this," Professor Holt conceded. "From a historical perspective, this would have to be someone well-entrenched in the subject matter – obsessive almost. He'd probably be attending lectures and talks or maybe even giving them. His home would be full of writing – both legitimate historical information and possibly even propaganda that would fuel his rage. Did I hear he used antique weapons?"

"Yes, both a knife and a gun."

Professor Holt locked eyes with her. "Have you heard about The Founders?"

CHAPTER 21

"Their name has come up several times," Kate said, wondering if she was the only person in Boston who hadn't heard of them before this case.

"Last night when I heard the news, that's who I thought of first. I was a member for several years," Professor Holt admitted. He explained much the same tale as Walter Kelly had the evening before. "I left when it became too militant for me. I'd almost say cultish."

Kate crossed her legs and sat back. She felt a real warmth for Professor Holt. There was something about the way the corner of his eyes crinkled up when he spoke. His body language was open, too. She asked, "What makes you say cultish? I had been thinking along those same lines, but I'm curious about your perception of that."

"I didn't think that until I decided to leave," Professor Holt explained, leaning back in his desk chair rocking it back and forth as he spoke. "When Parker Gage took over, many of the members were almost followers of his. There was talk of violence, and as members started to pull away from them, some of us faced retribution. There were several calls placed here to Harvard accusing me of things I never did and would never do. Plagiarism for one. Being involved with a young female student for another."

"What did you do?" Kate asked surprised.

"I had to defend myself against these allegations, but of course, it went away quickly because there was no proof of anything. It was just the embarrassment of the accusation and the investigations into the allegations. That alone could have ruined me had I been new to the school or not tenured. I got the benefit of the doubt where I might not have otherwise."

"That certainly is a hallmark of a cult. Most attack their members in some way when they leave. There are even some who send private investigators and other members to harass and follow them. The cults with huge followings and lots of money often go after ex-members through lawsuits."

Professor Holt caught her eye. "You have to understand it wasn't like that when it first started – far from it. The goal was discussion and an exploration of history in comparison to the current political climate. If anything, when we started, we had too many diverse voices. Sometimes we had to narrow down the discussion focus because we were all over the map. It was quite fun."

Kate ran through some questions she hadn't had time to ask Walter the night before. "Do you think Parker Gage is capable of violence like this?"

Professor Holt nodded. "He was contemplating violence in meetings. As I said, things took a turn."

"What kind of violence?"

He pursed his lips in thought. "There was some early discussion about what if the group could bump off certain figures in government." Kate started to speak, but Professor Holt asked her to wait. "At the beginning, it wasn't focused on killing anyone, but more what if a political figure was no longer living or removed from their position, how would that change the landscape. Later, that turned to discussing assassination. That turned to a discussion about bombing historical sites. It became the kind of group I could no longer be a part of. I knew some members went to the authorities – the FBI, I think."

"You didn't?"

Professor Holt looked down at his desk ever so slightly and then back up at Kate. "Other members were going to the FBI, so I didn't see the purpose in calling them as well. The other members knew I was willing to give a statement if it was needed."

Kate raised her eyebrows. "Were you ever contacted?"

"No, but then again you have to understand much of these discussions were theoretical. I never once heard an actual plot with plans. They were more 'what if' discussions."

Kate wasn't sure she bought that. It might have been that way in front of the whole group, but there was something Professor Holt wasn't telling her. She just wasn't sure what. "What does Parker Gage do for a living?"

He leaned forward in his chair and laughed. "Parker doesn't do much, but his father and grandfather had considerable wealth that he inherited."

Walter Kelly didn't know that much about Parker, but it seemed like Professor Holt might. "We heard The Founders mentioned and Parker's name came up a time or two, but we don't have much information about him. Care to share what you know?"

"I don't know that I know all that much, but I'd be happy to." Professor Holt paused and expelled a breath. "Let's see. Parker is in his late forties now, but I'm not certain his exact age. He lives in the Back Bay right on Commonwealth Avenue in a massive brownstone. My understanding is that he's moved the meetings from the Boston Public Library to his home. I've never been there, but it's what I heard." He paused and said to himself, "What else? What else?"

"Anything you can think of that might help me. Is he married? Children? Siblings?"

"Not married that I know of. No children either. He has a sister who is a professor at Yale. I don't think they see eye to eye. I never heard him say a nice thing about her. When I said he doesn't work, that's not exactly true. He's been an angel investor for several companies so he is still making money. He also had a hand in some commercial land development. But he's not with a formal company or runs a business that I know of."

"Do you think he's capable of something like these murders?"

"It wouldn't surprise me," Professor Holt said. "I think…" he trailed off when there was a knock on the door. He called out for whoever it was to enter and then waved in a petite young woman with short dark hair. "Ashley, this is FBI Special Agent Kate Walsh."

"Ashley Barrett," she said reaching her hand out to Kate. "I'm Professor Holt's teaching assistant. I saw you on the news last night."

"Nice to meet you," Kate said. "Yes, I'm here meeting with Professor Holt about the case. I thought he might have some insight into the historical angle of the case."

"I found it…" Ashley started to say but was rudely cut off.

"You can go now," Professor Holt interrupted. He handed Ashley a book and stack of papers from his desk and shooed her out the door. She offered Kate a shy smile as she left and closed the door behind her.

"She could have stayed," Kate said. "I'm open to any help I can get."

"No, no," he assured. "Ashley is an intelligent woman, but she would have talked your ear off all day. I doubt she would have had much to offer." Professor Holt looked at Kate. "Now, where were we?"

Kate didn't like the way he had dismissed Ashley. It turned her off the man completely. "I was asking if you thought Parker Gage was capable of these crimes," she said coolly.

"Ah, yes, that." Professor Holt's mouth set in a firm line. "I do, but I think you need to be very careful about going after him and make sure you have a rock-solid case."

"I'm aware of how to do my job," Kate snipped. "What I was

asking you was if you ever saw Parker get violent. I know you said he mentioned violence in theory, but have you ever witnessed him commit a violent act or have an antique weapon around?"

Professor Holt didn't say anything for several moments. He sat there watching Kate. She held firm and barely moved a muscle. After a tense few seconds, he relaxed and laughed. "Your father always said you could come out swinging if you had to. I believe he was right. No, Agent Walsh, I never saw Parker get violent or have weapons around him. As I said though, I've never been to his home."

"Is there anything else you think might be able to help me with this case?"

Professor Holt flashed her a grin. "Why don't you let me take you to dinner tonight and we can discuss more."

"I'm busy, but thank you." Kate stood to leave.

He jumped up from his seat and blocked her way. "I've offended you. I'm not sure how we got off track. We were having such a pleasant conversation. I apologize for whatever I did."

"Hardly a legitimate apology if you don't even know what it is you're apologizing for."

Professor Holt put his hands up. "Fair enough."

Kate stood her ground. "I've seen professors like you. You routinely interrupt your teaching assistants and treat them disrespectfully. It happens a lot with male professors and their female staff. I don't like it, and I didn't like the way you spoke to Ashley. It's certainly none of my business, but it shows me your character." Kate shook her head and smiled. "It's not something my father ever would have done."

"You're right about that," Professor Holt said and stepped out of the way. "I didn't mean to offend you. Ashley and I have had a difficult working relationship and my temper with her is probably too quick at this point."

"Understood," Kate said, but she still didn't back down. It might be a slight thing she was making too much of but some instinct in her was put off by him now. "Thank you for the information. I should be heading out."

Professor Holt stood where he was for a moment more but then gave up and moved back to his desk. "I would like to explore this a little more with you. Can I call you if I think of anything else to share?"

"That would be helpful," Kate said as she stepped out into the hallway. "I appreciate your time."

As Kate made her way down the hall back toward the front of the building, she contemplated going upstairs to her father's office but thought it might be too emotional so she skipped it. As she turned to the left down another hall, she ran right into Ashley.

"I'm sorry about disturbing your meeting," Ashley said, looking down at her feet.

Kate wanted to give the young woman advice to stand up for herself more, but it wasn't her place. Professor Holt was right that she didn't know the dynamic between them, but it didn't matter. "You didn't interrupt, Ashley. I welcome your thoughts on the case."

The young woman raised her head. "I was just going to say that there was a man on campus not too long ago trying to recruit male history students into a local academic society called The Founders."

"Here on campus?" Kate asked, wondering why Professor Holt hadn't mentioned that.

"Yes, but they didn't want female students, just male. When they started recruiting here, they were asked to leave. It was kind of a big deal."

"How long ago was this?"

"Maybe a year ago." Ashley squinted. "Didn't Professor Holt tell you?"

"He told me about The Founders, but didn't mention their recruitment strategies, but then again, I didn't ask." Kate played it off, but it was still strange he hadn't brought it up.

"Professor Holt was embarrassed because they recruited his former teaching assistant. He tried to warn Justin, but he joined them anyway. Eventually, Professor Holt let him go as his assistant."

Kate felt like marching right back to his office, but she didn't think that would help. "What's Justin's last name?"

"Lewis. He's still on campus getting his Ph.D. if you'd like to speak to him." Ashley stepped closer to Kate. "Between you and me, I wouldn't be surprised if he were the killer. He's had some infractions here on campus and there are rumors he was thrown out of his fraternity in undergrad for violence."

"Where did he go to undergrad?"

"Dartmouth, I think. I'm not positive. As I said, it was a rumor." Ashley's face reddened. "I don't want you to think I'm purposefully ratting out a student, but after what I saw on the news last night about the murders, it was Justin who immediately came to mind." She shrugged. "I thought you should know."

Kate assured Ashley she was glad for the information and that it was the right thing to do. She said goodbye and walked back to her car. Kate wouldn't go interview Justin alone, but she'd see how quickly Declan could make it to campus.

CHAPTER 22

"How did it go with the nerdy professor? Solve the case yet?" Declan asked sarcastically instead of saying hello. The street noise coming through the phone made it difficult for Kate to hear him.

She spoke louder than she probably needed to. "Professor Holt was a member of The Founders. He was able to corroborate Walter Kelly's statement from yesterday so that saves us a step."

"Where are you now?"

"Still on the Harvard campus. Can you come over? There's someone we should speak to."

Declan spoke to someone whose voice Kate didn't recognize. He got back on the line and said gruffly, "I'll be there in twenty." He hung up without saying goodbye.

Kate texted him the directions of where he could find her. She hoped his foul mood from last night wasn't still with him today, but if that call was any indication, she might end up regretting calling him at all.

While she waited, Kate plugged Professor Holt's name into a search engine and scanned through the numerous articles that came back. All were either research articles he had written, guest lectures he had given, or awards he had won. Kate clicked page after page looking for anything bad or nefarious about the man but came away with nothing.

Maybe she had overreacted based on her own experiences when she was a teaching assistant. The male professors, particularly the tenured ones, often had sexist attitudes. She had heard from friends that they had been sexually harassed during their grad school days. That hadn't been Kate's experience, but she believed them wholeheartedly.

Kate lost herself reading an article about one of Professor Holt's papers on George Washington's military strategy. She was so consumed by the article that she lurched forward with a jolt and her hand went to the gun on her hip when she realized a man was standing next to her car watching her.

She opened her car door and left her phone on the seat. "Professor Holt, did you want something? You startled me."

He handed Kate a thick manila envelope. "I'm sorry, I didn't mean to startle you. After you left, I went through a few files I had on The Founders and came across some old membership lists. It was for the last couple of years I was involved, so many might not be active. I thought you might want it in case you want to speak to some other people. I was going to call you later to see if I could drop it by, but I was headed to a lunch meeting and saw you sitting there. I called your name, but I guess you didn't hear me."

Kate smiled, thinking maybe she had read the situation wrong earlier. "Thank you, I appreciate it. This will help."

"Are you waiting for someone?"

Kate nodded. "My partner and I have another interview here on campus."

Professor Holt furrowed his brow. "Would it be improper to ask who you're interviewing?"

"No, it wouldn't be improper," Kate said, stalling. Given Professor Holt hadn't told Kate about his teaching assistant she wasn't sure she wanted to disclose it now. The benefit of getting some inside info before tracking Justin Lewis down won out. "Professor Holt, I'm looking for Justin Lewis, he's a grad student here and I understand was your teaching assistant at one time."

Professor Holt stepped back slightly and frowned at the mention of Justin's name. "I had thought about mentioning him to you, but I don't have any real reason to suspect him of any wrongdoing. I didn't want to speak out of turn."

"I understand," Kate said, but she didn't. "I want to speak to him much in the way I did with you. I'm looking for information. I understand Justin is a current member of The Founders. That might be helpful for us."

"If he's willing to speak to you. I don't believe Justin will be very forthcoming with information. He wasn't the best teaching assistant. He cut a lot of corners with his grad school work and since joining The Founders, he's completely fallen off the grid. I heard he's fallen far behind on his dissertation work and his advisor is about done with him."

"Why would Harvard put up with that? I remember it being quite different when I was here."

"His father donates large sums of money to the school for research each year. As a result, I believe some have cut Justin some slack." Professor Holt looked around and stepped toward Kate. He said quietly, "Justin has a bad temper so I'd be careful. He had some issues at Dartmouth both hazing a freshman at his fraternity and punching right through a wall in his undergraduate advisor's office. I don't believe that's on any permanent record. His advisor was encouraged not to make a police report at the time, but people talk."

"Do you know where on campus he lives?"

"He doesn't anymore," Professor Holt said, contradicting what Ashley had told her. "I believe he lives off-campus. The administration office will have the address." Professor Holt rattled off Justin's cellphone number in case all else failed.

Out of the corner of her eye, Kate saw Declan's car pull into the lot. She gave him a wave and then turned to Professor Holt. "My partner is meeting me here to speak to Justin, but I appreciate the information."

Professor Holt looked at his watch. "I have to go. Please call if you need anything more."

"Do you want to meet Agent James?"

Professor Holt had already backed away and turned to leave. He called over his shoulder, "Another time. I'm already late."

"Who was that?" Declan asked as he sidled up to her. "Do you always scare off men so easily?"

Kate elbowed him right in the side. "You were miserable last night and earlier today, so if you're going to be in a mood, I can do this interview without you."

Declan grinned from ear to ear and looped his arm over her shoulders. "You love me and can deal with my mood. I'm over it anyway."

"Do you want to talk about it?"

"Nope."

Kate turned her head to look up at him. "Can we get to work now?"

"Of course. What am I doing here?"

Kate gave Declan an overview of her conversation with Professor Holt including her perceptions both good and bad. She explained how his teaching assistant Ashley was the one who gave her the tip about Justin. "Professor Holt told me he didn't want to say anything and potentially get an innocent person in trouble, but he had no problem sharing some background with me after I asked. Did you find anything of interest this morning?"

Declan nodded. "A few good things, but let's go talk to this kid, and then I'll fill you in. We might have some good leads."

Kate knew that even if she tried to get Declan to tell her what they had found, he wouldn't. She wriggled out of his embrace and headed toward the administration building. The walk didn't take long at all. It had turned out to be a nice fall day. Kate had toyed with the idea of teaching at a college level if she ever left the FBI. She could see herself as a professor.

They entered the administration building prepared for a fight to get Justin's address information, but the woman was eager to hand it over. "I figured the cops would show up here sooner or later for something he's done."

"He's caused a lot of trouble here?" Declan asked.

"I'll just say that I'm surprised it took you this long to get here."

Kate glanced down at the address and was surprised to see that he lived in an apartment in a brownstone not too far from her. She assumed his wealthy parents paid his rent, which would have set them back a few thousand every month. She thanked the woman and headed back out the way they came in.

Kate told Declan the address. "Let's drive back to my place and we can walk the few blocks."

About twenty minutes later, they bounded up the steps of the brownstone and entered through the front door, which had been unlocked, and took the stairs to the third-floor back apartment. There was no doorbell outside the apartment door. Declan knocked with force.

"Coming! Coming! Stop banging!" a man yelled from behind the door. He yanked the door open and came face to face with Declan. "What do you want?"

Declan held up his badge. "Agent James and this is Agent Walsh with the FBI. We need to speak to Justin Lewis."

The man, who had messy dark hair and two-day-old stubble, looked like he had rolled out of bed. His Harvard tee-shirt stretched across his muscled chest and his blue flannel pajama pants hung low on his hips. "I didn't kill those people," he grumbled, stepping out of the way for Declan and Kate to enter the residence.

"Does anyone else live here?" Declan asked. There was a staircase off to the right that ran up to what was probably an attic bedroom. There were piles of clothes and magazines littering the stairs.

Off to the left was a small sparse living room that attached to an open dining room and kitchen. It amazed and saddened Kate the way developers had carved up what was once one-family brownstones into several apartments now. If there was a spot to sit down in the living room not covered by debris, Kate didn't see it.

"No, just me here." Justin went to the couch and pulled clothes, a pizza box, and papers from it and tossed it all in a heap on the floor. "Take a seat and let's get this over and done."

Neither Kate nor Declan sat down, but they did walk farther into the living room and stood. Justin shrugged and sat down on the spot he had cleared on the couch. "You said you didn't kill those people. What people are you talking about?" Kate asked.

"The ones all over the news." Justin grabbed the remote off the coffee table and turned on the television mounted to the wall. "The ones in the church and cemetery. I didn't do it, man. I knew you'd talk to someone at Harvard and hear about my affiliation with The Founders and you'd be down here. We already heard how you harassed Mark Boyle."

"Who'd you hear that from?" Declan asked with an edge in his voice.

Justin glanced up at him. "People talk. Now, ask me what you need to ask or get out. Consider yourself lucky I'm even willing to speak to you. I can call my father and have a lawyer in a matter of minutes."

Declan and Kate shared a look. This wasn't going to be quite the interview they thought.

CHAPTER 23

Kate stepped toward Justin. "If you'd like to have a lawyer, by all means call one, but we are only here to gather some information. We don't have any reason to suspect you of these crimes right now."

"Right now," Justin snickered. "Fine, what do you want to know?"

Kate didn't know how much time they'd have, so she wasn't going to waste it. "You said you know we spoke to Mark Boyle. Do you think he could have killed those people?"

"Mark?" Justin asked incredulously. "He's a wimp. No way could he ever kill someone. He'd wet his pants thinking about it."

Kate ignored his tone. "Who do you think is capable of something like this?"

"I don't know. You're the cops. You figure it out."

Declan exhaled a breath, and Kate worried he'd lose his temper, but he kept his response controlled. "Where were you in the early hours of Sunday morning through the early hours of Monday morning?"

"I don't have to tell you that."

"No, you're right, you don't," Declan said, "but it would go a long way in helping us clear you of these crimes."

Justin leaned back on the couch and raised his arms open wide. "I don't have anything to hide. I didn't kill those people. Some sicko did and there's no way I'm that messed up in the head."

Declan glared down at him. "Then you should have no problem telling us where you were."

"I was here getting high on coke and screwing my girlfriend all weekend." Justin shot them a smug look that dared them to say anything about the drugs. Kate wouldn't bother. She'd already seen the small baggie of cocaine on the edge of the coffee table. She could have brought him into the Boston Police Department right then, but she had other plans.

Kate pointed to it. "I think you left some of your stash out here in the open."

Justin inched forward and looked to where Kate pointed. Red crept up his face and flushed his cheeks. "That's not mine."

"Doesn't matter," Declan said, trying to hide his grin. "It's enough for us to get a warrant right now. That's enough to get you tied up in court for a while, too. Even your fancy lawyer won't be able to help because Agent Walsh and I will testify against you at your trial."

Justin shifted his eyes between them. "How do we avoid that?"

"Cut the crap and tell us what we want to know." Declan glanced around the living room. "We might also want to search. The drugs will allow us a search warrant, but we'd have to arrest you and bring you in. We could skip that if you allow us to search now."

"Isn't that like blackmail or extortion or something?"

Kate shrugged. "We aren't lawyers." She motioned for him to stand and started reading him his rights. Justin shook his head and wouldn't move. Kate looked down at him. "We can do this the easy way or you can go to jail. It's entirely up to you."

"We're cutting you a break here, Justin. I'd take it before you make Agent Walsh angry," Declan cautioned.

"Whatever," Justin said in an exhaled breath. "I don't know who killed those people, but I know you're interested in The Founders, which yes, I'm a member of. Yes, we have been talking about the murders. Some members think it's great. They are praising whoever is doing it, but I haven't heard much talk from anyone who knows who is behind it."

"You talk to Agent Walsh while I search your place, okay?" Declan asked. Before Justin could respond, he peered down at him. "Do you have any weapons in the house?"

"No."

Declan left the room, and Kate went to a chair that had a pile of clothes. She looked at Justin and then raised her eyebrows at the pile. He promptly got up and cleared a spot for her. The pile didn't go far, he dumped it on the ground near her feet.

"You said you were here with your girlfriend. What's her name and how can I reach her to verify?" Kate asked.

Justin rattled off a name and number and reached for his phone. "I'll call her right now and you can ask her."

That wasn't necessary, but Kate wasn't going to turn down the offer. If she wanted to follow up and ask more detailed questions later, she had the girl's information. Justin hit the speakerphone button and introduced Kate to his girlfriend, Bryanna. Kate motioned for him to hand her the phone.

She gripped the phone in her hand and clicked off speakerphone and spoke directly to Bryanna who did confirm Justin's alibi. She had been with Justin from Thursday night through Monday night and there was no way he was out of her sight for more than a few minutes at a time. She thanked the girl and ended the call.

"Your alibi checks out," Kate said. It didn't mean his girlfriend wasn't lying, but Kate had to work with what was right in front of her. "Tell me about The Founders."

"What do you want to know?" Justin said, a hint of relief washing over his face.

"We have reason to believe these murders might in some way be tied to The Founders. You know we spoke to Mark Boyle, but I'd like to hear what you have to say."

"Why?"

"Harvard grad student carries a lot of weight. My father was a professor at Harvard for years before he became an ambassador. I did my undergrad at Harvard. I think we are afforded a unique way to perceive the world others might miss." Kate smiled, hoping that appealing to his ego might elicit a better response than what she had been getting. It seemed to work, too, because he perked right up.

Justin sat up straighter and puffed out his chest. "I've been a member of The Founders for about a year. I know people think they are controversial, but the things we talk about make real sense. America clearly can't manage itself. Look at how many things are completely messed up."

He shook his head. "I get it. Things probably won't ever change, but Parker Gage, our president, said that we can get involved and make people see things our way, and maybe over time, real change will come."

Kate wasn't going to argue the merits or lack thereof of his position. "Does the group talk about acts of violence to meet their goal?"

"Before I joined, they did a lot, but I haven't heard talk like that in a long time."

"What made them stop?"

"I thought you would have known," Justin said with confusion in his voice. When Kate didn't respond, he went on. "There was an FBI investigation from what I understand. Members don't like to talk about it. I don't think anyone was going to do anything."

"What do you do at meetings?"

Justin smiled. "I can't tell you that. We take a secret oath to keep things confidential."

Kate wasn't surprised, but it was a clear indication something more was at play. "Are there any meetings with members that the whole group isn't a part of?"

"What do you mean?"

Kate leaned forward. "Does the board meet in private? Are there cliques or factions of the group that might take more of an extreme stance than the rest of the members?"

Justin shook his head. "I don't know. I wouldn't know that. I go to meetings maybe twice a month, but that's it. I don't get involved like that."

"What have you heard people say about these murders?"

"I don't know. I haven't been to any meetings in the last week. I don't talk to people outside of the group."

Kate knew he was lying. "You said earlier that you know we have been harassing Mark Boyle, so you've talked to someone."

Justin glared at her like he wanted to leap across the couch and attack. He didn't say anything to defend himself or offer up an explanation. It interested Kate how quickly he could go from sitting calmly on the couch to full-on simmering rage. She figured she was seeing the side to Justin that had gotten him into trouble in undergrad and at Harvard more recently.

Kate was about to ask another question when Declan bounded down the steps and barged into the room. He motioned for Justin to get on his feet. Declan had handcuffs in one hand and a large bag, containing what looked like smaller bags of pills and powder, in the other hand. Kate jumped up from her seat and took the bag of drugs from Declan to free up his hands.

"Let's go, Justin. Stand up," Declan commanded, but Justin didn't move. "You told me you didn't have any weapons and I found two handguns upstairs. I already ran a check and neither are registered to you. I could excuse a little cocaine, but you're dealing and have illegal guns. I can't brush that under the rug."

Justin tried to argue, but Declan wasn't having any of it. "I said on your feet now!" Declan reached down and pulled Justin up by force. He spun Justin around in one movement and snapped the handcuffs in place.

"I want my lawyer," Justin said as tears formed in his eyes.

"You can call down at the police station." Declan moved him forcibly toward the door. "I don't like being lied to. Where are your keys to lock the door?"

Justin hitched his jaw in Kate's direction. "Table by the chair. I didn't lie. That stuff isn't mine."

"Holding it for a friend, right?" Declan laughed. "We keep hearing that. You guys need to get better friends."

Kate grabbed the keys and followed them. "We don't have the car here with us," she reminded Declan.

"Boston police are already on their way and they are getting a warrant for a more thorough search." Kate and Justin hadn't even been talking that long. She said as much to Declan who just smiled. He explained, "He had everything shoved in a hole in a wall in his bedroom. Lucky for us he forgot to cover it."

Justin groaned at his stupidity as Declan walked him out of his apartment, down the flights of stairs to the waiting police cruiser. Declan handed Justin off to the local cop and promised he'd be down to the station to provide more details.

Justin continued to screech that he had been set up and demanded his lawyer as they left.

CHAPTER 24

"We can use this to our advantage," Kate said as they waited for the Boston crime scene unit to arrive. "He wasn't telling me anything we didn't already know, and I caught him in a lie. As soon as I called him out on it, his temper flared."

"What are you thinking?" Declan asked, checking his phone.

"We'll have to talk to Det. Briggs and the district attorney, but what do you think about seeing if we can cut a deal and have Justin wear a wire to get us inside The Founders?"

"I like the way you think." Declan texted Det. Briggs and explained what was happening. A minute later, the detective responded that he'd set up a meeting right away with the district attorney. Declan looked over at Kate. "I think it's going to depend on what the rest of the search finds if they would be willing to cut a deal, but given the seriousness of the murder cases, the DA might be willing to negotiate."

"Do you know Carmen Langston well?" Kate asked. She was so rarely in the city she barely knew the Suffolk County District Attorney.

"She's a firecracker in the courthouse. She worked her way up from assistant district attorney taking sex crimes and then homicide cases. She even took on the Irish mob." Declan whistled. "She's five-five, maybe, but the way she commands that courtroom is like nothing I've ever seen. I'm pretty sure she'll be willing to work with us unless the search brings back something worse than I found."

That was good news. Kate couldn't imagine too many more hiding places in that apartment, so she hoped they were in the clear. The Boston crime scene techs showed up and went to work. Kate tossed the supervisor Justin's key before she and Declan walked back to her house.

On the walk back to her house, she asked, "What did you find this morning?"

"I found a witness who saw a man fleeing the Old North Church around ten-thirty that night. She said she heard a commotion, someone yelling and looked out her window. She didn't see anyone at first, but moments later, a man rushed out of the church and headed in the same direction as Mark Boyle's house."

That was a huge break. "Could she see what he looked like?" Kate asked, side-stepping a piece of broken sidewalk.

"It was dark, and she's not sure. Det. Briggs is sending over a sketch artist. It's better than nothing though. We checked the area for cameras and nothing. The few that the city has

haven't been running. Det. Briggs said some of them are just up there as a deterrent but aren't in use."

"At least it's something," Kate said.

Declan's phone chimed and he read a message and then held it up for Kate to see. Det. Briggs said that Carmen Langston wanted a meeting as soon as possible. Declan texted that they were on their way to his office. "I think it's a good sign she wants to meet right away. Hopefully, she can strategize with us."

After getting back to Kate's and grabbing her car, they made it to Det. Briggs's office in record time. Det. Briggs and Carmen Langston were already waiting for them at the conference room table.

"You're late," she teased as they walked in the door. She had a broad smile and shoulder-length sandy brown hair. Her pantsuit and makeup were flawless. She shook their hands. "Agent Walsh.

Agent James. Take a seat."

Declan started to address her formally, but she stopped him. "I think the four of us are going to be spending a bit of time together so let's drop the formalities. Just call me Carmen and in turn are you fine with Kate and Declan?" She looked over at Det. Briggs. "Do you even have a first name? I've always just called you Briggs."

He laughed. "Harris, but no one other than my mom uses it, so Briggs is fine."

Kate and Declan agreed dropping the formality worked for them. "Have you been caught up to speed on the recent homicide cases, Carmen?" Kate asked, getting comfortable in her chair.

"I've been briefed, but tell me again so I make sure to understand from the FBI's perspective."

Kate and Declan took turns giving Carmen the run down from start to finish – from their initial call about the murder victim in Granary Burying Ground to date. Declan finished detailing the potential eye witness they found this morning, and then Kate gave her the overview of The Founders and Mark Boyle's connection. She gave Carmen a detailed account of Parker Gage's rise to power in The Founders and his connection to a very significant ancestor.

Carmen waited until they were done. "That's pretty much everything Briggs said has happened, but tell me what led you to Justin Lewis. That connection is unclear to me."

Kate tried to pull the most important facts to the forefront without a lot of weighty unimportant detail. "Charlie Crain, the reporter for the *Boston Globe,* suggested I speak to Professor Anthony Holt at Harvard. He teaches American history. While I was meeting with him today, I met his teaching assistant Ashley who tipped me off that his former teaching assistant, Justin Lewis, was currently a member of The Founders. We have several people connected to this group." Kate counted on her fingers. "Former members include Walter Kelly and

Professor Holt and current members Mark Boyle and Justin Lewis. This group's focus fits the profile of the kind of person who would commit these crimes and their members, mostly white affluent men, fit the killer's psychological profile."

Carmen made a few notes on a legal pad in front of her. "Do you think Justin Lewis is the killer?"

"No," Declan and Kate said in unison. Kate glanced at him and smiled. She spoke directly to Carmen. "He has an alibi for the last two murders and is a complete slob. Add in the drug use and there is no way he pulled off murders like these, but that said, I think we can use him."

"How exactly?"

Declan explained seeing the small bag of drugs first and then asking if he could search the place. "I explained to him given the drugs, we could easily get a search warrant, which we'd be happy to do, or I could go ahead and give the place a search with his permission. We used it as leverage. The goal was to rule him out as a suspect. Kate spoke to his alibi while I searched. Upstairs in his apartment, there was a hole in the wall with a large bag of drugs and two handguns. It was in open view. The drugs were assorted pills in smaller baggies and baggies of cocaine. I called Det. Briggs to get a search warrant and send crime scene investigators over. We weren't there for the drugs but couldn't let that slide either."

"Right, I get that," Carmen said, letting her words hang, "but how do you think Justin could help us now?"

"We were hoping you'd be willing to cut him a deal in exchange for him wearing a wire and getting close to Parker Gage, The Founders' president," Kate said. The more she thought about the plan, the more she believed it could work. "Justin already has an in being a member of the group, motivation to keep himself out of prison. If he goes to jail, Harvard will kick him out, so there goes years of work towards his Ph.D. He will be motivated to help, for sure."

"But is he capable of pulling it off?" Carmen asked.

Declan leaned forward, resting his arms on the table, and spoke directly to Carmen. "I think with enough coaching and support, he can pull it off and be as effective as any informant we use. Of course, there are risks. But right now, we don't have a way into this group, and they seem to be the best lead we have. If it's not Mark Boyle, and we have no real leverage to turn him, I truly believe it's someone inside The Founders committing these crimes."

"You make a compelling case." Carmen sat back and considered it. "Why not send in one of your agents to go undercover or a seasoned Boston detective?"

Kate shook her head. It was something she had already considered and scrapped. "Bringing in Mark Boyle, they are going to know we are looking at them. Justin told us he already heard the FBI was harassing members. We can't send in a new guy right now. It will be too obvious, and it will take too long to build trust. This killer will kill again and probably soon."

Carmen didn't say anything in response. The silence hung and tension rose as they waited, making Kate nervous for the first time that Carmen might not be on board. If she wasn't, there was no deal to be had. Often prosecutors saw things very differently than law enforcement.

Finally, after what seemed like an eternity, Carmen smiled. "You have a deal on one condition. I understand what you're saying about sending in a new guy blind. Your reasoning makes sense, but I don't trust Justin, so let's make him an offer and send him in with an FBI agent or undercover Boston detective. Justin can make an introduction and say the new guy is someone from Harvard who supports the cause. Maybe we can give him a military background, explosive expert or something appealing to a group like this. If their goal is domestic terrorism, a person like that is going to appeal."

Kate hesitated because she wasn't sure it was a good idea. If she was Parker, she'd be on high alert, but maybe having someone like Carmen described might outweigh his common sense. "We still need to interview Parker Gage."

"Do that first. Let's stir him up and then we can send in Justin complaining about the FBI harassing him and introduce the new guy who hates the cops, particularly the FBI. It might win Parker over quickly," Carmen speculated. "Besides, if you're at Parker's door and then send a guy in with Justin, I don't think he'll think we are quite that ballsy."

Declan slapped his hand down on the table. "I like it."

"I do, too," Det. Briggs echoed.

They all turned to look at Kate. She was still hesitant, but it could work. At that point, they didn't have much to lose. "I'm in," she said finally.

"Great," Carmen said, pushing her chair back and standing up. "I'll head over to lock-up and make the deal with Justin's lawyers. I'll call Det. Briggs tonight if he takes the deal. Tomorrow afternoon, they can report here with whoever you choose to go undercover. We will give them forty-eight hours to get up to speed and then send them in wired. In the meantime, Kate and Declan, you can interview Parker Gage."

The plan sounded good to Kate. She still needed to pick up the older FBI report on the investigation into The Founders, but she'd take care of that after this meeting ended. Carmen said goodbye and left. Declan had been right. She was a force to be reckoned with.

"I think I might have someone we can use undercover," Det. Briggs said, turning his attention to Kate and Declan.

"I hoped you would," Declan said. "I'm sure we can pull an FBI agent off another case, but they are spread a little thin over there right now.

Who do you have?"

"We have an undercover detective who has worked on all types of cases. He's a master of disguise and can change up his appearance. He is seasoned in undercover work and is in his late thirties but looks about twenty-five. Before joining the police force, he graduated from Columbia University so he can blend easily with The Founders members."

"Sounds like he's perfect," Declan said. "Bring him in tomorrow and we can get him prepped."

CHAPTER 25

On the way home, Declan swung by the FBI office to grab the case file on the previous investigation into The Founders. Before getting out of the car, he said to Kate, "When I talked to the agent who handled the case, he said it didn't get very far. Only a handful of members were willing to talk. He was able to get a statement from two of the remaining members. They never found much evidence. It sounds like there were threats of violence, but no plan the agent could confirm. He has some formal statements and interview notes."

Kate waited in the car while Declan ran into the office. The feeling of impending doom grew in her stomach. She knew the killer would strike again soon and probably before they could get the undercover team in place. Kate was grateful Carmen was on board, but she felt antsy about how long it would take to gather intelligence from inside The Founders.

There was a chance, too, that the murders had nothing to do with The Founders, but if that was the case, they didn't even have a starting place. The killer had been meticulous and left no evidence behind, at least that Sharon could tell. Kate pinched the bridge of her nose and closed her eyes. A tension headache spread across the front of her forehead and made her temples pulse.

"You look like you're about to have a meltdown," Declan said as he slid an evidence box in the backseat. He closed the door and then opened the passenger's side door, but thought better of it. "I'll drive us home. You okay?"

Kate got out of the car and walked around to the passenger side. She didn't let anyone other than Declan drive her car. She rested her head back and closed her eyes. "Not really. We have no real leads other than The Founders, and the killer is out there planning, or worse, executing his next kill while we've got nothing."

"Something will break as it always does." Declan started the car and pulled out of the lot. He kept the radio off and let them sit in silence, which they did most of the ride home.

When they got home, Kate headed upstairs to shower and change while Declan went into the kitchen, promising he'd cook something that would make her feel better. A little while later, comfortable in a tee-shirt and pajama pants, Kate wandered downstairs and the delicious aroma hit her nose as soon as she got to the bottom step. She found Declan putting the last touches on what he called sausage and pepper pasta.

Declan pointed to the table in the alcove. "I found a few things to work with in the fridge. You weren't totally barren. Go sit. There's a salad on the table for you, too."

"Why are you being so nice to me?" Kate asked as she sat and noticed how neatly he had set the table.

Declan looked over his shoulder as he stirred the pasta on the stovetop. "You're letting me live here for free. Don't be crabby and suspicious."

Kate picked up her fork and dug into her salad. After a few bites, her bad mood seemed to fade. By the time Declan brought over the pasta, Kate had a smile on her face and chatted with him amicably. "We are getting far too domestic," Kate said with a laugh. "Anyone that came in right now would confuse us for husband and wife."

Declan raised his eyes as he took a bite. "I kind of like it."

"Didn't you have this at home with Lauren?"

"Never." Declan finished chewing and put his fork down. "Lauren would have dinner ready by six and expect me home. If I had to work late, there would be an angry barrage of text messages so by the time I finally made it home, I wasn't even in the mood to eat."

"I know I told you I didn't think she'd understand your work, but I meant more along the lines of the travel we face and being gone for long periods. I didn't know it was that bad. You should have told me."

Declan took a sip of water. "Easier not to talk about it. That's why the divorce isn't so bad, but you know me, Katie, it feels like failure."

"Maybe it's just redirection to a better path," Kate offered, taking a generous bite of pasta and giving him a knowing glance.

Declan shrugged and they continued to eat chatting as old friends do. Kate hated to admit it, but if she was going to stop all the traveling for work, it felt nice having someone to come home to. The house was too big and quiet for just one person.

After they were done, Kate offered to clean up since Declan cooked. When she was done and hit the button on the dishwasher, she joined Declan in the living room to go through the evidence from the previous investigation into The Founders.

"You find anything of interest?"

Declan handed her a case file. "Parker Gage is as arrogant as people have told us he is. His statement shows that clearly. I haven't seen anything of interest in these files. I understand why people leaving The Founders were concerned and called in the FBI, but I'm not seeing any real plan in place to bomb anything. It sounds like a lot of hateful rhetoric though."

Kate scanned through the statement in front of her and then picked up another. She read with interest, but Declan was right. There wasn't anything that the FBI would have been able to do with this information. No crime had been committed or seemed to be in the process of being committed.

Kate set the files down and left the living room, promising Declan she'd be right back. She remembered something Professor Holt had told her earlier in the day, and she wanted to check it out. Kate went into her bedroom and grabbed her laptop off her dresser and carried it downstairs.

"What are you looking for?" Declan asked when Kate returned.

"Professor Holt mentioned that when he left The Founders Parker Gage had gone to Harvard to accuse him of plagiarism and being involved with one of his students. I was looking to see if Parker Gage or The Founders were named in any lawsuits."

"What would that prove?" Declan asked, grabbing another file from the evidence box.

"For one, it would prove that Professor Holt was telling me the truth. Secondly, there might be some discovery in one of the cases that might have relevance for us." Kate flipped through the database after she plugged in Parker Gage's name but nothing came back. She did the same with The Founders and again nothing.

"Did you doubt Professor Holt's credibility?"

"No, I didn't get the best vibe from him, but I can't put my finger on it." Kate paused from scrolling through the database and looked up at Declan. "If someone told me he was having an affair with one of his students, I wouldn't be surprised."

Declan nodded but didn't say anything. They both kept reading for a while longer but grew frustrated about not finding any evidence of wrongdoing. They called it quits and shut off the downstairs lights and headed upstairs at the same time. As Kate went into her bedroom, she turned to Declan who had moved down to the second-floor spare room as she had suggested.

"What if we're wrong? What if this has nothing to do with The

Founders at all, and we are wasting time?"

"Try not to stress yourself out, Katie" Declan said, leaning on the doorframe. "We can only work with what we have."

"It's easier when I'm called in to interrogate a suspect someone else found."

Declan grinned at her. "You've been spoiled," he teased. "Here you are complaining about needing to take a break, and you've been coddled. I'm out there doing real detective work. I should be the one retiring."

Kate rolled her eyes and shut the door to her bedroom. After she finished washing her face and brushing her teeth, she crawled into bed hoping for a good night's sleep. She fell into a sound dreamless sleep.

It was four in the morning when her worst fear came true. All at once, phones started ringing. Kate's cellphone rang from her bedside table and Declan's rang from the other room. She sat upright and adjusted her eyes to the light. She fumbled for her phone and brought it to her ear. She listened to Det. Briggs on the other line. It took her a moment to piece it all together. Bunker Hill. Stabbed. Difficult to identify.

She hung up and threw off her covers and dashed into the bathroom. Kate splashed water on her face, threw on enough makeup to be presentable, and found clothes. Within minutes, she met Declan in the hallway and they ran out the back door of the house. They got into Declan's car and raced out of the driveway toward the Charlestown neighborhood of Boston where the Bunker Hill memorial was located.

"Det. Briggs called me, so who called you?" Kate asked, her voice cracked as she spoke.

"Sharon. Det. Briggs called her first and told her to get her team out there. She said she'd call me while he called you." Declan glanced over at her. "I don't think they realize we live together."

"What do you know? Det. Briggs told me some, but he spoke so fast I don't know if I have the details right."

Declan stopped at a red light, looked both ways, and then went through it. There was no traffic on the road at that hour of the morning. "Sharon said the victim is male. Looks like one gunshot to the head." Declan paused and swallowed hard. "It also appears he was stabbed multiple times after death."

Kate turned her head to look at him. "How many times?"

"Sharon said it was too many to count."

"Just like Dr. Joseph Warren," Kate said softly.

"What?"

"Dr. Joseph Warren, who thwarted the British at Lexington and Concord, was killed in the battle of Bunker Hill in 1775. General Thomas Gage said Warren's death was 'worth the death of 500 men.' He was shot in the head by a British soldier and then stripped of his clothes and stabbed until he was nearly unrecognizable. His body was thrown into a shallow grave with another Patriot killed in the battle."

Declan gripped the steering wheel tightly. "The victim was found naked."

"Where did they find him?" This was the work of the same killer. Kate knew there was no question.

"On the grass off to the side of the monument."

They drove in silence the rest of the way. Kate's thoughts spun and guilt for not solving the case washed over her. As if sensing her thoughts, Declan reached a hand out to her. "We are doing the best we can. This killer is prolific. Look at the short window in between each kill. No one could have caught him yet."

Logically, Kate knew he was right, but the desire to catch the killer burned in her even more. He killed right under their noses and flaunted it.

CHAPTER 26

Declan pulled into a parking space along the road and cut the engine. The Bunker Hill monument sits in the middle of the city and has no formal parking lot. Most tourists walked to the national history site that had long ago been designated as a memorial to Dr. Joseph Warren, a Patriot and Freemason. The land around it had long ago been sold off and developed. There was a chance that someone in one of those houses might have seen activity, although tree coverage might have blocked the view, especially at night.

The monument, a two-hundred-twenty-one-foot obelisk, sits in the middle of a squared-off grassy area with sidewalk access on all four sides. A statue of Colonel William Prescott, which depicts his moments before giving the command to open fire at the start of the battle, stands in front of the monument on one side. There is also a granite lodge that houses a statue of Dr. Joseph Warren.

"It's so lit up it looks like daylight," Declan said as he opened the car door and glanced up the hill in the direction of the monument.

While they couldn't see much from their vantage point, the area was lit up like a ballfield for a night game. Kate and Declan climbed a few steps and raced up the sidewalk toward the action. Boston cops had set up barriers around the body to block the public view. They had brought in large lights to illuminate the area to aid crime scene techs who were hard at work assessing the scene. The medical examiner and his team had already arrived.

Kate couldn't count how many people were on the scene but identifying them was easy enough. Their blue jackets identified them as FBI, Boston Police Department, or Suffolk County Medical Examiner. "The whole team is out here," she said as they approached a uniformed cop blocking off the entrance. They each flashed their FBI badges and were let through. Kate reached up and tightened the ponytail she had twisted her hair into before leaving the house.

Det. Briggs saw them approaching and stepped out from behind the barrier. He blocked their path to the body. His face tightened. "This is the worst I've ever seen in all my years of doing this work."

Kate and Declan had seen it all. They were brought into the worst of the worst. But as they went to step around him, Det. Briggs held out his arm.

"I'm not talking about the condition of the body. I'm talking about the identity of the victim." Det. Briggs glanced back at the barricades which surrounded the body and then locked eyes with Kate. "After I called you, one of the cops recognized him. There's no easy way to say this. It's Justin Lewis."

Kate had been rendered speechless.

Declan, always calm and steady, asked, "Justin Lewis, who we arrested and who was going to wear a wire for us?"

"The very one." Det. Briggs shook his head in disgust. "This killer is watching us. He knows what we are going to do before we do it."

Kate expelled a breath. "Who called it in?"

Det. Briggs put his hands on his hips. "We believe it was the killer. At least, we can be lucky that no unsuspecting family found the body in the morning. That's about all we can be thankful for."

"How do you know it was the killer?" Declan asked what Kate had been thinking.

"He told the 911 operator where he left the body. He said that's what happens to traitors."

"We need Justin's cellphone records and to see all of his movements after he got out of jail yesterday," Declan said. "We need to know every minute of every hour after his release and pinpoint exactly who he interacted with. This killer is connected to him."

Kate looked back at the crime scene and then to Declan. "This deviates from his pattern of killing strangers, but it at least answers the question I had before about how he lures his victims. I couldn't imagine how he'd get anyone here in the middle of the night. But if the killer knew Justin, that would be easy enough to do."

"Let's go take a look." Det. Briggs parted a group of cops standing around on the outside of the barrier and let Kate and Declan walk ahead of him into the sectioned off crime scene.

Kate and Declan stood a few feet from the victim's body. Kate looked and turned her head away quickly. Justin was nearly unrecognizable. Had she not been with the man just yesterday and recognized his facial features, she might not have been able to discern his identity. Justin had a bullet wound in the middle of his forehead, and his face had started to swell from trauma. The rest of his body had been horrifically marred with stab wounds all over it. Kate forced herself to look back again. She stopped counting at twenty.

Kate turned her head in the direction of the medical examiner, who was talking to his team a few feet away. She called over to him. "Do we know if all the stab wounds were post-mortem?"

Dr. Graham walked over and stood beside her. He pointed his finger toward Justin's torso. "From what I can see here, based on preliminary blood evidence, I'd estimate all of them were post-mortem. I believe the victim was shot first, stripped of his clothes, and then stabbed."

"How do you know he was stripped of his clothes after he was shot?"

Dr. Graham bent down toward the body and motioned for Kate to lean in. He pointed to a blood trail that went up the victim's forehead. "The blood trail goes up. It was most likely caused by a shirt being pulled over his head. Otherwise, we wouldn't see that kind of blood trail."

As Dr. Graham spoke, Sharon walked up on the other side of the body. She waited until he was done. "I don't see much sign of a struggle. Looks like this guy met someone up here, he shot him in the head and that's it. My team is still looking around the area, but we aren't finding much. It looks as clean a kill as the others, but we'll continue to search."

Kate nodded lost in thought about how the crime might have gone down. She didn't know if it was as simple as Sharon had described it. Kate knew she'd have questions later, but right now she didn't have any. She turned to Declan. "Anything you want to know?"

"I'm good for now." Declan walked away back toward Det. Briggs. Kate thanked Sharon and Dr. Graham and left them to do their work uninterrupted.

"What's the plan?" Declan asked Det. Briggs.

Det. Briggs rocked on his feet hyped up and ready to go. "I have five officers coming to start canvassing these surrounding properties to see if anyone saw or heard anything. I want to talk to them early in the morning before anyone leaves for the day so we can hit the ground running."

"I'll work on getting Justin's phone records and his computer and have one of our tech guys go through it," Declan offered.

"We have his laptop down in evidence from the search warrant yesterday. I'll get one of my guys to bring it to your team," Det. Briggs explained and then turned to Kate. "Will you still interview Parker Gage today?"

"I don't know yet," Kate said unsure of her response. "I want to get a handle on Justin's last few hours. I think one of us needs to speak to his attorney. Has anyone called Carmen?"

"Not yet, too early," Det. Briggs said. "I figured one of us should be able to get some sleep."

Declan toed the dirt in front of his foot. The frustration in his voice was evident. "One of us will have to tell her and then strategize what we are going to do about The Founders. I think we might have to send in your guy on his own."

Det. Briggs shook his head. "Not on your life. I'm not having him walk into this. It's too dangerous until we can get a handle on what's going on."

Declan started to argue, but Kate stopped them both. "Not here and not now. Let me call Carmen and tell her. I want to speak to the 911 operator and then I'll track down Justin's attorney. We can go from there. If this is Parker Gage's handiwork, there's no point sending anyone in undercover. He got the jump on us, and we're going to have to figure out a new plan."

Det. Briggs seemed satisfied with that answer, but Declan didn't. He shot Kate a look of annoyance and stalked off toward the car.

"How long does he stay angry?" Det. Briggs asked. "He doesn't seem like someone I want angry for too long."

"He'll be over it by the time we get home. He's frustrated, that's all. Try not to take his moods personally. I don't." Kate turned to leave, but Charlie Crain stood speaking to Declan on the sidewalk near the road. No other media had made it out to the site yet, which had been a blessing. Kate saw Charlie hand a bag to Declan, and he immediately waved Kate over. She turned to Det. Briggs. "Looks like Charlie got another letter from the killer. Got a minute to check it out?"

Det. Briggs moved in step with Kate as they walked down the sidewalk to meet Charlie. "Did you get another letter?" Kate asked as they approached.

Charlie's face paled when Kate asked the question. "Not to my office.

This one came right to my apartment door."

"On the stoop outside?"

"No," Charlie said with a crack in his voice. "I live on the top floor of a brownstone, and he got into the building and left it right in front of my apartment door. My office is one thing. Knowing where I live, being that close to my home, it's too much for me."

Kate expelled a breath. "I get it. I'm still freaked out about the dagger he delivered to my door. Are there any cameras in your building?"

"I've already asked my landlord. We have a camera at the front door. It's hidden from view, so most people wouldn't even realize it was there," Charlie explained. "My landlord lives on the first floor and put it in a few years ago because he got tired of solicitors. I stopped before I came here and asked him to get it ready because the FBI would want it."

"How did you know about the murder?" Det. Briggs asked. "Thankfully, no media has made it out here yet."

Declan handed the letter to Det. Briggs. He took it in his hands and read it through the plastic. Then he handed it to Kate. It was simple, succinct, and terrifying.

Those who betray me deserve no better than Warren.

Charlie rubbed at his stubbled chin. "I assumed he meant Dr. Joseph Warren, and Bunker Hill is where he was killed, so I came here immediately." He pointed up the hill from where they stood toward the swarm of law enforcement. "I assume there's been another murder."

Kate handed the letter back to Declan. "There has and it was someone we believe the killer knew."

"Was he killed as brutally as Dr. Joseph Warren?" Charlie asked, wincing as he asked the question.

"Yeah," Declan said, "it's a mess up there. If you want the story, it's yours, but let's wait until they remove the body."

"If you run a basic story now and call me later today, we'll sit down with you again and give you a statement." Kate looked to Declan and Det. Briggs. "Since the killer is reading Charlie's column maybe we can use it to our advantage. We can send messages directly to him in the article."

CHAPTER 27

"For a petite classy lady, Carmen Langston sure can cuss like a trucker," Kate said, hanging up the phone. She and Declan were in the FBI office at desks, running down leads and making plans for the day. After leaving the crime scene, they went back to Kate's house to pull themselves together and prepare for the day. On their way to the FBI field office, they picked up the surveillance video from Charlie's landlord.

Kate couldn't remember the last time she had used the desk officially assigned to her at the FBI field office. She was never there and it hardly felt like her own. Someone had been kind enough to keep it stocked with office supplies, but other than that, the desk remained sparse and sterile. It would have been obvious to anyone who happened by that Kate wasn't someone in the office frequently.

"I don't think I've ever heard someone so furious," Kate said about her call with Carmen.

Declan turned his chair from his desk to hers. "What did she say?"

Kate rested her arms on her desk. "Carmen is as horrified as we are. She's not sure what we should do next. She asked for a meeting and said she'd be on her way over soon. She wants Det. Briggs, Dr. Graham, Charlie and Sharon here."

"Why Charlie?"

"She liked my idea of using the newspaper to communicate with the killer, but we are going to have to give Charlie all the info so he can help strategize with us. We can't piecemeal it to him anymore."

Kate didn't like it. Charlie seemed trustworthy enough, but he was a reporter and could run anything they told him without repercussion. Kate didn't like giving anyone outside of law enforcement that much access to case information.

"Makes a certain kind of sense, I guess."

"Whether we agree or not, Carmen said she was going to ask Det. Briggs to call him. I assume they will all be here within the hour. We are going to have to grab some conference room space."

Kate grabbed for her phone just as Declan's desk phone rang. He spun back around in his chair and grabbed it. He spoke to the person in clipped one-word responses and then hung up. He stood and turned to Kate. "They have the person clear as day going into and leaving Charlie's building at two this morning."

Kate finished reserving the conference room with the unit secretary and dropped the receiver back in the holder. Finally, a break in the case. "Don't tease me, Declan. They can see the person's face or is it some shadowy hooded figure?"

"They tell me they have a close-up of the guy's face."

Kate stood. "Let's go see it before everyone gets here." They walked to the elevator together to head to the computer forensics and video surveillance experts' office. "It can't be this easy," Kate said as she stepped into the elevator.

Declan hit the button for the fifth floor. "You're so pessimistic. It can be this easy if he had no idea there was a camera there. Charlie said it's well-hidden. Maybe the killer didn't know."

Kate knew there was a catch no matter what Declan said. Her stomach dropped as she rode the elevator up and stepped out onto the floor. They turned right and went all the way down the hall until they reached the office door. Normally, it was locked, but a tech stood waiting for them.

"I'm Matt," he said, reaching for Kate's hand. "Follow me and I'll show you what we found."

Kate scanned around the room at the nameless faces sitting behind computers focused on the tasks at hand. Because she wasn't in the office frequently, she didn't know many of her colleagues who worked in the building, but they were all vital to the work of the FBI. She nodded and smiled at those who looked up from their computers to acknowledge her.

Matt walked them into his office and he went behind his desk. He turned the monitor so Declan and Kate could see the screen. "I'll set it up for you a few seconds before he arrives. But basically, he shows up right at two. He picks the lock in less than a minute, pushes open the door, and is out of sight for roughly three minutes and twenty-one seconds. Then he heads back out, shutting the door behind him and disappearing into the night. It's when he's leaving that he turns in just the right angle toward the camera and the picture of his face is the clearest."

Before Matt played the video, Declan had a question. "You said he picked the lock. Did he have tools with him to do that?"

"Yeah, you'll see. He's skilled at it, too. This is someone who has broken into quite a few places. I haven't seen skill like that in a while."

Declan motioned for him to play the video. Kate and Declan kept their eyes focused on the screen and the black and white video started. When he first appears, his ballcap shields most of his face from view, but there was something about his build and the way he moved that was familiar to Kate. She inched up on her toes in anticipation. The man pulled tools from a backpack that he had slung over his shoulder, easily unlocked the door, slipped the tools back in the bag, and headed inside. The seconds ticked by, Kate growing more uneasy as they waited for his return.

"He looked familiar, right?" Declan said just above a whisper.

Kate nodded but didn't say a word. All at once, he appeared again and what Kate saw knocked her back two steps.

"What the f…" Declan didn't finish his thought. His words hung in the air, but his point was made. Kate felt his confusion, too. He turned to look at Kate for an explanation, but she didn't have one.

"Is this someone you know?"

Declan raked his hand through his hair, and this time, cursed loudly. He didn't hold back as he did before. "It's the murder victim from this morning." Declan pointed to the frozen image of the side of Justin's face. "He can't be the killer. That's not possible."

"Unless he's working for the killer." Kate reached back for support but found open space. She needed to sit down and think this through. The air in the office grew warm and Kate needed fresh air. She took a few short breaths hoping to clear her head, but the space seemed to close around her. "I have to get out of here," she said, turning abruptly and heading out the way they came in.

Behind her, she heard Declan thank Matt and instruct him to make a copy of the video and send it to his phone. "Wait up, Kate," he called and jogged to catch up to her at the elevator.

Kate stepped into the elevator and pushed the button for the first floor once and then jabbed at it with her index finger several more times, like it would go faster the harder she hit it. Declan reached out and grabbed her hand to stop her.

"We missed something huge yesterday and got him killed." Kate dropped her head into her hands.

"I know, Kate, I know." Declan reached his hand out and put it on Kate's back to comfort her. "Justin made a choice. He chose to work with the killer. He could have told us yesterday. We could have protected him had we known."

Kate appreciated Declan trying to reassure her, but it fell on deaf ears. By the pained look on his face, Kate knew he didn't believe his own words. Once they got to the first floor, Kate beelined for the front door, pushed it open, and stepped into the sunlight. She took gulping breaths of fresh air. No agent liked to feel like the choices they made got anyone killed, innocent or not. Kate also had no idea how to make sense of what she saw.

Declan paced back and forth while Kate stood still. "What does this mean, Kate? Justin was working with the killer. How?"

"Maybe delivering the letters. Possibly setting up the victims. We've had questions about how the killer got the victim to the cemetery. It's possible Justin knew the victims. I think we have to explore that."

Declan looked over at her. "If Justin was the one who delivered the dagger to your door, do you think he would have seen you before we showed up at his apartment? He didn't act like he had seen you before."

"I have no idea. He might have just been the delivery person, but at this point, we know beyond any shadow of a doubt he was connected to the killer. At least, now we have a starting point." Kate ran through her interactions with Justin the day before. Her guilt at his death started to ease. He had made his mistakes and he paid for them with his life.

Kate decided the best course of action going forward and shared it with Declan. "I need to speak to Justin's girlfriend. She said that he was with her during the time of the other murders so she knows more than she told me yesterday. Then I need to speak to his attorney and see what he's willing to share."

"Attorney-client privilege extends beyond death, Kate. Do you think he's going to share anything?"

"I don't know, but if he doesn't, he is impeding our investigation into who murdered his client. He might be willing, but either way, it's worth a try." Kate spun around to head back into the building to call

Justin's girlfriend, but Declan's whistle stopped her in her tracks.

"It's going to have to wait," he said, pointing to a sleek black car with tinted windows pulling to a stop in front of the building. "I think the illustrious Carmen Langston has arrived."

Carmen stepped out of the car one Manolo Blahnik hitting the concrete after the other. She was all business and raring to go. She clicked her heels on the pavement and strutted toward the building like she owned the place. "I didn't expect a welcome committee," she said as she pulled the door open.

Declan laughed and called back to her. "I didn't expect you to arrive with a driver. How do you rate a car service?"

Carmen tossed her hair off her shoulder and winked at him. "Perks of being me. Now come on, we have a killer to catch."

CHAPTER 28

After everyone assembled and were seated around the conference room table at the FBI office, Matt, who Declan had invited to the meeting, carried in a laptop and placed it on one end of the table facing everyone. He got the video queued up and played it once and then twice, freezing the image on Justin's face as he exited Charlie's building. Carmen gasped when she saw him. Det. Briggs had the same visceral reaction Declan had and let out a string of curses.

"Well, that certainly fits with the time of death, which is the only update I have for you," Dr. Graham said. "I have my assistant working on the autopsy right now. I believe the victim was killed around three this morning, which would make sense given the call to 911 at three-thirty. Now, seeing him on video here at two, I assume he went from this residence to Bunker Hill. It's about an hour walk along the Dr. Paul Dudley White Bike Path."

"We should check cab and rideshare records in case he was dropped off," Det. Briggs said. He looked at Matt. "Do we have Justin on surveillance at all after he leaves Charlie's house?"

"No," Matt said. "This is all we were provided. I don't know of any other street cameras in the area that are working and would have picked him up. I can double-check though."

"I didn't think there would be," Det. Briggs said and exhaled a breath.

He turned to Kate. "What do you think this means?"

Kate provided the information she had surmised earlier with Declan. "The bottom line is Justin was working with the killer. I assume he informed the killer he was arrested and asked to be an informant or the killer somehow found out. I believe the killer had Justin unwittingly deliver his murder notification letter to Charlie and then he was killed." Kate looked at Charlie. "When you received the letter was the envelope open or sealed?"

"It was sealed. I used a letter opener to slice it open from the top and not disturb the sealed part in case there was DNA that could be taken from it."

"Smart thinking," Declan said, turning to Sharon with raised eyebrows.

Sharon grunted. "No luck there. I tested all the envelopes we have to date and the killer is using an adhesive, not saliva. He's not stupid."

"Kate, you don't believe Justin killed anyone?" Carmen asked, tapping her finger on the table.

"I don't think so."

Carmen narrowed her eyes. "What are you basing that on? Don't tell me alibi because clearly, the girlfriend lied about something."

Kate appreciated Carmen's candor. "I'm basing it on his apartment. It was a mess, and this killer is anything but a mess. Given his murder, there is another killer."

Carmen shrugged. "Could be a partner."

"It could," Kate agreed, but her voice gave away her doubt. "It's more likely that Justin was a stooge. The killer used him to do his dirty work with things he might get caught doing."

"Such as?"

Kate spoke gesturing with her hands. "Luring the victims from one spot to the other and delivering the letters and the dagger to me. The killer is hiding until it's time for him to kill. I think that's becoming most obvious to me. It always bothered me that he'd risk delivering the dagger to my door. I thought maybe he'd used a courier service, but the more I thought about it, the killer would still be interacting with someone and could be traced. Using Justin, he minimizes his risk."

Det. Briggs spoke from the end of the table. "Why trust Justin? What was it about him the killer thought he could trust? Justin sounds like he was a drugged-out drug dealer prone to violence. That seems more unstable to me than risking doing it himself."

Declan glanced at Det. Briggs and then at Kate, who sat next to him. "He's got a point."

"He does," Kate agreed. "I can't account for every decision this killer makes. I can only tell you what this looks like on the surface. Looping back to Carmen's original question – no, I do not believe Justin killed any of the victims."

Carmen sat back with a satisfied look on her face. "You're the best, Kate. Your reputation is stellar on these cases, so if you believe that's true then that's what we are going with until we have evidence to prove otherwise." She glanced around the table. "Let's suppose then Kate's theory is correct and the killer was using Justin to help him. What does it mean now that the killer is without someone to help? Is he done?"

"I don't think he's done," Det. Briggs said. "I think we'll know when he's done, which is either when we catch him or something big happens. Kate, do you think he's going to stop killing and slip quietly into the night?"

Kate frowned and shook her head. "He wants the credit for his cause. His ego is too big to walk away without a big statement."

Declan cleared his throat and looked at Kate. "What's the big finish?"

"I'm not sure."

Declan screwed up his face the way he did when he was thinking.

"You know what's been bothering me?" When no one had an answer, he went on. "This killer is trying to make this statement to get revenge or whatever for England losing the war, but he's not going after anyone that matters. He's toying with Charlie and Kate, both of whom have ancestors tied to the Revolutionary War. The victims though, no ties. Can he not find victims with ties? Is it too much effort so he's choosing victims at random, except for Justin?"

"Maybe that's the big finish," Charlie said his voice low, fear spreading across his face.

"I don't think we can rule out that possibility," Declan echoed. "Charlie, you need police protection. You need to get off the grid right now. Do you have someplace safe you can go?"

Charlie hit his fist on the table and his face grew red. "I said this before, I'm not going into hiding. I have a column to write. I'm not letting this deranged killer drive me from my home."

Kate thought everyone would argue with him at once, but no one did. She didn't have anything to say because she wasn't going into hiding either. Plus, they needed Charlie. Everyone had their eyes cast down at the table not wanting to address the obvious – if someone could leave a letter at Charlie's door, they could have easily broken the door down and killed him. At least, Kate had Declan and knew how to defend herself.

Finally, it was Sharon who broke the silence with a whistle. "You are some kind of crazy," she said, shaking her head. "Charlie, if you're dead, you can't do your job. Go spend a week at a nice hotel on the FBI's dime. Go get a big suite that overlooks the river. Swank it up for a few days. Enjoy yourself. You can write from anywhere."

"She's right," Declan said. "Name the hotel, we will cover it. You are an asset to us, Charlie, so we can't lose you. You can check in with the newsroom from there. You can order room service to your heart's content. You can crank out story after story from a safe location."

Everyone had their eyes on Charlie as he sat there silently debating. "What about communication from the killer? If I'm not home, I won't see anything he leaves. If I'm not at my office, I won't get it."

"We'll take care of it," Det. Briggs assured. "I'll assign an officer to go by your place every day and the newsroom can call us and we'll pick up anything that's left. We need you out of sight. If we do this quietly enough, the killer might not even realize you're in hiding. If you go, it will be one less thing for me to worry about."

Det. Briggs cast his eyes up to Kate. "I'm guessing even if I tried to argue this point with you, that there's no way you're leaving your house? You shouldn't be alone there."

Declan reached his hand over to Kate's, which was resting on the table. "She's not alone. I'm living there now."

Det. Briggs fumbled for what to say. Sharon slapped her hands on the table, and Carmen's eyes shot up like she had just heard the best gossip of the century. She pointed between them. "I thought there was something between you two."

Kate let out a nervous laugh, pushed his hand away, and shot Declan a look of annoyance. "That is most definitely not what Declan means. He has been staying at my house while he's dealing with a personal matter, but I do appreciate that he's there. You're right, Det. Briggs, while I know how to defend myself, I shouldn't be there alone." She effectively changed the subject by turning to Charlie. "That's why it's critical you do as Sharon and Det. Briggs said and go stay at a hotel. It's not hiding. It's seeking safety so that you can most effectively do your job right now."

Charlie held his hands up in defeat. "You're a tough crowd to argue with. I'll do whatever you want." Together, they sat there making a plan for Det. Briggs to send two officers with Charlie back to his apartment to gather his things and take him to Fairmont Copley Plaza. Charlie reasoned he'd be right near the Boston Public Library in case he needed extra research on anything. Kate was pleased with the decision. It was also right near the Boston Common and public enough that Charlie might very well blend into the background with all the tourists should he need to step out of his room for anything.

"We need to plan what you're going to write," Carmen said, bringing their main reason for the meeting back to focus.

Kate sat back and thought for a few minutes while the rest of the team discussed their ideas. She wanted to get the message right. When the rest of the conversation died down, Kate spoke up. "I think we need to drive home the point that killing Justin brings us a step closer to the killer. We need to allude that we've made great strides in the investigation and are zeroing in on a suspect, but that the public needs to remain vigilant and call in with any information they may have."

Turning to Det. Briggs, Kate asked, "Do you want to set up a tip line or do you want the FBI to handle that? We have the manpower for it."

"Feel free, one less thing off of our plate."

"Charlie, I'll give you the number for a tip line once I have it." Kate also explained to him that she'd give him an exclusive later to run about the FBI's perceptions of the killer. "We can chip away at his self-image a little, rock his confidence."

After Charlie received his orders, he thanked them all and headed out to meet the two officers Det. Briggs had called. As the team started to get restless, Carmen commanded them back to attention. "We still have things to discuss."

CHAPTER 29

"Det. Briggs, give us a rundown of what your team has been doing to date," Carmen said, motioning for everyone to settle down.

"I think the most important," Det. Briggs started, "is that none of my researchers have found any ancestry connection of importance for any of the three victims. We won't know about Justin for a few days. I have a team running down cellphone records of all the victims, including Justin's, during the days leading up to the murders, looking for connections among the victims or any connections they might have had to a common person. I have officers out today questioning neighbors around Bunker Hill. There's been no word that anyone saw anything. It's a bit tree covered and not all the leaves have fallen. It wouldn't surprise me if there weren't any witnesses. I do have an officer going back to Justin's apartment to look for surveillance footage to trace his steps last night and see if anyone was at his place. They will speak to neighbors, too."

Declan interrupted. "We also have the FBI forensics team with Justin's computer going over everything. I want to know how the killer contacted Justin last night when he got out of jail. If we can figure out how they interacted, then we got the guy."

"I want to speak to Justin's attorney," Kate said, looking at Carmen. "Do you think he'll speak to me or invoke his attorney-client privilege?"

"I'm not sure. His attorney is Frank Flynn. Decent guy and a good criminal defense attorney. He's on Boylston Street. Visit him and see what he says. I'd call him, but he doesn't like me." Carmen smiled. "He's lost against me too many times for us to be friends."

Before Kate could respond, Dr. Graham held up a hand to grab their attention. His head had been bent down reading a text. He read the message from his assistant to the group and when he was done, he explained the meaning. "What he's saying is that the pattern marks on the skin are the same as the previous victims. The same knife was used in Justin's murder as the others."

"How many stab wounds?" Declan asked, leaning forward to look across Kate at Dr. Graham.

"Nine deep stab wounds in total, including one clean stab wound to his heart like the others. There were several shallower jabs with the knife just making a mess of him. The stab wounds are confirmed post-mortem. The victim died from a gunshot wound to the head. The same antique gun as the first murder." Dr. Graham looked around the table. "The killer used precision with the deep stab wounds."

Det. Briggs blew out a breath and cursed softly under his breath. Declan echoed the statement. Kate sat shifting through historical knowledge in her head, stories her father had long ago told her.

"What is it, Kate?" Declan asked.

"Nine," she responded, dragging out the word as she connected the dots in her mind before sharing the rest. When Kate had her thoughts together, she explained, "This killer does everything with meaning. I think that's even true on the number of stab wounds. The Loyal Nine, as they called themselves, were a group of unassuming merchants and tradesmen who came together as a sort of secret men's society to strategize how best to oppose the Stamp Act. They met in a small room in Chase and Speakman's Distillery or under a large elm tree in nearby Hanover Square. The tree became known as the Liberty Tree and ended up as the meeting place for speeches and a staging area for protests and demonstrations. These Loyal Nine garnered support from others and started activity to disrupt the Stamp Act."

Kate let out an embarrassed laugh. "I could sit here all day and give you a history lesson, but I won't bore you. Suffice it to say that ultimately it was the Loyal Nine who were the spark for the Sons of Liberty, which as you know, were the driving force for the Boston Tea Party and other important events leading up to the American Revolution."

Declan rubbed his temples. "You think the killer connected all these historical dots and used it in the murder?"

"Yes," Kate said. "I know it sounds crazy, but think about it. Justin's murder was about disloyalty. He was killed in the same way as Dr. Joseph Warren who had the information about Bunker Hill because Gen. Thomas Gage had been betrayed. The nine deep stab wounds could easily reflect the Loyal Nine who in this killer's mind were anything but loyal to England."

Carmen clicked her tongue. "When this goes to trial, you're going to be on that stand testifying for days to help a jury make sense of it."

Det. Briggs narrowed his eyes. "First, we need to catch him. Kate, I understand all this symbolism and how it's important to the killer, but how can we use it to help stop him?"

"Unfortunately, we can't. It's useful for creating a profile and matching that up to a suspect once they are caught and in narrowing down the field of suspects, but it's not predictive," Kate explained. "I don't know who he will kill next or when, but these historical connections matter to this killer. We should expect more of the same. I'd start putting officers near historical sites on the Freedom Trail, for instance."

Declan nodded. "Like they did in Atlanta with the serial murders there in the 1980s. They knew the killer was dropping bodies in the river and bodies of water, so the cops staked out the bridges and eventually caught the guy."

Carmen seemed to consider and looked to Det. Briggs. "Do we have some undercover cops we can get out there on the streets in the evening? He's killing late at night. Most of the murders have occurred between ten and early morning hours, right?"

"Yes, that's right," Kate said. "He's also leaving bodies along the Freedom Trail of historical sites. The cops need to be undercover. If he sees uniformed cops, it will spook him. They need to stay out of sight if there isn't much traffic on the street."

"We can do that," Det. Briggs said. "Let me step out and make some calls."

Dr. Graham stood as well. "I need to get back to the office, but I'll send the final autopsy report over as soon as I have it. It will take a while for toxicology." He gave a simple wave of his hand and headed out the door.

"I need to leave as well," Carmen said, pushing her chair back from the table. "Keep me posted. This city isn't going to last much longer with this killer on the loose. The only thing the news and talk radio is covering is this case. People are catching on to what's happening. You know how it goes. It takes a couple of days for the news to settle and then everything breaks loose."

"What are you going to do now, Kate?" Declan asked, leaning back in his chair and stretching his arms over his head.

"I need to pull an address for Justin's girlfriend and I need to go see Frank Flynn." Kate looked at her watch. "I don't like it, but we are going to have to put the interview with Parker Gage off until tomorrow. Running down leads connecting to who Justin might know and his involvement feels like a better angle to run with right now than talking to Parker, who probably won't tell us anything. Are you coming with me today?"

Declan stood. "No, I'm going to have a chat with Mark Boyle. I want to see if he knows anything about Justin and also confirm his alibi for last night."

"He lawyered up," Kate reminded him. "We can't talk to him."

Declan shrugged. "It's worth a try. I want to see Mark's face when I mention Justin's name. He seems like an emotional guy. He might just give me everything I want to know right on his face."

Kate didn't think it was a bad idea, but she didn't want Declan going off half-cocked and ruining a potential suspect if Mark turned out to be the killer. If they had more evidence, they'd be at his door right now, but nothing other than being in The Founders tied him to Justin. She said as much to Declan, but he dismissed her as being paranoid.

As they both headed out of the conference room, the unit secretary walked toward Kate with a swiftness that immediately garnered Kate's attention.

"There's a young woman in the interview room. She's hysterical and wants to speak with you. She said you called her yesterday. I didn't get a name because she's crying so hard."

At once Kate and Declan turned to each other. "Justin's girlfriend," they said at the same time with the same level of excitement in their voices.

"Do you want to sit in?" Kate asked.

"No, I want to get over and talk to Mark. I might hit his office, too."

"You're asking for trouble."

"Just a friendly man to man chat. He can call his lawyer if he likes. Don't forget, Kate, he might be willing to help if it means we get off his back."

Kate knew no matter what she said to Declan, he'd go sauntering into Mark's office and stir up trouble. She didn't even bother trying. She was too interested in why Justin's girlfriend had come to the FBI office.

Kate made her way down the hall and found the interview room where the unit secretary had left Bryanna. Before Kate even opened the door, the sobbing could be heard from the hallway. Sobbing was probably an understatement. The girl sounded inconsolable.

Kate took a breath, braced herself, and opened the door. A young woman with a gray sweatshirt sat at the table with her head in her hands, tears flowing down her face. Her mousy brown hair had been thrown up in a messy knot on her head.

Kate cleared her throat and started to speak, but the girl snapped her head up and stared into Kate's eyes. "Are you the one that got my boyfriend killed?"

CHAPTER 30

Kate hesitated at the doorway for only a brief moment. She closed the door behind her and took a seat across from Bryanna. "I'm Agent Kate Walsh, I spoke with you yesterday."

The girl cursed and called Kate names she'd never heard a woman call another before. She took it stone-faced. There was hurt behind the anger that Kate understood. She let Bryanna tantrum herself out until nothing was left except tears that flowed freely down her face. If Kate knew anything, it was that Bryanna had truly loved Justin.

Kate stood and grabbed a box of tissues that were on a table behind Bryanna. She set them on the table. "Can I get you anything? Coffee? Water?"

Bryanna grabbed a tissue and blew her nose and then grabbed another to wipe her eyes. "No. I don't even want to be here, but I figured you got him into this mess so maybe you can find who killed him."

Kate sat back in her chair and crossed her legs. She never found it easy to hit the delicate balance needed to not speak ill of the deceased but to help their loved ones face the reality of the situation. Kate struggled to find the right words. "Bryanna, I know that you loved Justin very much. That's obvious, but I don't know the person responsible for his death. We have reason to believe he knew the person, and you might be able to help me with that. First question, how did you find out that Justin had been killed?" To Kate's knowledge family notification had barely been made.

Bryanna grabbed another tissue and blew her nose again. "He left me a note at his apartment. When he didn't answer his phone when he got out of jail yesterday, I went over and found it on his bed. He said he was sorry and that he loved me, but he'd probably never get to see me again. I slept in his bed last night and this morning his mother called crying, saying that Justin was dead – he had been murdered."

"Did Justin say anything in the note he left about why he thought he'd never see you again?"

Bryanna shook her head. "I thought it was about drugs and going to jail. Last night, I thought he was arrested again after he got out on bail."

Kate rested her hands on the table palms down. "It's important you tell me the truth. There is no reason to protect Justin now. It won't help him. The most important thing you can do for him is to help us catch whoever killed him."

Bryanna raised her eyes to Kate. "I don't want to say anything bad about him."

"I understand that," Kate sympathized, understanding more than Bryanna would ever know. "Nothing you say can hurt Justin. The truth might help bring his killer to justice. It's important, Bryanna, or I wouldn't ask it of you."

Bryanna let out a breath. "What do you want to know?"

"I assume you know about the murders that have been happening in Boston. I was on the news talking about them and then I spoke to you about where Justin was last weekend." Kate waited until Bryanna confirmed she knew what Kate was talking about and then she went on. "I believe Justin was involved."

"No! He didn't kill anyone!" Her tears flowed down her face again.

"Bryanna, listen to me. I don't think Justin killed anyone, but I think the killer got Justin to help him. I'm not sure how Justin helped, but we believe because Justin was going to help the police catch this guy, he was murdered. Justin was going to do the right thing, and now, I need you to do the right thing."

Bryanna shook her head in disgust. "The right thing got him killed."

"We can keep you safe." Kate waited for the girl to respond. When she didn't, Kate continued. "You told me Justin was with you last weekend. Was that true?"

"Partially true," she admitted, shifting in her seat. Bryanna searched Kate's face for a reaction, but she gave none. Kate didn't say anything. She sat back and let the silence hang in the air for Bryanna to start talking again.

After a moment, she did. "Justin and I spent the weekend together, but he kept getting calls on a cellphone he didn't use all the time. I thought it was some of the guys buying drugs from him. I asked if he had switched phones for that. Justin said no that the new phone wasn't for that, but he wouldn't explain why he had it."

"What kind of phone was it?"

"It was one of those cheap pay-by-the-minute phones." Bryanna glanced at Kate. "I know what you're thinking – where is that phone now, right? Justin threw it out after that weekend. He said the guy he was doing some work for was paranoid, so he kept giving him new phones to use. That way they'd never be traced. Justin told me he'd have a phone for like three or four days, and the guy would take it and give him a new one."

"Did Justin ever mention the guy's name?"

"No, he never mentioned a name. Last weekend was the first time I even noticed the other phone. Justin was secretive about it. At first, I got jealous thinking maybe it was about another girl, but Justin assured me I was being silly. He said it was work, but he never told me what kind of work."

Kate narrowed her eyes. "Justin never mentioned anything?"

Bryanna shrugged. "He said he had to deliver a few things. He never told me what. Even when I bugged him to tell me, he never did. He wasn't like that normally. If I wanted to know something, he'd tell me but not this time."

"Did he say why he wouldn't tell you?"

"Justin said it was just safer that I didn't know." Bryanna looked down at the table and sniffled. "If I had known, maybe I could have protected him or talked him out of whatever he was doing."

"I doubt that. Justin was right to keep you out of it." Kate tapped her finger on the table to get Bryanna's attention. When the young woman raised her eyes to look at Kate, she said, "Tell me about last weekend. You said Justin wasn't there the whole time. Was he out delivering things?"

Bryanna relaxed back in her chair but kept eye contact with Kate. "I don't know what he was doing, I swear. There were a lot of text messages back and forth, but Justin wouldn't let me see what he was texting. Around one in the morning, we were snuggled up on the couch when he got another text. Justin got up and said he had to go. He told me he had to go find a guy and that he'd be back in a few hours. That's when I started thinking maybe it was another girl."

Kate knew Bryanna wasn't telling her the whole truth. "What happened after Justin left?"

"Nothing. He left and came back around two-thirty in the morning. I was asleep by then. The next morning, Sunday morning, we went out for brunch when he finally got up at noon."

Kate cocked her head to the side and smiled. "Bryanna, I remember being your age. You were home on a Saturday night with your boyfriend. He's texting on a strange phone he won't tell you about and then suddenly leaves at one in the morning, refusing to tell you where he's going. That's going to cause a strain in even the most trusting relationship. So, I'll ask you again, what did you do after he left?"

Bryanna wouldn't meet Kate's gaze. Her voice quiet, she admitted, "I followed him."

That was not the answer Kate had expected. She had figured Bryanna would have argued until Justin told her something to satisfy her and end a fight, but Kate never thought the mousy-looking girl in front of her would have hit the streets spying on her boyfriend in the middle of the night.

"Where did he go?"

"He walked to a bar on Newbury Street. I watched him go inside, and I could see through the window what he was doing." Bryanna took another breath and wiped a tear from her eyes. "He first ordered a drink at the bar and started talking to people. Then he met up with a guy and they had a drink. They left together shortly after and walked to Granary Burying Ground. At that point, I assumed it had to be about drugs and Justin didn't want me to know how much he was dealing. It was cold so I went back to his apartment."

"You said Justin got back around two-thirty?"

Bryanna nodded. "I was asleep in his bed by then, but I heard him come in. There's a clock right next to the bed. It said two-twenty-seven."

It was enough time for Justin to have killed the victim at Granary Burying Ground. Kate pressed further. "Did you talk to Justin when he came back?"

"I got up to see if he was okay. I thought maybe he'd tell me more since he was done with whatever he had been doing." Bryanna wiped more tears from her eyes. "But he didn't. All the color had drained from his face and he looked shaken. I'd never even seen Justin look scared before. He kept saying that he thought he should call the police, but he wouldn't tell me what he was talking about. I finally got him to calm down and come to bed with me. I figured maybe if he slept, he'd be better in the morning. I thought it was a bad drug deal gone wrong, but the next day, I knew. That guy he walked to the cemetery with had been murdered right there in the Granary Burying Ground."

Kate swallowed and cleared her throat. "When Justin arrived home, did he have blood on him or a weapon of any kind with him?"

"No blood or dirt or anything like that. He looked exactly how he did when he left the house. I don't know about weapons because he was in the apartment a few minutes before I got out of bed, but I didn't see him leave with anything and he didn't have anything when I walked out into the living room. He was on the couch with his head in his hands, debating back and forth about calling the cops."

Kate wasn't sure how Bryanna would react to her next question, but it had to be asked. "Once you found out the guy with Justin had been murdered, did you have any concern that your boyfriend might have killed him?"

"For maybe a minute when I first heard the news report, but then I read about how the guy died and no, absolutely not."

"Why is that?" Kate asked, confusion apparent in her voice.

Bryanna gave a half-smile. "Justin was freaked out by blood. He couldn't even stand cutting himself shaving. He acted like the biggest baby. There's no way if he was going to kill someone that he would have used a knife like that or cut the guy's neck. I assume Justin had witnessed the murder."

It was clear to Kate that Bryanna hadn't made the leap to understand that Justin had probably set the guy up to be murdered, and she wasn't sure she wanted to tell her. "Did you see Justin last night after he was released from jail?"

"No." Bryanna started to cry again, big tears rolled down her cheeks "He wouldn't even talk to me. He said he had a few things to figure out. That's why I went to his place, but I was too late. He was already gone."

CHAPTER 31

Kate let Bryanna leave the FBI office without taking a formal statement. The girl balked at doing it when asked, and the last thing Kate needed was to alienate a potential witness. Bryanna had provided substantial information connecting Justin to the killer, and Kate had no idea if they'd need Bryanna to testify to anything later. The entire interview had been audio and video recorded, so they had the info one way or the other. Keeping Bryanna cooperative was the only thing that mattered. Before Bryanna left, Kate had given her information for victim services in case she felt like she wanted to talk to anyone.

Kate got back to her desk emotionally spent and a million thoughts running through her head. She sat down and noted the blinking light on her desk phone. She picked up the receiver and hit the button for messages.

Frank Flynn said he'd be waiting for her at his office for an afternoon meeting. It seemed Carmen had changed her mind and called him to let him know the FBI would be calling him. She had strongly suggested that it would be good if he cooperated. Frank asked for a meeting an hour from his call. Kate checked her watch. She'd have just enough time to get to his office if she hurried. She clicked off from the voicemail and called Frank's office, getting his administrative assistant after two rings. Kate assured them she'd be over to the office as soon as she could get there.

Kate gathered up her things and left the office only realizing once she was outside that Declan had driven them that morning and he had left to go speak to Mark Boyle. She raised her eyes to the sky and shook her head at her forgetfulness. She pulled out her cellphone and called rideshare. She had become far too domestic with Declan in too short a time. Kate never had anyone to rely on after her parents' deaths. Now, here she was, a few days with Declan living in her home, and they were practically attached at the hip. She fumed, not exactly sure why it bothered her so much, as she waited for her ride.

Ten minutes late and out of breath, Kate shoved open the glass door to Frank's office and came face to face with a young woman who gasped at the sight of her and dropped a stack of papers on the floor.

"You startled me," the young woman chided Kate as she bent down to pick up the papers. She raised her head slightly to look at Kate. "I assume you're FBI Special Agent Kate Walsh?"

"Yes," Kate said, dropping her bag to the floor and bending down to help the young woman. "I didn't mean to startle you. I ran up to the fourth floor. I didn't want to miss Mr. Flynn before he left."

The young woman accepted a stack of papers from Kate and they both stood at the same time. "You're fine. Hardly anyone is on time to see Frank." She pointed to a hallway off the small reception area. "Second door on the right. He's waiting for you. Can I get you water or anything?"

"No, thank you." Kate smiled at the young woman and made her way down the hall. She nudged open a dark wood door and stuck her head inside. "Mr. Flynn, I'm FBI Special Agent Kate Walsh."

A squat heavy-set man with deep-set dark eyes sat behind an oversized wooden desk. He had sunk so low in his chair that his chest barely reached the top of the desk. He waved her in with a meaty hand and motioned to the chair in front of the desk. "Sit, don't worry," he said in between sips of coffee. "You're not late. Barely anything happens on time here."

Kate smiled as she sat, setting her bag on the floor at her feet. She crossed her legs and rested her hands in her lap as she assessed the attorney. He had loosened his tie at some point that day because it hung just off to the left of center. The buttons on his shirt strained to maintain his heft, but a broad smile and ruddy cheeks made Kate, and probably anyone else that entered his office, feel at ease.

"Your assistant said as much," Kate said. "I'm glad you called me. I wasn't sure you'd be willing to speak with me."

Frank offered a hearty chuckle. "Carmen Langston is not to be trifled with. She called and didn't leave me any room to say no."

"I hope she didn't strong-arm you too much."

Frank waved his hand. "All bark no bite." He seemed to think better of what he just said. "Let me rephrase. She's never had to bite me. I'm generally compliant."

He exhaled loudly like all the air had been let out of his body. "I assume you're here about Justin. As I told Carmen, I don't know who the killer is. I have no idea who he was working with or selling drugs for, but I know Justin was in deep trouble. That's a bit like stating the obvious now that he's been murdered, but it was more than that."

"What do you mean?"

"Justin's parents hired me, and they have money, Agent Walsh. Lots of money. They could have afforded an attorney from one of the most prestigious law firms in Boston. They came to me though."

Kate wasn't sure if Frank was being humble or what his point was. He had successfully defended some high-profile clients. "I'm not sure I understand what you're saying."

Frank dipped his chin and raised his eyes to her. "Discretion, Agent Walsh. I may very well be one of the best criminal defense attorneys in the city of Boston, but you'd never know it. I don't garner press attention. I make backroom deals with the best of them, but I don't talk out of turn. Clients who come to me know they are flying under the radar, and that's what Justin's parents wanted. They knew their kid was trouble. It's not the first time I've represented him." Frank shook his head in disgust. "This time Justin got in over his head."

Kate relaxed back in her seat. "I understand what you're saying about discretion, Frank, but does that mean you're not willing to speak to me now?"

Frank moved papers around on his desk like he was searching for something. "I wouldn't have had you come over if I wasn't going to tell you anything. I don't know much though. I said what I said so you'd understand why his parents hired me. They are going to want to sweep all this under the rug, so if you need anything from them, you aren't going to get it."

Kate let out a sigh of relief. "We shouldn't need anything from Justin's parents. They don't even live here in Boston, right?"

"No, out of state," Frank said and pushed his chair out from his desk. He leaned back and rested his folded hands on the top of his protruding belly. "I wish I knew who killed Justin, but he was working with someone and it wasn't about the drugs."

"I believe he was working with a serial killer." Kate waited to see if Frank would flinch or argue, but he didn't. "That doesn't seem to surprise you. I had a witness come in today to tell me that last weekend Justin met one of the murder victims in a bar and then walked with him to Granary Burying Ground. Soon after, he was at home and quite distraught. I don't know for sure what Justin was doing, but it sounds like he lured that victim there to be murdered."

Kate locked eyes with Frank. "Brutally murdered, Frank. This wasn't a run of the mill homicide. An antique blade was shoved so hard into the man's chest the handle left bruising. Then the killer sliced across his neck and nearly decapitated him. Justin's body had been left in a similar state."

Frank winced at the description. "I wish I could tell you more. When I got Justin out of jail, we came back here to my office. He sat right where you're sitting. It was obvious he knew he was in over his head."

Kate leaned forward slightly. "What did he say when he was here?"

"Justin told me that someone he had trusted asked him to get a guy to go with him to Granary Burying Ground. I knew that much, but Justin said he had no idea what this other person had planned. Justin was caught up with some crazy people – The Founders or something like that."

Kate nodded. "We are aware of them. My partner is speaking with a person of interest from that society right now. Was it someone from The Founders that Justin had been working with?"

"I don't know, Agent Walsh. As I said, Justin only gave me bits and pieces of information. He only got part of the story from the killer. From what it sounded like, Justin trusted this person – at one time anyway. I never got a full story, but Justin did leave me with one thing."

Kate raised her eyebrows. "What was that?"

Frank pulled a small key from under a stack of papers on his desk. He held it out in his hand to Kate. She stood and leaned over far enough to take it from him. The small gold key belonged to a safety deposit box or a locker of some sort. "Did Justin tell you what this key goes to, Frank?" she asked as she sat back down and continued to examine it.

"When Justin and I were talking after his release from jail, but before Carmen came over, Justin was angrier than I'd ever seen him. He didn't trust you and your partner. He said he needed to get back to fulfilling his mission. I tried to impress upon him the seriousness of his crimes but he didn't want to hear anything about the drugs. When Carmen called to make a deal, I told Justin he needed to do whatever he felt was best, but that if he didn't take the deal, he was looking at considerable jail time." Frank moved his chair to get comfortable. "He had two FBI agents who were willing to testify against him. When I reminded Justin of that, he said he'd at least hear what deal the district attorney was willing to offer."

Kate wasn't sure what this had to do with the key, but Frank seemed to want to tell a story, so she let him. "Was Justin going to take the deal?"

"The deal Carmen offered was more than fair. You weren't sending him in alone. All he had to do was make a connection to Parker Gage, who Justin had mentioned a few times. Justin was adamant that he couldn't do that. He said trust was everything in The Founders and life. He wouldn't be a rat even if it meant he'd go to prison. We argued back and forth for a while. Finally, he relented, but Justin said that from that point forward, he'd be in danger. He left me the key should anything happen to him. There is a safety deposit box at a local bank." Frank leaned forward and jotted down the name of the bank and safety deposit box number along with the security code to access it. He slipped the piece of paper to Kate across the desk.

Seeing the excitement on her face, he managed her expectations. "You're not going to find anything there. What you'll find is another key to a locker down at the train station." Frank sat back. "I have no idea what's in the locker, but whatever it is, it was important to Justin and important enough he kept it well-hidden."

CHAPTER 32

Kate left Frank's office and walked the few blocks to the bank. She kept the key in her pocket and her hand closed tightly around it. As she rounded the corner a block away from the bank, Kate had the distinct feeling of being watched. It wasn't paranoia but years of training kicking in. She kept her head focused forward and quickened her pace. The feeling didn't leave her but only intensified. Kate couldn't look around without being obvious, and the last thing she wanted was to tip off whoever was watching her that she was aware of their presence.

Kate saw an opportunity up ahead and she took it. At just the right moment, she turned right and ducked down a small narrow alleyway between two brownstones where she had assumed people would store their large trash bins. Her bet paid off. Kate immediately ducked behind a large black trash bin. She leaned into the wall and looked through the tiny sliver of space back out at the sidewalk. A moment later, she nearly fell back at who she saw. Ashley Barrett, Professor Holt's teaching assistant – the one who had tipped her off to Justin in the first place.

Kate stayed in place as Ashley entered the tiny alleyway but only took a few steps. There wasn't much space, so she'd have to look carefully to spot Kate behind the bin. Kate knew she was safe when Ashley turned and walked back to the sidewalk and in the direction that they both had been heading. Kate stayed still, and a few moments later, Ashley was back again. Kate had to decide right then if she'd confront her or wait. She had no idea why the girl was following her. Kate let her breathing go shallow and even, waiting for her to leave. Confronting Ashley now wouldn't serve any greater purpose, but it was another lead Kate would have to explore. She turned and let her bottom rest on the dirty ground. She pulled out her cellphone and texted Declan to meet her back at her house in twenty minutes if he could. She needed his help.

Kate put the phone back in her bag, peered around the bin, and didn't see Ashley. She stood, brushed herself off, and went to the end of the alleyway to peer around the wall in each direction. When she didn't see Ashley, she took off to the bank.

The process was easy enough. She asked for the box and typed in the code she had been given. When she was alone in the room, Kate unlocked the safety deposit box. Sure enough, just as Frank had said, there was a locker key sitting at the bottom of the box with a small index card with the number 64 on it. If Frank hadn't told her the locker was at the train station, she would have had no idea. Nothing else was in the safety deposit box. No money or other valuables.

Kate tucked the safety deposit box key and the locker key in her pants pocket and closed the lid on the box. She let the bank official know she was done and left the bank. She walked back to her house without incident.

Kate paced the living room waiting for Declan to arrive. He had responded to let her know that he'd be there but was running late. Kate wanted him to come with her to the train station. If she was removing evidence, she didn't want to do that alone. Her mind spun thinking about why Ashley might have been following her. That wasn't who Kate had expected. She assumed maybe it was the killer or someone after what Frank had given her. Unless Ashley was, but that didn't make much sense.

By the time Declan arrived, Kate rushed at him, holding out the key in her hand. "I met with Frank Flynn today. Justin is hiding something important at a locker in the train station. He gave me a safety deposit key, which had this key inside of it."

Declan nodded and made his way to the kitchen. His lack of response frustrated Kate.

"Don't you find that kind of strange?" she asked, trailing after him.

Declan opened the fridge and grabbed a bottle of water. He undid the cap and gulped it down. "Justin was a strange guy. Nothing surprises me on this case." He carried the bottle of water over to the center island and sat down. "I'll go with you. What else did you find out today?"

Kate sat down next to him and relayed the entire day including her meeting with Justin's girlfriend, Bryanna. She didn't realize until that moment, she hadn't told Declan what Bryanna had said about Justin bringing the murder victim to the cemetery. "Declan, he met the victim at a bar and walked with him to Granary Burying Ground right before he was murdered. Justin was involved in this. It means he's the key to solving it."

Kate finally had Declan's attention. "You have eyewitness proof that Justin met with the murder victim right before he was murdered?"

"Yes," Kate said and explained in detail again everything Bryanna had told her. "She was suspicious he was seeing another woman, so she followed him. Her story makes sense when you think about it. He had a secret phone and was getting texts all night and then he leaves. What was Bryanna supposed to think?"

Declan shrugged. "He was a drug dealer. Wasn't she used to strange people being around and Justin taking off without explanation?"

"No. Bryanna said that Justin told her what he was doing all the time. That's what made this situation so strange for her." Kate paused trying to remember exactly what Bryanna said. "A drug deal is what Bryanna ended up thinking when she saw them in the burial ground – that it was just a drug deal. It wasn't until Justin came home and he acted so strangely that she became suspicious. Then when she saw information about the murder on the news the next day, she put two and two together."

"She didn't call the police?"

"Come on, Declan, she's young. Would you have called the police and told them your girlfriend murdered someone if you didn't know for a fact that's what happened?" Kate waited for a response, but Declan didn't give one. She asked, "What happened with Mark Boyle today?"

"He spoke to me against the advice of his attorney, but he doesn't have an alibi for last night." Declan ran a hand through his hair and cursed. "I don't know, Kate. Everyone looks guilty."

"Did you tell him Justin had been murdered?"

Declan explained that he had gone first to Mark's office thinking he'd be working, but his secretary said he hadn't been to the office in a few days. She said Mark was now working from home. "I get there, Kate, and it's crazy. He answers the door and I tell him about Justin. He didn't seem surprised. Mark didn't say anything at all. I told him and he went to close the door in my face without any reaction at all, but I asked if I could speak with him. He let me in."

"How well did he know Justin?" Kate asked, getting up and grabbing a bottle of water from the fridge. She grabbed another for Declan and slid it across the island for him. She leaned against the counter waiting for an answer.

"He said that Justin was involved with Parker Gage. That they knew each other well. There's some connection between Justin and Parker, but Mark wasn't sure what it was."

"Could they be related?"

"I don't think so, but I think it's worth looking into, especially now if you think Justin was working for the killer." Declan shrugged. "We still need to interview Parker."

Kate let out a frustrated sigh and took a sip of her water. "We don't have anything concrete on him yet, and I was hoping we would before we went to speak to him."

Declan hopped off the chair and threw his water bottle in the recyclable bin. "Come on, let's go see what Justin is hiding in the locker. It might give us some greater insight."

"Are you okay?" Kate asked, following him to the backdoor of the house. "You seem distant and aloof, more so than usual."

Declan opened the back door and held it open for Kate as she walked through. "Yeah, I'm fine. Lauren texted me a few times today asking me if I'm getting a lawyer or how I'm planning to respond to the divorce. She also wanted to know where I'm living."

Kate shifted her eyes toward him. "She sent the divorce papers to my house. I would have thought she assumed you were staying with me."

"You'd think, Katie, but she's digging for information." Declan climbed into the passenger seat of Kate's car. They backed out of the driveway and headed toward the train station on Atlantic Avenue. Kate hit the gas only to have to hit the brake. It was stop and go traffic the whole way there, which wasn't far. The train station was a few miles drive, but too far to walk. She hated driving and this was why.

Kate grew frustrated behind the wheel. "You think I'll find a spot to park?"

"Nope. Throw the flashers on and double park in front. We won't be long, and I'll track down a transit cop and flash my badge while you head toward the locker." Declan leaned across the console and dug around in the backseat. He pulled gloves from a box and an evidence bag. "This is why you're driving," he said readjusting in the passenger seat. He held up the gloves and bag. "You're always prepared, and I ran out of my supplies the other day."

Kate pulled the car to a stop right in front of the train station as Declan had suggested. She didn't even look for another place to park. As she turned off the ignition, Kate asked, "How did you leave it with Mark Boyle?"

Declan had a hand on the door to open it, but he looked back at her. "I told him I'd be in touch. He insisted on his innocence once again. He said he's afraid he's being set up." Declan shut the door behind him and jogged over to a transit cop standing in front of the door. They spoke briefly and were waved in. Kate grabbed the evidence bag and gloves and got out of the car.

Kate and Declan walked into the train station together and found the lockers fairly quickly. "Number 64," she told Declan as they both started scanning the rows.

Declan found it first and slid the key into the lock. Before he turned it and opened the metal door, he glanced around. "I'm almost a little afraid of what's going to be in here."

"What are you worried about?" Kate stood at his side impatient for him to open the door. She resisted the urge to reach out and shove his hand away and do it herself.

"I don't know." Declan glanced once to his left and his right and then slowly turned the key. He pulled open the door, dropped his eyes to the bottom of the locker, and let out a gasp. "What the..."

Kate sucked in a breath. "I know," was all she could say. She stared at the thick handle and scanned down the shiny silver blade covered in dried blood.

CHAPTER 33

Kate stood frozen in place as she stared at the knife. Declan shook himself free from the shock and called Sharon at the lab to bring over a team. He ran to the closest transit cop and asked him to help block off the area. Declan insisted on connecting with the person who could expedite the surveillance footage from the last few days.

Kate heard all of this from behind her while her eyes remained glued on the knife. It looked exactly like the one that had been delivered to her home, probably by Justin. The dried blood covered the entire blade. It had to have been used in at least one of the murders. A blood and DNA analysis would tell them whose blood it was, but it directly implicated Justin in at least one murder.

More than that, it didn't make any sense. If Justin had committed murder, then who killed him? Sharon said the same dagger that was driven into the chests of the two stabbing victims was also used to kill Justin. He had the same bruising on his chest. Did that mean there were three of the same antique daggers? One was hard enough to fathom. A matching pair was a stretch for as old as they were, but three? Kate couldn't make sense of it.

She felt a growing crowd swarm around her. Kate wanted to turn and tell the onlookers to back up, but her eyes fixated on the dagger and her body wouldn't do what she wanted. The spell broke when

Declan came over and put his hand on her back and asked if she was okay. When she didn't answer, Declan assured her that the transit authorities were doing everything they could and an FBI forensics team were on their way. Kate mumbled a response and stalked off to find a bathroom to throw some water on her face.

What were they missing? The question plagued her as she shoved the bathroom door open and moved to the end of the line of sinks. She asked the question again as she checked her reflection in the mirror. Dark circles had formed under her eyes from a lack of sleep. Kate hated to admit it, but the last few nights she had tossed and turned. When she did sleep, she awoke sweating and gasping for breath from a nightmare she could barely piece together. All Kate knew was that her dreams had been haunted by murder and cries for help, but she was left powerless to do anything.

Kate turned on the taps and cupped her hands under the running warm water. As she brought the water to her face, the creak of the bathroom door garnered her attention. A young woman with a short blonde curly bob walked in. Kate expected her to head to one of the stalls but the girl just watched Kate. The water filled the palms of her hands and splashed over the sides.

"Do I know you?" Kate asked, sounding far meaner than she had meant.

The girl shook her head. "No," she croaked, "but I think I might be able to help you."

Kate pulled her hands back from the water and shook the excess free. She turned the taps off and wiped her hands on her pants. "Help me with what?" Kate asked as she approached.

"I saw the guy who put the knife in the locker," she said barely above a whisper.

That grabbed Kate's attention. "When? Who?" she barked, startling the girl with her intensity. Kate softened her tone. "I'm sorry, I didn't mean to snap like that. Do you want to talk here or would you like to find us a quieter place to talk?"

"Here is fine." The girl looked over her shoulder at the door. "I can't be too long."

"It's okay," Kate assured her. "I won't let anyone else come in."

The girl swallowed. "Two nights ago, I saw a guy standing in front of those lockers with a backpack on right before ten at night. I was on a late train and the place was empty except for the people getting off the train. I was one of the first people to get into the waiting area and that's when I saw him. He slipped the knife out of the backpack and put it in the locker. I saw the knife and what looked like blood, but I didn't know if it was real or not."

"Did the guy see you?"

"I don't think so." The girl shrugged. "I don't know really, but he didn't turn in my direction. It all happened fast. He heard and saw all the people coming from the train and he slammed the locker shut and left through the front door. I wasn't sure what I had seen, but it made me uncomfortable." She paused and squinted her eyes. "I'm probably not saying that right. He gave me a bad feeling. He kept looking over his shoulder and then when I saw the knife..."

Kate understood. "Did you tell anyone what you saw?"

"My mother when I got to her house. I thought about calling the cops, but I didn't walk over to the lockers so I didn't know the locker number or who the guy was or anything. It all sounded a bit crazy. I didn't think anyone would believe me."

"You're telling me now. That's all that matters. What are you doing here now?"

The girl bit her lip. "I've been coming back here to watch the locker and see if anyone came for the knife. I was trying to figure out what locker, but I haven't been able to. I figured I'd better call the cops, but I wanted to tell them what locker it was in. Then I saw you and you had been on the news recently about some murder cases. That's when I figured maybe it had to do with that."

"You've been sitting here at the train station watching the lockers this whole time?"

The girl shrugged. "In between classes, yeah. I told you I didn't like how that guy made me feel. It gave me the creeps. Even when I went home and told my mom and she told me to forget about it, I couldn't forget. It kept running through my mind." She tugged on a strand of her hair. "I know that probably makes me a weirdo or something, but it's the truth."

If Kate were the girl, she probably would have done the same thing and she assured her of that. "Do you remember what the guy looked like?"

She described Justin exactly as he had looked when Kate saw him at his apartment. The girl added, "I don't know how old I'd say he was. He looked like one of those guys who dressed younger than he is. Like he was purposefully trying to seem younger or maybe he was drugged out. There was something off about his appearance."

"Was anyone with him or was he talking to anyone?"

"No," the girl said, looking back at the door. "I didn't even see him for more than a minute or two if it was even that long. By the time I saw him, he already had the locker door open and was pulling the knife from the backpack. He dropped it in, slammed the door shut, and took off. Sometimes I question if I even really saw what I saw."

Kate asked the girl if she could get her name or any contact information. She refused because her mother had been adamant with her about not getting involved. She figured she'd be in trouble even being at the train station. Without anything else to add, the girl slipped out of the bathroom before Kate, who went back to the sink to splash water on her face. The girl hadn't told Kate much she didn't already know, but at least it was confirmation that Justin was the one to drop off the knife. Kate finished up in the bathroom and headed for the door.

Once back into the main area of the train station, Kate walked over to Declan and Sharon who stood side by side talking. Their heads were together and they appeared to be engaged in serious discussion. Kate waited and didn't want to interrupt, but Declan raised his head when he saw her. "I wondered where you were. I was just going to text you."

"I ran to the bathroom and a girl followed me in," Kate explained. "She said she saw who dropped the knife in the locker." Kate detailed the girl's statement to her. "Two nights ago was before we spoke to him. Frank Flynn had the safety deposit key since Justin was released from jail. We need to know whose prints and blood are on that dagger. I know Justin's will be, but who else is the question."

"You still think Justin didn't kill anyone?" Sharon asked, her hands propped on her hips looking up at Kate like she had lost her mind.

"Yeah, I still don't believe he killed anyone. I think he was involved, but I don't think he's the killer."

"Are you sure, Kate?" Declan asked, looking at her with skepticism all over his face. "You said yourself his girlfriend, Bryanna, saw him take the guy to the Granary Burying Ground. Now he's been seen hiding the murder weapon."

"I'm sure." Kate looked up to the ceiling and processed her argument before she opened her mouth. Locking eyes with Declan, she explained, "Justin didn't have to give Frank the key. He didn't have to tell Frank anything about the locker. That dagger could have sat in that locker for a long time before anyone found it. I don't know how or why Justin got possession of it, but my guess is he took it from the killer." Turning to Sharon, "I think you're going to find someone else's prints on that knife."

Sharon shook her head. "I don't understand what you're saying. Are you trying to tell me you think he stole a murder weapon and hid it? That doesn't make a lick of sense to me."

"Me either," Declan echoed. "How did Justin steal it?"

"I don't know," Kate said, her voice nearly yelling and tinged with frustration. "I don't have all the answers, but I know Justin didn't kill anyone. If he had, he would have gone home to his girlfriend covered in blood. Instead, he looked shaken up like he had seen something that freaked him out. If Justin was the killer, he wouldn't have stashed the knife in a locker and given Frank the key. He could have thrown it in the river or wiped the knife clean and thrown it out. You don't leave a bloody knife in a locker someone else knows about if you're the killer." Kate narrowed her eyes. "Besides, who killed Justin?"

Sharon held her hands up in defeat. "This is all above my pay grade. You'll excuse me while I get back to work. I should know something more in the morning. I'll call you then." Sharon gave them each a nod and went back to her team standing at the lockers. They were in the process of bagging the dagger and evaluating the locker inside and out for fingerprints and other potential evidence.

Declan pulled Kate to the side. "What's our next move?"

"We wait." As Declan started to argue, Kate shushed him. "I'm frustrated, too, but we need to see what comes back from the evidence on the dagger. I know other prints will be there. Let's go home and talk. There's something I didn't tell you earlier."

"You're always holding back on me."

CHAPTER 34

The season's first snow fell lightly against the windshield as Kate parked. She stepped out of the car and tipped her head back to catch the snowflakes against her cheeks and eyelashes. She closed her eyes and instantly smiled. It was something she always did as a child.

The first snowfall brought a wonderment of the season. The flakes glimmered in the glow from the light at the back of the house that came on automatically at dusk. For Kate, there was something serene about snow at night as it shimmered to the ground. The first snowfall always brought excitement for the season that Kate knew would eventually dull to drudgery around March when everything was brown and the city threatened to revolt if one more snowflake made an appearance.

Declan laughed at her childlike act. "You still do that," he said more statement than a question.

"Of course," Kate said, glancing over her shoulder as she unlocked the door. "It's snowing early this season. I have to enjoy a happy moment when I can get it." She pushed open the back door and they stepped into the warmth of the house. The heater had kicked on and a rush of warm air hit Kate in the face.

"I need something warm to drink. Got any whiskey?" Declan asked, throwing his keys and wallet down on the center island and shrugging off his coat.

CHAPTER 34

Kate pointed to a low cabinet next to the fridge. "How about some coffee and Bailey's instead? I have that, too." She glanced over her shoulder, and he agreed. "We shouldn't drink too much. We have no idea when we are going to be called out again. This killer isn't done. We both know that."

Declan kicked off his shoes by the back door, tugged off his tie, and pulled his shirttails out from his pants. "I'm exhausted and not going anywhere. He can start killing at a decent hour."

Kate knew Declan didn't mean that. He didn't want the killer to claim any more victims, but what he said made her wonder if there was a reason the killer always struck at night or the very early morning. She asked Declan as much.

"Easier to get away with it at night," Declan suggested but admitted he had no idea. "He's probably busy working a day job and can hunt his victims at night. Isn't that usually how it goes?"

"I guess, but I wondered if it was significant." Kate made a pot of coffee while Declan went upstairs, yelling to her that he was changing and would be back down in a few minutes.

A few minutes turned into forty, and by the time Kate saw him again, she had already made the coffee, ordered pizza for dinner, and changed her clothes. She sat on the couch, a throw blanket across her lap, dressed in leggings and a sweatshirt and sipping her Irish coffee.

Declan went into the kitchen and came back with a mug of steaming coffee. He plopped himself down on the end of the couch and tugged on Kate's blanket for her to share. He sipped his coffee. "You said you didn't tell me something earlier, but I need to go first because I keep forgetting." He glanced at Kate and she motioned for him to go on. "I called the president of the local chapter of Daughters of the American Revolution, and they had some threats a few months back. Anonymous calls and emails. I went to their office and spoke to them today."

"Do you think it's connected?"

"I don't know yet. I passed the emails off to our tech team to see if they can trace the IP addresses." Declan leaned back into the couch and sipped more of the coffee.

"What kind of threats were made?"

"The emails made threats to blow up their building. The caller said similar things. One call threatened to shoot each one of them as they came out of their regular monthly meeting."

Kate set her cup in her lap. "Did they call the police?"

"They took the threats seriously, but nothing was ever done. No detective was even assigned, but I called Det. Briggs and he said he'd pull the incident reports for us." Declan turned his body to look more at Kate. "I don't know if it's connected, but it sounds promising."

"Did they have any idea who was making the threats?"

Declan nodded. "That's the strange thing. They brought up The Founders. The woman I spoke to said that Parker Gage had interrupted their meetings a few times and had sent members propaganda videos and materials. I requested those be sent to us, too. They assumed Parker had been making the threats, too, but nothing was ever confirmed. If it's not him, they have no idea."

"I assume there was no follow through with the threats?"

"No, we certainly would have heard of that. I think if it was Parker Gage, he was trying to scare them. I was told Parker vehemently denied making any of the threats, but I don't think anyone there believed him." Declan locked eyes with Kate. "We have to go interview him, Kate. Everything is leading back to this guy."

Kate knew Declan was right. She wasn't stalling so much as making sure they were in the right position and had some leverage before they went to speak to him. Sometimes they only had one shot at an interview. "Let's do it tomorrow at his house. I want to see inside his place if he will let us."

Declan's lips turned up in a grin. "He's not going to give us access the way Justin did if that's what you're thinking."

"I didn't think he would, but I want to invade his space and see how he reacts. If he's the killer, he invaded my space sending that dagger here, so I'm going to do the same to him."

Declan reached over and patted her legs under the blanket. "That's why I love working with you. You have a subtle ballsy-ness that most people don't have."

Kate laughed as he made up words. "I know you'd rather go in with a full SWAT team and take him down, busting down doors and shooting, but that's not going to work on this case."

"You're right. The woman I spoke to today said she could connect us with an antique weapons collector who specializes in weapons from the Revolutionary War. I know Sharon said she had someone look at it and confirm the daggers are authentic, but I want to know more."

"It's on my growing list of things to do. Message Det. Briggs now and see if we are clear to reach out to the guy that was recommended to you today. I'd like to get moving on that tomorrow if we can easily connect with someone. I want to learn more about the daggers, too."

Declan reached for his phone and shot off a quick message to Det. Briggs. Within seconds, the detective responded to Declan that all was clear and to go for it. Declan went upstairs to find the phone number of the contact he had been provided. As he placed the call, Declan's voice echoed through the house and carried down the stairs. Kate heard him agree to an appointment for tomorrow afternoon. That would give Sharon some time to confirm any DNA evidence and fingerprints from the dagger found in the locker.

As Declan bounded back down the stairs, he said, "I assume you heard that." Kate confirmed she had, and he slumped back down on the couch. "Tell me what you're been trying to tell me for hours now."

Kate had nearly forgotten again. She took another sip of her coffee.

"I'm fairly certain Ashley Barrett followed me from Frank Flynn's office to the bank where Justin had his safety deposit box."

"Who?" Declan asked, confused.

"Professor Holt's teaching assistant who turned me onto Justin. She's the one who told me to check into his activities connected to The Founders."

"What do you mean she was following you?"

Kate relayed the story as it happened, including ducking down the alleyway to avoid her. "I'm not even sure why I did that," she explained, laughing at herself. "Normally, I'd have turned and confronted whoever it was, but I didn't know at the time. We need to keep watch and go speak to her again."

"Why don't you talk to Professor Holt first and get some more information on her. Maybe she knew Justin had hidden the knife or she could know more than she told you before. I wouldn't jump to conclusions on why she followed you," he cautioned.

Kate had thought of talking to Professor Holt, but there had been a weird vibe between him and Ashley while she was in the office. Kate wasn't sure she wanted to wade back into that. She did need to talk to Professor Holt about Justin though so maybe she'd pay him a surprise visit in the morning.

Kate and Declan sat there talking about the case until the pizza arrived. Declan got up to answer and refused the money in Kate's outstretched hand. He grabbed the pizza from the delivery guy and dropped the box on the coffee table and went into the kitchen. He came back moments later with plates, napkins, and glasses of soda for each of them. He arranged it all on the coffee table.

"You didn't have to pay."

"I wanted to," Declan said, reaching for a slice of sausage and mushroom pizza. After he took a bite and wrangled the gooey cheese in his mouth, he said, "I'm going to owe you anyway. Lauren is convinced we are having an affair, so that means if this divorce goes to trial, you're going to be called to testify."

"Is that why you've been so grumpy today?" Kate asked, pulling a slice onto her plate.

"I want to keep you out of this divorce, but I'm not sure how I'm going to do that. It looks even worse with me living here." Declan chewed and swallowed. "I'm thinking of moving out."

"No, don't," Kate said more quickly than she had meant to. She didn't want Declan to know how much she enjoyed him living there even if she had felt like they were getting far too domestic with each other.

With a bit of pizza still in his mouth, he turned his head around to look at her, a look of surprise on his face. "You want me here that much? I figured I'd already be driving you crazy."

Kate offered a sheepish shrug. "It's a big house and gets lonely. If I'm not going to be traveling and I'm at home more, it's nice to have some noise. Besides, I feel safer with you here. Is Charlie settled into the hotel?"

"As far as I know." Declan took another bite and grinned into his pizza. He mumbled barely loud enough for Kate to hear him. "I knew you'd love me living here."

"I'm fine with testifying if Lauren is going to call me. We've never had anything romantic between us, so it's not like I need to lie to cover for you. Don't stress too much. We have enough to worry about."

Kate and Declan finished off dinner and carried everything to the kitchen to clean up. As Kate was about the throw the dishes in the dishwasher, her phone chimed with a text message. She grabbed her phone from the center island and read it. "What do you know…" she said, trailing off and continued reading. "Professor Holt wants to meet me tomorrow at his house rather than his office. He saw the news about Justin's murder and has some information for me. He gave me his address and asked me to come alone."

Kate texted him a quick response to let him know that she'd be there and then looked up to Declan. "Because he's asking me to come alone is exactly why you're coming with me."

CHAPTER 35

The next morning at nine, Kate and Declan stood on the second step of Professor Holt's three-story brick rowhouse on Pinckney Street in Boston's Beacon Hill neighborhood. The house had black shutters on all the windows right up to the third floor and a green door. An antique-looking lamp hung above the door.

"How does a Harvard professor afford this?" Declan asked, letting a loud whistle escape his lips. "This has got to go for five or six million."

Kate reached out and pulled the black door knocker back and dropped it twice against its metal plate. "He's tenured and has written a few books. He also does well on the lecture circuit." She glanced back at Declan who stood slightly behind her to the right. "How did my parents afford the house? It was willed to my father. Old family money."

Kate was about to knock again, but as she reached her hand up to the door knocker, someone on the inside turned the door handle and tugged it open. Professor Holt stood in socked feet with a simple gray sweater and jeans on. He smiled as he saw Kate, but his face noticeably fell when he spotted Declan.

He forced a smile and raised his eyebrows. "I had hoped you'd be here alone, Agent Walsh. I'm a bit uncomfortable with what I have to tell you."

Kate ignored his comment. "Professor Holt, this is my partner, Special Agent Declan James. We are working the case together, so anything you need to tell me is important for both of us to know."

"I see," he said curtly and stepped out of the way to let them in.

A winding staircase with hardwood floors and wrought iron railing sat off to the right. The foyer, with shiny hardwood floors and white painted walls, provided a straight shot to the back of the home. The living room was the first room off the hallway. Two couches sat facing each other in front of a fireplace that looked original to the home.

Kate and Declan sat down on one couch while Professor Holt stood, seeming unsure if he should sit or stand. It was clear Declan's presence had thrown him off his game.

Declan noticed it, too. "You'd probably be more comfortable if you sat, Professor Holt. I assure you everything you tell me is as confidential as if you were meeting with Agent Walsh alone." Declan locked eyes with the man. "Regardless, if I'm here or not, Agent Walsh would have shared the information with me after the interview. This is saving us a step, and as you can imagine, with a case like we are dealing with any saved time is critical."

"Of course," Professor Holt said, smiling and taking a seat. "It's silly of me, but given the connection to Harvard, discretion is important. As an alumnus, Agent Walsh would know that better than anyone."

Declan gestured with his hands. "Discretion is important but so is catching a serial killer. You texted Agent Walsh that you had some information about Justin." Declan leaned back on the couch and clasped his hands in his lap. So far, it was playing out as Kate had hoped. They had determined before they arrived that Declan would take the lead, which she hoped would throw Professor Holt a curveball

"Yes, well, Justin had been my teaching assistant for some time." He paused and reached up and scratched at his head. Kate had noticed he did that while she was in his office, almost like a nervous tick. He cleared his throat. "It's my fault Justin got involved in The Founders. I left the group a couple of years ago around the time Justin first started working with me. I had taken him to a meeting and he was enthralled with them since that time. He knew Parker Gage, which surprised me. He hadn't mentioned it before the meeting, and Justin was never clear with me about how they had met."

Kate asked, "What can you tell us about Justin recently? My understanding is he was fired from his teaching assistant job with you."

"Regrettably, that is true. Justin became so involved with The Founders that he started missing classes. He'd be scheduled to give a lecture for me and wouldn't show up. He had papers to help me grade that wouldn't get done." Professor Holt winced and shook his head. "It was more than that though. Justin started showing a propensity for violence that had me concerned. A few of my students came to my office hours to complain about some of the topics Justin had started discussing in classes."

"Could you be specific about that?" Declan asked.

Professor Holt remained silent for a moment and then explained. "I have an advanced class exploring pivotal moments in the Revolutionary War – major battles and war-time decisions that helped shape the outcome. Justin decried the Patriots and started trashing American heroes as traitors." Professor Holt gestured with his hand. "For the British, yes, in a technical sense, they were traitors, but Justin hammered it home. He stood in front of the class and said that he wished George Washington had been hung. He described what should have happened to him in graphic violent detail. The students, of course, were concerned. A few used the word unhinged to describe Justin."

"It seems like there might be more than that," Kate encouraged, knowing full well he knew more.

"Well, there were drugs. Many students knew Justin was using cocaine and selling it. There were all kinds of pills, too. All in all, it spiraled out of control, and I couldn't keep him on any longer."

Declan turned his head to look at Kate. She knew there was still more Professor Holt wasn't telling them. She pressed, "Forgive me, Professor Holt, but we know all of this. It's hardly the earth-shattering confidential information you made it out to be. I assume because Agent James is here you are holding back. Please tell us what you wanted me to know. I made time to come here and speak with you, and as Agent James said, time is a commodity we don't have a lot of right now."

Professor Holt brushed his hands down the front of his pants and balled them into fists and then relaxed them. He looked only at Kate when he spoke. "Justin came here and attacked me one night. It was after I had left The Founders and probably two months after I fired him. It was clear he was high on drugs because he rambled on, violent and angry, about turning America around. He said we shouldn't be wasting our time studying American history but making history. We needed to right the wrongs that had been done. He wanted my help."

Kate remained focused and kept her voice calm. "Help with what exactly?"

"He suggested the very thing that's happening now. Killing people and getting revenge for America's past sins, as he called it."

Kate blew out a breath. "You didn't think this might have been important to tell me before today?"

"I didn't think he was serious. The Founders had been making all kinds of threats. I told you that. Many people gave statements to the FBI. I assumed I wasn't the only one Justin told this to. When the murders happened last weekend, I could barely believe it." Professor Holt scratched at his head again. "I didn't think there was any way this was Justin. He's a smart guy, but not smart enough to pull off something like these murders and get away with it. He's messy, unplanned, and unpredictable. Tell me if I'm wrong, Agent Walsh, but that doesn't seem like the kind of person who would commit these crimes and get away with it."

Kate didn't respond.

Declan took that as a sign to take over again. "Did Justin have access to any antique weapons?"

"Yes, he did," Professor Holt said and shifted his eyes to the floor.

"What specifically did he have?"

Professor Holt stood. "Let me go get a photo for you. He brought them into my office once, and I was so impressed with the condition, I snapped a photo."

When Professor Holt walked out of the room, Declan turned to Kate. "You still think Justin is innocent?"

"I never said he was innocent," Kate argued. "I said that I didn't think Justin killed anyone. He's involved somehow in the murders. Let's not forget, Justin is dead, killed in the same manner as the others."

Professor Holt walked back into the room and handed a large printed black and white glossy photo to Kate. "I blew it up because I was so impressed with the quality and detail of the daggers."

At the mention of daggers, Declan's head snapped to the side and he glanced down at the photo in Kate's hand. He raised his eyes to hers, but Kate gave nothing away. She stared down at the photo and asked, "You believe these are antiques?"

"Not believe. I know they are." Professor Holt pointed down at the photo. "These daggers belonged to General Thomas Gage. He received two matching sets right before the war. They were a gift from his superiors in the British Army when he was sent back to the Colonies. Most people believed they were lost to history or some antique dealer had them hidden away. Some people never believed they existed at all and were the thing of legend. I had heard about them, but hadn't thought much about the story until Justin brought them into my office."

Kate handed the photo to Declan so he could get a better look. "You said there were two sets. There is only one set in that photo. Do you know anything about the other set?"

"No, Justin didn't mention anything about it either. He had an antique mahogany box he kept the daggers in side by side. The box had General Gage's initials on the top. I could barely believe what I was looking at when he brought them in. That's why I took the photo."

Declan stared at the photo as Kate watched for his reaction. He had no emotion on his face. Finally, he tipped his head back to look at Professor Holt. "How did Justin come by these?"

"I asked him that and he said his father had bought them off a collector."

"Did you believe him?"

"It didn't make a lot of sense to me."

"Why?" Declan asked, handing the photo back to Kate.

Professor Holt clicked his tongue. "This would be a huge find so if an antique dealer truly had these, they would have been at auction for millions of dollars. It would have made the news, at least, in the circles I'm in. I had never heard about a dealer having these."

"Could it have been before your time – say maybe it wasn't Justin's father but a grandfather who had bought them years and years ago?"

"Sure," Professor Holt said, "but there would still be news clippings about them. When I tell you there has been nothing but speculation about the existence of these daggers, I'm not exaggerating. No one has ever been able to confirm their existence until Justin brought them into my office. I could barely believe he let me hold one. It was heavier than I would have expected, but then again, they were never meant for battle."

At the mention of the daggers, a memory tugged at the corner of

Kate's mind, but she couldn't bring it into focus. It was a feeling of déjà vu she couldn't shake. She only had one question. "How do you know they are authentic and not a replica?"

Professor Holt shrugged. "I guess I don't. They looked the way the daggers had always been described to me. Justin said they were real and I took him at his word."

Kate took out her cellphone and snapped a photo of the photo and then handed it back to Professor Holt. "How do you think these daggers play a role in the murders?"

Professor Holt's eyes grew wide. "I don't know if they do. I'm certainly not suggesting they do. Given everything Justin had told me about the murders he wanted to commit, I assumed when the news said an antique dagger had been used that this is what they meant."

Kate accepted that answer and wanted to move on from the subject. "Tell me more about your teaching assistant Ashley. Any idea why she'd be following me?"

Professor Holt took a step back and stared down at Kate. "I was afraid this was going to happen."

CHAPTER 36

"Why is Professor Holt more worried about Harvard's reputation than he is bringing information to law enforcement?" Declan asked as they stepped onto the sidewalk after leaving Professor Holt's home. He made sure the door closed behind them and then he expressed frustration Kate assumed he had been holding in while in the house.

"I don't know. You could have asked him that," Kate said, walking side by side with Declan.

"You think he would have answered me. Man, he hated that I was there. Did you see his face when we walked in?"

"I told you there's something about him I don't trust." Professor Holt's response as to why Ashley had followed Kate hadn't done anything to decrease the vibe that she had about him. He said that Ashley had a crush on him and had questioned him after Kate left his office the other day about whether he was interested in dating her. Kate could not imagine that a teaching assistant would ask a tenured professor that question unless boundaries between them were regularly crossed.

Declan said Kate's name and snapped her back to attention. "I said you probably get that vibe from him because he wants to sleep with you."

"With me?" Kate asked, her voice an octave higher, but Declan wasn't wrong. She had thought Professor Holt might be interested in her given the way he had been acting when they first met. He had asked her out after all. She winced. "Is it that obvious?"

"It's that obvious. I can see why you don't trust him. I'm not sure I believe what he said about Ashley."

"I was just thinking the very same thing," Kate said, excitement in her voice. She always got a bit giddy when she and Declan were on the same page and she didn't have to convince him. "I think there is more going on between them. Also, am I supposed to believe that just as I'm coming out of Frank Flynn's office Ashley decides to stalk me because she thinks I'm interested in dating Professor Holt and she's jealous? That doesn't make any sense."

"We need to pay her a visit." Declan glanced down at his phone. "Want to drive over to Harvard now and track her down?"

"I think we should. I assume he is probably going to tell her I know she followed me, so the sooner we can talk to her the better." Kate and Declan walked a few blocks before either one of them spoke again. Kate broke the silence and said, "Professor Holt said there were four daggers, at least according to legend. We know about three of them – the one sent to me, the one in Justin's locker, and I think we can safely assume, the one used to kill Justin. If Justin had one set of them that means someone has the other."

As Declan glanced down at Kate, his face scrunched up in disbelief. "That's if we believe Professor Holt."

"About the legend or that the daggers were Justin's?"

"All of it."

"I'm sure the legend is easy enough to track down." Kate stopped on the sidewalk and Declan nearly bumped into her. "What time are we meeting with the antique dealer? I completely forgot we have that scheduled today."

Declan reached out and tugged on her arm. "Don't panic. We have a couple of hours. More than enough time to get over to Harvard and back to the FBI office to meet with him. I already told Sharon to have the daggers ready for him to inspect."

Kate breathed a sigh of relief. There were so many balls in the air they were juggling, she couldn't keep everything straight. They walked down the narrow alleyway that ran behind Kate's street and up the small brick walkway into the back of her house and took her car. Declan said he'd text Sharon on the way to see if she had made any progress on the dagger pulled from Justin's locker.

Declan sent a text as soon as they were buckled into the car, but it took Sharon nearly the whole twenty-minute drive to text back. As soon as his phone chimed, Declan reached for it and read the text. "We got lucky. There are fingerprints – a few different sets of prints. Sharon is working to get clean prints of each so she can run them in the system. She should know more in about an hour."

Kate changed lanes and slowed for a red light. "I was just thinking of something Professor Holt said that didn't mean much to me at the time, but now that I'm thinking of it, it's significant. He said he held the dagger and that it was heavier than he had thought it would be. That could account for the different sets of prints. If Justin let Professor Holt hold the dagger, then he could have done that with countless others. Fingerprints might not tell us what we hoped."

Declan cursed. "We can't seem to catch a break here, but let's wait and see what Sharon finds. At least, we will know who is in Justin's circle."

"I didn't think of it that way." Kate found a place to park not far from the history building. They found their way back to Professor Holt's office. It occurred to Kate once she was there, she didn't know where Ashley's office was located. Kate ended up knocking on a few doors until someone answered and they directed Kate and Declan to the third floor where most of the graduate teaching assistants had space. As soon as they stepped off the elevator, Ashley's voice echoed down the hall. "That's Ashley," Kate said. "At least I know she's here."

They approached the office door where Kate heard Ashley talking. When Kate stepped into view, Ashley's head snapped up, and she nearly dropped the phone. She fumbled with it as it slipped from her fingers. Catching it before it crashed to the desk, Ashley told the caller she had to go and then hung up. She stood from behind her desk. "Agent Walsh, can I help you with something?"

Kate introduced Declan who made his way into the office and took a seat like he owned the place. Declan had a way of using his body to make his presence and power felt. He popped his ankle up on his knee and assessed her.

"Why were you following Agent Walsh yesterday?" he asked, keeping his eyes trained on her.

"I didn't—" Ashley started to say, but Declan cut her off.

"Let's not start with a lie, Ashley. That isn't good for anyone. Agent Walsh knows you followed her, what street you were on, and even where she lost you. We don't have time for games."

Ashley blinked rapidly as she tried unsuccessfully to come up with a response. She slumped back down in her chair without uttering a word.

Declan turned to look at Kate who stood behind him. "What do you think, Agent Walsh? Do we have enough to make an arrest?"

"We might, but I'm not sure if that's necessary." Kate sat down next to Declan and pulled the chair closer to Ashley's desk. "Harassing a federal law enforcement officer does carry some significant jail time, but Ashley was the one who gave us the lead on Justin, so maybe we can cut her some slack."

"No, I don't think so." Declan leaned in with a menacing look, and all the blood drained from Ashley's face. She gulped once and then again. "Ashley, I can't always be with my partner, but if anything were to happen to her, I'd drop my badge and gun at the office, turn in my credentials, and handle things the way they do in Southie where I'm from," he threatened. "Do you understand what I'm saying?"

Ashley said quietly, "I didn't mean any harm."

"A moment ago, you said you didn't follow Agent Walsh. Now, you're saying you didn't mean any harm. What am I supposed to believe?"

Kate held her hand out to push Declan back. "Let's give Ashley a chance to explain." Turning to the girl, Kate said, "Ashley, you'll have to excuse my partner. We've worked together for a long time, and he's protective of me. It would help if you could tell us what you were doing."

Ashley, seeming to have a little more confidence, sat back in her chair. "I saw you and wanted to ask a question about Justin, but then you disappeared and I couldn't find you. I wasn't following you as I had started to say."

Kate asked, "What was your question?"

"I wanted to know if he was the killer you had been searching for. I saw on the news he had been murdered and that didn't make a lot of sense to me since I thought he had been the one killing people."

Kate pursed her lips. The girl was lying and Kate knew it. "You would have heard mention of that on the news."

Ashley nodded once. "I guess you're right about that. I wasn't thinking. It's all been so upsetting. Is there anything else you need?"

Declan, who had been quiet while Kate played good cop, suddenly stood and took a few steps toward the back wall to a small bookshelf in the corner of the room. He picked up a simple silver photo frame and then turned around and peered over at Kate. She had no idea what had caught his eye.

"Who is this, Ashley?" Declan asked, holding out the photo to her.

"My boyfriend."

"He looks significantly older than you."

"That's not a crime. We are both consenting adults."

Declan walked over to Kate with the photo frame in his hand. He held it out to her without saying a word. Kate took the frame in her hands and looked down at it. It took everything she had not to register on her face the feeling that ran through her. The man staring back was someone Kate recognized from The Founders' materials Professor Holt had provided her.

Kate asked, "Ashley, what is your boyfriend's name?"

Ashley's eyes shifted from Kate to Declan. She had to know something was up by their reactions, but it was clear she had no idea what the response would mean to them. "I don't understand why this is important, but his name is Parker Gage."

Kate's tone became more serious, all businesslike. "Ashley, you mentioned that you knew Justin was involved in The Founders. You said you knew Justin was up to no good, but you failed to mention your relationship to Parker Gage. Why is that?"

Ashley folded her arms over her chest. "I don't see how it's relevant."

Several thoughts ran through Kate's head at once, and she wasn't sure what she should ask or how far she should push. She looked to Declan, but from the look on his face, he was unsure, too. Kate slowed the rush of thoughts and narrowed her focus. "Tell me about your relationship with Parker. How long have you been seeing each other?"

"I've known him for a few years, but we have been dating about a year," Ashley said, confusion on her face. The girl appeared to have no idea why this mattered. "I don't understand—"

"Are you a part of The Founders?" Declan asked, interrupting.

"No. I don't believe in the same things that they do."

"Doesn't that make it a little hard to have a relationship with Parker?" Declan asked. By the look on Ashley's face, she seemed to not understand. He rephrased. "Parker is the president of The Founders. By all accounts, he is fanatical in his beliefs. We have heard that he's advocated violence – bombings here in Boston against historical sites. Several prominent members left when Parker took over."

Ashley shrugged and rested her hands on her desk. "I love him, and we make it work. I don't have to believe everything he believes. He's not like what most people think he is. He was never serious about violence. People took things he said out of context. What he was saying was that that's how the Patriots rose to power – with violence. What he was saying was that's what it would take to undo it. If America showed it was incapable of ruling itself, England would have to take over again. But he never told anyone to go commit violence."

Since Declan hadn't made a dent, Kate asked, "Do you ever attend The Founders meetings?"

Ashley looked directly at Kate. "No, it's for men. That's the way Parker wanted it. There had been some women in the group, but he prefers it to just be men, so I'm not involved. I wouldn't be anyway. As I said, I'm not interested."

Kate was about to press the young woman further, but she turned to Declan and noticed his head bent, staring down hard at his phone, completely distracted from the conversation at hand.

"What's going on?" Kate asked.

He hitched his head toward the hallway. They both excused themselves from Ashley's office and stepped out into the hall, closing the office door behind them. Declan reached for Kate's arm and tugged her down the hall. When they were far enough away from Ashley's door, he said, "Sharon found two other sets of prints on the knife – Parker Gage and Ashley Barrett."

"Ashley's fingerprints are in the system?"

Declan nodded. "Dismissed underage drinking arrest from when she was an undergrad. The case was dismissed, but her prints were on file."

CHAPTER 37

"What do you think it means that her prints are on the dagger?" Kate asked, her voice rushed and low.

Declan pointed down the hall to Ashley's office. "It means she had her hands on the dagger that was found in Justin's locker. That's probably why she was following you. She knew with Justin dead that he had the murder weapon with her prints out there. I bet she was trying to get to it first."

"Do you think she's working with the killer or do you think, like Professor Holt, she had held the dagger at some point because Justin showed it to her?"

"That's a good point. No one else's prints were found so either the dagger was wiped off after Professor Holt held it or it wasn't the dagger he touched."

It was time to press Ashley harder than they had before. Kate paced back and forth in the hall considering the best approach. "Leave me alone with her," she said finally. When Declan started to argue, Kate turned to him. "No, listen. Ashley could be caught up in something and feel like she doesn't have any way out. You were rough on her went we first when in and that didn't work at all. She didn't tell us anything. I'll tell her you had to take another call, and I'll bond with her and see what I can get. At the very least, we need her alibi."

Declan threw his hands up in the air frustrated with her, but as he normally did, he relented. "I'm not leaving this hallway. If she's the killer, you shouldn't be alone with her."

"Whatever." Kate turned and marched back to Ashley's office, putting on her game face with each step. She turned the door handle and pushed the door open. "Sorry about that. Agent James had an emergency to handle. I'll catch up with him later."

Ashley raised her head and locked eyes with Kate. "I'm busy and need to get some work done before I teach a class in forty minutes. I think you should go."

Kate returned to her seat and sat. "I don't think so. We need to talk. You're in some trouble, Ashley. I'd like to help you out of it, but you have to work with me. We can either talk here or I can bring you formally into FBI custody. It's up to you how this goes."

Ashley moved some papers on her desk and leaned her arms on it. "What kind of trouble?"

"We will get to that. First, tell me where you were last weekend." Kate specified the dates and times of the murders.

"I was at home, alone. I have quite a bit of work to do towards my Ph.D. and this teaching assistant job keeps me busy. I worked all last weekend at home."

"You didn't see Parker at all?"

"No, he said he was busy and I was busy. We don't spend all of our time together."

"I see," Kate said, crossing her legs and making Ashley wait. Kate mentioned the night of the first shooting, but Ashley had no idea where she was. That didn't surprise Kate. She'd be hard-pressed to tell anyone what she was doing on a random night a few weeks back. Unless there was an event or something significant that happened, most evenings blend one into another for people.

Kate tried another date. "What about the night Justin was killed?"

"You think I had something to do with that?"

"I'm trying to rule it out."

Ashley's voice rose an octave. "Why would you think I did anything to Justin? I told you I was suspicious of him and I was, but I'd never hurt him!"

"If that's true, Ashley, then simply tell me where you were that night."

She sat back and closed her eyes, shaking her head. "I was home alone again. Before you ask, no one can confirm that." She opened her eyes and gave Kate a pleading look. "You have to believe me. I'd never hurt Justin. Why do you think it's me?"

"Ashley, the call Agent James took was to let us know that your fingerprints were found on a dagger believed to be the murder weapon."

A look of shock came over Ashley's face.

Kate asked, "Are you surprised I found the dagger or that your fingerprints were on it?"

Ashley didn't say a word, but she lowered her head so Kate could no longer see her eyes.

"Let me tell you what I think happened." Kate waited for Ashley to look at her, but when she didn't, she continued anyway. "You touched that dagger when Justin showed you. After you found out about the murders, I believe you thought it was Justin because you had seen and touched the murder weapon. He probably even talked to you about some of the violence he wanted to commit, but you didn't take him seriously then. When you saw me in Professor Holt's office, you knew that was your chance to tell me about Justin. When you found out he was murdered, I think you remembered your prints were on a dagger. You might have even worried that it was the murder weapon. I think you panicked and were following me. You saw me go to Frank's office, and I think you thought it was your shot to find the dagger before I did."

Kate had no idea if her theory was correct. There were parts of it she had completely made up just to get Ashley's reaction. She waited in silence to see what Ashley would do. When she said nothing, Kate pushed her harder. "Ashley, Agent James wants me to arrest you. He's convinced you were working with Justin to murder people. Believe it or not, he thinks you're the one who killed Justin, and then in a desperate attempt, you tried to find the dagger before we did. You're going to have to give me something so he doesn't come back up here and arrest you."

Ashley hesitated to digest what Kate said. Tears ran down her cheeks. "I didn't kill anyone, but you might as well arrest me."

Kate sat straighter in her chair not sure she had heard correctly. "Are you admitting that you committed a crime?"

"I am," Ashley said softly. She stacked up papers on her desk, and when it was in satisfactory order, she stood with her arms outstretched to Kate. "Arresting me is the safest thing you can do for me. If he got to Justin, he can get to me."

"Sit back down, Ashley. Tell me who you're afraid of."

"I don't know, that's why I'm afraid."

"That doesn't make any sense to me. Tell me what's going on," Kate urged.

Ashley rubbed at her eyes, which had grown red from crying. Mascara ran down one side of her cheek under her eye. She dragged the back of her hand across it and smeared it more. "I don't know if I can explain," she said, sniffling back tears.

"Just try."

Ashley grabbed a tissue from a box on the shelf behind her and blew her nose. She reached for another tissue and wiped her eyes and face. "I think I must know the killer, but I don't know who it is. I thought it was Justin, but someone killed him, so I guess I was wrong. I followed you because I knew I had touched that dagger. You're right about that. I thought if I could get to it first..." Ashley trailed off not finishing her thought.

"What were you going to do if you found it?"

Ashley shrugged. "I wasn't sure and that's the truth. I was worried. I knew I didn't have an alibi for the nights of the murders because I was home studying and grading papers. Then knowing I had touched the dagger Justin showed me, I knew I might be in trouble."

Nothing Ashley said made much sense to Kate. There was something she was missing. Kate asked the question she thought she had asked before, but felt now, the answer was more important than ever.

"Why were you suspicious Justin was the killer? I know he had a violent streak. I know you said he had been talking about murders like this, but there had to be something more definitive."

Ashley nodded. "Parker told me that Justin had done it. He said that Justin had taken things too far, and he worried that it would come back on him and The Founders. Parker worried that everything he had built would be destroyed. That's why I told you about Justin. I figured if you caught him it would stop and Parker would be okay again." Ashley looked down at the desk. "But then when Justin was murdered, it occurred to me that I had touched the daggers he had. I read in the newspaper that the murders had been committed with an antique dagger. I worried that it would come back to me."

"Did Justin ever tell you or Parker he had committed these crimes?"

"He never told me. I have no idea what, if anything, he told Parker. I just got the information from Parker."

"If Parker thought that strongly that Justin had committed these crimes, why wouldn't he have called the FBI himself?"

Ashley sniffled. "Parker figured he'd be blamed. You had already gone after Mark Boyle. He figured he'd be next. I thought if I could convince you it was Justin that you'd catch him and Parker's connection would never come up."

"Ashley, the same dagger you touched also had Parker's fingerprints on it. Have you stopped to consider that Parker might be the killer?"

Ashley didn't say anything for several moments. Then she raised her eyes toward Kate. "I don't want it to be him."

Kate felt a moment of sadness for her. "You said yourself that someone killed Justin, so at the very least, he was working with a partner. That partner could be Parker."

Ashley held up her hand to stop Kate. "Parker was angry that I told you about Justin. He said I should have stayed out of it. What if it is Parker and he comes after me next?"

"Why would he come after you?"

"I can't say." With that Ashley closed down. She wrapped her arms around her body and sank back on her chair, refusing to make eye contact with Kate. They sat like that for several moments until she spoke again. "I need protection. If you can get me to someplace safe, I'll tell you everything I know."

CHAPTER 38

"Do you trust Ashley, Kate? That's the only thing that matters right now." Declan sat in the chair with his feet propped up on another in the FBI office conference room.

Kate had been pacing around the room since they arrived back at the office. After Ashley said she'd tell them everything she knew if the FBI got her some protection, Kate had been torn about the decision. There was something about Ashley that Kate didn't trust, but at the same time, even Declan had speculated that killing a woman – a representation of General Thomas Gage's wife – might be the next step the killer would take.

If it was Parker, who better than his girlfriend? Either way, Kate couldn't look the other way if Ashley felt like she was in danger. The responsibility of Justin's death already weighed heavily on her. Still, though, Kate couldn't shake the feeling they had been played.

Kate stopped pacing and threw up her hands in frustration. "I don't trust her, Declan. That's why I'm so keyed up."

"What do you want to do about it?"

Kate yanked a chair out from the table. She sat down and folded her arms across her chest. "It's a lose-lose for us. If we don't protect her and something happens, I won't be able to live with myself. If we do protect her, and Ashley is somehow involved, how can we live with ourselves for harboring and protecting a serial killer or their accomplice?"

Declan didn't seem as bothered by Kate's conundrum as she did. He shrugged. "It's the risk we have to take."

Kate exhaled. This was the third time she and Declan had had this conversation. The first time had been when she left Ashley's office to speak to him in the hall and ask what he thought they should do. The second time was when the Boston cop came to escort Ashley from the building back to her apartment to gather her things and bring her to the hotel they had arranged.

Before she left with the cop, Ashley had called the Harvard administration office and informed them she needed a two week leave of absence to attend to a family issue. While Kate stood in front of her desk, Ashley called Professor Holt and told him she had to leave school for a few weeks. He had been furious. Kate could hear him yelling through the phone, but Ashley had remained strong. By the time the call had ended, Ashley wasn't sure she'd even be able to keep her teaching assistant job, but the job wasn't worth risking her life. Ashley promised as soon as she was settled and felt safe that she'd reach out to Kate and tell her more.

Declan dropped his feet to the floor and inched up in his seat. "Kate, I can't have this discussion again. You'll know in a few days, once Ashley is settled, if we made the right choice or not."

This was the side of Declan's personality that infuriated her. Blasé decision making. The "let's see what happens" attitude. Declan thought Kate was uptight and rigid and she thought him too cavalier about important decisions. That said, Kate couldn't do anything about it at this point, so she'd have to let it go. She checked her phone for the time. "What time is this guy getting here?"

"Now." Declan stood and pointed to the hallway.

A tall, slender man with jet black hair wearing jeans and an emerald sweater came in the door. Declan shook his hand. "Albert Hill, I'm

Special Agent Declan James and this is my partner, Special Agent Kate Walsh. We appreciate you coming here on such short notice."

Albert took a seat across from Kate. "It's nice to meet you. I know this is a murder investigation, but the idea that you might have come across General Thomas Gage's daggers is thrilling to me. It would be an astounding find."

Kate didn't fault the man for his excitement. Declan grabbed the evidence box from a side table and carried it over to Albert. He set the box down on the table and pulled out the first dagger, the one that had been left for Kate.

Declan handed the dagger, sealed in a clear evidence bag, to Albert. "Here it is. I'm hoping you're able to assess it in the evidence bag, but if we need to open it, that's fine, too. I have some gloves here you can use."

"I would like to open it to see it in better detail," Albert said, reaching into his pocket. He pulled out a pair of thick blue surgical gloves. "I carry gloves. Always prepared in my line of work."

Declan pulled on a pair of gloves he grabbed from a box on a side table and carefully pulled the dagger from inside the evidence bag. He handed it over to Albert and the man's eyes lit up. Kate didn't want to read too much into his expression, so she sat there holding her breath while he examined it. She had no stake whether the legend was real or not, but still, there was a tinge of anticipation in the air over the possibility.

After what seemed like an eternity, Albert set the dagger down on top of the evidence bag. He looked over at Kate and then at Declan. "That's the real deal. I don't know where you came across it or who the owner is, but that is most definitely a real Revolutionary War dagger."

"How do you know that?" Declan asked, skepticism tinging his voice.

"The craftsmanship is exactly of that time. The materials that made the handle and blade and the design are consistent."

Declan didn't seem convinced. "Could it be a forgery?"

"If it is, it's the best one I've ever seen." Albert sat back and smiled at Declan. "You called me. I'm among the most respected in the field. People hate seeing me because more times than not, I have to break the bad news that their antique find, that they think is going to bring them millions, was a knock-off made in the 1980s." Albert picked up the dagger. "I'd stake my entire career that this is an original dagger from the time around the Revolutionary War. It's British, too. Not American."

Kate leaned forward and rested her arms on the table. "How do you know that?"

Albert turned the dagger toward her and pointed with his finger at the rounded top of the dagger handle. "See this design, right here?"

"Barely, but I did notice there was a design there."

"It's faded with time, but there are some swirly lines and a small fox. It's part of General Thomas Gage's family crest." Albert set the dagger down. "I know everyone says that the Gage daggers are legend, but I've known they were out there for a long time. There were documents found about forty years ago in a home in London that were from a commander of the British forces at the time of the Revolutionary War who commissioned the daggers for Gage. It was a parting gift when they sent him back to America as governor of Massachusetts in April 1774."

"Is this the first time you've heard that anyone has laid eyes on hem?" Declan asked.

"No, the legend has persisted for more than one hundred years. I'm not even sure how that came about. Back in the 1960s, a man in New York claimed to have found the daggers, but upon inspection, they were deemed fake. Later, in 1992, there were rumblings and rumors man here in Boston had found a pair of the daggers. No one was ever able to confirm the man's identity or see the daggers, but people believed that this mystery man had found them. To be honest with you, I believed it, too."

Declan raised his eyebrows. "Are you okay with blood?"

Albert turned his head up to him. "I guess, as long as it's not my own. What did you have in mind?"

Declan excused himself and left the room. Kate assumed he was going to get the dagger that had been in Justin's locker. She explained that to Albert who sat with a confused expression on his face.

"We have two of the daggers," Kate explained, "but I've heard there are four. Is that true?"

"It is true. Gage had four daggers on his family crest so the understanding is that the daggers were representative of that, which makes sense since some of the family crest is engraved on the dagger handle."

"What does the legend say about the daggers? Were they all missing?"

Albert shook his head. "Only two were believed to be missing here in America. The other two were thought to have returned with Gage when he went back to England. I suspect they were probably passed down his family line or maybe even lost to history."

Kate latched onto something he said. "Do you believe they were passed down his family line? Is it likely to have gone that way?"

"I don't know, but that's always been how the story goes. If the daggers made it back to England with Gage, there is no reason they wouldn't have been passed down through the generations. A gift from the British forces was significant. The daggers were handmade and have his family crest. It makes sense that such a gift would be passed down from one relative to the next."

"Do you know much about Gage's family line?"

Albert laughed. "Not really. I know you might think because I'm obsessed with antiques I'd care where they came from. Sometimes I do, but I don't get into genealogy. I don't even know my own beyond my great-grandparents. It's never been too much of an interest to me." He eyed the dagger. "I'm more of an object person than a people person."

Kate understood, but she wanted to push a little more. "Were there any stories about the daggers that went along with Gage's family line?"

Albert gestured with his hand as he spoke. "As I said, I only heard that the other pair might have remained with his family, but I never heard much beyond that. I couldn't even tell you Gage's children's names. If memory serves me, I think he had three sons and a few daughters."

"He had nine children that I'm aware of," Kate said.

"You know more than I do." Albert smiled and turned his attention to Declan who carried an evidence bag in his hand containing the bloody dagger. Albert pointed. "Was that used in a murder?"

"Three murders that we are aware of," Declan said and handed the evidence bag to Albert.

This dagger Albert did not take out of the bag. He moved it around inside the evidence bag and brought the rounded end closer to his face. "Same design on the end of the handle. I'd say this is the other half of the pair."

"You said two daggers probably remained with the family and the ɔther two were lost here in America," Kate started, pointing at the lagger. "Do you have any idea how two got out of Gage's possession?"

Albert handed the evidence bag back to Declan. "There were stories hat the Governor's mansion could have been robbed and looted and hey were taken then. We don't know though and never will. The egend is that they were gone here in America, probably a treasured aul of a Patriot getting one more win over on the British."

Declan folded his arms over his chest. "So, the stolen daggers were one more humiliation that General Thomas Gage suffered at the hands of the Patriots then?"

Albert, mouth set in a firm line, nodded his head once. "You could definitely look at it that way."

CHAPTER 39

After Albert Hill left, Kate and Declan sat back down at the conference table. Declan toyed with the dagger in the evidence bag. "It seems to me that the killer is out for revenge for General Thomas Gage. If what Albert said is true, that a set of daggers were stolen from Gage, then it's the perfect murder weapon to exact his revenge. Not to mention, Parker Gage could have the pair passed down through the Gage family line."

Kate didn't disagree. "I think we either have a killer who has a massive fascination and loyalty to Gage's image or we have someone, like Parker, possibly related to him. Either way, I'm pretty sure now that revenge is the motive. Not the typical motive for a serial killer, but we learn something new every day."

Declan nodded. "I think that's a fair statement. I wonder how far Det. Briggs has gotten with genealogy research. He said he had two researchers on it tracing Gage's family line. We know about Parker, but there could be someone else."

Kate drummed her fingers on the table, thinking through the events of the morning. They had avenues to explore. There were Gage's family tree and the daggers' history – which would probably prove impossible to trace since it was mostly legend. Still, something about that legend and the daggers kept niggling at a memory she couldn't quite grasp. No matter how hard she tried, Kate couldn't recall the information that seemed to sit in the corner of her mind just out of reach, cloaked in the shadows.

Declan grabbed for his phone and typed out a text. "I'm going to ask Det. Briggs if they made any progress. What's next for us?"

Kate wasn't sure, but she had a reprieve as Sharon stuck her head in the conference room door, waving a paper at them.

"I got some DNA off Justin's pants, which the crime scene techs found in a heap far from the body." She slapped the paper down on the table and wiped strands of hair away from her face. "I've been looking for a break like this, but there's good and bad news." Sharon took a breath but didn't stop long enough for Kate or Declan to ask anything. "The good news is, we got some DNA. The bad news is we haven't gotten a hit in any of the databases. Right now, we have unknown male DNA."

"That's more than we had before," Kate said, reaching for the paper. She read the few lines on the report that didn't say much more than Sharon had just explained. "We have a comparison now if we bring in a suspect."

Sharon pulled out a chair and sat down. "There was a lot of DNA, too. It was blood DNA, and after looking at the report that Dr. Graham sent over from the medical examiner's office, it looks like Justin put up a fight. Whoever your suspect is, he left with some bloody clothing. He didn't get out of this kill unscathed. I couldn't say for sure, but he might have some bruising or scrapes if Justin got into it with him before he died."

Declan set his phone on the table and leaned back in his chair. He linked his fingers together behind his head and blew a breath up to the ceiling. "I think it's time we visit Parker Gage. We probably have agitated him by putting Ashley in hiding. She said he was already annoyed that she said anything to the police about Justin. Now, with some potential DNA evidence, if we get enough of a statement or suspicion in the interview, we might be able to get a warrant for a DNA sample."

Kate pursed her lips. Declan wasn't wrong. It was past time to interview Parker Gage. She glanced over at Declan. "We can go find Parker Gage now. I think you're right that we should interview him. I don't think we are going to get more ammunition before we go." Kate went to stand, but before she was fully upright, she asked, "What did Det. Briggs say about the genealogy?"

Declan picked up his phone and read off the message. "There were some already created online, but they couldn't authenticate them. His team is recreating the family tree. There's a line of relatives back in England, but so far, there is no one in the United States involved in anything nefarious or even looks like a viable suspect other than Parker Gage. It's a slow-going process."

Declan hitched his jaw toward Sharon. "Some good things are happening with genealogy and DNA to solve cold cases. You think we can drop the DNA sample you have into GEDmatch and see if we can start creating some family trees that way?"

Sharon looked at him, the skepticism written on her face. "I don't know much about all that, and I certainly don't have the time. Let me check around in the lab and see if anyone knows much about it."

Declan smiled and waved her off. "Get one of your interns on it. That's what we have them for. Plus, those young kids know more about this new-fangled technology than we do."

Kate rolled her eyes at him and Sharon laughed. "You're a riot. You're thirty-eight years old. Hardly an old man." Sharon stood and slapped Declan on the leg as she walked out. "I'll put an intern on it and be in touch."

"You did sound like you were about sixty," Kate cautioned as they walked back to their desks.

"I feel like I'm about sixty on some days. The science is ever-evolving, and it was never something I quite understood to begin with. Someday it's going to make us all obsolete."

"We will never be obsolete. The science can connect the dots for us, but the human element will always be there. Are we going to try Parker at his house first?"

Declan checked his watch. It was already late in the day, nearing close to five. "I think by the time we get over there, it will be after the workday is over. By all accounts though, Parker doesn't work much. He does some investing but doesn't work for a company that I know of. If he's not there, we are going to have to wait for him to get back."

Kate had thought as much, but she hadn't been sure if Declan had found other information. It sounded like a solid enough plan for her. They finished up the last of their work. Declan sent a few emails, and Kate gathered her things to go.

An hour later, they stood on Commonwealth Avenue on a wide cement front stoop that had wrought-iron railings that ran its length. They waited in front of a massive oak door that had glass panels framing each side of it. The house inside was dark, so they couldn't see much other than the formal foyer.

"You ready?" Declan asked, his hand hovering just over the door knocker.

"I expect Parker to be tightlipped and not share much. My expectations are low for this interview, but as always, we'll give it a shot."

Declan smirked at her. "I like that you're managing your expectations better. It's better than perfectionist Kate who gets angry when she doesn't get the confession the first try."

"Just knock," Kate said, shaking her head at him.

Declan raised the brass door knocker and dropped it against the metal plate. He rapped three times in a row and then waited. About thirty seconds later, he did it again. Finally, after several moments passed and they were both ready to leave, a middle-aged woman in black pants and a white blouse came to the door.

"May I help you?" she asked, looking down her nose at them.

Declan pulled up a chain he had around his neck attached to his FBI badge that sat in the middle of his chest. "I'm FBI Special Agent Declan James. This is my partner Special Agent Kate Walsh. We are here to speak to Parker Gage."

The woman took a step back, surprised, but she didn't step out of the way to let them in. "I can't imagine why you'd want to speak to Parker Gage."

"I'm not at liberty to discuss that with you." Declan placed his foot on the landing and inched forward. "Is he here?"

The woman nodded and moved out of the way to let them into the home. "He is up in his study working. He hasn't finished work for the day. I'm his house manager, Lillian Dale."

Kate extended her hand to the woman who took it. "Ms. Dale, if you could please go get Parker or direct us to his study that would be helpful."

She shook her head. "No, I can't possibly let you into Mr. Gage's study. I'm not even allowed in there, but follow me to the sitting room and I'll get him for you."

Kate and Declan followed the woman as they went through a hallway with dark wainscoting on the walls and marble flooring that looked as if it was polished by hand every day. There wasn't a scuff mark or smudge in sight.

Lillian Dale slid open pocket doors and stepped through the center as she ushered them into a formal sitting room. The marble flooring gave way to hardwoods, but the dark wainscoting continued into the room. Two large floor-to-ceiling windows on the far wall had heavy gray drapes on each side and a sheer panel down the middle.

The most striking thing in the room was the massive portrait of

General Thomas Gage in full military dress. The painting was encased in an ornate gold frame. Other than that, there wasn't much in the way of any personal items in the room. Overall, the room gave off a dark and masculine feel. Deep gray sofas and straight-back chairs with tables strategically placed around the seating space were the only furniture in the room.

Neither Kate nor Declan sat. They stood together waiting in the center of the room. Lillian left as quickly as she had brought them in, leaving the pocket doors open and giving them a sliver of a view into the hallway.

"Is this what you expected?" Declan asked, looking around the space.

"It's formal, not a personal item or effect in place. It's in keeping with what I assumed but doesn't give us much to explore while we wait." Kate pointed to the portrait. "That's certainly an imposing and striking image of the man."

Declan walked over to the portrait and stared up at it. "It's hard to imagine that this man and his legacy could cause such a murderous killing spree."

A man chuckled from the doorway. He spoke in a posh clipped British accent, which surprised both Kate and Declan. No one they had spoken to had even hinted Parker Gage wasn't American. "You haven't studied your history. The rage that General Thomas Gage stirred in your so-called Patriots practically burned down this city I'm certainly not an advocate for what's happening now, but it's understandable."

Parker gave off a regal appearance with his crisp white shirt with French cuffs and gray flat front slacks. In his left hand, he held a highball glass filled three-quarters of the way with a brownish-gold liquid. His strong jaw had a small three-inch scar down one side His long thin nose had been broken at least once. It gave his face character it might not have otherwise had. Parker looked no more than forty if that. His trim waist went into narrow hips and long runners' legs. Kate assumed the man couldn't have been more than a few percentages of body fat.

It was Parker's right hand that garnered most of Kate's and Declan's attention. A white gauze bandage had been wrapped around the hand several times down to his knuckles. Only the very tips of his fingers were visible.

"Parker Gage, I assume?" Kate asked, and the man nodded once. "What happened to your hand?"

He swished the alcohol around in his glass and took a large swig, tipping his head back. He swallowed, righted his head, looked Kate right in the eyes, and gave a sinister leer. "You think that's bad, you should see the other guy."

CHAPTER 40

Declan's hand immediately hovered over his sidearm, ready to unholster and draw his weapon if needed. "That's why we are here, Parker. We've already seen the other guy – dead on a slab at the morgue."

Parker waved him off. "You're dramatic, and we haven't even been formally introduced. You know I'm Parker Gage. You know that you came to my home in search of me. Who are you? Ms. Dale mentioned you were with the FBI, but I'm not sure why you'd need to speak with me."

Parker walked farther into the room, brushing past Kate and Declan, and sat down in a high-back chair. "Please, sit down and we can discuss anything you'd like. I've had a long day, and there's no point in standing when the furniture is so comfortable."

Kate shifted her eyes over to Declan and his face said everything she needed to know. He wasn't going to sit and get comfortable even if she dragged him kicking and screaming to do so. He'd remain standing at the ready, looking tough and mean. At least, he was good at it.

Kate needed to bridge the divide so she moved around the couch and took a seat on the end near Parker. She glanced back over her shoulder to see that Declan had moved to stand behind the couch.

Kate introduced Declan and herself and explained why they were there. "You can imagine, Parker, you'd be of interest to us given the specifics of these homicide cases. There is a killer in Boston leaving bodies at Freedom Trail historical sites and sending letters to the newspaper with his grievances. It's clear we have a killer set out for revenge at what happened to General Thomas Gage." Kate paused and let that sit with Parker for a moment. When he didn't respond, Kate went on. "Given your familial relationship to General Gage and your leadership with The Founders, of course, you can imagine your name has come up during our investigation."

Parker shifted his shoulders in a way that indicated he heard her but offered nothing else. His eyes shifted from Declan to Kate. "You think I'm somehow involved?"

"Are you?" Declan barked.

The corners of Parker's lips turned up. "If I were, do you think you can barge into my home, ask me one question and I'm going to confess?"

"That's not a denial."

"That's not an admission of guilt either, Agent James." Parker swished his drink around in the glass and took another drink. When he was done, he rested the glass in his lap and looked up at Declan across the top of Kate's head. "I'm not a killer. I've been accused of a lot of things, including inciting violence against historical sites. The last time the FBI visited me, they said I was planning a series of bombings, which was ridiculous. I'm a businessman. I barely even know how to cook myself dinner. I'm not creating bombs. I'd blow myself up trying to put one together. The FBI found no proof and left. You would know that if you had done your research."

"We did," Kate said, folding her hands in her lap. Parker had a tone of grievance but also pain like he couldn't believe the FBI would be suspicious of his activities. Kate wasn't sure if it was faked or real at that point. "We can understand if you're doing nothing more than providing a forum for intellectual conversation, but many people who have been a part of The Founders and left have indicated that the society might be fanatical in its mission. I'm sure you can understand why we'd end up here at your door."

"Fanatical or passionate about our cause? I think there is a fine line." Parker relaxed more into his chair and crossed his legs. "There have been many in the media and academia who have left us. That much is true. We get people all the time who want to join our society but struggle when they are challenged intellectually. They are at the top of their industries and they think one way, and when challenged on their opinions, they quit." Parker held his glass up and knocked back another sip. "They are free to go. I don't hold anyone here who doesn't want to be here. It's certainly not a cult, which is another word I've heard thrown around."

Kate knew from what Professor Holt had told her that what Parker said wasn't necessarily true. She felt the need to press him on that. "Parker, while I can appreciate that you might not see things from the perspective of your members, we've heard that leaving The Founders isn't always easy. Some of your members have felt threatened and have had their livelihoods threatened."

Parker glanced at Kate. "It depends on how they leave. If I'm thinking of the same person you probably spoke to, he didn't leave in a way that felt respectful. He threatened me. He challenged me, and deserved everything he got."

"Let's get back to the murders," Declan said, interrupting.

"What about them? I think they are terrible. I don't condone them and I think using my ancestor as an excuse for this kind of nonsense tarnishes his reputation more. It's not something I'd ever do."

"You don't enjoy that someone is getting revenge for the slights your family suffered at the hands of the Patriots?" Declan asked, folding his arms across his chest and smirking at Parker.

"You and I think very differently." Parker took the last sip of his drink and set the glass down on the floor next to the chair leg. "General Thomas Gage did the best job he could at the time given the historical circumstances. Now, do I think the founding of America should ever have happened? No, I think we are clear where I stand on that position. America has been out of control since its founding. It would have been much better for the global economy and politically for it to have remained under British rule. I think you'll see soon that politically the whole country is going to split itself in two. It was founded on some nice ideas that don't work in the real world."

Kate held her breath waiting for Declan to argue back. Even she wanted to argue how wrong Parker was, but nothing good would come of it.

When neither of them said anything, Parker when on. "I don't see these murders the same way as you do. I think it's someone who wants to continue to tarnish my family name. There's no good going to come of it." Parker uncrossed his legs and leaned forward in his chair. "How would a series of murders undo the damage to General Gage's reputation? It can't. It can only tarnish it more, so I'm as eager as you to see these killings stopped. It's bringing unwelcome focus on The Founders and our mission and negatively impacting my family name."

Something he said gave Kate an idea. "I assume you have an alibi then for when the murders took place?"

"Give me the dates, and I'll give you access to my calendar. I don't leave home much. There isn't a need. I work from here and run The Founders from here. I wouldn't say I'm a recluse, but when your home is as comfortable as mine, there's rarely a reason to leave. My staff might be able to account for my time or members of The Founders who are here often."

"What about your girlfriend?" Declan asked.

"Ashley?" Parker asked, his voice going up an octave. "What about her? It's more of a casual relationship than serious. She's young. I'm not pleased with her for bringing Justin into the fold at The Founders. From news reports, my opinion that he was trouble was correct."

"Ashley brought Justin into The Founders? My understanding was that you met Ashley through Justin who was a serious member. We heard Professor Anthony Holt brought Justin to his first meeting," Kate said surprised at the information.

Parker shook his head and looked her right in the eyes. "No, Ashley came to me and wanted to join The Founders. You can call me sexist, but I don't have women as members. We did at one time, but I've cultivated a forum where men can be free to be men. Ashley and I did strike up a conversation. She's an intelligent woman and I invited her to dinner. A casual romantic relationship followed from there. As a result, she introduced me to Justin. I believe you're right that Professor Holt at Harvard also made an introduction to Justin, but by then I had already met him. I never got the best vibe from the kid and kept him at arm's length."

Kate started to speak, but Declan talked over her. "What did you think about the daggers that Justin claimed to have found?"

Parker nodded. "I wondered when we were going to get around to them."

Kate swiveled on the couch so she was positioned looking more directly at Parker. "After talking to a Revolutionary War antique weapons expert, we have confirmed that the daggers are authentic and ones most likely owned by General Thomas Gage. My understanding is that two daggers were taken from here in America at that time, but two others made it back to London with him when he left. Are you aware of anyone in your family having possession of the daggers?"

Parker shook his head. "We've all heard the story, but until Justin showed me a set of daggers and asked me to authenticate them, I had not seen them in person. My grandfather had an old photograph from the 1920s that showed the daggers in a box. What my grandfather said was that one of his uncles had possession of the daggers at one time. I never saw them. I don't even think my grandfather saw them. He only heard about it and saw the photo. I couldn't tell you right now who has the daggers or where they are. The two daggers Justin brought to me seemed authentic. They had markings from General Gage's family crest and were similar to daggers of that time. I couldn't authenticate them though. I don't know what materials were used to make the daggers. Either way, it angered me that Justin might have had the ones stolen from General Gage, but he wouldn't tell me how he came into possession of them. It became a source of contention for us."

Declan narrowed his eyes at Parker. "That explains why your fingerprints were on the murder weapon."

Surprised, Parker asked, "One of the daggers I touched was used to murder someone?"

"Yes, that's what led us to your door, among other reasons."

"I swear to you I had nothing to do with these murders. I will account for my time and whereabouts for each murder if you give me the dates you need," Parker reassured.

"We can get to that," Kate said. She had something else on her mind though. "It doesn't seem that you liked Justin much at all."

"That would be a correct assumption on your part, and I never acted otherwise, Agent Walsh. Justin pushed and pushed to be in among my inner group at The Founders, and I did everything possible to keep him out. He didn't have the intellectual capacity and tenacity that I like in our members." Parker shifted to look up at Declan. "Frankly, he also had a drug habit. I may have a glass of whiskey now and then, but I'm not into the drug scene and certainly don't want that among my members. I told Justin more than once he wasn't welcome. He insisted on coming to meetings, and some of our other members wanted him around. The more I tried to push him out, the more insistent Justin became. I finally figured it was better to keep an eye on him, but he became increasingly more hostile and erratic. I worried that he might carry out some violence in our name."

Declan asked the obvious. "Why not call the police when you became aware of these murders?"

A mocking laugh escaped Parker's mouth. "And say what exactly? I was already on the FBI's radar from the past because of unhappy members who spread lies about me. You were already interrogating some of my current members. Frankly, I think you're fools to think Mark Boyle would have anything to do with this. He is the most mild-mannered man I've ever met. He spooks if you speak too loudly. I had no proof Justin did anything. Why would I draw attention to myself?"

"So," Declan said, pausing for effect, "you're telling us you have no idea who the killer is?"

Parker raised his eyes and a slow smile spread across his face. "I never said that."

CHAPTER 41

Declan glanced down at Kate and then took three quick steps around the couch toward Parker. Kate thought Declan was going to grab Parker by the shirt and pull him up, but he didn't. Declan stopped right in front of the chair with his hands firmly planted on his hips.

Declan's tone remained firm and no-nonsense. "What is it that you're trying to say then? You're wasting our time with these games. If you know who the killer is, you have a responsibility to tell us. Otherwise, we will assume you're an accessory to murder."

Parker held his hands up in defeat. "I don't know who it is, but I assume it's someone close to me. I think they are trying to tarnish my family name and take down The Founders."

Kate didn't understand. She asked with skepticism in her voice, "You think someone is purposefully trying to frame you? All indications are that they are out for revenge for General Thomas Gage. They are doing this to right the wrongs against him."

Parker uncrossed his legs and inched forward in his seat. "Aren't you dealing with a bit of a madman? Why would you believe anything he tells you? That doesn't make a whole lot of sense to me. Isn't he the one with the most motivation to lie?"

Kate could understand his point. She often heard that from people not well-versed in criminal profiling and forensic psychology. If it were that simple to figure out, she'd be out of a job.

"It's more complex than that," she explained evenly. "We aren't taking him at his word, but rather, looking at his method of murder, the words he's using in his letters, and his overall action. This is a killer with an agenda. If he wanted to frame The Founders, he could have carried out what you were accused of before and blow up a building. Leave the criminal profiling to us, but I don't think you're far off in thinking this person could be close to you."

Declan waited for Kate to finish and then asked, "Have you spoken to your girlfriend Ashley today?"

"No," Parker said, his voice rising in suspicion. "Should I have?"

"She's currently in protective custody. She believes the killer is close to her. If it's someone the two of you know, how long is that list of people?"

Parker threw his hands up. "I've introduced her to The Founders members. She knew Justin, who by all accounts is either the killer or connected to the killer. It could be anyone, Agent James, but I do think it's someone close to me. I've been going over the member roster of The Founders past and present and trying to narrow it down. I don't have a clue."

Declan turned his head to look at Kate and then back to Parker "Are you willing to give us that list?"

"Absolutely not," Parker said emphatically. When Declan started to argue, Parker dug in deeper. "I'm not going to have the FBI harass my members. You have my word if something comes to my attention or if I have concerns, I'll call you."

Declan scoffed. "Like you called us with concerns about Justin?"

Parker didn't say anything. He gestured dismissively with his hand and then stood. "I think this conversation is over. Let me get you Ms Dale who can confirm my whereabouts on the dates in question."

Declan reached his hand out to Parker's arm and stopped him from walking by. Fire lit in Parker's eyes and he shoved him off. "Don't touch me."

Declan held his hands up. "You never told us what happened to your hand."

Parker held it out for them to see. "I was up in the attic going through some old files and had to move a bookshelf to get a box. The thing tipped over on me and scraped my hand. Ms. Dale can attest to that. She was here when it happened. I went to urgent care and needed a few stitches. I'll go get the medical report for you."

When Parker left, Declan turned to her. "What do you think, Kate?"

Kate stood and faced him. "He seems aggravated by the whole thing. Parker isn't what I expected. I walked in here thinking he was the killer and it would be obvious to us by the time we left. That isn't what we saw at all."

"I'm bothered by the fact that he didn't seem concerned we have Ashley in protective custody. He didn't even blink or ask if she was okay," Declan explained, watching the door for Parker's return. "Don't you think he'd be concerned?"

Kate didn't know. "Parker acted like the relationship was more casual than Ashley might have led us to believe. He also might have spoken to her and didn't want to tell us. I can't explain that, but the man we just met has me thrown. I'm not seeing what others have described to me."

Declan ran a hand through his hair. "Are psychopaths ever?"

"That's just it, Declan. Parker isn't presenting as a psychopath. None of what he's saying or doing seems in any way off to me. If anything, he strikes me as someone who wouldn't get his hands dirty killing people. I expected more simmering rage at the surface. The person who wrote those letters certainly had that."

Kate rushed out the last few words as Parker returned to the living room. He had a medical report in his hand which he extended to Kate.

His assistant Lillian was right behind him.

"Ms. Dale has my schedule and can account for my time on the dates in question. If I was meeting with anyone at the time and you need to speak to them, I can certainly provide you the contact information."

Kate didn't think that would be the case since most of the murders were committed later into the night. "Does Ms. Dale live here at the house, Parker?"

"Yes, I have three staff who do. Ms. Dale plus my housekeeper and a chef live in residence."

Kate raised her eyes to Lillian. "Ms. Dale, you can account for Parker's whereabouts while he is at home?"

She nodded once. "It's an old house. It's hard to slip in or out without anyone noticing. Every sound echoes."

Kate pulled out her phone and scanned down the times and dates of the murders and provided Lillian the information.

"Those times are in the middle of the night," Lillian said surprised. Only flustered for a moment, she regained her composure and opened the book in her hands that contained Parker's schedule. She scanned the pages reading off that Parker was at home at each of the times. She snapped the book shut when she was done. "I haven't taken any time off and neither has the housekeeper or our chef. We were all here with Parker at those times. I can tell you that if he left the house in the middle of the night, we'd know, and I don't believe that happened."

Declan moved to stand near Kate. "What happened to Parker's hand, Ms. Dale?"

She recounted the story from her perspective, but it was what Parker had described. He had gone into the attic to go through some files and close to an hour later, he had come down into the kitchen with his hand completely torn up and bloodied. Lillian had gone with Parker to the urgent care because he had limited use of his hand. "The doctor said it was a minor injury but because of how deep the cuts were stitches were needed."

Parker held his hands out to his sides. "Are you convinced now that I'm not a deranged serial killer, leaving bodies along the Freedom Trail?"

Kate didn't want to give confirmation one way or the other. Parker had been very different than she had anticipated, which rarely ever happened. She wasn't ready to let anyone off the hook though. She smiled at him. "We appreciate all the information you provided and will be in touch if we need anything further."

Parker's face constricted with annoyance, probably because Kate wasn't going to say he was no longer a person of interest to them, but he walked them to the front door without saying a word. As Kate and Declan hit the sidewalk, she felt eyes on her and looked back at the house once to see if Parker was looking.

Standing in between the drapes of a side window stood Parker. Kate's eyes scanned over the rest of the house and realized he wasn't the only one. Lillian Dale stood at a second-floor window and across the house on the other side of the second floor stood a man. He had one hand pressed against the glass as he looked at them on the street below. Kate shivered at the scene.

"It seems the entire house is watching us leave," Kate said quietly to Declan as they started to walk down Commonwealth Avenue.

"I hope you're not discounting Parker as a suspect because I don't trust him," Declan said. Before Kate could argue Declan kept talking, his voice rushed and tinged with frustration. "I know what you said in there, but there is something about him I don't like. It's all too perfect if you ask me. As far as I'm concerned, if the only people who can give you an alibi are people you employ and that depend on you for a living, then that's no alibi at all. No matter what you say, Parker Gage is still top of my list."

Kate smiled to herself. It was rare to see Declan so worked up about a case. She reached out her hand and squeezed his arm. "I'm not dismissing anything you're saying. That was a lot to process. You know I'm rarely thrown by an interview, but this time, I'm feeling a bit off my game. There are things about him that match the criminal profile and then there are others that do not. He's a creepy guy for sure. We are still on the same page."

"That's good. I'm glad we can agree." It was like all the anger and frustration had let out of Declan and he didn't quite know what to do with himself. He reached his arm around her and pulled her close and dropped a kiss on the top of her head. "If I haven't said it before, thanks for being such a great partner and friend."

Kate wriggled under his affection. "What's gotten into you?" she asked, laughing.

"I figured you were going to fight me on it. I got all geared up for a good rumble with you and then you let me off the hook. It feels weird." Declan took his arm back and shrugged. "Let's stop and get dinner and not talk about the case or my divorce or anything stressful for an hour. Then we can get back to it."

"Fine by me," Kate agreed. "I need to give my brain a rest. I've felt like there is something important I'm trying to remember that might help the case, but I can't quite recall it. It's been driving me crazy. Maybe some downtime will help."

Kate and Declan stopped at a pub two blocks from her house. It had been a regular dining spot for her family while she was growing up. She knew the owner, but most of the staff had changed over time With Kate's constant travel, she didn't have much time to stop in as regularly as she once did. The place reminded her of her parents and was a welcome home away from home.

Kate and Declan grabbed a back booth near the window, read their menus quickly, and had their food and drink order in the first time the server stopped at the table. They chatted easily as they waited for their food. Kate nursed an Irish coffee while Declan enjoyed a pint. The small pub filled up with couples and families having dinner. As the server dropped food at the table, snow started to fall again.

Kate glanced across the table at Declan chatting happily as he sipped his beer and dug into his burger. Her heart swelled just a little. The words he had said to her earlier about being grateful for their friendship reverberated in her head. She had been caught off guard by his affection, but the older she got, the more she appreciated him in her life. Kate felt the same as he did, and she realized then, she should probably tell him that more often. As FBI partners, they often clashed on cases, and sometimes that spilled over into anger in their friendship. No matter what though, she had no idea what she would have done without him in her life to this point.

As they were taking the last bites of their food, Declan's phone rang. He reached for it on the table, read the messages, and cursed loudly. 'We were lucky we got more than an hour to unwind. Det. Briggs got a call about a woman's body propped up against a tree in Boston Common. She's been stabbed."

CHAPTER 42

Night had fallen and the streets were dark, only illuminated by car headlights and streetlamps. The snow had begun falling at a faster rate. The flakes were smaller now and sticking to the ground. Kate and Declan quickly walked the few blocks from the pub toward Boston Common. They cut through Boston Public Garden and sidestepped people on the sidewalks as they cut their way through to the other side. Neither spoke as they weaved and dodged their way past people who were coming home from work or heading out for the evening.

Once they made it into Boston Common, they stopped on the edge of the path. Declan looked at his phone again for specific directions to where the body had been found. Det. Briggs mentioned they were not far from the frog pond, which later in the winter was used as a skating rink.

He turned to Kate. "It's got to be out of the way someplace. I can't imagine someone carried a body from the street and placed her there without countless witnesses seeing him."

Kate had already thought of that. The area had heavy foot traffic, but there were nooks and corners of Boston Common off the sidewalks where a murder could take place unseen. "I assumed he lured the victim there and killed her on the spot. There is no way he carried the body there."

The two made their way past wide-open grassy areas until they saw a crowd of people standing around. Boston police had made quick work of setting up tenting over the area and roping it off to onlookers and foot traffic.

Declan and Kate flashed their badges to the uniformed officer standing guard and he moved the barrier out of the way so they could pass through. They came upon Sharon first. Kate was glad to see Det. Briggs hadn't wasted any time bringing in the FBI forensics team.

"Sharon, what do we have?" Declan called out as he approached.

She motioned for them to walk with her back to the body, which was on the far side of a tree shielded from view of onlookers. "When Det. Briggs first called me, I thought there was no way a body could have been dumped here. It's too obvious, but as you'll see, it's dark at night. Where her body was placed is out of the way of streetlights. Someone could easily commit murder back here and leave the body."

"Do you think she was killed where she was found?" Kate asked, watching the ground as she walked.

"Without a doubt," Sharon said. "You'll see the ground is disturbed ike she might have put up a fight. Her body was staged and even covered with a blanket up to her chin. If someone walked back here, hey might have thought she was homeless propped up against the ree the way she's positioned. You can't tell until you get close to her hat she has blood down the front of her shirt. That was partially covered with the blanket. You'll need Dr. Graham to tell you the particulars but looks like she was stabbed once right in the chest. A good amount of blood, too."

Declan asked, "Any idea how long she's been dead?"

Sharon glanced over her shoulder at him. "That would be Dr. Graham's call, but to me, it looks like she was just killed. I wouldn't ay more than an hour. She is still warm to the touch and blood is still ripping from the stab wound."

Kate and Declan shared a look as he checked his phone for the time. "We've been gone from Parker's house at least two hours. The timing doesn't rule him out."

Sharon raised her eyebrows. "You were with Parker Gage?"

Kate explained their meeting without going too much into detail. "He could have easily slipped out of his house and come over here to meet the victim. He doesn't live more than a ten-minute walk from here."

Sharon nodded and continued walking toward the victim. When they were around the backside of the large tree, Sharon pointed at the young woman who Kate assumed couldn't have been more than twenty-five. Her straight dark brown hair was cut in a severe bob at her chin and she wore simple understated makeup. She had the kind of soft, pleasant features with high cheekbones, full lips, and porcelain skin that didn't require much enhancing. The killer had closed the victim's eyes as he posed the body or she had shut them as she died. If not for the mortal chest wound, she could have simply fallen asleep next to the tree.

Declan grabbed gloves from Sharon and snapped them on. He crouched down low next to the body and checked her over. He carefully pulled the blanket down and then looked up at Sharon. "Did you check her for any identification?"

"We haven't gotten that far. Det. Briggs said not to disturb too much until you and Agent Walsh were on scene."

"That's good," Declan said as he reached out and pulled the blanket back even more. "Got an evidence bag, Sharon? We can put this right in there now."

Sharon left them for a moment and returned with a large evidence bag and marker to jot down the information needed on the front. Declan stepped out of the way to let Sharon work. After she finished and the blanket was secured in the bag, Declan and Kate looked over the victim and were surprised by what they saw. The woman's hands had been folded in her lap, and in between her fingers was a folded note.

Declan bent down and tugged the note free from her hands. Blood had dripped from her chest to the outside of the note. He unfolded the piece of paper carefully so that he did not spread the blood or disturb the writing. It was the same precise cursive penmanship as previous notes. Declan read it aloud for Kate and Sharon.

This victim probably doesn't surprise you. This is exactly what Margaret Kemble Gage and every other traitorous woman deserved. We underestimated the role of women during the Revolution but never again. Cunning, cruel, and manipulative – they deserved to die right along with their "Patriot" husbands.

"He's right. We knew he'd kill a woman. It was only a matter of time," Kate said, her voice tinged with frustration and sadness. She wasn't sure why but she felt this murder deeper than the others. "It's why we hid Ashley. At least, now I feel like that was the right choice, but this poor young woman was murdered in her place."

Declan shook his head. "Kate, you don't know for sure that the killer would have murdered Ashley. We were right to give her protection." He handed the note to Sharon for her to bag as evidence and then bent down again to inspect the body. He patted down her legs, trying not to move the body or disturb the scene in any way. When he was done, Declan stood. "I don't see a wallet or anything. We are going to have to wait until Dr. Graham pulls some prints."

As Sharon finished labeling the note, she looked between Kate and Declan. "Do we have any hope of catching this guy? We are doing everything we can. I did as you asked and got an intern to work on GEDmatch for me. He said it's a slow go because not much is coming back. It's like this guy is a ghost."

"He can't hide forever," Kate said, not sounding too confident.

"The Zodiac killer hid forever. He terrorized northern California in the 1960s, sent letters to the media, and then vanished into thin air," Sharon reminded them. "This city can't have a Zodiac killer. We have to catch him."

Declan nodded. "It's not the 1960s. Look at how high-tech DNA advancements are. You'll probably be the one to break the case, Sharon. Don't give up now."

It was clear Sharon was frustrated. They all were, but Declan's words seemed to spur a fire in her and she trudged off in the direction of her colleagues.

When she was gone, Declan turned to Kate. "We are going to catch him, right?"

"You don't sound as confident as you did seconds ago."

"I'm not, Kate. I said it for Sharon's benefit. We have to rally our team, but between you and me, this guy has me stumped."

Kate took a deep breath and let it out slowly. "Me too. I wonder who called it in."

"Let's go find Det. Briggs."

They walked away from the victim's body, but Kate glanced back once and made a silent promise that the young woman did not die in vain. She would find the killer and ensure they were brought to justice. Kate rarely made that promise to anyone.

It didn't take them long to find Det. Briggs among the other Boston police staff. "Det. Briggs," Declan said, approaching. Once he had the detective's attention, the three of them moved off from the others Declan detailed the note he had found on their first assessment of the scene.

"Do you know who called 911?"

"It was the killer. That's how we got out here so fast. He said he had just killed a woman and described where he left the body." Det Briggs pointed off in the direction of the victim. "Hidden away behind the tree like that, it could have been hours or into tomorrow until someone spotted her. Even if they saw someone sitting against the tree, if they didn't leave the walking path and walk around to the other side, they'd have no idea she was dead."

Kate glanced back to the victim, feeling the same sadness wash over her as before. She shook it off and refocused her attention. "I assume there are no witnesses."

Det. Briggs motioned with his finger for them to follow him. "We have one woman who has some information for us. She lives right off Boston Common, and when she saw the police lights and the crowd of people, she rushed over to tell us what she had seen earlier this evening."

"Did she see the killer?" Kate asked, the hope apparent in her question.

"I think you should talk to her. She was shaken up and I don't think I got the full story. I believe she saw the victim twice."

Det. Briggs walked them to a woman who stood with two uniformed cops. She wrung her hands and stood expressionless as Kate and Declan approached. Det. Briggs made introductions. "Maryanne came forward quickly with what she saw. We appreciate she didn't waste any time letting us know."

Declan didn't reach his hand out because he was still wearing gloves, but Kate did. "Let's walk over to the side here away from everyone and we can talk."

Maryanne shifted her eyes to the side and followed Kate away from the uniformed cops. Kate wanted to give the woman some space without everyone hovering around her. Even Det. Briggs had caught n to what Kate was doing and stepped back to let Declan and Kate e alone with the woman.

Maryanne breathed out loudly. "I appreciate that. It was getting a ttle overwhelming standing there. What do you want to know?"

"Just start at the beginning," Declan said. "First tell me how you know the woman you saw is the one who was murdered."

"Det. Briggs showed me her body, and I'll never forget her face." Maryanne swallowed hard.

"Understood," Declan said.

Maryanne seemed to gather up her courage. When she spoke again, her voice was stronger than before. "I got home from work right around five and had to take my dog for a walk, which I do here in Boston Common every night. As we passed by, I saw the woman standing near the tree talking to a man."

Declan and Kate shared a look. At once, they both asked, "You saw the killer?"

CHAPTER 43

Maryanne took a visible step back, a brief look of shock on her face. "Well, I…" she trailed off and then took a moment to compose herself while Kate and Declan tried to contain their excitement. Maryanne continued. "Let me tell you what I saw and then you can ask questions. I don't know if the man I saw is the killer or not. I came by with my dog and saw a woman standing by the walking path in the grass. She was talking to a man. I noticed her because she had a folded blanket in her hand, and I couldn't imagine anyone sitting out at night the way people do during the day. The temperature had already dropped and the snow had started. Big fat flakes at first, but you knew more was coming. Anyway, she and the man were talking. I walked by and that was that."

Declan started to ask a question and Maryanne shook her head. "Let me finish," she insisted. "I walked to the other end of Boston Common, the same path I take every evening. When I came back through, the couple was no longer visible to me, but I heard their voices hushed and angry. It was obvious they were arguing, but they hadn't looked happy when I saw them the first time. She looked stressed and he was trying to get information from her. She was stalling. I didn't hear what they were arguing about later, but I assumed the same thing. He was very angry the second time. As I walked off and got closer to my house, his voice got louder. I thought to myself that a public place isn't appropriate to argue like that, but it's none of my business. I didn't think anything of it again until thirty or forty minutes later when I saw all the cops around. From my window, it looked to be about the same area where I saw them so I rushed right over."

Kate had so many questions, she wasn't sure where she wanted to start. Declan looked at her to take the lead. "Did you see the man the second time you walked by?"

"No, I heard them arguing, but at that point, they were out of sight. I assumed they had stepped farther off the path for some privacy. I didn't see anything but shadows."

"Do you have any idea if the man you saw talking to her near the walking path was the same man she was later arguing with in the shadows?"

Maryanne stopped to think for a moment. She shrugged. "No, I guess I can't be certain. It was an assumption on my part that it was the same person. Why would she be arguing with two different people?"

Kate didn't know anything at that moment, but they couldn't make any assumptions. "Tell me about the man you saw with the victim the first time you walked by."

Maryanne described the man – tall, with dark hair, and wearing a tan wool sweater. She said there wasn't anything distinct about his face, she only saw a side profile. "I think he was handsome, if not a bit plain. An everyday sort of guy. There wasn't anything odd-looking about him. He stood near the woman but not touching her. At first when I passed by, it was obvious that they were discussing something. They were deep in conversation, but he wasn't angry then. He looked frustrated. Like she was holding back something he wanted to know. I heard her say, 'Charlie, I can't speculate like that. I can't tell you something I'm not sure of.'"

"Charlie?" Kate asked, not sure she had heard Maryanne correctly. "She said the man's name?"

"Yes, just once. I'm fairly certain that's what she called him, but that's a common name around here. I could count on both hands the number of men I know named Charles who go by Charlie."

"What are you thinking?" Declan asked Kate.

Her eyes shifted toward him, but she didn't say a word. She wasn't even sure she could articulate the horror of what she was thinking. Kate reached into her pocket and pulled out her phone. She typed a few words into the search engine and pulled up a photo. She showed it to Maryanne. "Does this look like the man you saw speaking to the victim?"

Maryanne took the phone and peered down at the photo. It didn't take her long. "Yes," she said, handing the phone back to Kate. "That's him. I'm sure of it. The same handsome if not plain face. I told you he looked like a million other men in Boston, but I'm sure this is him. Who is he?"

"Just give us a moment, please." Kate pulled Declan to the side and handed him her phone.

He squinted down at the photo and then furrowed his brow. He raised his head to Kate for some explanation. "This doesn't make any sense, Kate. This is Charlie Crain, the *Boston Globe* reporter. He can't be the killer. The killer was sending him letters."

"I know, but stranger things have happened. Killers put themselves in the middle of cases all the time. What if the letters came from him and he mailed them to himself to make it look like he was receiving them? He walked right into the middle of our investigation."

"Why would he do this? I think we would have had an inkling before now if it was him. Don't you think?"

Kate exhaled a breath. She would have liked to have thought so, but nothing about this case made sense. "Let me finish speaking to Maryanne. I'll see if I can get more information from her. You go and find Charlie. The hotel is only a few blocks away from here. You can walk it in less than fifteen minutes. Ten, maybe, if you're walking fast enough."

"There's supposed to be a uniformed cop at the hotel standing watch. They would have known if Charlie slipped out."

"This should be easy enough to confirm. Let's be discrete about it though, Declan. You're right. It's odd. Let's do what we can to protect his reputation until we have more information. This woman he met could have been a source on one of his articles for all we know."

"Are you going to tell Det. Briggs?"

Kate wasn't sure but withholding information from him probably wouldn't do anyone any good. "I'll stall until you can get over there and speak to him. Let me know as soon as you know anything."

With that, Declan left. Kate waited until he was out of sight and then walked back over to Maryanne. "I'm sorry about that. Charlie is someone we are familiar with, but not a person of interest. Can you tell me more about the interaction between Charlie and the victim?"

"I've told you everything I know, Agent Walsh." Maryanne paused and seemed to gather her thoughts. "When I walked by the first time, as I said, I thought it was odd because she had a blanket in her hands. I assumed she was planning to sit on the grass, which for the time of evening and the snow, I thought odd. That's why I got a good look at her. Otherwise, I don't pay much attention to people. The man, Charlie, stood next to her. They were facing each other, and he seemed to be trying to get information from her. She kept refusing. I have no idea what they were talking about. I wasn't close enough to hear everything they were saying."

"What about their body language? How were they interacting?"

Maryanne pursed her lips. "They were standing face to face. It was clear they knew each other. I wouldn't have been surprised if they were romantically involved. She didn't seem afraid if that's what you're after. If I'm remembering correctly, at one point, he reached out and touched her arm. She didn't pull back, but she did look anxious or stressed by the conversation. Her face was constricted, and she shook her head a few times as they spoke. He was calm though. He wasn't angry. If anything, he was too calm for an argument. He was trying to get something from her. But there was no shouting or yelling at that time. It was a marked difference to the vibe I got when I walked back and passed them the second time."

"Did they look at you or speak to you when you walked by the first time?"

"No, they seemed to be in their own little world. They were focused on each other."

The next point was critical, and Kate hoped Maryanne could give the details needed. "This is important, Maryanne," Kate stressed. "How long was it between the first time you saw them and when you walked by again?"

Maryanne didn't even need to think. "Twenty to twenty-five minutes. This is a path I walk every night. You and I can walk it right now if you'd like to test it out." Maryanne turned and pointed to a gate in the fence that surrounded the outside of Boston Common. "I came right through that gate from across the street. I pass by here first and at the end of my walk. My total walk time is usually thirty minutes."

That was more than enough time for Charlie to have given up and left and someone else to have joined the woman. It might not be likely, but it was possible. "Tell me the first thing you noticed when you came back through and passed them again."

"I had forgotten about them on the rest of the walk. My mind was on work, but the first thing I noticed was hushed angry voices. I couldn't see anyone so I was a bit startled. Boston Common is generally safe, but I'm still a woman walking alone at night in a dark park. I'm always cautious, so the voices startled me. It was worse I couldn't see anyone.

I knew there were people off in the distance someplace that I couldn't see. I heard a woman, but her voice was muffled and I couldn't make out what she was saying. That's when I remembered the couple who had been talking earlier. I assumed it was them. I figured maybe they had stepped back from the path as their conversation grew more heated. By the time I reached the gate, his voice was louder and angrier."

"Could you hear what he was saying?"

"Not really. Although his voice sounded angrier and louder, their voices were somewhat muffled. I didn't hear their conversation. I heard words here or there."

"That's okay," Kate said, excited. "Anything will help at this point."

Maryanne nodded. "I heard one word above the others loud and clear. He called her a traitor. Then I heard the word punished. That's it though. Out of context, it didn't make much sense. Traitor and punished aren't words you hear in conversation every day. Who even speaks like that to a grown woman?" Maryanne reached her hand up to her face and rubbed her jawline. "Do you think if I went over and intervened, I might have saved her?"

Kate reached out and patted Maryanne's hand. "No, you might have ended up a victim as well. It was good you kept walking and went to the safety of your home. I'm glad though you noticed the cops and came back to tell us what you saw. It's important and might even be the break we need in this case."

A tear ran down Maryanne's cheek. "Will I ever forget her face? It's so horrific. I know the police had to show me her body so I could identify if it was the same person, but I don't think I'll ever get the image of that poor girl dead against the tree out of my mind."

"I don't know if it will ever leave you," Kate said honestly. "It will fade in time as most things do. Don't hesitate to reach out for some counseling to talk about it. It's helped a lot of people."

Maryanne nodded and Kate walked her back to the uniformed cops where she had been standing before. One of the Boston police detectives walked Maryanne back to her house and would take a formal statement there. As they walked off, Det. Briggs turned to Kate for details about the interview. He only started to speak when Kate's phone rang. She apologized and stepped off to the side to take it.

"Kate, you need to get over here right now and bring Det. Briggs. Charlie has been gone for the last three hours and no one has seen him. His room is trashed."

CHAPTER 44

"I don't understand what you're saying," Det. Briggs shouted a bit out of breath as he and Kate raced across Boston Common toward Boylston Street and the Fairmont Copley Hotel a few blocks down on St. James Street. "What did the witness say?"

"She said the woman was arguing with a man named Charlie. I pulled up a photo of Charlie Crain, and she made a positive identification." Kate stepped around a couple who were walking slowly hand in hand.

Det. Briggs did the same and caught up to Kate. "He's in the safety of a hotel with cops watching him. How could it be him? That doesn't make any sense."

"I know. I know," Kate said frustrated. "That's what Declan and I thought, too. That's why I sent Declan over to the hotel to speak to him while I finished with the witness."

They shoved past a few more people and both resisted the urge to run along the crowded sidewalks. Kate turned to him as they found a clearing. "Det. Briggs, there was enough time in between when Maryanne saw Charlie and then when the victim and killer were arguing back farther out of sight. Twenty to twenty-five minutes had passed. I'm not insinuating Charlie is the killer, but I am saying he has to be a person of interest. Given he's gone, it's even more concerning."

Det. Briggs cursed under his breath. "How can he be gone? Wha were my officers doing?"

"I don't know. I didn't get the full story from Declan. You know everything I do right now."

Kate and Det. Briggs didn't say anything else as they walked. They turned on Arlington Street and walked two blocks to St. James. Once there, the sidewalks opened up even more and they moved quickly to the hotel. Inside, they found two Boston cops standing in the lobby.

"How could you lose him?" Det. Briggs shouted when he saw them.

Both cops paled when they saw the detective but didn't say a word. Other guests in the hotel turned around and were watching them. Kate put a hand on Det. Briggs's back and pushed him toward the elevator. "Let's not cause a scene," she said. She turned and waved for the officers to follow her.

They rode the elevator to the fourth floor. Declan had said Charlie's room was at the very end of the hall. It would have been hard to miss. Two more uniformed cops stood in the hallway outside the room. As Kate approached, Declan stepped out.

"It's a mess. His laptop is gone, but his clothing is still here. It looks like some papers and files were tossed as well. Someone was looking for something."

Det. Briggs caught his breath and, with his hands on his hips, asked his question again. "How did he get away?"

A tall dark-haired cop responded, "He said he wanted some fresh air. We had been letting him walk down to the main lobby and step outside. We have one officer outside the room door and another in the lobby. He has gone down and back several times without incident. The officer watched him step into the elevator and radioed down to the other officer that he was on his way down. He never got off the elevator down there. We have been searching for him since."

"Did you call it in?" Det. Briggs asked.

"No, we didn't and we should have because the officer up here left the room and started a search. That's when the room was trashed. He got back up here and the door was open. That was the same time Agent James arrived."

Declan stepped forward. "Det. Briggs, it was an honest mistake. Charlie wasn't a prisoner. He wasn't confined to his room. He had the freedom to do what he needed. He was here for his protection only."

Det. Briggs nodded and calmed down a bit. "Has anyone checked the security footage?"

Declan responded, "We've requested it and are waiting for hotel security to call us when they have it ready."

"Any incoming or outgoing calls?" Kate asked, relieved that Det. Briggs had calmed down. They couldn't focus on the task at hand if they were all hyped up placing blame.

"One call outgoing," Declan said and caught her eye. "It was to 911."

"911?" Det. Briggs asked.

Declan nodded. "We are waiting for the report of that call. Either Charlie came back up here and was in some distress or maybe the killer called 911 from here to report the body."

"Let me make a call," Det. Briggs said, reaching for his phone and moving down the hall away from them.

Kate stepped around Declan and into the hotel room. It was a larger suite with a small living room area and desk and bedroom. There were papers strewn all over the floor in the living room area. As Kate moved farther into the next room that had the bed, the destruction was even worse. The bedside table drawers had been pulled out, and the bed linens had been ripped off and tossed in a heap on the floor. Even the pillows had been torn out of pillowcases and ripped open. Charlie had file boxes stacked against the wall. Those had been tossed with pages pulled out of file folders and then thrown to the ground. Even the clothing he had in dresser drawers and the closet had been taken out and searched, left in a heap on the floor.

"I don't think Charlie did this, Declan. This was the work of someone else. Are you sure the cops didn't search his room and leave it like this?"

Declan stepped toward her. "I'm positive. They were standing outside the door when I arrived. You should have seen the cop's face. He had no idea what was going on. I was the first person in the room."

Kate took another minute to glance around, taking in the mess and destruction. Whoever did this was in a hurry and had something specific in mind that they were searching for. Charlie wouldn't need to make this kind of mess to access something he needed.

"What are you thinking?" Declan asked, snapping Kate out of her train of thought.

"It doesn't look staged. Charlie wouldn't need to do this to find something of his own. I was wondering if he might have staged it to look like this, but why leave and then come back and do this. That doesn't make any sense."

"What do you think happened then?"

"I have no idea, but we need to find Charlie. I'm going to call his office and check there for him and then we can check his home. If no one has seen him, we need to put out an all-points bulletin to local police to be on the lookout for him."

"Should we go public with it right now?" Declan asked.

"Not yet. Not until we can get a handle on what's happening here. We don't know if he's a suspect or a victim."

"That makes sense."

"Agent Walsh. Agent James," Det. Briggs said as he walked into the bedroom. "I have some information. I tracked down the caller information from the 911 call that told us there was a body in Boston Common. It came from here in the hotel. I don't know if it was specifically this phone, but the number traces back to the hotel phone number."

Kate let that information sink in, but she still wasn't sure what it meant. The obvious was that Charlie killed the girl, came back to his room, tossed the place, and made the call. Then he managed to get past the cops and escape into the night. But that didn't feel quite right.

She turned to Det. Briggs. "We need the surveillance footage to see who was coming and going from this room and at what time."

"I'll make the call to security again." Declan placed the call and spoke to someone for a moment, answering in clipped one-word responses. When he was done, he said to Kate and Det. Briggs, "They have the surveillance footage ready for us down in their office. We need officers standing guard here though. I don't want anyone coming or going from this room. Sharon has a team coming over here to dust for prints and see what other evidence they can collect."

Det. Briggs called officers from the hallway and gave them explicit instructions not to enter the room or allow anyone else to enter who didn't have an FBI badge. The officers assured him that the instructions would be followed.

Declan, Kate, and Det. Briggs made their way down to the first floor and navigated two long corridors to the staff entrance. There, the chief of security was waiting for them. He introduced himself as Ken Miller and directed them back to his office.

Ken pointed to his desk and computer, which had a still image of Charlie standing in the hotel hallway outside of his room. "I have the video set up from when the guest first left his room today. You can see he speaks to the cop standing guard in the hallway and then proceeds to the elevator. He does not go down to the first floor. He gets off at the second. It took me a while to find him, but he headed for the stairway and down to the first floor in the back of the building. From there, he slips out of a side door that leads into an alleyway and then the street. We lose him after that."

Kate, Declan, and Det. Briggs moved closer to the screen as Ken hit play. They watched exactly what Ken had just described. Charlie didn't look upset or worried or even in a hurry. He made pleasant conversation with the cop and then headed down to the elevator. The video showed him checking his phone and putting it back in his pocket. He remained calm and emotionless the whole time. Kate understood how the cop standing guard was so easily duped.

They watched the surveillance feed until Charlie slipped out the side door and was gone from sight. Kate glanced at the time stamp and it was shortly before five. He would have had just enough time to make the quick walk to Boston Common and be seen by Maryanne speaking to the victim. What's absent from the video is telling – no note and no weapon. That's not to say he didn't have it stashed someplace or in his pocket, but Kate thought that unlikely.

Declan glanced back at Kate and she was sure he was thinking the same thing.

He asked, "Do you have the next video when someone returns to he room?"

"I do," Ken said, clicking a few buttons on his keyboard. "You can't ee his face because he has a hood up and stays shielded from view of the cameras like he knew they were there. He comes up the back tairway, waits until the hallway is clear, and then enters the room. He s in there approximately twelve minutes and then leaves with some apers and a laptop."

"How does he get in a locked room?" Det. Briggs asked.

Ken craned his neck around to look at him. "He has a key card."

"Just play it," Declan said, blowing out a frustrated breath.

Ken clicked play and the screen came to life again. This time a man n black pants and a black hooded sweatshirt made his way into the allway from a stairway entrance. Given the proximity of Charlie's oom to the stairs, the man didn't have to take more than ten steps to the hotel room door. He pulled a keycard from his pocket and entered the room. As Ken said, he left, heading to the same stairway twelve minutes later.

"That's not Charlie Crain," Det. Briggs said. "There is no way that's him."

He was right, that wasn't Charlie, which meant in all likelihood he was in danger or already dead.

CHAPTER 45

Kate didn't want to talk in front of Ken so she motioned with her head for Det. Briggs and Declan to follow her out. She wanted to find a place where they could speak privately and Kate could call Charlie's work. Before they left, Declan thanked Ken for the surveillance footage and instructed him to make the FBI a copy. He told them someone from the crime scene unit would be down to collect it shortly.

They made their way back to the main part of the hotel and stepped into the corridor. "We need someplace private to talk," Kate said. "Where can we go?"

"I asked the hotel staff for a conference room earlier we can use as a command center. They gave me space." Det. Briggs set off down the hall. Kate and Declan followed behind him as they traversed hall after hall. The room Det. Briggs had been given was across the hotel lobby to another part of the hotel, but the space was quiet and far away from hotel guests. Declan and Det. Briggs pulled out chairs and sat at the table. Kate, keyed up and anxious, paced in front of them.

"What do we know so far?" Declan asked.

Kate spoke as she paced. "We know Charlie left the room right before the meeting with the victim. We know he ditched his protection detail and had enough time to walk to Boston Common before Maryanne would have seen him. We know shortly after the time we suspect the murder happened, a man who was not Charlie was back at his room with the keycard and tossed the place, taking papers and a laptop. The man on that video the second time wasn't Charlie. He was taller and slimmer not to mention dressed differently than Charlie who was in jeans and a sweater when he left."

Declan leaned back in his chair. "What does all that add up to for you?"

Kate stopped pacing and turned to face him. "I think it leaves us with three options – Charlie is working with the killer, he's in danger, or he's dead. I don't think we can assume anything else at this point. Your thoughts?"

Declan shrugged. "Same, I guess. I have a hard time thinking Charlie is the killer. I don't think he's working with him either, but I don't think we can rule that out completely. I'm willing to leave it on the table."

Det. Briggs remained silent, but his furrowed brow and the concern in his eyes told Kate he had something important to say. She encouraged him to speak up and not hold back.

"I don't want to think Charlie is the killer. I don't. I like the guy. He seemed genuinely freaked out by the case and wanted to help, but can we rule out he is the killer? Maybe this person who tossed his room is someone helping him and making it look like Charlie is in danger Maybe it's all a big con to throw us off his trail."

It was an astute observation that Kate hadn't wanted to consider but Det. Briggs was on the mark. She did not argue with him. "You're right, Det. Briggs. Let's add that possibility to the list. I'm going to call his boss and try to track him down at the newspaper. Then Declan and I will go over to his house and see if he's there. We might need to get a search warrant for his place."

Declan motioned with his hand for Kate's attention. "What about Ashley?"

Kate had forgotten all about her. "She's here in this hotel, right? We put her and Charlie on different floors to save on manpower in the lobby. Has anyone spoken to her?"

Declan shook his head. "I only thought of her right now. We should at least check on her while we are here. If the killer knew Charlie was here, there's no reason he wouldn't know Ashley was here, too."

Declan decided to find Ashley while Kate called the newspaper. Det. Briggs would reach out to Carmen Langston and work on a search warrant for Charlie's residence. After they left the room, Kate called Charlie's office. There was no answer on his work line so she called his boss, Vince Darcy. Kate had to leave a message asking him to return the call as soon as possible. It was late and she assumed he had already left his office. Kate had no more than set her phone down when it rang. It was Charlie's boss returning the call.

Kate answered quickly and explained who she was and that she was looking for Charlie. "Have you heard from him at all today?"

"I have. I spoke to him earlier in the day. He had made a plan to meet with Amy Wheeler, one of the researchers here at the newspaper. I told him it was risky to leave the hotel away from his protective details, but he insisted that Amy had the information he needed. Charlie had her working on something related to the murder investigation. He said the information that Amy found might break the case wide open, but he wouldn't disclose it in our call. He said he had to confirm a few things before he could go public with it."

A wave of fear washed over Kate. She asked, "Do you know what time they were supposed to meet?"

"I don't, Agent Walsh." Vince paused and then with concern in his voice asked, "Is everything okay? You're starting to worry me."

"Have you heard from Amy since the meeting?"

"No, I haven't spoken to either one of them."

Kate wasn't sure what information she should disclose or the best way to go about it, but there was a nameless victim headed for the morgue. The truth would have to win out over any confidentiality at the moment.

Kate sat down in a chair and explained the situation. "There was another murder this evening in Boston Common. We have a witness who places Charlie speaking to the victim shortly before her death. Charlie is now missing from the hotel. We don't believe he ever came back to his room, but someone did and they were looking for something. They trashed the room and took his laptop and paper files. We must find him. We have not searched his home yet, but do you know of any place he might go?"

Kate was met with dead silence on the other end of the line. It lasted so long she wondered if they had been disconnected. "Vince, are you there?"

"Yes, I'm sorry. I don't know what to say. Are you sure the victim is Amy?"

"No, we are still waiting on identification of the victim, but Charlie was seen speaking to the woman who was murdered. I'm waiting for word from the medical examiner's office after they pull her prints but it could take a while."

"Is there any way we can meet in person? I might be able to provide identification." Vince paused again and took an audible breath. "Amy is my niece, Agent Walsh. I'm the only family she has in the area."

"Yes, of course. I can call the medical examiner right now and tell him we are on our way."

"Do you think Charlie killed her?" Vince asked, but didn't give Kate time to respond. "I'm sorry, I can't believe that he would do that. Charlie and Amy were close. I thought they might be dating, but we have a policy against office relationships, so I never knew for sure. can't imagine he would hurt her."

"We don't know Charlie's role in this, if any, or if he is in danger."

"Do you need to access his apartment? I have the key and permission to enter. I've taken in his mail and watched the place for him when he's traveled. Charlie and I have worked together for a long time. I'm more than his boss. I thought we were friends."

"I planned to head to Charlie's residence right after I got off the phone with you. We are working on getting a search warrant, but let me get back to you on that. I'll call Dr. Graham at the medical examiner's office and let you know when to meet us. I'll be in touch soon."

Kate ended the call and quickly called Dr. Graham. She had no idea if they had even removed the victim's body from Boston Common yet. She hoped they had, but Kate had no idea how long the scene would take to process. Dr. Graham didn't answer his cellphone but his assistant did. They were in the process of moving the body to the morgue now and hadn't taken fingerprints yet. It would be at least an hour before they'd be ready for someone to come view the body. Kate confirmed that they'd be there then.

In the meantime, Kate would go to Charlie's apartment and see if he was there. As Kate left the conference room in search of Declan, she ran into Det. Briggs in the hall. He confirmed that Carmen was in the process of getting a judge to sign off on a search warrant for Charlie's apartment. Carmen indicated it shouldn't be a problem given the witness statement and the fact that Charlie was missing.

"That's good," Kate said. "We might have a lead on the victim's identity." She explained the call to Vince at the newspaper. "Unfortunately, the victim might be his niece. I'm going to meet Vince at the morgue in about an hour for identification. At least, this gives us more to go on."

"What do you want me to focus on?" Det. Briggs asked, walking with Kate to the main lobby of the hotel.

"Running down leads and canvassing to see if there are other witnesses out there who might have seen anything in Boston Common. I think we should put the basics on the news and ask people to call in. It would be fresh in anyone's mind. The longer we delay, the more difficult it will be for people to remember accurately. You know how witnesses can be. We also need to make sure that you have officers on Ashley."

As they reached the lobby, Declan stood in the middle of the room speaking to two uniformed Boston cops. He waved Kate and Det. Briggs over. "Ashley is secure in her room. She has no idea anything is going on. I didn't tell her anything. I told her I was checking in to see if she needed anything. She'll know once this hits the news, but I didn't want to say anything right now in case you want to tell her."

"It can wait. We have more important things to do." Kate turned her attention to the two cops. "We need to make sure Ashley doesn't leave her room. Send up room service. Let someone run errands for her. Under no circumstances does anyone enter or leave that room unless escorted by a Boston police officer. Understood?"

Both men nodded and assured Kate they wouldn't move from her room and wouldn't let her leave. As they walked off, Kate gave Declan a quick overview of the call with Charlie's boss and the update about the victim. "We have a lot of ground to cover tonight. Let's head over to Charlie's apartment first and make sure he isn't hiding out there."

Declan and Kate said goodbye to Det. Briggs and then headed off into the cold Boston night air. The snow blew across their faces and the ground already had at least an inch piling up. Neither was dressed for the storm that had arrived.

CHAPTER 46

Kate and Declan walked from the hotel to Charlie's brownstone apartment in record time. As they climbed the last few steps to the third floor, it was clear someone had recently been there. Charlie's door, the only one on that floor, was open and papers had drifted into the hall. Someone had left lights on in the apartment, so at least they weren't in total darkness.

As they reached the landing and saw the mess, Declan and Kate stopped in their tracks and both immediately reached for their guns. Declan looked back at Kate, and without saying a word, motioned with his hand and shifted his eyes in the direction he needed her to take. Kate nodded once in understanding and then Declan advanced. Kate took the left side and Declan the right, advancing first to the door while she covered his side and back.

"Charlie Crain, it's Agents James and Walsh. If you're here, please come out with your hands up," Declan yelled loud enough that the whole building probably heard him. There was no response, just dead air. Declan took another step toward the door and stepped over the papers to enter the apartment. He called out Charlie's name again.

They entered the living room, which led back into a dining room and kitchen in the back. Off the dining room was a small hallway with a bathroom and two bedrooms. They walked through looking in closets and small spaces until they were sure it had been cleared and they were alone.

It wasn't until they were back in the living room that they noticed some small droplets of blood near the front window. Declan reached for a light switch on the wall and turned on the ceiling light.

He went closer to the spot and inspected. "It's fresh, Kate. It looks like it would be sticky to the touch. We are going to need to get the crime scene unit up here."

Kate looked around the living room. The furniture seemed in place and there didn't appear to be signs of a struggle, but like the hotel room, it appeared to have been thoroughly searched. "I can't say by looking that there was a struggle, but something happened here."

"Let me search again. Give Det. Briggs a call and let him know we need a crime scene unit here as soon as possible. See if they can rush the search warrant, too."

Kate reached for her phone and made the call. Det. Briggs answered on the first ring and listened. He asked a few questions and seemed as confused by the situation as Kate and Declan. Det. Briggs informed her that the FBI crime scene unit had just arrived at the hotel and he'd speak to Sharon and give her an update. In the meantime, he offered to send a crime scene unit from the Boston Police Department. Kate declined – not because they weren't excellent – she wanted the continuity of the FBI on the scene. Det. Briggs understood.

Kate stood in the middle of the room feeling paralyzed by the circumstances in front of her. She had no way to stop the killer who was terrorizing the city, and it didn't seem like he would stop anytime soon. He was close enough to the people around the investigation that he knew Charlie and Amy were making headway in identifying him. He knew to strike quickly and with precision to ensure that information didn't come to light. Kate had the sinking feeling she had already met and interacted with the killer. She just had no idea who it was.

Declan came back into the room and headed for the door. "I'm going downstairs to speak to the neighbors and see if they saw or heard anything. There should be video surveillance that the landlord can access. Did you call Det. Briggs?"

Kate explained the call and the delay in Sharon and her team coming to the apartment. "I told them we'd wait. I'd rather have the FBI gather evidence than the Boston Police Department and have evidence scattered between departments."

"Good call but that means I'm going to need to wait here while you go to the morgue."

Kate had thought of that and she had no problem going alone, but Declan wasn't so sure.

He turned back to her. "Kate, take a cab. I don't want you to walk back to your house alone at night and get your car. Take a cab, and I'll meet you over there if Sharon gets here soon enough."

"I'll be fine," Kate assured him, but her voice faltered. She thought better of it. "I'll take a cab."

Twenty minutes later, Kate stood in the lobby of the morgue waiting for Vince Darcy. She had spoken briefly to Dr. Graham and explained the situation. His normal unflappable demeanor seemed a bit shaken by the events of the evening. Kate wanted to ask if he was okay, but she assumed he wouldn't like that she had noticed he was off his game. She offered him a reassuring smile instead and promised the FBI was working as hard as they could to solve these crimes.

Soon after Dr. Graham left, Vince arrived. He was about her height with wavy dark hair. He had crinkles around his blue eyes and a warm smile, even under the circumstances.

He reached out his hand to her. "I appreciate you meeting me here. I didn't want to do this alone."

"We'd never make you do that. If you'd rather not do this at all, there are other ways we can identify the victim."

"No," Vince said, shaking his head. "This is the fastest way, and if it's my niece, I want to know. I think it's not knowing what to anticipate that's the hardest part."

Kate understood that better than he knew. "Let's go then and get this over as quickly as possible for you."

Kate walked Vince through the door into the main morgue office and down a long sterile corridor to the room Dr. Graham had indicated. She looked through the square window in the door and saw that he was ready for them. The body had been laid out on a stretcher and covered with a white sheet. Kate turned the handle and opened the door. Dr. Graham looked up as they entered and introduced himself to Vince.

"I appreciate you coming down here so quickly. I know this is hard for a family member to do, but it does expedite the identification process," Dr. Graham explained.

Vince nodded and walked tentatively toward him and the body Once they were standing nearby, Dr. Graham pulled back the sheet from the victim's face. Vince sucked in a sharp breath.

"That's Amy," he said barely loud enough for Kate to hear him. "How did she die?"

Dr. Graham pulled the sheet back over Amy's face. "She suffered a chest wound with a dagger, we believe. I've not had an opportunity to examine further, but that's the initial assessment from the scene."

Vince looked at Kate. "Like the others then?"

"From what we can tell, yes, it appears so."

"Do we know anything about Charlie yet?"

Kate shook her head. "He wasn't at his apartment, but like his hotel room, it appears to have been thoroughly searched by someone. Agent James is there now waiting for a crime scene unit. We still don't know Charlie's whereabouts though." Kate put her hand on Vince's arm. "Let's go out front and let Dr. Graham continue his work. There are few things I want to ask you."

"Feel free to use my office," Dr. Graham offered. "It's two doors down on the right."

Kate appreciated the gesture so they wouldn't have to stand in the front lobby and talk. Kate and Vince found Dr. Graham's office. Kate flicked on the overhead light as they entered and she sat down in a chair at a small round table. Vince sat down across from her.

"I'm very sorry for your loss," Kate said. "You said that you're her only family here in Boston. Do her parents reside someplace else?"

"No. Unfortunately, Amy lost both of her parents in a car accident when she was in her twenties. She grew up in New Hampshire and moved here for college and stayed. She bounced around from job to job for a few years but came to the newspaper about a year ago. She is one of the best researchers we have. She had a real knack for it."

"Do you have any idea what Charlie had her working on?"

"Not specifically, no. We have three researchers at the paper who assist with fact-checking and research to help our reporters who are working on bigger or more complex stories. Charlie and Amy had worked together several times. She is the only researcher he used because she was that good. As I said before, I think their relationship might have developed outside of work, but I don't know that for sure."

Vince paused and rubbed his eyes. It looked as if he were trying to hold back tears Kate was sure he'd shed as soon as he left the building.

Vince rested his hands on the table. "These murders were personal to Charlie. He was very upset after receiving the killer's letters. I'm surprised he dodged his protective detail. He had expressed to me more than once that he was glad you had convinced him to go into protective custody. Charlie didn't even tell me where he was going. You've mentioned his hotel room a few times. I didn't even know he was in a hotel. I figured it was some sort of safe house. That tells me that whatever he thought Amy knew was critical to solving this case.

Charlie was willing to risk his safety to get the information."

Kate locked eyes with Vince. "Does that mean you don't believe Charlie could have killed your niece?"

"Absolutely not. The more I've thought about it, the more it's impossible. Charlie has never shown any propensity towards violence, and I've known him for more than twenty years. He has worked the crime beat for most of his career and he takes great pride in seeing justice prevail. There is no way he is a killer."

Kate thought as much, but hearing someone so close to Charlie say it was the final confirmation she needed to remove him as a person of interest. "Is there anything you can tell me about Amy's final hours?"

Vince dropped his head, looking down at the table. "I wish I could tell you more. I wish I had spent more time with her or taken her to lunch or something meaningful, but it was a regular day. I saw her at her desk. She mentioned Charlie had reached out to her and wanted some of her research. She wasn't sure she should share it yet because it wasn't complete. I think she was worried it might have been a slanted opinion, but she didn't share the specifics of the research. Amy was very fair. If she dug up dirt on someone, she made sure to search for counterarguments. She went out of her way to nail down facts that painted the whole picture rather than just told the side of the story the reporter might be hoping for. I called Charlie on his cellphone and asked what his plan was concerning this research. That's when he told me he was going to ditch his protective detail long enough to meet with Amy and convince her to give him what she found. I wish now I had talked him out of it, but I figured he knew best."

Kate sat back and considered what Vince said. She bit at her lip in thought. "Is there anyone else who might have known about Amy's research? Someone else at the newspaper perhaps?"

"I don't think so. Amy remained tightlipped about her work sometimes even after the story ran. Her discretion was what made her so good."

"Someone knew," Kate said stressing the point. "If Charlie isn't the killer, and I'm fairly convinced he's not, then someone else knew Amy and Charlie were close to identifying the killer. It's someone close. If I mention a few names to you, would you know if they were men your niece might have known?"

"Try me."

Kate listed off a few names of members of The Founders, throwing Parker Gage and Mark Boyle into the mix. She didn't want to bias him, so she added several other names to her list.

Vince shook his head at each one. "None of those names sound familiar to me, but I don't know everyone my niece knows."

Kate asked a few more questions, and when it was clear there wasn't anything else Vince was able to provide, she told him she'd follow up as she knew more. Vince asked if she'd walk out with him. Kate got up and followed him through the lobby and outside. When they were in the parking lot, Vince reached out and shook Kate's hand. From his palm to hers, he passed her a small thumb drive.

Vince looked around and then said in a hushed tone. "I don't know who to trust either, but this is everything from Amy's computer in a file she had marked for this case. I didn't look through it, but I thought this might help. Some of the names you mentioned might be on there."

Kate felt the weight of his words and the coolness of the thumb drive against her palm. She slipped it into her pocket. "I appreciate this more than you know."

CHAPTER 47

It was quarter past midnight when Declan arrived back at Kate's house. He called her name from the kitchen and thanked her for having the house well-heated. He shook his head free of snow as he met her in the living room. She sat curled up on the couch under a blanket while she scrolled through Amy's research.

"I can't believe the storm came on like that. They weren't even calling for snow and we have at least six inches out there." Declan sat down next to her and peeled off his wet socks. "We got nothing on the surveillance video. The landlord shut it off after he had to turn the video over to the FBI when Justin dropped off that letter. He figured with Charlie gone, nothing would happen and he didn't want to get mixed up in the case again. Not the smartest man."

Declan filled Kate in on the rest of his time. He had remained at Charlie's apartment while the crime scene investigators did their job. They'd have to test the droplets of blood and compare them to see who it belonged to, and that probably wouldn't happen until morning. Sharon's team had burned themselves out, going from scene to scene. Declan made sure they were all sent home for a good night's rest. He had also worked with Det. Briggs to make a statement on the eleven o'clock news about the search for Charlie Crain, making sure to mention he was a witness and not a person of interest.

Declan pulled the corner of Kate's blanket around him and moved in closer to her. "What do you have there?"

Kate had texted Declan earlier after meeting Vince to confirm that the victim was his niece. Declan suggested that there wasn't anything else she could do and he'd meet her back at the house. That was fine as Kate wanted to start digging into Amy's research, but she hadn't had the chance to tell Declan about it. She moved her laptop screen so he could see. "Vince Darcy from the *Boston Globe* gave me a thumb drive with Amy's research. He said he pulled everything from her computer that was in a file labeled for the case. He's nervous about who to trust, and he should be. He even made me leave the medical examiner's office to go out into the dark parking lot to slip the drive to me as he shook my hand."

"I'd be nervous, too, if I were him. You said earlier you think the killer is someone close to us. It has to be, Kate. It's someone watching very closely. They know where you live. They knew where Charlie lived and where we were keeping him." Declan read the page Kate had pulled up on the screen. It was research on Mark Boyle. "It seems she had zeroed in on Mark."

"It's more than Mark," Kate explained, pulling the laptop closer to her and scrolling through some files for Declan. "She researched almost all The Founders members. Somehow, she got a roster of names that she was working from. She also pulled research on former members, but it doesn't look like she got as far with that."

Declan whistled. "Amy put in a good deal of effort to help Charlie. What did she find that was so interesting to him?"

Kate gestured with her hand toward her laptop screen. "That's the problem. I don't know. It's not clear. She has files on each person, but there is nothing significant that's jumping out to me. She hit on something, but I don't think she confirmed it based on what Vince told me and the witness said. Amy was hesitant to give the information to Charlie. Vince said Amy took her job seriously and that she was overly cautious about ruining anyone's reputation. She told Charlie enough that it was worth the risk to ditch his protective detail and meet up with her. It was significant enough that the killer targeted her."

Declan rested his head back on the couch and stared up at the ceiling. "Is that bothering you at all?"

"What?" Kate asked, turning to look at him.

"Most serial killers start with people close and then branch out. This killer seemed to target people at random like Jordan Williams and Pete Amato. There's no connection that we know of. It seemed like random victim selection for the most part. Now, he's killing people close to him. First, it was Justin and now Amy."

"We don't know that he knew Amy," Kate countered.

"True, but I'd assume this wasn't random."

Kate considered what Declan said because it was unlike other serial killers, but then again, this guy wasn't like any killer she had encountered before. She tried to explain her reasoning to Declan.

"We have to throw out the usual playbook with this killer because his motivations aren't like other killers we have dealt with before. This is part political and part revenge. Killing Justin made sense. Maybe the killer felt Justin wronged him somehow, and Amy may have identified him. She was in a way the perfect representation for Thomas Gage's wife. A spy and someone willing to do him in."

Declan shrugged. "I guess that makes sense. Do you think Charlie is dead?"

Kate sighed. "I don't know. I've been thinking about him all nigh I think we'll know very soon. This killer is all about the show. If he kills Charlie, the killer will direct us to his body. I think, for now, w have to consider him missing. Whether he is in hiding or the killer has him, I don't know. He is a direct descendent of Benjamin Franklin I'm worried the killer is moving to people with stronger ancestral ties to the Revolutionary War."

Declan sat forward. "That means you're more in danger now than you were before."

Kate shook her head. "I wouldn't say that. This killer knows where I live. He could have tried to strike at any time, but he hasn't. I think, if anything, he's enjoying playing cat and mouse with me."

Declan's phone chimed and both of their heads snapped to attention, looking at his phone on the coffee table. "I'm almost afraid to look at it." He reached for it and read the text. "It's Sharon. Even though I told her to go home after leaving Charlie's apartment, she went back to the lab. We used his toothbrush for a DNA sample and she matched it to the blood we found on the floor. It's Charlie's. Whatever happened, he made it back to his apartment. It didn't look like there was too much of a struggle other than the place had been searched. I can't explain it, Katie."

"I can't explain it either," Kate lamented.

Declan stood and stretched. "I need a shower and then I'm going to bed. I told Det. Briggs that I'd meet him at the police station at eight."

"I'm headed up in a minute, too." Kate focused her eyes on her laptop and Declan headed for the stairs. As he started to climb, Kate stopped him. "Unless you need me to go with you, I thought tomorrow I might stay here and go through more of this research. There's something that's been nagging at me. I feel like there's something I heard a while ago or read in my father's papers that might be relevant. I want to spend some time going through that. It's annoying me I can't remember."

Declan walked back down two steps to the floor and leaned on the banister. "Are you sure you want to stay here alone? Wouldn't you rather go to the office and do that?"

Kate smiled. "I'll be fine here. Besides, I can take this research with me, but I can't drag all the boxes my father has upstairs down to the office. The doors are locked. I'm armed. I'm probably safer here than I am out there." Kate could tell by the look on Declan's face he wasn't buying it, but he didn't argue with her. She assumed he was too tired to put up a fight, which is precisely why she told him tonight and not in the morning.

"I'm calling Det. Briggs in the morning and having him send a squad car to sit out front. You're having a security detail whether you like it or not." With that, Declan turned and walked upstairs not giving Kate any chance to complain.

Kate wasn't even going to bother. She knew Declan would do whatever he wanted to whether she wanted him to or not. She wasn't going to let on, but she appreciated that he worried about her. In this case, Kate believed it wasn't needed, but it certainly couldn't hurt.

Kate refocused her attention on the laptop. She went back to the research file on Mark Boyle. It listed his employment, length of time with The Founders, and some of his activities. Amy had even taken screenshots of questionable social media posts. There was nothing in the file though that they didn't already know.

Kate closed Mark's file and opened a file for another member of The Founders but found, after reading for about ten minutes, her eyes grew heavy. She decided fighting sleep wouldn't do her any good. She shut down her laptop and set it on the coffee table. She'd get back to it in the morning.

Kate double checked all the doors to make sure they were locked and looked out the back window after she shut off the light to make sure there was no one out there. Kate would never admit it to Declan but she was concerned about her safety. The killer had struck to close to home for her liking.

Kate made her way up the stairs, shutting off lights as she went. Declan's door was partially closed and his soft snores drifted through the hall. Kate made her way to her bedroom and barely made through her nighttime routine before she fell soundly asleep in her bed.

Thankful for an eventless night's sleep, Kate woke early the next morning around six, showered and got herself ready for the day, and went directly to the third floor to start going through her father's files. She was up there for probably an hour when Declan's footfalls echoed off the stairs.

"I have coffee for you," he called.

"I'm in here," she yelled from the last room in the back of the house.

Declan entered the room with his hand outstretched with a steaming cup of coffee. "I figured you might need it. How late did you stay up last night?"

Kate stood from behind her father's desk, which she had piled high with folders, course binders, and Harvard documents her father had kept over the years. She took the cup from Declan and took a sip. "I went to bed shortly after you. I figured a good night's sleep was better than trying to force myself to stay awake. We don't know what today will bring, so better to get sleep when we can."

Declan sat down in a chair near the desk. "Found anything so far?"

"I haven't searched anything too in-depth yet. I've mostly organized it into piles."

Declan kicked his ankle up to his knee and assessed the organized mess on the desk. "You think your father has something from his Harvard days that can help solve this case?"

Kate shrugged and took another sip of her coffee. "I don't know if it will help us solve it or not, but something is nagging at me telling me to look through his things. Call it women's intuition."

Declan laughed. "I thought you were all logic and none of that nonsense, as you called it, like the last time a psychic tried to get involved in a case."

Kate rolled her eyes as she looked at him over the cup. "I didn't say anything about being psychic, which is nonsense. I said I had a gut feeling. You have those all the time and they are valid. Give me this one."

Declan held his hands up in mock defeat. "Do what you have to do. I got a message from Dr. Graham. He said he left one for you, too. He finished Amy's autopsy."

"That was fast." Kate would have to remember to do something nice for him. He had made their case a priority and that didn't always happen in some jurisdictions. "What did he say?"

"Amy had one stab wound to the chest. He said the murder weapon appeared to be the same dagger used in the other cases based on the bruising on her chest. She didn't appear to struggle, so Dr. Graham reasoned that maybe the killer took her by surprise and quickly overpowered her."

That might be a blessing if it had happened that way. At least, Kate reasoned, Amy wouldn't have had enough time to suffer and be in fear. "Did he find anything else of significance?"

"He still has to wait for the toxicology report to be back, but he's not expecting anything strange. None of the other victims, except Justin, had drugs in their system." Declan stood. "I'm heading out but come down and lock up behind me. I called Det. Briggs. He's going to request a squad car come over, but they are short-staffed today because of the storm and another homicide case they are working."

"I'll be fine, Declan." Kate pointed to her holstered gun sitting on the edge of the desk. "I'm as trained as you are to defend myself."

Declan headed for the door, but turned back and locked eyes with Kate. "That may be so, but I'd never forgive myself if something happened to you. I'm meeting Sharon at the lab and then I'll be with Det. Briggs. Call if you find anything, and I'll do the same."

CHAPTER 48

Once Declan left, and Kate was sure he had gone, she went downstairs and checked to make sure the doors were securely locked behind him. She made herself a bowl of oatmeal, poured herself more coffee, and enjoyed a moment of peace and quiet in the kitchen while she ate her breakfast. When she was done, she listened to the message Dr. Graham had left her. He updated her about the autopsy and provided the information Declan had told her, but he also mentioned that it might be beneficial to tell Amy's uncle that she had not suffered, at least not for long. Kate would do hat this afternoon.

Even though Kate felt silly for doing so, she checked the doors again on her way up the stairs. Peeking out the front window, Kate watched plow as it went by. She hadn't realized that it had snowed well into the night. The ground had been covered and her front stoop would eed to be cleared. Kate stood at the bottom of the steps and debated going back upstairs and digging into her father's files or going outside and taking care of the snow. Kate groaned aloud. She'd never focus n work if she knew snow removal hung over her head.

She went to the front closet and pulled out her coat, gloves, and boots. Then she dug around in the back of the closet for a shovel. As much as she loved fall, she didn't relish winter in Boston.

Kate unlocked the front door and stepped out onto the front steps clearing a path as she went. She took a deep breath of cold air and let it out slowly. The fresh air would probably do her good. She made quick work of clearing the steps and then got down to the sidewalk and dug the shovel in and tossed the snow into a pile at the curb. Kate worked for nearly a half-hour when she was interrupted by someone calling her name. She snapped her head up and looked around.

Her neighbor Larry from across the way waved to her as he looked both ways to cross the street.

"I've been looking for you," he said as he walked around the snow pile and met her on the sidewalk. "I didn't even know if you were back in town, but then I saw you leaving the other day. I guess you didn't hear me yell your name."

Kate smiled at her neighbor who had lived in the same house across from her parents for as long as she could remember. "I'm sorry. I've been consumed with a case I've been working. Is there something you need?"

"I wanted to let you know I've seen a guy lurking around the front of your house for the past week. He walks up and down the block but he seems to slow in front of your place."

Kate squinted up at him unsure. "I have my FBI partner, Agent Declan James, staying with me. He has been in and out of the house frequently especially over the last few days. Could it have been him you saw?"

Larry shook his head and said seriously, "No, I've met him. He introduced himself to me while you were still out of town the last time you traveled. This is someone else. I'm concerned, Kate. I've been watching the news and know what's going on."

"What does he look like?"

"He was an inch or two taller than me and fit. He is always well dressed and when I spoke to him, he had a British accent."

Wide-eyed, Kate asked, "You spoke to him?"

"I did two nights ago. I got tired of seeing him around here. I had been waiting for him, and when I saw him, I came out of my home, pretending I was headed out and I waved to him. I asked if he had moved into the neighborhood. I said I had seen him a few times walking up and down the street. I told him outright that most people on this block have lived here for a long time and we know our neighbors. I figured it couldn't hurt to put a scare into him if he was up to no good."

Larry had always been a watchful neighbor even when her parents were alive, but Kate was surprised he had gone out of his way for her like that. She smiled at him. "That was brave of you, Larry. I appreciate it. I possibly know who you saw, and I'll certainly have a word with him. Do me a favor though and don't confront him again. Between you and me, he is a person of interest in this murder investigation. I had no idea he knew where I lived, but he doesn't live far from here, so there might be an explanation. I don't need you to risk your safety though. If you see him again, give me a call on my cellphone. Declan and I will address it."

Larry reached out and bumped Kate on the arm affectionately. "You have a deal. When you get some time, my wife and I would love to have you and your new fellow over for dinner."

Kate laughed. "Not my new fellow. Declan and I are friends and partners."

"You sure?"

"Of course, why do you ask?"

Larry shrugged and his lips turned up in a mischievous grin. "The way he talked about you hinted at more. He seemed to have a real affection for you."

"Long-time friendship, that's all. We went through the FBI academy together and have been friends and partners for a long time."

Larry winked at her. "Well, if you say so, but don't forget to have fun, Kate. Your parents wouldn't have wanted you to live a life of all work." With that, he turned and headed back across the street.

Unnerved by what Larry had told her, Kate let out the nervous breath she had been holding while speaking to him. The last thing she wanted to do was scare Larry or show that she had genuine fear of what he told her. Kate glanced down the sidewalk one way and then the other and dug the shovel back into the snow. She finished as quickly as possible and got herself back in the house and closed the door. Her hand shook as she turned the lock into place. The safety of her home had been compromised for the first time on a case and that only drove her to solve it even more.

Kate pulled off her boots, gloves, and coat and rested the shovel against the back wall of the closet. She'd have a puddle of water to clean up later from the wet shovel and boots, but she didn't care. She made a beeline to the kitchen and found her phone on the counter. Kate sent a quick text to Declan informing him about what Larry had said. She closed the text telling him they'd have to pay Parker Gage another visit later.

Kate poured herself more coffee and carried her cup and phone up the stairs to the third floor. She remained determined to find the information she knew was there in her father's work papers. Kate set the cup and phone down on the desk and reached for a pile as she sat down. Her father had kept everything so tidy and organized that it should be quick work going through it all. She only wished she had an inkling of the nagging memory that had yet to make itself known. If she had even a hint, it would make for easier work.

Kate spent the next hour pouring over her father's files, flipping from folder to folder and page to page without any luck. It was only when her phone chimed that she set the page down and grabbed the phone. Declan had texted back that he was at the FBI office and that Sharon's intern had made some headway on GEDmatch and was in the process of building out a family tree for the killer. They didn't have a significant match yet locally to Boston and no names they were familiar with had come up, but it was more than they had accomplished before. Declan told Kate he could meet her at Parker's residence around four that afternoon if it worked for her.

She texted back that it was perfect timing and then put the phone back down. She leaned back in her chair and stared at the ceiling. She closed her eyes and asked her father to help her. Kate wasn't even sure she believed in the afterlife. She had been raised Catholic but faith had never come as easy for her as it seemed to others, especially after she lost her parents. Kate preferred to believe in what she could confirm with her senses.

Kate leaned forward in her chair and grabbed for another file. She opened the manila folder and started reading through each page. Moments later, she could barely believe her eyes. She found exactly what she was looking for. She read the note written in her father's hand and nearly leaped out of her chair with excitement.

The information wasn't complete though, but it was the first clue that had felt solid in the entire investigation. Kate sat back and strummed her fingers on the desk, thinking about the next step she should take. She needed more information and the only person at Harvard she knew that had been there with her father was Professor Holt. She had no idea if her father had told the man the information he just read, but it was worth a shot.

Kate picked up the phone and scrolled through her contacts until she found his number. She called, but he didn't answer. She left an urgent message for him to return her call without giving the details she'd found. She couldn't sit there though. She sent off a quick message to Declan, letting him know she found something and was headed to the Harvard campus to speak to Professor Holt in the hopes he could shed more light.

She flipped off the office light and went downstairs. She pulled open the closet door and grabbed her coat and headed to the kitchen. She found her keys sitting on the island and dashed to her car, which Declan had been kind enough to clean off that morning.

Kate pulled out of the alleyway and resisted the urge to speed on the still snow-covered roads. She made her way to Harvard's campus hitting every green light and never once stopped by the normal Boston traffic. She assumed many people had remained at home given the snowfall because the streets had been mostly empty.

Kate found a place to park outside of the history building and ran the distance from her car to the door, pulling it open with such force she startled a student sitting in the lobby studying. She offered an apology as she raced toward the stairway up to Professor Holt's office. The building lacked the normal hustle and bustle and din of student noise. It occurred to Kate as she made her way down the hall toward the office that classes might have been canceled for the day. Professor Holt's door was not only closed but locked when she tried to turn the handle. She knocked once and then twice, but his office remained dark.

"Professor Holt!" Kate called out even though she was sure the man wasn't there.

Three doors down the hall, a young man stuck his head out of his office door. "He hasn't been here for two days. He called in yesterday and said he was home not feeling well. Most of the early classes were canceled this morning because of the snow. He should be in tomorrow if you want to try him then."

Kate cursed under her breath. "That's okay. I can try him at home."

The young man started to say something, but Kate rushed by him and didn't hear what he said. All she cared about was getting to Professor Holt.

CHAPTER 49

Kate found the only on-street parking spot left two blocks over from Professor Holt's house. She pulled the car to the curb, shut off the ignition, grabbed her things, and ran to his house, slipping twice on the snow and ice. By the time Kate got to he door, a surge of energy being so close to solving the case bubbled up inside her. She didn't bother with the door knocker and instead pounded her fist on the door. "Professor Holt!" she yelled over and over again.

Finally, the door sprung open, and much to Kate's surprise both Professor Holt and Mark Boyle stood there. She stepped back, uncertainty taking over the energy she felt a moment before.

"I had no idea you two knew each other," she blurted not meaning o have said it aloud.

"We've known each other for a long time." Professor Holt stepped ut of the doorway and allowed Kate to enter.

She stamped off her snow-covered boots on the mat before stepping inside. "Do you know each other through The Founders?"

The two men shared a look, but it was Mark who explained. "We ave known each other for years well before The Founders. Boston n't that big when you run in the same circles."

"I didn't mean to interrupt your meeting. I need to speak with you, rofessor Holt, about an urgent matter." She turned to Mark, hoping that he would take the hint and leave.

Mark smiled and nodded his head. "I'll leave you to it then, Anthony. Give me a call later and we can finish our discussion."

Professor Holt drew his lips together, annoyed at the intrusion, but he didn't argue with Kate or Mark, who was already in the process of getting his coat out of the hall closet and slipping it on. "Yes, Mark. I'll do that. I apologize for the interruption. I had no idea that I'd be needed by Agent Walsh."

"I left you a message on your cellphone," Kate told him. "I went to your Harvard office first and they said you've been home from work."

Professor Holt smiled stiffly. "I didn't realize you had been tracking my whereabouts."

"Not tracking you, no. As I said, something urgent has come up and I need your assistance."

Mark, who had bundled himself up for the cold, had one hand on the door. "Better help her, Anthony. The FBI can be quite dogged when they are after information."

"Yes, we generally are when there is a serial killer on the loose and the public is in jeopardy."

Mark left without saying another word, but the paling of his skin said everything. It was clear Mark was afraid of Kate and what she might have on him. His moment of bravery came and went within seconds. It was the first time Kate wondered if Parker Gage had been right about the man and that he wouldn't have had the stomach for murder.

After Professor Holt closed the door behind Mark, he turned to Kate. "Let's go into the living room. I have a fire burning and it's warmer." He turned and walked down the hall and Kate followed. "Can I get you something to drink?"

"No, thank you. This shouldn't take up too much of your time."

"I would hope not. You've already inconvenienced me, forcing me to allow Ashley to take a leave of absence to go into hiding or whatever ridiculous thing she's doing." Professor Holt walked into the sitting room and gestured toward one of the couches for Kate to sit.

The fire threw enough heat to warm Kate who had been shivering since she left her house. Kate sat and waited for him to take a seat across from her. "I didn't mean to inconvenience you, but Ashley requested protection and given the case, Agent James and I felt it was the best course of action. Have you heard from her?"

"Other than when she initially told me what was happening, no. Should I have?"

"I was curious if she had told anyone where we are keeping her."

Professor Holt shrugged. "I can't account for anyone but myself, but I haven't heard from her. I have to make the hard decision now if I can even continue having her as my teaching assistant or I need to let her go."

Kate didn't want to get involved, but she offered a thought. "It's your right to choose your teaching assistant obviously, but if you can, consider this is not a normal circumstance. The FBI would not be paying for her protection unless we truly felt there was a risk to her life. At least, weigh that in your decision making."

Professor Holt leaned forward and lifted the cup he had sitting on a coaster on the coffee table that separated the space between Kate and himself. He took a sip and smiled at her as he set it down on his lap. "I'll consider, but I'm sure this is not why you're here. What can I help you with?"

Kate leaned back on the couch and folded her hands together. "You were close to my father at Harvard, correct?"

"I'd say so. He was my advisor for a time." Professor Holt paused and seemed to weigh his words. "Your father was a brilliant man. His knowledge of history was unlike any I'd met before or since. It wasn't just his knowledge. He was open to debate and learning about the implications of decisions in history and how it impacted modern life."

Kate remembered that fondly about her father. He'd tell her all the time history may have already happened, but the decisions made then were still felt. He loved exploring the meaning and why things happened the way they did.

"Your father would have made an excellent member of The Founders," Professor Holt said, snapping Kate out of her memory. She must have had a strange look on her face because he clarified. "The way it was when I joined. Not what it's turned into." He laughed to himself. "Forgive me, but I'm sure you didn't interrupt my meeting with Mark to walk down memory lane. Go on."

"My father kept everything from his time at Harvard – every bit of curricula he developed, his research, and even notes on his students and other faculty." Kate tapped at the side of her head with her inde finger. "There's been something nagging at my memory since this case started and the dagger showed up on my doorstep. I was a chil for most of the time my father taught at Harvard, but I can remembe snippets of conversation he would have with my mother. One of thos conversations must have caught my attention and implanted itself i my memory, but for the life of me, I couldn't remember it. I just kne it related and was important. So, this morning I went through m father's things, and there it was."

Professor Holt took another sip of his drink and then gestured wit his free hand. "You have me on the edge of my seat."

"My father left a note among his papers that he was shown Genera Thomas Gage's daggers, two of them from a person at Harvard wh claimed to have been related to the man. The only problem is, m father didn't mention in his note who had shown him. He simpl stated that the history department had a surprise that day and detaile what he saw and heard. After reading the note, I clearly rememb him coming home to tell my mother the miraculous find. I think I w probably eight or nine at the time so that was more than twenty-five years ago. If he mentioned the person who had the daggers to my mother either I didn't overhear that or I don't recall."

Professor Holt showed no emotion on his face, so Kate couldn't read if this was news to him or not. He simply said, "Is there a question in there?"

"Well, yes. Were you there then, and if so, do you remember who it was?"

"It had to have been before my time or maybe I wasn't there that day. I don't recall anything of the sort." Professor Holt stood as if the conversation were over.

Kate wasn't having any of it. She had done the calculations and Professor Holt was most definitely at Harvard at the time. She told him as much. "You must remember something. My father said it had the whole department buzzing."

"Memory is a tricky thing, Agent Walsh. How can you be sure you remember that or even remember it correctly? You may be only thinking you remember – a false memory so to speak. Since your father didn't indicate when it happened, it could have been before my time. I don't recall it at all. I can't tell you I remember something I do not."

A phone rang off in the distance and Professor Holt left the room without saying another word. Kate wasn't going to be brushed off that easily, not after she was so close to figuring it out. She stood from the couch but had nowhere to go. She walked close to the fire and reached her hands out to warm them. It was then she heard it.

Faintly at first and then a touch louder. Her name coming from the wall or maybe the floor. She stepped closer to the wall and then leaned in above the grate on the floor. There it was again, faint and distant, but distinctly her name.

Kate got down on the ground and put her ear directly above the grate and heard it again. She couldn't be sure, but it sounded like Charlie Crain.

"What on Earth are you doing?" Professor Holt barked from behind her.

Kate sucked in a breath and put her hands flat on the floor. She did not doubt that Charlie Crain was here in Professor Holt's home and that could mean only one thing. Kate reached her hand down to unholster her gun, but she never got the chance.

Professor Holt, suddenly on top of her, yanked Kate to her feet by her hair. Every ounce of training Kate had coursed through her. She threw an elbow back, landing it in his gut, and turned to swing at him. She stopped short when she realized they weren't the only two people in the room. Mark Boyle stood in the doorway holding a gun pointed directly at her.

Professor Holt righted himself and caught his breath. He too had a gun in his hand – an antique pistol and Kate wasn't sure if it was loaded or not.

"I wouldn't take another step if I were you," Mark said, walking with sudden confidence toward her. "Give me your gun. Now!"

In seconds, Kate thought through every scenario of how this could play out. All of them ended with her dead on the floor. She held her hands up in defeat. "We can talk this out."

"We are beyond talking," Professor Holt said, now aiming his gun at her.

"Okay," Kate said slowly. She explained every move to them as she reached her hand down to her hip holster and unclipped it. She inched the gun out still debating if she had any moves left, but playing along for now, seemed to be the best option. She bent down and put the gun on the floor near her feet.

Mark scoffed at her. "Don't be coy. Kick it over to me. Then, you can give us the one on your ankle. I know how this works."

Kate nudged the gun with her foot enough to move it forward but not enough to reach Mark. She lifted each pant leg and showed them how tight her ankle boots were. "No ankle gun today. I didn't bother to put it on I was in such a hurry."

Seeming satisfied with the response, Professor Holt shoved past moving to the wall right behind her. He pushed on one section and the wall gave way, revealing a doorway. He turned and grabbed Kate by the wrist. "You're coming with me until we can figure out what to do with you. You destroyed my plan, and for that, you'll need to pay."

"What was your plan?"

He shook his head in disgust. "I thought you were supposed to be he best. There should be nine victims to fulfill my mission. You made ne kill Justin, and then I had to kill that stupid nosey researcher for he newspaper. That's only five. I have four more to go." Professor Iolt shoved her forward and then stopped. "I guess with you and Charlie that will bring me to seven. I'm nearly there."

Kate knew that nine had meaning to him. She tried to pull her arm ack to free herself, but his strength overpowered her. "The FBI and he Boston police know that I'm here," she lied.

Professor Holt pulled Kate through the doorway and onto a narrow anding that led to an old wooden staircase. He pushed her in front of im and nudged her down the stairs. "No matter. You didn't suspect ne even after you read your father's note about my find. It was me, ou foolish girl. I'm related to General Thomas Gage and had his aggers. No one will ever suspect me."

Anger flamed through her body. He was right, of course. She hadn't gured it out. She hadn't even suspected him. "They will come for ne," she said with force.

"I will send them away and tell them you were headed to Parker age's house. My dumb cousin makes the perfect patsy."

Kate didn't even have time to react to the fact that Professor Holt and Parker were related because they hit the bottom of the stairs and came face to face with a thick metal door. Professor Holt pulled a key from his pocket and unlocked the deadbolt. He pulled the door back and shoved Kate through it with enough force that she fell forward and landed on her hands and knees.

As the door slammed shut and locked behind her, she leaned back and brushed off her hands.

"I guess there's no hope of rescue now," Charlie Crain said with fear in his voice from the corner of the darkened space.

CHAPTER 50

I wouldn't say that." Kate stood and brushed off her pants. She took her phone from her pocket and held it up.

"There's no cell service down here." Charlie lifted his phone rom beside him on the bench where he sat. "I've tried everything to get out of here. There's one door, no windows, and no way to get out."

Kate checked her phone and found that she didn't have cell service ither. She attempted to send a text to Declan anyway in the hopes it might go through.

"He told me he's going to hang me in Boston Public Garden as a traitor, which is what they should have done to Benjamin Franklin. m surprised I'm still alive."

Kate reached under her jacket to the back waistband of her pants. he pulled out her second gun and checked the chamber. She had six ullets. "Professor Holt isn't going to kill either of us. If I had a shot p there, I would have taken it, but he has help."

"I know," Charlie said wearily. He toed the dirt ground in front of im. "His teaching assistant saw me at the hotel. It was right after at he attacked me at my apartment."

"Ashley?" Kate said, confusion in her voice. "You saw Ashley at the otel? I was talking about Mark Boyle."

"I don't know about him," Charlie said. "One of the Boston cops ought Ashley to my room. She convinced him that she needed to speak to me. I guess they figured since we were both in FBI custody on the same case that it would be safe. She introduced herself to me and asked me a ton of questions about what I knew so far."

"What did you tell her?"

Charlie threw his hands up. "Of course, I didn't answer her, but she knew I was there and my room number. She saw some notes on my desk from my researcher, Amy. I knew then it was a setup. I didn't know what to do. I didn't think the cops would believe me. It's not like I had proof. I would have sounded crazy."

"Is there any chance she stole one of your keycards when she was in your room?"

Charlie's eyes got wide. "I couldn't find one of them. I thought I had lost it."

Kate cursed under her breath. "Why did you meet with Amy?"

"She said she had found some possible information about another of Gage's relatives living in Boston. We already knew about Parker Gage, but finding another couldn't have been a coincidence, but when I met her in Boston Common, she wouldn't tell me what she knew. She said that just because someone was related it didn't mean the person was the killer. We argued and I went to get research I had left back at my apartment."

Kate walked over to the bench and sat down next to him. "Why did Amy have a blanket with her?"

He turned his head to look at Kate. "How'd you know about that?"

Kate held up her hand. "Tell me about what happened at your apartment first."

Charlie dropped his head and looked down at the ground. "I was there maybe an hour, maybe longer. I was in my home office going through some research when someone knocked on my door. I went to answer it and there was Professor Holt with a dagger in his hand. He forced his way in and we struggled. In the process, he sliced me acro the stomach." Charlie held up his shirt to show Kate the makeshift bandage he had across his middle. Blood had seeped through the material. "He pulled out a gun after he cut me and told me that if I didn't come with him, he'd kill Amy. I figured Ashley had told him I was suspicious and he had followed me."

Kate realized Charlie had no idea that Amy had been murdered. "What happened then?"

"He assumed I had research that named him there at my apartment. He tore apart my office and then the bookshelf in the living room. He didn't find anything. After he gave up, he stuck the gun in my back and marched me out of my place. We walked to this house, and I went willingly. I figured saving Amy was worth the risk." Charlie sat quietly for a moment and then lurched forward and moaned at the same time. "Amy's dead, isn't she? That's why you asked about the blanket. If she were alive, you could have asked her yourself. I'm so stupid."

Kate reached out a hand and placed it on Charlie's back. "He must have been watching you with her in Boston Common. He killed her minutes after you left her there."

Charlie turned his face to Kate's and he had tears in his eyes. "Did she suffer?"

"No," Kate said, shaking her head. "Her death came quickly. She might not have had time to even be afraid or know what was happening."

That seemed to comfort him. "Amy had the blanket because she picked it up from the dry cleaner before we met up." Charlie smiled to himself. "We were dating, and the last time I was at her place, we had spilled wine on her comforter. The dry cleaner said he could remove the stain and he did."

"When Professor Holt came to your apartment, did he have your laptop or any files with him?"

"No, why?"

"He ransacked your hotel room first."

Charlie leaned back and rested his back against the wall. Kate withdrew her hand. "Check Ashley's room. I bet he went through my room and took everything to her. I don't know how she's involved, but I'd bet money that she is."

Kate believed Charlie was right. Ashley had to be involved, and she'd be dealt with later. The most important thing Kate needed to focus on was getting out of Professor Holt's house alive. "What has Professor Holt said to you? Has he fed you? Let you out to go to the bathroom?"

"Yes, to both, although I don't know why he's feeding me if he's planning to kill me. He hasn't said much to me. There is a bathroom down here. I've tried a few times to get away from him, but it only results in pain. He struck me in the head once. Another time, he punched me in my stab wound. That's why it started bleeding again. I've tried to ask him questions about why he's doing what he's doing, but I never get a response." Charlie turned to look at Kate. "Does anyone know you're here?"

"Agent James knew I was headed to speak to Professor Holt, but I didn't say specifically that I was headed to his house. I told him I was going to his office at Harvard. He'll figure it out though." What Kate didn't add was her worry that Declan might figure it out too late. "Has anyone else been here?"

"Just that madman upstairs that I know of."

"I heard you yelling my name. How did you hear me upstairs?"

Charlie stood and walked over to the far corner of the room and pointed to the ceiling. "There's a heating vent. I could hear you talking to him. I wasn't positive it was you, but I figured it was worth trying. I'm surprised you could hear me. I think he soundproofed this room. It's hard to hear anything."

Kate got up and walked to the vent first. She didn't hear anything

CHAPTER 50

"You said you tried the door?"

Charlie nodded. "Unbreakable."

Kate believed him, but she still wanted to see for herself. The thick steel door had a handle that didn't even turn from the inside. There were no seams or anything to stick a tool in to pry it open. Not that they had any tools. There was nothing else in the room. The walls were made of cinderblock and the floor dirt. The ceiling looked like wooden boards original to the home.

"What do we do?" Charlie asked.

"We wait. In the meantime, I'm going to teach you a few self-defense moves I learned at the FBI academy. If he comes back, even if he has a gun, I have mine and we can overpower him."

Charlie laughed. "I'm not much of a fighter."

"You don't need to be."

"I'm willing to try my best if it means we get out of here alive."

Over the next hour, Kate showed Charlie several self-defense moves. Ie picked up the information quickly, and even with his injury, he eemed to be able to handle his own. Kate had no idea what she was oing to do, but she didn't want to tell him that. Her only goal was eeping Charlie's spirits up and focused on the goal at hand. Kate had o idea if Declan would figure out where she was, so she might be eir only hope. She'd go down fighting if she had to.

After they practiced the moves one last time, Kate patted Charlie n the arm. "You're better than you think you are. Let's rest up. How ften does he come down here?"

"Every few hours or so. There doesn't seem to be a regular schedule."

Kate sat down on the bench and mapped out a plan in her head of hat would be the best approach if he came down for them again. e wouldn't admit it to Charlie but fear had crept in. Kate had to main focused and alert. She checked her phone again and the text ill hadn't gone through. An error message appeared, indicating her phone couldn't connect to the network. She let out a long deep sigh.

For two more hours, Kate and Charlie sat in the basement locked away from the world. They stood, stretched, talked, and tried to keep the mood as light as possible right up until the moment they heard voices coming from the floor above.

Kate looked in the direction of the vent. "Someone's here."

Charlie got up immediately and went to stand under it. Kate did one better and balanced herself on the bench to get even closer.

"I tried that, but I tipped the bench over," Charlie explained to her.

"I'm lighter, but it is hard to balance." Kate held onto the wall and tried to get up on tiptoes, but the bench swayed under the movement. She settled back down on flat feet and motioned for Charlie to lift her. "Do you think you can lift me to the vent?"

"Definitely." Charlie wrapped his arms around her below her backside and hoisted her up toward the vent. Kate practically knelt on his shoulders as she tried to reach it. She was high enough though to hear what was happening upstairs.

"It's Agent James and Det. Briggs," Kate said excited. She screamed their names into the vent not once but three times. She also screamed directions to find the panel on the wall that opened to the stairway. When she still wasn't sure they had heard her, Kate pounded on the ceiling with her fist and smacked at the vent grate. She didn't stop pounding or yelling until she heard a commotion and Declan's angry voice.

"They know!" Kate yelled, looking down at Charlie. She yelled again for good measure and kept yelling until a shot rang out. Kate screamed and Charlie lost his footing and dropped Kate to the ground. She landed hard but scrambled to her feet.

"Someone is on their way down here. Go get in position."

Charlie ran to the side of the door hidden from view. He stood poised and ready to pounce. Kate took her position dead center of the room and aimed her gun at the door. If it was Professor Holt, she'd kill him before he ever got the chance to enter. Kate held her breath as the moment passed, waiting either to be rescued or to kill a man. She was ready for whatever she'd have to do.

Someone unlocked the deadbolt and pulled the door open. Kate's finger twitched on the trigger as Declan screamed Kate's name. As soon as she saw that he was alone, Kate relaxed her arms and let the hand with the gun fall to her side. Charlie slumped down against the wall and groaned with relief.

Declan rushed to her and wrapped her in a hug, which she returned not caring how unprofessional that might look to Charlie.

"Katie, I thought I lost you," Declan said, burying his face into the side of her neck.

"I'm fine. I'm fine," she assured him and let him go. She stepped back out of his embrace. "What happened upstairs?"

"Sharon's intern finally finished that family tree." Declan looked between Charlie and Kate. "Professor Anthony Holt appeared on the family tree as a distant great-nephew of General Thomas Gage. We didn't have his DNA to do a match, but he's the only name that was familiar to us. Then you wouldn't respond to calls or texts. I came here as soon as I could."

"Is Mark Boyle upstairs, too? He's involved."

Declan pointed to the ceiling. "We got them both. Neither is talking right now, but it appears they were working together."

"There's someone else we need to go see right now, but Charlie needs medical attention. Let's get him upstairs and go visit Ashley at the hotel."

CHAPTER 51

"You ready, Kate?" Declan asked as they rode the hotel elevator to Ashley's room. "You went through a trauma today. I can handle this if you want me to. No one will think less of you if you go home and curl up in bed and have a good cry."

Kate grimaced. "Is that what you think women do?"

"It's what I would do!"

Kate laughed. "No, this is payback. I knew Ashley wasn't giving i to us straight. I'm doing this myself, and you're here to make sure don't kill her with my bare hands."

"Angry Kate. We haven't seen her in a while."

The elevator doors opened and the sea of Boston cops that De Briggs had arranged parted like the sea as Declan and Kate charge down the hallway side by side toward Ashley's room.

Declan, Kate, and Charlie had come up out of the basement to fin Det. Briggs standing over Professor Holt and Mark Boyle handcuffe and sitting on the floor. The shot Kate had heard was Declan shootin Professor Holt in the shoulder as he went for his gun. Mark ha immediately dropped his weapon and put his hands up.

Kate had explained Ashley's role and Det. Briggs immediatel radioed the message over to the hotel that she was not to leave th room under any circumstances, but she also wasn't to be told wh was going on.

The man at the front desk in the hotel had given Kate the keycard to Ashley's room. She slipped the card in, turned the handle, and shoved the door open, startling Ashley who sat at the desk hunched over a laptop.

"Is that Charlie Crain's laptop you're going through?" Kate snarled, moving swiftly into the room. She grabbed hold of the arm of the desk chair and pulled it away from the desk and shoved it back toward the window. She bore down on the young woman who appeared utterly terrified of Kate.

"I, well, I…" Ashley couldn't get out a word.

Declan bent down and looked at the file. He clicked a few buttons. "Yes, Agent Walsh, that's exactly what she's doing."

"Care to explain yourself?" Kate asked, standing over Ashley not giving her any space to move or even get up from the chair.

"I want a lawyer," Ashley said, gaining a bit of confidence.

"That's fine," Kate said and turned on her heels. "Agent James, please read Ashley her rights, and then we can take her to lockup." She turned back to Ashley. "It's okay. Professor Holt and Mark Boyle already told us you were the mastermind in this. You're looking at life in prison with no possibility of parole. In another state, you'd be looking at a death sentence."

Ashley didn't move, but tears welled up in her eyes.

Kate fought the urge to smack her. "I don't buy it, so you can turn off the crocodile tears. You think you fooled me once, but I was suspicious of you the whole time." Kate headed for the door.

"Wait!" Ashley called her back. "I didn't kill anyone. I didn't mastermind it. That was Professor Holt. I'll tell you what you want to know. I'll tell you how we're all involved."

"It's too late for that." Kate walked to the doorway, but before she could turn the handle and step into the hall, Ashley begged.

"Please. I don't want a lawyer. I swear I'll tell you everything!"

Kate and Declan had been wired for sound before they came up to the room. In a van outside of the hotel sat the prosecutor Carmen Langston and Det. Briggs. It had played out exactly as they planned so far. Kate turned to Ashley and read the woman her rights. "You are waiving your right to an attorney to speak with me. Is that correct?"

"Yes, please. I'll tell you anything. I can't go to prison for the rest of my life." Ashley wiped tears from her eyes.

"I won't be sentencing you so I can't determine that, but I have on good authority that the prosecutor is willing to work on a reduced sentence for your cooperation and testimony at trial."

Ashley said she understood. "This was all Professor Holt's doing. He's the one who killed the people. Mark Boyle wrote the letters for him. I don't even know how much Mark was involved. I only saw him once. He wasn't involved in killing anyone that I know of. He might have helped find people to kill. I don't know."

"What was your role?" Kate asked sitting on the edge of the bed across from her.

"I recruited Justin and stayed close to Parker to set him up. I fed Parker so many lies that the police were closing in on him that he even went by your place a few times but couldn't get the courage to speak to you. I was supposed to call you in the morning and tell you that I knew Parker had committed the murders. The dagger Professor Holt used as one of the murder weapons has Parker's prints on it. It's hidden in Professor Holt's upstairs library. He wore gloves." Ashley took a breath. "Justin didn't kill anyone, but he lured victims to where they were killed. We were both working with Professor Holt. We had a mission, and we fulfilled it."

"Your twisted ideology doesn't even make any sense," Declan said leaning back against the desk. "You all participated in the murder of innocent people to satisfy the need of a deranged man bent on revenge. You did nothing but take innocent lives and ruin families."

Kate nudged Ashley's chair. "You've done more than what you're saying. Tell me the rest."

Ashley didn't respond. She wouldn't even look at Declan. "I also did some research for Professor Holt and covered for him at Harvard when he'd miss a class. I also misled you, Agent Walsh, so I could find out where you were keeping Charlie Crain. Professor Holt wanted to kill him next."

"Charlie Crain is perfectly safe. It's Professor Holt who has been shot and is in police custody."

"There's something I don't understand," Declan said. "Why would you rat out Justin to Agent Walsh? He could have tipped us off on the whole plan."

"He was getting too unpredictable. Professor Holt was worried he'd tell someone so he planned to kill him, but I told him you'd then know it was someone close to Justin and you'd figure it out. Professor Holt didn't care. He planned to kill Justin that night but then you arrested him. When he got out of jail, Professor Holt said he couldn't wait any longer so he killed him for betraying us. That's why I knew I had to find that dagger. He stole it from Professor Holt!"

Ashley calmed down and spent the next hour going over the details of how the entire plot came to be. Professor Holt had always been radicalized by the idea of going back under British rule. He had spoken at length to Parker Gage. Once Parker realized that it was Holt who had been making the bomb threats in The Founders name, he kicked him out. That spurred Holt on to not only commit the murders but pin it on The Founders to take them and Parker down in the process. Mark was a willing patsy in the whole thing.

Ashley explained that Justin was easy to radicalize. He'd already held some of the core beliefs Professor Holt espoused and had a violent temper. The fact that Justin's father had two of the daggers and Professor Holt had the other two felt like fate. There was a natural synergy between them. When Kate asked how she had become radicalized to the idea, Ashley was less forthcoming, but it had started because of her extreme respect for Professor Holt. From there, he convinced her of the mission. Once the players were in place, the plan went into action immediately.

When Ashley was done and Kate was sure they had the information she needed, Declan slapped the handcuffs on her and led her to a Boston detective who was waiting in the hall.

He came back for Kate who had remained in the room. "You ready? I think we can call it a day. Det. Briggs and Carmen Langston can take it from here. Sharon will be over soon to process the scene and collect any evidence."

Kate, now that it was over, felt the emotion of the day coming over her. She wasn't going to cry in front of Boston cops. She swallowed the emotion down. "Sure, let's go get this audio off us, and then maybe we can get some dinner. Spade called me, but I haven't listened to the message yet."

"He can wait for once."

Kate and Declan walked out of the hotel room and into the hall. The Boston cops cheered them on and congratulated them on a job well done. Kate hoped Det. Briggs and Carmen would take center stage with the media because she didn't have it in her to make a statement. They left the hotel and stopped at the surveillance van.

"I couldn't have done this without the two of you," Det. Briggs said as he took the wires off them.

"Yes, you could have. You're one of the best that Boston has," Kate said, "but we were happy to help. This is our city, too."

Kate and Declan said goodbye and promised to be around if anyone needed anything. Carmen said she'd be in touch regarding prosecution.

As Kate and Declan walked the few blocks to the pub near her house he explained, "I called a lawyer who I'm going to retain for the divorce. I'm probably going to lose everything and have to live with you for the rest of my life, but at least, it will be settled."

Kate bumped him with her hip. "As I said before, as long as you're cooking, you can stay. A woman has got to eat."

Declan laughed. "What are you going to do about work? Still going to quit?"

"I don't know," Kate said and meant it. "I might just need a break, some downtime."

"Makes sense. You've been doing nothing but traveling for years, but Spade will fight you on it."

"That's probably why he's calling."

Later, when they got to the pub and ordered their dinner, Kate listened to the message. He left direct precise orders. When the message ended, Kate set her phone down on the table and let out a long dramatic sigh. "Spade needs us on a flight to Miami in the morning. A serial killer is murdering wealthy single women in South Beach. They are calling him the Miami Ripper."

Declan took a sip of his beer and watched her over the rim. "You in?"

"I'm in," Kate said dryly, wishing she didn't feel such a sense of duty. "At least we can escape the Boston cold and snow."

"That's something at least." Kate and Declan finished their food, had more drinks than they should, and stumbled home to pack for the flight the next day. Kate's decision about the direction of her career would have to wait.

About the Author

Stacy M. Jones was born and raised in Troy, New York, and currently lives in Little Rock, Arkansas. She is a full-time writer and holds masters' degrees in journalism and in forensic psychology. Stacy is an avid reader of the mystery genre. She currently has three serie available for readers: paranormal cozy Harper & Hattie Magica Mystery Series, the hard-boiled PI Riley Sullivan Mystery Serie and the thriller FBI Agent Kate Walsh Series. To access Stacy' Mystery Readers Club with three free novellas, one for each serie visit StacyMJones.com.

You can connect with me on:

- http://www.stacymjones.com
- https://twitter.com/SMJonesWriter
- https://www.facebook.com/StacyMJonesWriter
- https://www.bookbub.com/profile/stacy-m-jones
- https://www.goodreads.com/StacyMJonesWriter

Subscribe to my newsletter:

- http://www.stacymjones.com

Also by Stacy M. Jones

Read FBI Kate Walsh Thriller Series Book #2 - Miami Ripper

Have you read The Curators - the series novella? Access it free with Stacy's Free Mystery Readers' Club Starter Library. Three books included:

PI Riley Sullivan Mystery Series novella The 1922 Club Murder
FBI Agent Kate Walsh Thriller Series novella The Curators
Harper & Hattie Mystery Series novella Harper's Folly

Hit subscribe at http://www.stacymjones.com/

Other books by Stacy M. Jones in series order:

FBI Agent Kate Walsh Thriller Series

The Curators
The Founders
Miami Ripper
Mad Jack
The Fuse

PI Riley Sullivan Mystery Series

The 1922 Club Murder
Deadly Sins
The Bone Harvest
Missing Time Murders
We Last Saw Jane
Boston Underground
The Night Game

Harbor Cove Murders

Harper & Hattie Magical Mystery Series

Harper's Folly

Saints & Sinners Ball

Secrets to Tell

Rule of Three

The Forever Curse

The Witches Code

The Sinister Sisters

Scandal Knocks Twice

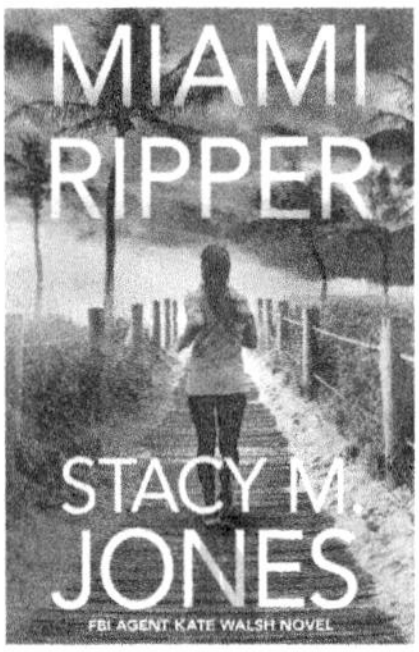

Miami Ripper

A killer is stalking high-priced escorts and leaving a trail of bodies in empty mansions along Miami Beach's intracoastal waterway. When the crimes become too much for the locals to handle, FBI Agents Kate Walsh and Declan James must find a killer walking among the city's elite.

Amid the glamour and money is a seedy underbelly that runs through the city like an electrical current. Young women are enticed into relationships with older men where sex and money are traded – creating a power dynamic that leaves the woman vulnerable and susceptible to a killer.

Agents Walsh and James must figure out who to believe in a city where everyone has an agenda, and even the local cops seem to have something to hide. A devastating break in the case reveals the potential killer, but the chase is on to find out who is harboring and potentially helping him. Can Agent Walsh use her profiling skills to figure out his plan before the next victim is found or will terror keep reigning in the city?

Made in United States
Orlando, FL
21 August 2024

50639161R00186